MISTLETOE AND THE BILLIONAIRE BOSS

by

SERENITY WOODS

ISBN: 9798870630014

CONTENTS

Chapter One

Missie

"I feel I should warn you," Juliette announces, "Alex Winters is the grumpiest guy in the history of the universe. Just so you know."

It's Friday the seventeenth of March, and we're walking past Hagley Park in Christchurch with the River Avon on our right, and beyond it the large gray buildings of Christchurch Hospital. A coxed four shell passes us, the rowers pulling hard on the oars, and a punter in traditional Edwardian costume steers two tourists through a flock of mallard ducks. Weeping willows trail their fingers in the water, and autumn leaves flutter down from the tall oaks.

I'm too anxious to enjoy the scenery, though, and say, "I wish you'd told me that before I signed Finn up for the program."

"Oh, don't let it put you off. Alex is gorgeous, and he's a genius—just a grouchy one. He's like a mixture of James Bond, Stephen Hawking, and Scrooge."

I try to imagine the combination and fail. "I wish you hadn't told me that. I was already nervous."

"Aw, no need to be. Don't worry about the interview. It's almost a done deal, as long as you don't do anything crazy to frighten him off."

"Oh God. Now I'm terrified."

She laughs and links arms with me. "Come on, I'm teasing you. How can he fail to love you? I don't know a single person who doesn't think you're amazing."

Well, I can think of one. How sad is it that I was married to him?

"Mind you," she says, "I rarely see Alex show interest in a woman. He's not dated for ages. Sometimes I wonder if he's like a Ken doll down below."

That makes me laugh. Juliette Kumar is of Māori-Indian descent, taller than me, and slender, with long dark hair, light-brown skin, and attractive dark eyes. She has a Māori tattoo on her arm and a red bindi between her eyebrows, and she's an intriguing blend of both cultures, while also being a modern Kiwi girl.

I met her at Christchurch Hospital when my son's physiotherapist first suggested he might be a good candidate for a new program nicknamed The Hands-On Robot or THOR for short. Kia Kaha—Māori for 'stay strong'—is a company formed by a group of friends who invented an exoskeleton to help people with spinal column injuries to walk. They've recently developed a smaller model for children, and they're looking for volunteers to take part in a series of trials.

Eager to help Finn any way I can, I put him forward for it, although I haven't told him yet. I don't want to get his hopes up until we've been given the green light. Being told you'll probably never walk again at the age of ten is hard enough without being given false hope.

I've become friends with Juliette, who is the chief physio at Kia Kaha, and it's her I have to thank for getting me an interview. She promised to meet me today and show me where to go.

"Is Alex the head of the company?" I ask as we turn away from the river and circle the large building before us.

"Five of us run it together," she replies. "Alex is kind of the unofficial boss, but don't tell him I said that."

As we climb the wide steps to the front of the building, I look for a ramp, which I'll have to use if Finn does get on the program. I can't see one though, and frown as I say, "Do you have wheelchair access here?"

"Of course. There's a ramp around the side, but most of our disabled visitors use this." She gestures to a small area next to the stairs that turns out to be a platform lift. An outdoor one! Very fancy. "We're focused on making people with disabilities comfortable here," she says. "We have a large disabled car park, Braille signage in the bathrooms, and overhead signage for people who are hard of hearing. And we're always open to suggestions for ways we can improve."

Impressed, I follow her across the paved square and through the automatic doors.

"The building has a biophilic design," Juliette explains as we enter the lobby. "We collaborated with the local *kaitiaki*—Māori guardians who advocate for elements of nature—when we designed the office, in order to make it as beautiful and sustainable as possible. You can see raw materials like punga logs, reclaimed Kauri timber, and river stones throughout the offices, and obviously we use lots of native plants."

The lobby is large and open plan, with a crescent-moon-shaped reception desk that curves around a seating area. The front of it is created from a carved light wood carved with pictures that the sign informs me tells the story of Tāne-mahuta, god of the forest. Autumn sunshine from the high windows falls across the scene, making it look like a forest glade.

"Oh, it's amazing," I say. "Wow, that painting is fantastic." It takes up almost all of one wall, a splendid representation of Ranginui and Papatūānuku, the primal couple in Māori mythology. Papatūānuku, the Earth Mother, lies on her back with her face and figure forming the hills and valleys of the world, while Rangi, the Sky Father, looks down at her from the heavens, his lips touching hers.

"Well, you have a special treat today," Juliette tells me. "The artist is a friend of ours who's here on business, so you'll get to meet him!" She takes me up to reception and introduces me to the young woman sitting behind the wooden desk. "Rebecca, this is Mistletoe Macbeth. She's here for a meeting with Alex."

"Hello," Rebecca says with a smile. "What a wonderful name."

"It's a weird name," I reply cheerfully, "but it means people won't forget me in a hurry."

She chuckles and turns the visitor's book toward me. "Could you sign in, please? And if you wouldn't mind wearing a sticker." She passes me one with the word 'visitor' on it, and I stick it to my jacket. I've dressed smartly today in my best gray pantsuit with a white blouse, and I've pinned my dark hair up in a neat bun in the hope of making a good impression.

As I sign the register, Juliette says, "Oh, here's James."

I turn to see a man crossing the lobby. He's wearing a smart, elegant, navy suit, he's exceptionally well groomed, and he's possibly the best-looking guy I've ever seen in real life.

"Hey, James," Juliette says. "Have you come to meet Missie?"

"Yeah," he replies, and he holds out his hand with a smile. "Pleased to meet you."

"James is a computer engineer and one of the owners of the company," Juliette says as I shake his hand.

"Juliette's supposed to be in a meeting," he replies, "so I'll take you through to Alex's office if you like."

She gives me a hug. "I hope it goes well!"

"Thank you so much for everything you've done for me," I tell her. I know she argued for me when some of the others said they'd rather start the trials with children who had two parents. "I really appreciate it."

"It's only what you deserve," she says briskly. She looks at James then with an impish smile. "I've warned her how grumpy Alex is, but I've tried to impress that his bark is worse than his bite."

"It might be worth having a tetanus shot anyway," James comments.

She snorts. "Good luck."

I watch her walk away. I wish she was coming with me!

"Don't listen to her," he says with a wink. "Alex is one of the good guys. We wouldn't be here without him. Come on, I'll take you through."

Somewhat mollified, I follow him across the lobby and into a glass-walled corridor that leads to an open-plan office. It's all designed the same way as the lobby—what did Juliette call it? Biophilic?—with lots of blue-and-purple pāua shells, stones, plants, and wood carved with pictures from Māori legends.

"It's a beautiful building," I tell him as he leads me through another set of automatic glass doors.

"Thank you, yeah, we love it, and it's a great place to work. Look, I can introduce you to the guy who's responsible for much of the design." He stops by two men who are standing by the water cooler, chatting. "This is Henry," he says, indicating one of the men. He's Māori and a big guy, maybe six-three or four, with wide shoulders. "He's a member of the South Island *iwi*, Ngāi Tahu, and he helped plan and design the new office. Guys, this is Mistletoe Macbeth."

"Missie, please," I correct. "Juliette was just telling me about how you worked with local *kaitiaki*. It's wonderful."

"Thank you." Henry gives me a big smile as we shake hands, his eyes creasing at the corners.

"And this is Damon," James informs me, gesturing at the other man. He's around six-two, not quite as big as his friend, but also handsome, with interesting gingerbread-colored eyes. "He painted the picture in the lobby."

My eyebrows rise. "Oh, really? Wow. It's amazing."

"Thank you." Damon also shakes my hand. I catch him and James exchanging a quick glance, and for the first time I get a tingle of suspicion.

"I get the feeling I'm being vetted," I tease. "Have I passed the test?"

"Aw," James says, "Juliette's been singing your praises, and everyone's keen to meet you, that's all."

"Eek." I pull a face. "Don't be misled by the name—I'm not that interesting."

They all laugh, and Damon smiles. "Good luck in the interview. I'm sure you'll do great."

"Thank you." I give them a parting smile and follow James as he gestures to the group of offices ahead.

"After you," he says, stopping in front of one to let me precede him.

I go to pass him—and walk straight into the glass door. It makes a huge clanging noise, and everyone in the vicinity, including Damon, Henry, James, and the guy in the room in front of me, look over and stare.

"Are you okay?" James asks with concern.

"Oops. Yes, I'm fine, thank you." Embarrassed at my faux pas, I go into the room. What was it Juliette said? *It's almost a done deal, as long as you don't do anything crazy to frighten him off?* Way to go, girl.

"It helps if you open the door first," the man inside states. He rises from the armchair he's sitting in. "You must be Mistletoe."

My face burning, I tuck the strand of hair that curls by my cheek behind my ear. "Um, Missie, please."

"I'm Alex Winters." He has a deep, slightly husky voice. He holds out his hand. I slide my hand into it, and his fingers close around mine.

He's tall, maybe six-two, but slimmer and not as big as Henry. He's wearing a dark-navy suit that's so smart and well-fitting it looks as if he's in uniform, a white shirt, and a navy tie with small white polka dots. His dark hair is cut in a low fade that's longer on top with the sort of volume Finn would kill for. He looks very sophisticated and well-groomed.

When I get back to school, the first thing I'm going to do is sneak into my best friend Carly's classroom and tell her how all the guys who work here are super-gorgeous. Maybe I should take a photo of them all to show her…

"Are you okay?" he asks as I continue to stare. "You don't have a concussion or anything?"

"Your windows are very clean," I say, deciding offense is the best form of defense. "At home I've got Transformers stickers in the middle of my sliding doors."

"What a great idea," he says. "James, make a note."

James just laughs, so I'm guessing it's not a serious recommendation. "Can I get you a drink?" James asks me. "Tea, coffee, a cold drink?"

"Coffee would be lovely, thank you. White, no sugar."

He nods and leaves.

I glance around the office. It's large and spacious, with a big wooden desk at an angle, and a sofa and two chairs on the other side. It's mostly glass, so you can see into the other offices, and it has a magnificent view out across the Avon. Today it's filled with autumn sunshine.

His desk bears a laptop, a phone, and a closed notepad—nothing else, no empty mugs, folders, or pieces of paper. Two pens sit side by side, neatly lined up.

"Wow, you're tidy," I say.

"I… uh… have mild OCD."

"Oh, shit, I'm sorry." Jesus, how many times can I put my foot in it? Embarrassed, looking for something else to say, I sniff the air, enjoying the subtle scent. "Have you been eating custard?" I joke, looking across at him.

He undoes the buttons of his jacket, flicks back the sides, and slides his hands into the pockets of his trousers. "My cologne has a touch of vanilla."

Fuck me. Apparently there's no limit to the amount of times I can insult this man. "Oh. I didn't mean to imply you smell like a trifle. It's nice. Um… warm, you know, friendly."

He gives me a look that suggests he's thinking *Jesus Christ, who is this woman?* "Would you like to sit down?"

"Oh. Sure." I walk over to the sofa and lower down as gracefully as I can. He sits in the armchair, leaning back and resting an ankle on the opposite knee.

His Apple Watch beeps, and he taps it lightly. "Just an alarm," he explains, seeing me look at it.

"To remind you to keep taking the pills?" I joke.

He lifts an eyebrow. "To remind me of our meeting, in case I missed the first alarm."

"So that was the second alarm?"

"I can sometimes miss appointments when I'm busy." He shifts in his chair. "You found your way here okay?"

"I met Juliette, and she brought me in. It's a beautiful building."

"Yeah, I think so. It's Henry's baby. James introduced you to him, right?"

"Yes. Juliette said you're all old friends."

"We went to university together."

"You're all computer engineers?"

"Apart from Juliette, yes."

"And you got into robotics and making the exoskeleton after one of your colleagues had an accident?"

"Yes, our friend Tyson suffered a spinal column injury."

"Juliette said he's doing well."

"He's getting married tomorrow. We've all been working hard to help him so he can stand for his vows."

"Oh, how wonderful. That must be so rewarding for you all. I bet his wife will be thrilled. Does she know?"

"Not yet." He looks a tad amused, and I realize I'm babbling.

I flush. "I'm sorry. I talk too much when I'm nervous."

The door opens and James comes in with two takeaway coffee cups.

"Thank you," I say as he passes me mine.

He glances from me to Alex. "Everything okay?"

"Fine." Alex takes his coffee cup. "Cheers."

James looks back at me. "You sure you don't want that tetanus shot?"

I bite my bottom lip, and he grins and goes out.

"Tetanus shot?" Alex asks.

"Um… Juliette said your bark was worse than your bite, and James said it might be best to get a tetanus shot anyway."

He holds my gaze, and I can't tell whether the comment has amused or annoyed him. I clear my throat. "Sorry."

"You can't get the staff nowadays," he says.

My brow furrows. "I feel as if I've got off on the wrong foot."

"You haven't."

"You seem annoyed."

"I'm not. I'm very dry."

I give him a helpless look. "I know I'm flaky and a bit hopeless. But I really, really want to do well in this interview. Finn needs this so much, so all I want to say is that even if I drive you nuts, please don't hold it against him."

"I wouldn't be much of a man if I did," he says. He leans forward, elbows on his knees, holding his coffee. "Missie, let me clear a few things up. Juliette put Finn forward for the trial, and I trust her opinion one hundred percent. The team here at Kia Kaha has read through Finn's records from his physio and doctor. We've already given him the green light."

I stare at him. Finn's in?

"I know I referred to it as an interview in the email," he continues, "but this meeting is just a formality. I wanted to meet you, that's all, and discuss your role in Finn's treatment. You know him better than anyone, and I want to talk to you about his motivation and whether you think he'll be able to commit to the treatment, which involves a significant time investment for a young lad, as well as a physical strain that can be tough for a parent to deal with. I know you're a single mother, and I believe you work full-time. You already have a lot on your plate, and I wanted to make sure you have enough support, because your wellbeing is as important to us as your son's."

My jaw has dropped. His speech didn't mention his business's needs once, even though I'm sure that's in the forefront of his mind. I have no doubt that the success of these initial trials will impinge greatly on Kia Kaha's future, and I wouldn't have blamed him if he made that very clear. Instead, though, despite his somewhat stern visage, he's just made me feel like the most important person in the world.

Emotion rushes through me without warning, and I press my fingers to my mouth in horror as tears well in my eyes.

To my surprise, he doesn't frown or look impatient. Instead, he gets up, retrieves the box of tissues from his desk, brings them back, and offers me one before taking his seat again.

I try to blot the tears that tip over my lashes, hoping it's not giving me panda eyes. "I'm so sorry." My voice is little more than a squeak.

"It's all right," he says. His voice is gentle. "You've been through a lot. Your only child suffered an appalling injury. I can't imagine how stressful it's been for you."

"Oh my God, please stop or I'm going to bawl my eyes out."

Leaning an elbow on the arm of his chair, he rests his lips on his fingers and doesn't speak again as I compose myself.

When I'm finally back in control, I blow my nose, then have a couple of gulps of coffee. "I'm sorry about that," I say finally. "Things have been a bit tough lately, and I've been so nervous about this meeting. I thought I had to convince you to take Finn."

"I wouldn't have put that pressure on a mother," he replies, frowning. "The interview, such as it is, works both ways. It's important that you ask all the questions you need to, so we can decide whether you feel Finn is a good fit for the program."

I nod and blow out a breath, trying to calm myself. "I appreciate that."

He picks up his coffee cup. Then he says, "I have an idea. Why don't we go for a walk? It's a beautiful day, and it's less formal and maybe less intimidating than sitting here, in the office."

"Oh, um, okay." Taken aback, I pick up my coffee cup, shoulder my purse, and follow him over to the sliding doors.

"You're okay walking in those heels?" he asks.

I look down at my strappy sandals. "Oh, yeah, I wear these all the time. I'm five-seven, but I like the extra few inches."

As soon as the words leave my mouth, I realize what I've said, and half expect him to reply with 'I bet' or something similar, but he doesn't. He doesn't smile either, but something about his expression—a slight sparkle in his eyes—tells me that my reply amused him.

He steps back to let me precede him through the doors, but he only moves a couple of inches. As I squeeze past him, I breathe in the scent of his cologne, warmed by his skin—a spicy sandalwood, with a touch of vanilla. I look up and catch his eye, and a shiver runs down my back. This guy is an enigma. I can't read him at all, and I have no idea what he thinks of me.

He closes the door behind me, then leads me down a series of steps on the private terrace to a gate at the bottom. We go through it and find ourselves on the pathway that follows the River Avon, and turn right, heading for Hagley Park.

He's right—it's a beautiful day, the breeze too cool for summer, but too warm for winter. Fluffy clouds scud across a bright blue sky, ruffling the feathers of the ducks. We stop and wait for a couple of them to cross the path in front of us with a group of tiny ducklings.

"Aw," I say. "How gorgeous."

"She's a bit of a helicopter parent," Alex says as the mother fusses around them to make sure none of them gets left behind.

"I think I would be too, if my babies could be snatched by a stoat at any moment."

"Fair point."

We watch them descend into the river and swim off, and then we continue along the path.

"Are you sure you've got time for this?" I ask him curiously. "You must be a very busy man."

"Nah. Most of the time I just play solitaire."

Again, he doesn't smile, but he told me, *I'm very dry*, so I know he's teasing.

"You're quite unusual," I tell him.

"I get that a lot."

"Juliette said you were a mixture of James Bond, Stephen Hawking, and Scrooge."

"I don't know whether to be flattered or insulted by that."

"Well, I understand you're the brains behind THOR, so I'm guessing the genius bit is right. You've got the James Bond look going for you. How do you feel about Christmas?"

"Bah, humbug."

"Yeah, so I think she was spot on."

I just get a wry glance, and I look away, flustered. Most people smile a lot in conversation to disarm or reassure you, and men sometimes flirt lightly, even if they're not single—it's just a way to connect, to feel comfortable with one another. But Alex doesn't do that, and I'm not sure how to handle him.

"All right," he says, "so I've read the file Finn's doctor sent several times. But maybe we should start at the beginning. Why don't you tell me about yourself and Finn in your own words, and then I'll go through the program, and you can ask me any questions you like?"

Chapter Two

Alex

Mistletoe Macbeth sips from her coffee cup while she thinks about how to start her story. Her gaze is fixed on the ground, and her forehead is creased in a frown. Juliette told me that Finn's mother had a permanently sunny disposition, but it's clear that this morning her emotion is overwhelming her.

She's wearing a light-gray pantsuit with a white shirt and a pair of nude-colored, strappy sandals with stiletto heels. How do women walk in those all day? Her toenails and her fingernails bear an elegant French tip.

Her dark hair is wound in a tight bun, but a thick strand spirals past her cheek, curling like a silk ribbon. She has full lips with a marked Cupid's bow, and dark-blue eyes. Her left hand still bears her wedding ring.

"What do you want to know?" she asks.

"Tell me a bit about yourself," I reply. "What wasn't in the reports. Just so I can build up a picture of Finn and his home life."

"Okay... um... well... I'm twenty-seven, twenty-eight on December the twenty-third, hence the Christmassy name. It was my father's idea. I still haven't forgiven him."

"It's certainly different."

"How very diplomatic of you."

"Diplomatic is my middle name," I tell her.

She gives a short laugh. "I teach at Clifton Primary School."

"What's your degree in?"

"Art. And I know what you're thinking—it explains the flakiness." She meets my eyes, and her eyebrows draw together. "Don't look at me like that," she scolds.

"Like what?"

"Like you think I'm batshit crazy."

"I'm really not. It's just my normal face."

"Your expression hardly changes. You're a very difficult guy to read."

"I'm laughing on the inside."

"Well, perhaps you should laugh on the outside occasionally, just to let the other person know you're not apoplectic with rage."

"I'll bear that in mind."

She obviously doesn't know what to make of me. "Being flaky isn't necessarily a bad thing," she states.

"I'm sure it isn't."

"I have a feeling that you're the type of guy who detests flakiness."

"What gives you that idea?"

"Let's say it's my sixth sense." She points a finger at me. "I saw that."

"Saw what?"

"You raised your eyebrow."

"No, I didn't."

"You don't believe in intuition?"

"Of course I do."

"I believe in psychic abilities. And crystals. And astrology." She speaks defiantly, obviously expecting me to scoff.

"Okay." I keep a straight face.

She frowns. "Aren't you going to crack a joke about the moon being in Uranus or something?"

"I wouldn't dream of it."

She bites her lip. "I shouldn't be telling you all this. I want you to think I'm serious about this trial."

"I told you, I wouldn't remove a child from the trial just because I thought his mother was…"

"Mad? Crazy mad? Crazy bonkers mad?"

"Unusual," I choose.

"I have many layers," she protests.

"Like an onion?"

"More like a lasagna."

"Unfortunately, I'm allergic to bechamel sauce."

She looks startled. "Really?"

"No, Missie. I'm not lactose intolerant. It was supposed to be a joke."

She presses a hand to her forehead. "You're doing my head in. I can't tell when you're being serious and when you're teasing."

"I can't be both?"

She stops walking and looks at me. I bear her scrutiny patiently, finishing off my coffee.

Eventually, she mumbles, "I'm going to put my cup in the bin. Want me to take yours?"

"Sure."

I watch her pass a general rubbish bin and walk a few hundred yards to a recycling bin, toss her cup in, then come back to me.

"What?" she says. "Don't you care about the environment?"

"I don't *not* care."

She clears her throat. "Maybe we should get back to Finn."

"Of course."

"You want me to tell you about the accident?"

"I'd like to hear it in your own words." We turn left into Hagley Park, taking the path that follows the Avon in the direction of the Botanic Gardens.

She's quiet for a while. I let her think about what she wants to say. A coxed four goes past us, the guys pulling effortlessly at the oars.

"The accident happened just before Christmas," she says slowly. "We lived in Dunedin. Lee, my late husband, was a real-estate agent. He was taking a client to see a property, but he'd just picked Finn up from school, and Finn was in the backseat—Lee often did that, if he had a late appointment. Finn would do his homework or play a game on his phone until Lee had finished. The police think Lee was distracted by something, because he ran a red light and drove straight into a lorry. He and the client were killed outright. Finn suffered a spinal column injury, and he's been unable to walk since."

She speaks calmly, showing no sign of the emotion she exhibited in my office.

"I'm so sorry for your loss," I tell her.

"Thank you."

Trees close around us on either side, the odd dry leaf fluttering to the ground.

"So, it's been three months," I say.

"Yes."

"Tell me about Finn's injury." I've read the doctor's and the physio's detailed reports, but I want to see what Missie understands about her son's predicament.

"He suffered damage to the lumbar section of his spinal cord," she says, "the L1, L2, and L3 vertebrae, to be exact. They're not sure yet how serious it is because there's still some swelling. He has loss of function in his hips and legs, and hardly any control over his bowel and bladder. He can't walk, even with crutches. He also had a concussion, and he can't remember the day of the accident. Maybe that's a blessing."

She's obviously listened to Finn's doctor and physio. I don't need to explain what's happened to her son. I just need to make it clear where we go from here.

"As I'm sure you know," I say, "spinal shock can last for several months. The most recovery occurs from three to six months, after the swelling has gone down, so he's at the perfect stage to start rehabilitation."

She nods. "So you think you can help?"

"Let me explain first what we do at Kia Kaha. I think Juliette told you about the exoskeleton?"

"A little."

"We've given it the nickname The Hands-On Robot, or THOR, for the children. It's a self-supporting mobility device that helps the patient to move and exercise their limbs with confidence. At the moment, we're using it primarily to help patients regain greater control over their body. When people have damaged their spinal cord, the brain can't control the bladder and bowel because the message carrier—the spinal cord—has been injured. We can teach the patient ways to help empty the bladder, and to control the bowel, and rehabilitation helps lessen the possibility of circulatory problems and regain muscle tone."

Birds hop between the lofty walls of the cork oak and sequoia trees of the Archery Lawn. I take the path to the right, deeper into the park, and Missie follows.

"There are other companies in New Zealand carrying out similar rehab," I say, "but THOR is different because we've integrated it with a gaming computer to encourage children to do their physio, and to make it more enjoyable."

"What kind of games are there?"

"A wide range—anything from sporting games like tennis, rugby, and football, to action games involving doing quests and fighting monsters. All of them are age appropriate, of course. If you decide to go ahead with the rehab, Finn will have to come into Kia Kaha after school three days a week for an hour each time. It will be intensive and tiring, but it's most likely to provide positive results."

She's quiet for a moment. We come to the end of the path, and I gesture for her to turn right.

"Have you seen the Regret Water Sculpture?" I ask her.

She shakes her head. We emerge from the trees onto the Archery Lawn, in front of a round pond with a sculpture made from steel rods. The statue of a partially submerged figure of a woman wearing a gown and a blindfold with arms outstretched reclines in the water.

"It's supposed to reflect the messy reality of human life," I tell her.

"Seems appropriate," she whispers. "It's beautiful."

"I thought you'd like it, as an artist."

She stops walking and stares at it for a moment. Then she turns to me. "Alex… can I ask you something?"

"Of course."

"Can you help Finn to walk again?"

I hold her gaze. Her eyes are a shade darker than the blue sky behind her.

"You know I can't promise anything," I tell her gently.

"I know. And I'm not asking you to sign your life away. I won't sue you if it doesn't work, I swear. But…" She hesitates. "That first week, Finn's specialist, Dr. Michaels, said it was unlikely he'd ever walk again because the damage was too severe."

I don't say anything, although I frown.

"Finn didn't take it well," she continues, "and it's been very hard on us both. I don't want to give him false hope, to put him through all that if there's little chance of him returning to the way he was. But if you think you can help, we'll both give a hundred and ten percent to the program. I'll get on my knees if I have to."

"That won't be necessary."

She blushes scarlet. "I meant to beg."

"I know."

"Oh God, I'm making such a mess of this."

"You're really not."

She raises her eyes to mine. They're glassy with unshed tears. "Is there hope?"

"There's always hope."

She drops her gaze and presses her fingers to her lips for a second. Then she says, "He's only ten. It's so young. I want him to have a normal life, to be able to run around again, to be independent, to have girlfriends and be able to… you know."

I know what she's saying—spinal cord injuries can affect a man's sexual performance. It's a valid concern.

"Can you help him?" she whispers.

I've read his reports and talked in depth with Juliette about his prognosis. The surgeon has done his best to repair the damage to Finn's spine. Initial scans have shown that the swelling is going down, and everything's healing as it's meant to. Nothing's certain with the human body, but what I do know is that his chances of getting better will improve significantly with intense rehab and physio. I can't promise Missie that he'll be running marathons in the near future, and I understand that she doesn't want false hope. But I'm confident that coming to Kia Kaha is what the kid needs.

"Yes," I tell her. "We can help."

"You're not just saying that because it's what you think I want to hear?"

"I don't lie. I say exactly what I mean. You don't have to read between the lines to figure out what I'm trying to tell you. I'm not promising miracles. And it won't happen quickly. It will be hard work on Finn's part, and it'll be tough at times. But I believe that with care and dedication, this time next year will see him on his feet again."

I can see she's struggling to retain her composure. "We should talk about the cost," she whispers. "My husband took out a life-insurance policy, so I have some money."

"That was astute of him."

"I didn't know he'd done it. A week after he died, I got an email out of the blue from Eastwood Insurance saying the policy was paying out. It was a real shock. Three hundred thousand dollars."

"That must make things a little easier."

"It's made all the difference to Finn—we were able to get him a quality wheelchair and other equipment, and to have improvements carried out at home to make it easier for him to move around. I don't know what I'd have done without it. I still have a good bit left. I'm saving it for him—I feel too bad about spending it on myself. I'll use it to pay for the treatment."

"Put it into a savings fund for him," I tell her firmly. "You don't have to pay a cent."

Her jaw drops. "Really?"

"Yes. Eventually it'll be funded through the public system, but we're fronting the cost of the initial trials. You don't have anything to worry about."

Her eyes fill with tears, and then they spill over her lashes.

"I'm sorry," she squeaks, fumbling in her pockets for a tissue.

"Here." I pass her my pocket square, then gesture to one of the park benches. We go over and sit. She perches on the edge as she dabs at her eyes.

"I'm sorry," she says again.

"It's okay."

"Carly's going to demand her ten bucks."

"Sorry, Carly?"

"My best friend. She's also a teacher at the primary school. She bet me ten bucks that I'd cry today."

"Well, that was easy money. You lost your husband three months ago, and you've had to go through all this with Finn alone. I'm shocked that you're not bawling your eyes out twenty-four-seven."

She swallows hard and looks at me with watery eyes. "You're such a strange man. One minute I'm sure you think I'm mad, and the next you say something like that."

I watch her as she gathers her composure. She takes several deep, shaky breaths, looking across the pond at the statue of the woman with the blindfold and the outstretched arms. "That's how I feel," she whispers. "Groping blindly in the dark."

"Well, hopefully we can provide you with a flashlight to help you see better."

She rubs her nose. "What's the next step?"

"I'd like to meet Finn. We should arrange for you to bring him in. I'll go over everything we've discussed, and then I'll show him around Kia Kaha and introduce him to THOR."

"I'd appreciate that. It has surprised me how often medical professionals talk to me and seem to forget he's in the room."

"He's the most important person in the whole equation. I want him to understand what we're going to ask him to do, and make sure he's on board with it."

"Okay."

"I'd like him to meet the rest of our team, especially Tyson Palmer eventually. He's a good friend of mine, and he's the reason we created MAX—the adult version of THOR. He suffered a spinal column injury when he was twenty-two, which put him in a wheelchair. His injury was more severe than Finn's, and it's taken him a lot longer to regain his mobility. But he's getting married tomorrow, and he's going to surprise his fiancée by standing to say his vows."

"Oh," she murmurs, "that's wonderful."

"Yeah, we think so. It's taken him five years of hard work, but he never gave up."

"Finn will work hard," she says. "I know he will. It was just... after what the doctor said, he was very down, and it was hard to get him to do his physio. I'm guessing he didn't want to give Finn false hope, but I don't think he should have told him that."

"He absolutely should not have said that. But anyway, why don't we get back to the office, and we'll make an appointment for Finn to come in?"

She nods, and we get to our feet and start walking back.

She holds out my pocket square to me. "Keep it," I tell her. "I have plenty of others."

"Um, okay, thank you." She slides it into her pocket.

"Is Finn back at school?"

"Yes, he started this week. He's in his last year at the primary school where I work. They have a Learning Enrichment Center, and they've allocated someone to stay with him during the day for a while, to take him to each lesson, and to the bathroom if he needs it." She bends to pick up a scarlet leaf. "He hates being treated as if he's disabled," she admits. "But I didn't want him to miss too much schooling."

"So we'll get him in after school. Three-thirty until four-thirty?"

"You don't work weekends?"

"Juliette doesn't."

"Oh, of course."

"Once Finn is comfortable with the physio program, another of our team can be there on Saturdays if you'd like to swap one of the days."

"It's tough for me to leave school at three-thirty," she admits, "that's all."

"You don't have to stay with him. You can drop him off and then go back to school for an hour. Or I can come and pick him up if you want."

Her eyes widen. "Seriously?"

"He'll be fine with us, once he gets to know us. There's not a lot you can do anyway—you'd just be sitting there, watching. You're welcome to, of course, but it's important that you carry on with your own life."

She lowers her gaze to the ground, and we walk quietly for a while.

"I really appreciate this," she says eventually. "Thank you, for choosing Finn, and for being so understanding."

"You're welcome."

She glances at me. "Seriously, though, you need to smile more."

"I'll take that under advisement."

"I like smiling. I'm a glass-half-full kind of girl."

"You're a primary school teacher. It'd be weird if you weren't."

"Is your full name Alexander?"

"It is."

"I'm going to call you Alexander from now on."

I stifle a sigh. "If you must."

"I'm going to make it my mission in life to make you smile more."

"Good luck with that."

"I'm pretty good at cheering people up."

My brows draw together. "After everything you've been through, it wouldn't surprise me if you were the most miserable woman in existence."

"Every cloud and all that." She studies me for a moment. "Do you find me annoying?"

"No."

"Irritating?"

"No."

"Are you sure you don't want to punch me in the face?"

That makes me laugh for the first time, and her eyes light up.

"I knew I could make you smile," she states happily.

"Don't tell anyone," I scold. "I have a reputation to maintain."

"It can be our little secret." But her eyes continue to sparkle.

We cross the road and head back to Kia Kaha. I let us through the gate, and we climb the terrace steps and go back into my office.

"Right, let's book Finn in," I say, going over to my computer. "I'd say tomorrow, but Tyson's getting married, so it'll have to be Monday. What time is best for you?"

"I can make three-thirty on Monday."

"Okay. Can I just double check, Finn's surname is Taylor, right?"

"Yes, it's his father's surname. I've always been known by my maiden name at school, and I decided to stick with it."

"Miss Missie Macbeth?"

She wrinkles her nose. "It does sound a bit ridiculous when you say it like that."

"Not at all. I like it."

"Oh," she says, and blushes.

I hide a smile. "Okay. Well, I look forward to meeting Finn."

"I hope you like him," she says somewhat shyly. "He's such a lovely boy, but the accident has changed him a lot."

"It's common for people, including children, to suffer from depression after an injury like this. And he's at that age anyway when you have all these conflicting emotions raging around inside you." I open the door for her, and we walk slowly through the offices toward the lobby. "I can remember being that age, and it's no fun."

"What were you like as a kid?" she asks.

"I was a nerd. Not a bad bone in my body."

She looks at me with her big blue eyes as we pause in the lobby. "Oh, I sincerely doubt that."

I hold her gaze for a moment. Then I say softly, "I'll see you Monday."

She clears her throat. "Goodbye." She hesitates, as if she's going to say something else. Then she gives me a quick smile, turns, and walks away.

I watch her cross the lobby. Her high heels give her butt an attractive wiggle as she walks.

I feel a presence at my side, and turn to see James standing there. I follow his gaze, and together we watch Missie go through the automatic doors and down the steps.

I drag my gaze away from her to discover him looking at me.

"Nice girl," he says.

"Her husband died three months ago, James."

His smile fades. "Yeah."

"She's having a helluva tough time with her son, and she has a lot of grieving to do."

"Yeah, I know."

We don't say anything more until we stop outside his office.

He pauses with his hand on the door handle. "She's pretty though," he says.

Sliding my hands into my trouser pockets, I just give him a wry look before I walk away.

Chapter Three

Monday 19th March

Missie

"Are you okay?" I help Finn out of the car and into the wheelchair. He's unusually quiet. I bend and fold down the footrests, then hold his hand and look up at him. "How was school?"

He shrugs. "All right."

"Did something happen today?"

"No." He rubs his nose. "I'm a bit nervous, that's all."

"Aw." I smile and rub his hand. "There's no need to be. From what Alex told me, it sounds like this physiotherapy is going to be a lot more fun than it was at the hospital."

"What's he like?" he asks as I lock the car and start walking with him toward the Kia Kaha building.

"He's tall and dark. Kinda gorgeous, actually."

"Do you fancy him?"

"A little bit. He thinks I'm crazy, though."

"I wonder why?"

"My son, ladies and gentlemen."

He chuckles. "So he's, you know, friendly?"

"He's… unusual." I don't want to scare Finn by saying Alex is stern and hard to read. He's easily intimidated by strict teachers. "He doesn't smile a lot, but he's quite funny."

Finn doesn't reply, and I decide not to say anything else.

The big car park has wide spaces so people with wheelchairs have plenty of room to maneuver, and it's only a short distance to the side entrance of the building. The doors open automatically, and we go into the lobby and across to the reception desk. I've already explained to

Finn about the biophilic building, and he looks around in awe at the Māori carvings and all the plants.

"Hello Rebecca." I smile at the young woman behind the desk. "We're here to see Alex again."

"Hello, Mistletoe!" She smiles at Finn. "And you must be Finn. Pleased to meet you." She offers him a hand, and he shakes it shyly. "I've already buzzed Alex, and he's on his way," she says.

I turn in the direction of the offices and spot him immediately, striding through the glass-walled corridor. He looks different today. He's not wearing his suit jacket, and he's rolled up his shirtsleeves. His hair also looks less styled, as if he's been running his hand through it all afternoon.

I've been thinking about this guy all weekend, and all day at school today. I didn't want to. I'm pretty sure he thinks I'm kooky—he was just too polite to say so. He makes me feel... unsettled, and I don't like that I can't guess what he's thinking. But there was something in his brown eyes when he watched me that caused goosebumps to rise all over me.

They're rising now, as he approaches, and his eyes meet mine.

"Hey, Missie," he says, holding out his hand.

"Hello." I shake it, tingling at the feel of his skin on mine. "Um, this is Finn. Finn, this is Alexander Winters."

"Alex," he corrects, shaking Finn's hand. "Don't listen to her."

"You shouldn't say that about his mother," I scold.

"I'll be saying it a lot," he says to Finn with a wink, and Finn grins. "Come on," Alex says, taking Finn's wheelchair. "We're in the boardroom. Everyone's waiting for the star of the show."

He strides off with Finn, pretends to steer him into a plant pot, then swerves at the last minute, and Finn laughs.

Taken aback, I follow them along the corridor to the end, where they turn right and enter a large room through a set of automated doors. It has a long wooden table surrounded by black chairs. The room faces a terrace with wide concrete steps that lead down to the Avon. The wall is nearly all glass, and they've opened the sliding doors, so it's full of afternoon sunshine.

The three people sitting at the end of the table stop talking as Alex enters with Finn. Alex steers him around the table, then slots him into a space without a chair. "This is Finn," he announces. "Finn, this is James, Henry, and you've already met Juliette."

James and Henry shake hands with him, and Finn's face flushes. He loves the way they're treating him like an adult.

"Great to meet you at last," James says. "We've heard a lot about you."

"Yeah," Henry says, "apparently you've finished Zelda: Tears of the Kingdom. I'm so impressed. I'm only about halfway through." He's referring to a game on the Nintendo Switch.

"We were just debating whether it's better than Breath of the Wild," James says.

"I've done them both," Finn says. "Tears is better."

"Told you he'd be cool," Alex says to them. He looks at me then, and his lips curve up, just a little. "Have a seat, Missie." He gestures to the chair beside his as he sits.

I lower myself down. The middle of the table is filled with plates of food—club sandwiches and rolls, small pies, sushi, and a variety of cakes and biscuits. "Are we interrupting you?" I ask, wondering whether they're having a board meeting.

"Nah," Alex says, "we were just about to have afternoon tea, that's all. We have to have food available whenever we meet, or Henry feels faint."

"That's true," Henry admits.

"Help yourself if you're hungry, Finn," Alex adds. "I was always ravenous when I got home from school." He pushes a plate across to him, then starts piling food on his own plate. Finn watches him, then looks at the sandwiches and starts helping himself.

I glance at Juliette, and she winks at me. I know then that they've ordered the food for Finn, and Alex is trying to put him at ease. Touched, I help myself to a few sandwiches and some sushi, as I only managed half my lunch because I was on playground duty today.

James lifts a large jug of water with ice and chopped fruit, and pours everyone a glass. Again, we're all on the same level—it's not the adults having coffee and the child drinking water.

I look at Alex, who's offering Finn the plate of sushi and telling him the chicken teriyaki ones are the best.

"What happened to your hair?" I ask.

He raises a hand to it self-consciously. "What do you mean?"

"He forgot to put product in it this morning, is my guess," Juliette states.

"You don't look quite as well-turned out today," I tease. The longer top that he'd combed so carefully last time has lost some of its height and is flopping over his forehead.

He scowls. "I've been working all day." He runs his fingers through it to try and keep it back. It doesn't work and just flops forward again. Finn giggles. "Don't you start," Alex says. "I was just beginning to like you."

Finn giggles again, revealing that he doesn't believe Alex's reprimand. "Have you really played Zelda?" he asks.

The others all laugh. When Finn glances around at them, Juliette says, "Alex has played every game in the universe."

"You make me sound like a nerd," Alex complains.

"If the cap fits," Juliette says.

"We're all gamers," Henry tells Finn. "We've all got PlayStations, Xboxes, and Switches."

"We play online together," Juliette reveals.

Finn's eyes widen. "What do you play?"

"Mostly MMOs on the PC," she says, "World of Warcraft, Final Fantasy, New World, Guild Wars 2. But some console games like Call of Duty Modern Warfare."

It's obvious from her terminology that she's telling the truth, and Finn looks impressed. "I'm not supposed to play World of Warcraft," he says. "It's for twelves and over." He glances at me.

"Actually, we both play," I admit, pulling an 'eek' face. "It's been something we can do together." I don't add 'since his accident' but I'm sure they realize that's what I mean. Gaming has been an escape for both of us over the last three months. "I know a lot of people would frown on that," I add.

"Actually, a New Zealand study found no evidence for a link between video games and aggressive behavior," James states, taking a bite out of a sandwich.

"I didn't realize that," I reply in surprise.

"I always feel that people who criticize gamers are missing the benefits that gaming provides," Juliette says. "As well as physical benefits like hand-eye coordination, it encourages teamwork, and improves strategy and leadership. And it's cool," she adds to Finn and elbows him, and he grins.

"Dad used to play Mario Kart with me," he says.

"Yeah that's fun," Alex says without missing a beat. "Which one?"

"Um, eight."

"We've all played it together," Alex says, gesturing at the others. "We'll have to invite you around for one of our gaming afternoons. We'll even let you win a couple of times."

"I'm faster than every kid in my class," Finn replies. "I bet I'll beat every one of you."

"Are you trash-talking me?"

"Might be," Finn says, and they both laugh.

So my son can make Alex laugh, even if I can't! The guy has attractive, straight, white teeth and a mischievous smile when it does appear. He should definitely smile more.

I like that he didn't blanch away or change the subject when Finn mentioned his father. In fact, I like everything about the way they're acting with him. I can see that Finn has relaxed, especially now he's had something to eat, too.

"Mum said that your machine is part of a game," Finn says.

"Yeah," Henry replies, helping himself to more sandwiches. "We all find exercise easier if we have something else to do like listening to music or watching TV. So we figured it would be more fun to do physio if it was connected to gaming."

"Do you like Transformers?" Alex asks.

"Yeah," Finn says. "I've got loads, and I've seen all the movies."

"Then you're going to have no trouble," Alex says. "THOR looks like a Transformer you can get in. Sometimes I have a go just for fun."

"He's telling the truth," Juliette tells Finn. "I've told him off several times."

Finn giggles again. He's obviously enjoying himself, and now I can see he's excited to take a look at the machine.

"So how's your day been, Mistletoe?" Alex asks, surprising me.

I give him a wry look at his use of my full name. "Fine thanks, *Alexander*."

"Mum calls you Alexander the Great," Finn says.

I go completely scarlet and say, "Finn!" while the others try not to laugh, and fail.

"More like Alexander the Mediocre," James says.

Alex's eyes meet mine and his lips curve up a fraction, although whether that's due to my nickname for him or James's comment, I'm not sure.

"Oh look!" Finn's gazing out of the window, and I turn to see that a flock of mallard ducks has made their way up the terrace steps and is looking at us through the glass.

"They come up for food," Juliette says. "They like oats. Shall we try them with one of these flapjacks? I don't think there's much sugar in them."

Finn likes the idea, so Juliette wheels his chair through the sliding doors and out onto the deck, and the two of them start breaking off pieces of flapjack for the excited ducks.

I look back at Alex and discover him watching me. "Sorry about that," I say. "The Alexander the Great comment, I mean."

"I can think of worse compliments," he says. "And it does explain my desire to sack Thebes."

That makes me laugh. He holds my gaze for a moment, his eyes full of amusement, before he lowers his gaze to the laptop resting on the table by his side. "So... we were thinking about starting Finn's program on Monday, April the third. How would that work for you?"

"Whatever's best for you," I reply, relieved it's so soon.

"Okay, we'll book him in. I think..." He trails off. He's looking past me, out of the window, and he suddenly gets to his feet.

"What..." I watch him stride past me toward the sliding doors, and then he breaks into a run. I spin around just in time to see that Finn's wheelchair has rolled back; he must have forgotten to put on the brake. He's bending to feed the ducks, but one of the back wheels is an inch from the top step of the terrace, and the chair is still moving backward. Juliette's talking to him, but she hasn't noticed.

As the three of us inside watch in horror, the wheel goes over the step and the chair pitches back. Alex reaches him a second too late to catch the arm of the chair, but he does manage to grab a handful of Finn's sweatshirt. Finn has sat up in shock as he obviously felt the chair tip, and the momentum of him straightening increases the speed at which the chair is falling.

The steps aren't steep, but they are concrete. I have a vision of him tumbling all the way down, cracking his skull on the way, and a scream hovers on my lips. At the last minute, though, with a superhuman feat of strength because Finn isn't a tiny boy, Alex hauls him out of the chair by his sweatshirt and catches him with the other arm, and the empty chair crashes onto the step below, bumps down a few, and keels over, one wheel spinning in the air.

Juliette stands in shock, and we all rush outside.

Alex slides his other arm under Finn's legs and lifts him up. Finn puts his arms around Alex's neck, visibly trembling.

"It's all right," Alex murmurs. "No harm done." He meets my eyes, and I can see the relief reflected in his. "Crisis averted," he says, walking past us back into the boardroom.

"Jesus." I'm shaking like a leaf, too.

"I'm so sorry." Juliette puts her arm around me and rubs my arm. "I was looking the other way."

"It wasn't your fault. I've told him time and again to double check his brake is on."

"He was distracted by the ducks," she says. "We both were. Come and sit down. I'll make you a cup of tea."

I let Juliette lead me back into the room and go over to Finn. There's no point in scolding him about the brake; his fear will teach him more than me nagging him.

Alex is still holding him, although as I walk up to them, he lowers Finn into a chair.

"Are you okay?" I ask, dropping to my knees beside him.

Finn nods and rubs his nose. "Alex saved me," he says, and leans forward to put his arms around me.

"I saw." As I rub Finn's back, I look over his shoulder at Alex and mouth, *Thank you.*

He ruffles Finn's hair. "If you're that keen on flying, I'll take you for a ride in my helicopter."

Finn lowers his arms, his eyes widening. "Really?"

"You've got a helicopter?" I ask, stunned.

"Yeah. It'll be a good excuse to get up in the air. I love flying. Remind me to check my calendar after we've seen THOR, and we'll book in a time."

Finn looks at me, eyes alight with excitement. He's been fascinated with helicopters since he was a toddler, but I've never been able to afford to take him up in one.

"The chair's fine," Henry says, bringing it in.

"There," Alex says, "everything's cool. So come on, bro, what do you say we give you a ride in our robot?"

"Do you want to rest for a bit first?" I ask Finn, worried the shock has affected him.

But he squares his shoulders, clearly intent on putting on a brave face for Alex and the others. "No, I'm fine."

"You have your cup of tea," Alex tells me. "Juliette can bring you through afterward." He glances at Finn, then back at me. He wants me to stay here for a bit. Maybe he thinks if Finn stays with the guys, it'll make him feel better.

"I'll be fine, Mum," Finn says. He doesn't want them to think he's a kid.

"Okay," I say softly, and Juliette goes over to the drinks table to make the tea.

Henry brings the chair forward, and without being asked, Alex bends and lifts Finn into it, making sure his feet are on the rests and that he's comfortable before taking the handles.

"Have you played Hogwarts Legacy on Switch?" he asks as he steers Finn toward the door.

"No, it's for twelve and up."

"I'll lend you my copy. Don't tell your mother." He disappears down the corridor, Henry and James chuckling as they follow.

I look at Juliette, who looks as pale as I feel.

"I thought I checked the brake on his chair," she says as she pours hot water onto the teabags. "I'm so sorry."

"You did—I saw you. He took it off so he could turn and face the ducks, and he obviously didn't put it back on. Well, he's learned his lesson today." I blow out a long breath. "Thank God Alex was watching."

"Did you see how he hauled Finn up?" She brings the cups over.

I take mine from her. "I know. I don't know how he did it. Finn's tall for his age, and I know he's lost weight, but he must be about eighty pounds."

She blows a raspberry. "Alex can bench press 175 pounds."

"Seriously?"

"That's nothing, Henry can do well over 200." Her lips twist as I raise an eyebrow. "Not that I've been watching them in the gym or anything."

I chuckle. "Seriously, though, that was impressive. And the way Finn put his arms around him... He's normally very reticent with people he doesn't know."

She blows on her tea. "He must miss his dad a lot."

My gaze drifts out of the window. The ducks have gone, and the sky is clouding over. "Yeah," I say.

We sip our tea, watching the first drops of rain appear on the glass.

Eventually, Juliette asks me about the primary school where I work, and we chat for a while about teaching and children, as Juliette works with kids a lot. In the end, it's about twenty minutes later that I say maybe we should check on Finn, as I don't want Alex to think he has to babysit him for me.

She leads the way out of the boardroom. Instead of heading back to the lobby, she turns the other way, following where the guys went, crossing the glass-walled main office and heading for the brick building at the end. We go through a set of doors and find ourselves in an area that looks more scientific, with clean white walls, and rooms with people in lab coats and lots of computers and machinery.

She takes me up a ramp and stops at the top, her hand on the door. "This leads to a balcony that looks down at the treatment room," she says, "so we'll get a good view of how they're doing." She puts a finger to her lips, then pushes open the door and goes in.

I follow her onto a wide platform with a balustrade at the front, and we lean on it and look down at the room.

I don't know what I expected to see—possibly Finn bolted into the robot equipment, with the guys giving him a lecture on its uses. Instead, the robot device stands in the corner, and Alex, James, and Henry are all in wheelchairs, playing office basketball with Finn. The ball is a soft one, and they're obviously in two teams—Alex and Finn against James and Henry. The plastic hoop is stuck to the wall.

There's lots of shouting and laughter, and my lips curve up as I watch Alex park his chair in front of James's to intercept the ball, then pass it to Finn, who neatly steers around Henry to shoot the ball through the hoop. Finn whoops and goes over to Alex, and they high five.

Finn spots us and waves, and Alex looks up. "We're unbeatable," he says, spinning his chair in a circle. Finn watches, then copies him, and Juliette sends me a smile.

"Come on," she says, leading the way down the stairs.

James and Henry rise from their chairs and fold them up, but Alex stays seated as we walk up to them, playing with the ball.

"How did you get on with THOR?" I ask Finn.

"It was brilliant," he says enthusiastically. "Just like a Transformer. I tried it on, and Alex showed me how to stand up and sit down using the controls. It's so cool." He laughs then as Alex throws the ball at him and it bounces off his head.

"He did great," Alex says, catching the ball as Finn tosses it back. "We went through some of the games, and he's going to try The Knights of Avalon. It's an Arthurian adventure where you have to quest for the Holy Grail."

"I play a knight wearing a suit of armor," Finn says. "You have to do all these exercises that real knights had to do."

"Tilting at windmills," Alex says.

I smile at Finn. "Did you get to—" I stop as the ball bounces off my head, and my gaze slides to Alex.

"Sorry," he says, not looking the least bit mortified, and Finn giggles.

"I think it's time we went home," I say wryly.

"Aw…" Finn obviously doesn't want to go, which I take as a sign that he's gotten over his accident and is enjoying himself.

"Thank you all so much," I say to them. "Except for you." I poke my tongue out at Alex, and his lips curve up.

I take the handles of Finn's chair. "We'll see you on April the third."

Alex hooks his foot under Finn's chair and turns him to face him. "What are you doing on Saturday?"

"Nothing," Finn says.

"Wanna go up in the helicopter then?" Alex asks.

Finn's jaw drops. He looks up at me, his eyes widening. "Can we?"

I meet Alex's gaze. As usual, he's not smiling, but his eyes are sparkling.

I still can't make this guy out, but I can't deny that I find him attractive. And it's clear Finn likes him.

And that's when I hear warning bells.

"Actually, we're busy this weekend," I say as graciously as I can. "But thank you for the offer."

"Aw, Mum."

"We should go now. Thank you all for your help."

They all say goodbye. I don't meet Alex's eyes as I turn Finn and take him out through the door and head for the lobby.

It's raining lightly outside. Finn is quiet, and I know he's disappointed. I feel a tug of guilt. The boy's been through so much, and Alex was offering him what might be a once-in-a-lifetime treat. Have I made a mistake?

But I know Finn. The accident obviously had a huge physical impact on him, but what we've been through with his father took an even greater emotional toll. He feels betrayed and abandoned, and he's going to gravitate toward any male who shows him kindness and friendship. I must be careful that he doesn't get too attached to Alex. The guy is obviously thoughtful and kind, despite his stern visage, but he's only doing his job.

I also have a lot of therapy to go through before I can put my ghosts to rest. So it's best that I keep my distance from any man who gives me anything approaching the feels.

I head back to the car, telling myself to concentrate on the fact that Finn's about to start his therapy. Alex's promise that Finn should be on the way to being back to his old self in a year feels realistic and achievable, a goal we can both work toward.

And that's all that matters.

Chapter Four

Alex

Finn's program begins on the third of April. That first day, Missie stays with him, but once she sees there's little she can do, and that he's fine staying with us, she begins dropping him off and coming back to pick him up when the hour is done. It gives her time to finish off her day at school or have a little time on her own, and it encourages Finn to take responsibility for his own rehabilitation, too.

Whenever I'm in the office, I try to make sure I'm present when Finn's there. He's not the only youngster in the trial, but he was the first to start, and I want to keep an eye on his progress. Plus, I like the kid. He reminds me a lot of myself. He's tall, and starting to be all elbows and knees. He's better looking than I was at his age, but he also has a neat fade haircut, and I can tell by the way he's styling it that he's trying to copy mine, which is kinda sweet. He's adventurous and funny, and he gets my sense of humor. He loves computers, and he's fascinated enough by what I do to suggest he could be a computer science engineer himself one day.

And being there with him, especially at the end of the session, when we try to finish with a fun game, has the added bonus that he's happy to chat. Without me having to ask, as the weeks go by, Finn gradually reveals details about his life and his mum. Nothing too intimate—guys don't normally talk about feelings. But enough to begin to form a picture.

I discover that Missie's mum is alive, but her dad died three years ago of a "substantial homatema," which I interpret as a subdural hematoma. She's an only child. Finn says his grandma is "like mum with the weird bits taken out." She lives with them and helps out with the cooking and cleaning, because his mum is "untidy and scatterbrained."

Despite these obvious flaws, "she knows every famous artist that's ever lived," and she likes to drag him around the art gallery and point out interesting (Finn's expression suggests he's being sarcastic) things about each painting.

She loves to dance, especially to ABBA, and she's seen *Mamma Mia* "at least a billion times." She complains about her hair and spends too much money on conditioner, trying to tame it ("and it never works.") She loves seafood, fudge, and lemon meringue pie, and the other day she ate a whole box of Jaffa Cakes by herself and put on five pounds. She adores fairy lights, and her favorite color is yellow.

He says the other teachers at the school call her Miss Sunshine, and that everyone thinks she's the most positive person they know.

"And Alex is the grumpiest," Juliette tells him. "Sounds like they're perfectly suited for one another."

Finn just laughs, but I glare at Juliette, and later, after Missie has collected Finn and left the building, I take Juliette to one side and say, "I'd appreciate it if you refrained from making comments like that to a boy about his mother when she only lost her husband four months ago."

Juliette studies her feet and looks appropriately remorseful. "Sorry."

I inhale deeply, then blow out a long breath. We've been friends for a long time, and I know she means well. "Missie has just been widowed," I say more gently. "She has a whole world of grieving to do before she'll be ready to date again. The last thing she needs is a guy coming on to her. And Finn's lost his father. I mean, Jesus, he's only ten. There's no good age to lose a parent, but he's heading toward puberty at a rate of knots, and he's going to be filled with all these conflicting emotions."

"He likes you," she says.

"I know, and that's why I have to be extra careful."

She looks up then and meets my eyes. Slowly, her lips curve up.

"You're quite gorgeous when you're telling me off," she says.

"Stop it," I scold.

"I mean it. I have no idea why you've been single for so long. You should be on Tinder, shagging your brains out."

"Jesus. This conversation is over."

"Don't you use Tinder? I would, if I were single."

"No, I don't, and I have no intention of doing so. The idea is abhorrent to me."

"Maybe if you stopped using words like abhorrent, you might get laid."

"Will you leave me alone?"

"You're a weird guy, Alex Winters. You realize she probably has no idea you like her?"

"I'm not listening."

"I'm just saying. It's hard enough nowadays when we all have to be careful with our signals. You might have to be a little more obvious."

"Stop interfering. I don't need your help."

"I think you do."

"I absolutely don't, and I thank you to refrain from being so meddlesome."

"There you go again. Meddlesome? Where are you from, 1852?"

Irritation flares inside me. "Do you really want to get into a discussion with me about our love lives and who we should be with?"

I've known for a long time that she has a secret crush on Henry, but when they first met, he was with the woman he eventually married. Juliette obviously thought that was it and met Cameron, an accountant, and they've now been together for several years. Then, just before Tyson's wedding, Henry announced that he and Shaz were getting divorced. That's shaken us all, and I can only imagine how it's thrown Juliette up in the air.

She flushes. We glare at each other for a long moment.

"That was a low blow," she says, and her eyes fill with tears, which is very unusual for her.

Immediately, my frustration vanishes. She's one of my very best friends, and the last thing I want to do is upset her.

"Aw, come here." I put my arms around her, and she buries her face in my chest. "I'm sorry," I murmur.

She shakes her head, not lifting her face. "We argue all the time."

I'm guessing she means her partner, Cam. "Ah, I'm sorry."

"I love him, Alex. I really do."

"I know. And he loves you. I know he does."

"Yeah. But sometimes I think he doesn't like me very much."

I rest my lips on her hair, feeling unutterably sad. Relationships are hard. I've had several long-term ones that ended, and it's always tough.

She turns her head and leans her cheek on my chest. "I don't mean to annoy you. I think she likes you, that's all, and it's so easy to miss the signs and let things slip by."

"I'm not an idiot, Juliette. I know what I'm doing."

She gives a short laugh and moves away, rubbing her nose. "Yeah. Sorry."

I frown. "You and Cam... are you going to be okay?"

She shrugs. "I guess time will tell." She walks away, leaving me with an uneasy sense that things are changing, whether we like it or not.

*

The weeks slowly tick by. I'm busy, working on half a dozen different projects, as well as keeping an eye on the progress of patients using both MAX and THOR, but I manage to keep an eye on Finn most times he's in. His birthday comes and goes, so he's now eleven. He's making good progress, and trying hard. Juliette eases him into the rehab program, beginning with exercises to strengthen the muscles in his legs that he hasn't used for a while and getting him used to the exoskeleton before starting to work on the psoas muscle that overlies the vertebral column, and other major muscles around his hips and lower back.

From what I've seen, patients on the program tend to be split into two different groups. Many get excited at the progress they're making, and their charts show a gradual rise in effort and improvement. But some people's charts are a series of peaks and troughs, especially in the early days. Once their initial enthusiasm wanes, they realize there's a long, tough road ahead of them, and suddenly it all becomes too hard.

Finn falls into the second group. After a few weeks, the novelty of working with a robot wears off, and as Juliette pushes him to work harder and do more, he reaches breaking point. One Friday, I'm in my office on a Zoom call with Damon in Wellington, discussing one of our joint projects, when my phone buzzes, and I see it's Kaia, one of Juliette's assistants.

"Can you hold on a sec?" I ask Damon. "I just need to take a call."

"Sure."

I answer the phone. "Hello?"

"Alex, it's Kaia. Can you come to THOR's room? Juliette's having trouble with Finn."

"I'll be right there." I hang up and go back to Damon. "Gotta go, dude, sorry."

"No worries. Catch you later." He ends the call.

I leave the office, jog along the corridor to the physio rooms, and go through THOR's door.

Juliette and Kaia are halfway through undoing the straps that hold Finn in place in the exoskeleton, talking to Finn, whose face is scarlet with fury.

"It's all right," Juliette's saying calmly, "I'm nearly done. Just a couple more."

"I want to get out!" he yells, tugging at the clips on his thighs.

I stride across to them and release the clip he's trying to yank off. "Hey, dude. What's going on?"

Juliette gives me a relieved glance. "We were doing some quite strenuous exercises, and I think he just got tired and a bit overwhelmed."

"I'm not tired!" he screams at her.

I don't reply, concentrating on the final clips, while the other two finish the ones on his lower legs. As soon as he's free, I lift him out of the exoskeleton and into his wheelchair. He pushes me away, then covers his face, his chest heaving.

I glance at Juliette, who looks upset. "I think I pushed him too far," she murmurs. "He was quiet when he came in, and I should have realized he was tired."

"It happens." I gesture at the door. "You two go and have a cup of coffee. I'll sit with Finn for a while."

"You're sure?"

"Yeah, go on."

I wait until they're both gone, then sit on the bench beside Finn. I lean forward, elbows on my knees, hands clasped, but I don't touch him.

"They've gone," I tell him. "It's just me and you."

He lowers his hands. He's trying hard not to cry.

"She kept saying I wasn't trying hard enough." He trembles with pent-up fury and frustration. "And I am. I'm really trying. But it doesn't matter. I'm not getting any better. My fucking legs won't work!" He hammers on them with his fists.

"Hey, stop." I get up and grab his wrists, then just manage to move back in time as he swings for me.

I straighten and put my hands on my hips. "Do you really want to punch me?"

"Fuck off!" he yells.

"Are you trying to shock me? Because it won't work. I'm pretty sure I know more swear words than you do."

"I hate you!"

"Fair enough. There's no law that says you have to like me. But if you think that'll make me give up on you, you're going to be disappointed. You can have today off, because you're obviously tired. But you're going to say sorry to Juliette for your behavior, and then you're going to work twice as hard for her next time, do you hear me? Because I'm not giving up on you, Finn Taylor. I'm going to see you walk out of here one day if it's the last thing I do."

He stares at me, and then his bottom lip trembles.

I sigh and drop to my haunches in front of him. "I know it's hard, and I'm sorry you have to go through it. But what doesn't kill you levels you up, right?"

Before I can stop him, he leans forward, throws his arms around me, and buries his face in my neck.

"Hey, whoa." Off balance, I tip forward onto my knees and freeze for a moment. When you're alone in a room with a kid, physical contact isn't advised. But at times like this, the human urge to comfort overrides everything else. He's lost his dad, and he's stuck in a wheelchair. Of *course* the poor guy's a mess.

"It's all right." I give him a hug and rub his back.

"I'm sorry," he whispers.

"It's okay."

"I didn't mean to swear at you."

"They're just words, Finn. They don't mean anything."

"Mum doesn't like me swearing."

"Then we won't tell her."

He gives a little laugh and moves back.

I take out my pocket square and hand it to him. He wipes his eyes and blows his nose, then holds it out to me.

"You keep it," I tell him. "I don't want your snot, thank you very much."

He laughs again and tucks it in the pocket of his jeans.

I sit back on the bench. "You want to tell me what's going on?"

"What do you mean?"

"If you're just tired and frustrated, that's okay. But there's nothing else that's gotten to you today?"

His smile fades, and he looks down at his hands as they twist in his lap. "I had an argument with Mum this morning."

"Okay. Do you want to talk about it?"

"I asked her if we could get a dog, and she said no."

"Okay."

"I really want one," he says. "It'd be so cool to have a puppy. I could teach it how to sit and lie down and stuff. I'd feed it and take care of it, I promise."

"But she doesn't want one?"

"She said there'd be nobody to look after it during the day."

"That's a fair comment. Puppies need feeding and taking out every few hours. Don't glare at me."

"I thought you were on my side."

"I'm on the puppy's side. It'd get lonely being on its own all day."

He scratches at a mark on the arm of his chair. "I guess." He huffs a sigh. "It's really annoying when she's right."

"Yeah, I get that. Luckily, she's pretty, so that kind of makes up for it." I get up and go over to the table against the far wall. I open the small fridge and take out two bottles of water, grab two of the oat bars from the box next to it, and bring them back.

"I'm not hungry," he says.

"Okay." I leave the bar next to him. "I'm starving though." I open mine and have a big bite. Finn watches me for a moment, then picks his up and opens it. I hide a smile as he takes a bite and sighs.

"How was school today?" I ask.

"All right. I came top in the class in a test we had in computer studies."

"Well that's pretty smart of you."

"It's *dull as*. It's all about spreadsheets. I want to do programming."

"Yeah, I get that, but spreadsheets are a big part of it. I couldn't do my job without them."

"Were you top of your class at school?"

"Sometimes. When I went to high school, I met my best mate, Damon, and he was smart, too, so sometimes I came top, and sometimes he did."

"My best mate's called Robbie. He likes computers, as well. We're going to run a company together like you do with your friends."

"Good idea. It helps to have someone to bounce ideas off."

His blue eyes, so like his mother's, survey me with puzzlement. "You don't make fun of me like other grownups do. Most of them say I'm too young to decide what I want to do now."

"Damon and I were twelve when we agreed we were going to run our own companies. It's good to know where you're going."

"Does he work here?"

"No, he runs a company in Wellington with his brothers, but he comes down to help me out with software issues sometimes. He was the one who helped integrate the gaming software with THOR's program."

"I'd like to meet him."

"I'll introduce you the next time he comes down."

Finn eats the last bit of his oat bar, then picks at the wrapper. "I don't want to be disabled. I want to be able to do stuff. Important stuff."

"Well, being disabled doesn't mean you can't do amazing things."

"Don't patronite me."

"The word is patronize, and I'm not. Have you heard of Stephen Hawking?"

"Was he an astronomer?"

"He was a theoretical physicist and a cosmologist. He predicted that black holes emit radiation. Nobody believed him at first, but eventually his findings were said to be a breakthrough in theoretical physics. He had ALS. Do you know what that is?"

"No."

"It's Amyotrophic Lateral Sclerosis, a neuromuscular disorder. It causes muscle weakness and muscle wasting, and problems with swallowing and speaking. Stephen Hawking was confined to a wheelchair, and he had to communicate through a speech-generating device using a muscle in his cheek. But despite all that, he married—twice—and had three children, and he wrote a book called *A Brief History of Time* that was on a bestseller list for 237 weeks."

Finn's cheeks have reddened. "I didn't know," he murmurs, dropping his gaze.

"You've gone through a life-changing incident," I say. "I can't imagine how hard it is for you to come here and have to push through the pain and work the muscles that won't do what you want them to. It's your life, Finn. Not your mum's, and not mine. If it's too hard, and if you want to give up, that's your prerogative. But I'll be disappointed if I hear you using your accident as an excuse for not achieving great things at school."

"I won't give up," he whispers.

"All right."

"I'm sorry I got angry."

I lean forward, elbows on my knees again. "I'll let you into a little secret—I get angry too, sometimes."

"Really?"

"Yeah. Most guys do. You know what testosterone is?"

"It's a hormone?"

"That's right. Your mum's told you about what happens during puberty?"

"Um, yeah."

"Boys' bodies produce thirty times more testosterone when they enter puberty."

His eyes widen. "Really? Wow."

"It makes you grow tall and strong, it deepens your voice, and it makes hair grow everywhere. But it also changes your behavior and mood. It makes you feel angry and fed up and frustrated. It's normal, and it's happened to every guy you know. But being grown up is about learning how to handle those feelings. Being an adult is about staying in control of your temper, your behavior, and your language. Does that make sense?"

He nods. He's quiet for a minute, and I take the lid off my water and have a few mouthfuls. When I look back at him, he's watching me.

"Dad had a temper," he says.

I meet his eyes. Slowly, I put the lid back on the bottle.

"A lot of men do," I say carefully.

"He shouted a lot," Finn says. "He used to get really angry when things didn't work. You know, cars and computers."

"Okay."

"I don't want to have a temper," he says.

"Well, it's good that you recognize that. Once we understand the things that frustrate us, we can work on how we react to those feelings. We had a male teacher at school in our Health class who used to tell us 'out of reaction and into observation'. It means learning to recognize when those angry feelings start bubbling up, and analyzing them and working out why we feel that way. He'd tell us 'to turn and walk away' if we were upset or angry."

"Don't tell Mum," Finn says, his brows drawing together. "She doesn't like me talking about it to people."

"I won't. It'll just be a secret between us, okay?"

He hesitates, his eyes meeting mine.

I debate whether to say anything. I'm not a therapist, and I can't imagine Missie would be happy with me talking to her son about this.

But I can see he wants to talk, and he told me a few sessions ago that he doesn't like his therapist. He said Missie doesn't have any brothers, and it doesn't sound as if he sees his dad's family much. Most primary-school teachers are women. Who else is the kid supposed to talk to?

"How did his anger manifest?" I ask gently. "Did he just yell?"

"He threw things. He punched a hole in the wall once. And he kicked over the table."

I let it fall quiet for a moment. Then I say, "Was he ever physical… with you?"

"No."

"With your mum?"

"Sometimes."

Ah, jeez.

"She cried a lot," he says. "She still does, even though he's gone."

That makes me feel as if someone has reached inside me and grabbed my heart. "I'm sorry," I say softly.

"I hated him," he whispers. "I used to wish he'd go away and leave us alone. And then he died. Do you think it was my fault?"

Pity rushes through me. "Nobody was to blame for the accident. These things happen in a split second. He didn't see the truck until it was too late. It's nobody's fault, and it's certainly not yours."

"I'm glad he's gone," he says, and then his eyes water. "Does that make me an evil person?"

"Of course not. It's okay to have mixed feelings about someone. I'm the same with my mum. You can feel frustrated or furious or resentful with them and still love them. He'll always be your dad, Finn. And I'm sure he loved you very much."

He swallows hard and looks at me. "Mum thinks it would be wrong for her to date anyone else until dad's been gone a year, but I wish—"

He stops then, though, as the door opens, and Juliette comes in with Missie, and the moment's gone.

As Missie walks toward me, though, looking gorgeous in jeans and a pink sweater, with her blue eyes giving me goosebumps the way they always do, I feel a surge of fury at the thought that her husband mistreated her, an emotion that I know isn't going away any time soon.

Chapter Five

Missie

I arrive early today, expecting to catch the end of Finn's session, but as I walk through the offices toward the treatment room, I meet Juliette coming out with Kaia. They both look concerned, and my pulse picks up at the thought that there's something wrong with Finn.

"Hey," I say as cheerfully as I can, "everything all right?"

"Finn's a bit frustrated," Juliette said. "He's okay, but I think he's tired, and he got a bit cross with me."

"Oh my God, I'm so sorry."

"It's completely my fault. I should have recognized he was tired and stopped the session early."

I go to walk into the room, but she says, "Alex is talking to him. Come upstairs with me."

Part of me wants to ignore her—if my boy's hurting, he needs me.

But Juliette's already halfway up the steps, so I follow her, and together we lean on the balustrade and look down at the room.

Finn is sitting in his wheelchair, his face red and contorted with anger, glaring at Alex, who's standing before him, hands on hips. Alex is talking, his voice raised, and I can just hear what he's saying. "I'm not giving up on you, Finn Taylor. I'm going to see you walk out of here one day if it's the last thing I do."

My heart seems to shudder to a stop, and I press my fingers to my lips. Next to me, Juliette does the same.

Finn's expression turns emotional, and Alex bends to look at him, lowering his voice so we can't hear him. But the next thing we see is Finn throwing his arms around Alex and burying his face in his neck.

Oh shit, poor Alex. He didn't ask for this. I twitch, about to turn and run down the stairs, but Juliette holds me there, and when she glances at me, she's smiling.

So I stay, and I watch Alex stiffen, then relent and comfort my son, giving him a big hug.

Juliette shakes her head. "This guy..."

We watch as they eventually separate, Alex making Finn laugh, and then Alex sits on the bench and the two of them chat quietly for a while.

"What do you think they're talking about?" Juliette whispers.

"I don't know." But whatever it is, I think Finn needs it.

Alex retrieves some water and a snack, and I can see Finn's resentment fade as his after-school hunger is sated. Very smart, Alex.

They talk for a long time. I wish I could hear what they're saying, but their voices are too low.

Juliette told me before the program started that Alex would prefer it if I didn't stay with Finn during his treatment. At first I felt a flare of indignation—I know my boy better than anyone, and I have a right to be present. What if he needs me? He's very self-conscious about the fact that he has no control over some of his bodily functions. It's bad enough that I have to leave him with an assistant at school.

But after the first session, I realized that Alex wants to build his own relationship with Finn, and he doesn't want me interfering with that.

It stung at first, and not just because of Finn. I know I cold-shouldered Alex when I refused his offer of a trip in his helicopter, but I'm woman enough to be hurt that he's not taking the opportunity to spend as much time with me as he can. But now, watching them together, I understand. He's putting Finn first. He really does want to help him, not just to get him walking, but to be there for the boy who's lost his father and who's struggling physically and emotionally.

Well, doesn't that just turn me into a mushy puddle for this man?

This afternoon, he's in smart mode again—he's wearing a dark-gray suit that fits him like a dream, a crisp light-blue shirt, and a sedate dark-blue tie. His hair is neatly combed—he obviously remembered to use product today. I can't smell his cologne from here, but I know what it would smell like because I've been dreaming about it—that delicious spicy vanilla scent. I'm trying not to obsess about this guy, but to be honest, when most of my dreams are haunted and full of shadows, it's a relief when he appears in them, even if he is glaring at me.

I bite my lip. I'm a grieving widow, and I'm not supposed to be showing interest in other men. But Juliette is turning out to be a firm friend, and somehow I don't think she'll pass judgment on me.

"Is he married?" I whisper to her.

She shakes her head and murmurs back, "He's single. Hasn't dated anyone that I know of since last year."

"Why? He's gorgeous. He must have women falling over themselves." My gaze lingers on his face as he listens to Finn speak. He has nice, neat eyebrows, not haywire and bushy like some guys have. Is it weird I've noticed that?

"Don't know," Juliette says. "He's never been one of those guys who's permanently got a woman on his arm. He's had two, maybe three, longish-term relationships that have ended quietly, without drama."

"He doesn't talk about any girls? Go on Tinder, you know, rate them out of ten, talk about what they're like in bed or anything?"

"Lord, no. He'd never do that. None of the guys here would, to be fair, but Alex is more respectful than most. He's openly disapproving of that sort of thing. He bollocked one of our junior programmers recently because he commented on a girl's figure when she walked past. I've told him several times he's far too strait-laced."

I kinda like that about him, though. I don't mind my son spending time with a man like that.

"Does he live on his own?" I ask. "I know that's a nosy question."

"Oh yeah. He has a huge house out on one of those private country estates where you need a code to get through the gate. You know he's loaded, right?"

My face warms. "That's not why I was asking."

"Yeah, I know, I'm just saying. His mum is the actress, Kaitlyn Cross?"

"No... really?" Oh my God, she's super famous.

"Yeah. She put some money into a fund for when he came of age. He invested the majority of it in Kia Kaha when he left uni. Well, James has a younger sister who has chronic asthma. While they were at uni, as part of a project for their final year, they created this piece of equipment that measures a kid's peak flow. It's connected to a screen that has a rabbit wearing a hat, and the kid has to blow in the tube and try to blow the rabbit's hat off. It's so simple, but it's really effective, and it can be produced relatively cheaply, so kids can have one at home. Have you heard of the Three Wise Men?"

"I'm guessing you don't mean the ones from the Christmas carol?"

"Well, that's where they got the name—their surname is King. They run a company that makes medical equipment for children. They bought the patent, and they also bought patents for a dozen other pieces of equipment, most of them invented by Alex. That's where they've made a lot of their money."

"Wow. I didn't realize he did all that."

"I'm not surprised. He's a very private guy. Hard to get to know."

"You like him, though, as a person?"

She smiles. "He's one of my very best friends. He works so hard. Always has. It was a struggle at uni to get him to leave his computer and come out with us all. He's incredibly driven and *smart as*, and he's loyal to a fault. He's calm in a crisis and laid back most of the time— he only ever raises his voice when I wind him up."

"I find that appealing. I haven't even heard him swear yet."

"He doesn't, even with us. I've sometimes wondered whether he does in the sack." She gives me a mischievous smile.

"Juliette," I scold.

"Don't tell me you haven't thought about it. He's so prim and proper. Such a good boy. Do you reckon he's a tiger when he lets loose?"

I can't risk thinking about him in bed—I think I'd implode. "I just wish he'd smile more."

"Oh don't be put off by his grumpy exterior. He's very funny. You need to get a few drinks in him to loosen him up—he's a lot different when he's drunk. But you should know, Missie, he has an incredibly strong sense of what's right and wrong. He likes you, but he would never make a move on you while you're grieving. You're going to have to let him know when you're ready."

I don't reply to that. Firstly, I'm not sure he does like me—he's not made it obvious. And secondly, I'm a mess, and I don't know how long it's going to take me to be un-messy. When is it acceptable to show interest in another man after your husband dies in a tragic accident?

"I'd better go down," I tell Juliette, and I turn and descend the steps, then push open the door to the treatment room. Alex gets to his feet as I go in, and his brown eyes are fixed on me. They hold a hint of disapproval or regret, or am I imagining it?

"Hey, you two," I say, going up to Finn. I know better than to ruffle his hair or kiss him in front of people, but I give him a smile. "How are you doing?" I say instead.

"Okay," Finn says. "I'm a bit tired."

"We were both knackered," Alex says, "so we decided to stop early today."

"Shall we get going then?" I ask Finn, and he nods.

"Is there something you want to say to Juliette?" Alex asks.

Finn looks up at her and reddens. "I'm sorry I lost my temper. I shouldn't have shouted at you."

She smiles. "That's okay."

"I was just tired," he says, "but I promise I'll try twice as hard next time. I'm not giving up."

"Glad to hear it," she says.

Alex holds out his hand and curls it into a fist, and Finn bumps it. "Have a great weekend," Alex says.

"Thank you," I say to Alex.

His eyes meet mine, and there's definitely warmth in them. But he just gives a short nod and turns away to start tidying up the straps on THOR.

I say goodbye to Juliette, and then push Finn out of the room and through to the lobby. "What were you two talking about?" I ask as we go out of the front door into the afternoon sunshine.

"Stuff," he says.

"Good stuff?"

"Yeah." He hesitates. "He said that boys have thirty percent more testosterone when they go through puberty, and that's why they feel angry all the time."

"That's true," I say, surprised.

"He said he gets angry too, sometimes."

"I'm sure he does."

"He said it's okay to be angry, but being grown up is about learning to control your temper."

We reach our car, and I stop and open the passenger door, then lean in to put my bag in the back.

"I didn't tell him anything, Mum," he says as I straighten.

I inhale, then blow out a long breath. "It's all right. I know you don't have any other guys to talk to."

"I like him, that's all. He's good with computers, and he's smart, but he's cool too, you know?"

"Yeah, I know."

"He said you were pretty."

My eyes widen. "Really?"

"Yeah. I said you were annoying when you were right, and he said you were pretty, and that made up for it."

My lips curve up, just a little. "Come on," I say softly, "let's get you in the car. Then maybe we'll get a pizza. What do you think?"

"Aw, yeah."

I don't get takeaways very often. Money's tight, even though my mother helps out where she can. I still have a good bit of Finn's insurance payout, but I refuse to touch that for myself, and I only dip into it if I need to buy him a new uniform, or anything else for school. But tonight I'll make an exception.

After he's in, I lift the chair into the back, then get in the driver's side.

"We'll get a large one each," I say as I start the engine, "and chicken wings, what do you reckon?"

"And onion rings?"

"Yeah, and all the dips, right?"

"I can't wait. I'm starving."

Smiling, I ease the car into the traffic.

I know I shouldn't place too much importance on Alex's comment, but my brain refuses to stop thinking about it.

He thinks I'm pretty. Well, that's better than a kick in the teeth, anyway.

*

I don't see him the next few sessions, and Juliette finally reveals he's in Wellington, working with his friend, Damon. It's July now, over six months since the accident. Finn is making good progress, she assures me. He's regaining muscle movement and feeling, albeit slowly, and she says it's a good sign. His strength and stamina are improving, and he can now get himself from his bed or a chair and into his wheelchair, and vice versa, which is something he couldn't do before.

They teach him how to weight shift to change the pressure on different parts of his body, and encourage him to be more independent with his bathing and dressing. I gradually learn to step back, even if he's getting frustrated, and only step in when he gets completely stuck.

The following Friday, I arrive a few minutes before four thirty, ready to pick Finn up, and walk into the treatment room to see Finn already in his wheelchair.

"All done?" I ask.

"Yes, it went well," Juliette says. "And because of that, we've got a special surprise for him."

I look at Finn, who shrugs but looks interested.

"Come on," Juliette says, taking his chair and steering him to the door. "Follow me."

She leads the way along the corridor toward Alex's office. As we near, I can see him behind his desk, although he's looking at something on the carpet behind him. I go ahead and knock on the door, and he looks up and gestures to come in, so I open the door, standing back to let Juliette and Finn go past me.

"Hello," he says as I let the door swing shut.

"Hey. Juliette said you wanted to see us?"

"Yeah." He looks at Finn and, to my surprise, gives him a mischievous smile. "Got a surprise for you."

"Oh?" Finn looks puzzled.

Alex bends and picks something up, then gets to his feet and turns around. He's holding the cutest Golden Retriever puppy in the world.

Finn inhales deeply and his jaw drops. "Oh my God."

Alex walks around his desk to stand before us. He smiles at Finn, and then he holds the puppy out and puts her on Finn's lap.

The pup is all elbows and feet, just like Finn. She clambers all over Finn, then puts her front paws on Finn's chest and stretches up to lick his chin. Finn laughs, then squeals as the puppy nips his fingers. "Naughty girl!"

Alex picks up a canvas chew toy in the shape of a hedgehog and passes it to her, gently pushing the puppy away from Finn's fingers. "No biting, Zelda!"

"Zelda!" Finn says.

"Yeah. Thought it was appropriate."

"I love it! Hello, Zelda!" Finn tugs the hedgehog, laughing as Zelda tugs back.

"When did you get her?" I ask Alex.

"Yesterday. She's eight weeks old." He slides his hands into the pockets of his trousers. "I thought Finn could play with her after his rehab."

Finn's jaw drops again. "Did you hear that?" he whispers to the puppy. "We're going to be best friends."

I meet Alex's eyes. He returns my gaze calmly, and we study each other for a good twenty seconds while I struggle to get my brain to work.

"Did you get the puppy for him?" I whisper eventually.

"No," he says.

Juliette clears her throat. "He's telling the truth. He's always had dogs in the office, but his last one died back in January."

"Took a while to get over her," he says. "But I'm ready for a pup."

He still holds my gaze, and I can't look away. Even though the timing might have been right for him to get another puppy, I know he got the dog for Finn. He couldn't buy him a puppy, because that wouldn't be fair, so he's done the next best thing. He's even named her after a character from Finn's favorite game.

I know it was for Finn, but it's quite possibly the nicest thing that anyone's ever done for me, too.

Emotion rushes through me, and I press my fingers to my mouth as tears sting my eyes. God, this guy, he keeps unraveling me.

Alex watches me for a moment. Then he takes a tissue from the box on his desk and brings it over.

He stands before me and holds it out. I take it, smelling the scent of his cologne in the air, the spicy vanilla aroma that pervades my dreams on a regular basis.

Before I can think better of it, I move up close to him and rest my forehead on his shoulder.

I feel him inhale, and then his arms come up around me, and he gives me a hug.

Behind us, Juliette kneels to talk to Finn and play with the puppy. But Alex and I stay standing, him holding me, as the afternoon sunshine spills across us.

He doesn't say anything, and neither do I. He's not wearing his suit jacket, and as I turn my head, I rest my cheek against his crisp white shirt. His throat isn't far from my mouth—I could reach up and kiss his Adam's apple above his tie, if I wanted. I don't. But I could.

I stand there for maybe a minute, composing myself, listening to Finn's laughter, something I haven't heard enough over the last six months. Alex doesn't move, and he doesn't lower his arms. I can feel the warmth of his body through his shirt. The cotton is stretched over his impressive biceps. The guy must work out in his spare time.

I can't stand here for much longer or it's going to look weird. I lift my head, and immediately he drops his arms, and we both step back. I don't look up at him, and he turns away and walks over to Finn.

"We'll have to train her," he says, and his voice sends aftershocks through me, leaving me trembling.

"Do we have to go yet?" Finn asks, sending me a pleading glance. "Can we stay and play with her for a bit?"

I look at Alex then, and he shrugs. "I've got twenty minutes. Want a cup of coffee?"

My lips curve up. "That would be nice."

"I'll get them," Juliette says. "Have a seat, Missie."

So I sit on the sofa and laugh as I watch Finn and the puppy playing together, filled with a warmth I haven't felt in a long, long time.

Chapter Six

Alex

Over the next few weeks, we develop a new system to encourage Finn to do his rehab—Juliette marks off the number of stars on a chart corresponding to the effort she feels that Finn has put in, and he's then allowed to play with Zelda at the end of his rehab for five minutes per star. It works like a dream. Every week, Juliette fills in all five stars, and I secretly (after consultation with his mother) add one more star for luck, so he has half an hour every session to play.

He comes to my office, and he sits on the floor and plays with the pup, trying to teach Zelda to sit, stay, lie down, and roll over. When Missie turns up, she comes into my office and I make her a cup of coffee, and we sit and chat and watch Finn until five o'clock, when she finally tells him it's time to go.

In the beginning, we talk mainly about Finn's rehab. I go into detail about how THOR works, and she asks lots of questions about how we came up with the idea, and how it integrates with the gaming software. We also talk about Finn's progress, and I explain the different muscles of the back, hips, and legs, and how Juliette is increasing the mobility and strength of each muscle with different exercises.

Missie is nervous about being alone with me, I can tell, so I wait for her to move the conversation on. It happens slowly, as September leads into October. She gradually relaxes in my presence, and she starts telling me about her day. I hear about the kids in her class, the lessons she's done, and funny stories about what the kids have gotten up to.

Eventually, she feeds me little personal nuggets of information amongst the general stuff. I discover that her mum's called Sandra and her dad's name was Martin. She secretly likes that he gave her the name Mistletoe, even though she tells everyone she doesn't.

She talks about her art, and for the first time I see a passion bloom inside her that hasn't been there before. She's converted a spare room in her home into a studio, and she spends a lot of her spare time there, working mainly with watercolors, mainly painting pictures of the sea, because she loves tackling waves and the movement of water. She's never traveled, but she says she'd love to visit some of the larger galleries in Europe: the National Gallery, the Louvre, the Van Gogh Museum, the Uffizi.

But she never talks about her past, and she never mentions her husband.

I do notice, though, that she's stopped wearing her wedding ring.

One day, because my curiosity gets the better of me, when she's talking about Finn going to high school next year, I comment, "You must have been very young when you had him."

"Seventeen," she says, giving me an 'I can't believe I did that' look. She glances at Finn, makes sure he's absorbed in the puppy, then mouths to me: "I got pregnant by mistake," and pulls an 'eek' face.

"Bet your parents were pleased," I say, thinking about how mine would have reacted if either of my sisters had fallen pregnant at seventeen.

"Yeah, they weren't too happy. My dad took Lee down to the shed and said, 'I hope you're going to do the right thing.' It was practically Victorian. I'm just surprised he didn't actually point the shotgun at him."

"He did, though? Do the right thing, I mean."

"Yeah. I have some lovely wedding photos with a bump."

"Good that he stepped up, though."

"Probably would have been better if he hadn't." She looks away, out of the window.

I think about what Finn told me, that his father sometimes got physical with Missie. I study her profile—her fine features, the beautiful curve of her Cupid's bow, her pale skin with the attractive flush to her cheeks—and wonder how on earth a man could ever raise his hand to her. I want to go prehistoric on his arse, but the guy's gone now. I just hope there's a God, because he deserves to have to answer to someone for his crimes.

"We'd better get going," she says to Finn.

He looks up from the puppy and glances from me to her. "You haven't asked him yet."

She looks embarrassed. "Uh... no..."

"Go on," he prompts.

"Spit it out," I say, amused.

Her lips curve up. "We're having a careers day at school next Thursday. Lots of different people are coming in to talk to the kids about their jobs."

"We wondered if you'd come," Finn says eagerly. "You can talk to everyone about working with computers. All my friends want to meet you."

Missie blushes at the fact that he's obviously told his mates about me. "Sorry," she mumbles. "I'm sure you're far too busy."

I bring up my calendar. I have a meeting I can't miss at two p.m., but I can shuffle everything else around. "I could make the morning, if that's any good?"

Her eyes widen. "Seriously?"

"Yeah."

Amusement lights her features. She obviously didn't expect me to say yes. "You'd come into the school and talk to a whole classroom of kids?"

"Sure."

"They're eleven years old."

"In that case, no."

She gives me a wry look. "I mean, you'd have to pitch it pretty low. It's not like a careers day at high school. It's more about the field you work in, you know, um, what it's like to work with computers, and, um..."

"So you don't want me to give a detailed comparison between Java and Python coding then?"

"Oh yeah," Finn says.

Missie narrows her eyes at me. "I just can't see you being all cutesy with primary school kids, that's all."

"What do you mean? I'm very cute," I say, and Finn giggles.

She purses her lips. "Well... if you're sure..."

I look at Finn, whose eyes beg me to say yes. I'm sure he was probably a popular kid at the school, and now he's been redefined as the boy in the wheelchair. I'm touched that he's talked to his mates about me. And that's when I get a lightbulb moment.

"I've got an idea," I say to Finn. "How would you like me to bring THOR into your classroom, and you can give a demonstration of how it works?"

Finn's jaw drops, and Missie's eyebrows rise.

"Would that be embarrassing?" I ask him. "Or do you think it would be cool?"

"It would be *cool as*," he says breathlessly. "Do you mean it?"

"I wouldn't say it if I didn't. But it's up to Miss Macbeth here."

She's too astounded to smile at my use of her name. "Alex, you can't possibly bring your valuable equipment into school." That makes me laugh, and her lips curve up. "You know what I mean," she scolds. "I'm glad I made you laugh, though."

I give her an amused look. "We actually have six THOR units. They're easily transportable, because we knew we'd need to be able to take them into the hospital."

"But you know what kids are like—I'd hate for it to get damaged."

"I'll bring Henry. He can stand guard. It'll be cool for the kids to see what Finn has to go through. And maybe give them an understanding into disability and the advances we're making with technology."

She hesitates. "Well… if you're sure."

"I'm sure."

"Okay. So we'll say eight-thirty next Thursday, ready for a nine a.m. start?"

"Yep, sounds good."

She helps Finn into his wheelchair, and I pick up Zelda and watch the two of them leave and go down the corridor. I lean back in my chair with the pup on my chest, and let her clamber up and lick my chin, her tiny tongue rasping on my stubble.

"Good girl," I murmur, ruffling her floppy ears. "Am I crazy, Zelda?" She sneezes, and I sigh. "Yeah, I thought so."

*

The following Thursday, I pull up in the van outside the front of Missie's primary school, and Henry and I go into the lobby. We're just signing the visitor's book at reception and getting our stickers when Missie comes out, looking a tad flustered.

"Hello," she says. I know she normally wears trousers to work because she's often sitting on the carpet with the kids or out doing PE with them, but today she's wearing a pretty light-blue dress with a daisy pattern. It's early November and the weather is very spring-like, but she brings a touch of summer to the bright day.

"Where's Zelda?" she asks.

"I've left her with James. Are you okay?" She looks anxious.

"Change of plan," she says nervously.

"Oh?"

"Um… so many kids said they wanted to watch your presentation that they'd like to put you in the school hall. I don't know how you feel about speaking in front of the whole school?"

"He's given a presentation to the Prime Minister," Henry says, "and he gave the keynote speech at a symposium in Sydney. He should be all right."

"Oh," she says. "Wow."

I glare at him, then look back at her. "I'll be fine, but how does Finn feel about giving a demonstration in front of everyone? I'd hate to embarrass him."

"He's okay. Everyone thinks it's cool that he's using an exoskeleton for his physio, so he's the talk of the town."

"All right," I say. "Let's get THOR into the hall, then."

The tailgate of the van turns into a lift, and we lower THOR down on its trolley, then wheel it through the building and into the school hall. Henry helps me remove the trolley, and then we retrieve a couple more pieces of equipment from the van and get ready for the presentation.

Missie introduces us to the principal, then disappears to her class. As it turns nine a.m. the doors open and kids start filing in, sitting on the floor in rows, the youngest at the front, the oldest at the back. There's a lot of nudging and pointing, especially when Finn's assistant brings him in and parks his chair at the front, to one side.

I see Missie come in with her class, and she sits with the other teachers at the edge of the hall. I know her well enough now to realize she's nervous, although whether it's on my behalf or Finn's, I'm not sure.

The principal comes to the front, and the kids gradually fall quiet.

"Good morning, everyone," she says, speaking into the lavalier microphone. "As you all know, today is Careers Day, and we have lots of people coming in to talk to you all about their jobs. But first we're lucky enough to have two of the directors from a company called Kia Kaha in Christchurch. Kia Kaha is a computer software and hardware company that makes medical equipment, and today they've brought in one of their amazing inventions to show you all. And now I'm going to hand you over to Mr. Winters and Mr. West, who are going to tell you all about their company and what they do."

The kids clap enthusiastically, and I walk forward and take the lavalier mic from her.

*

Missie

Oh my God, I'm so nervous. Poor Alex. I don't care what Henry says—nobody likes being thrown into the deep end. There are over two hundred and fifty kids sitting there staring at him. I have no idea what he's going to say. I'm sure he's not used to talking to children. If he focuses on the technical details, they're going to start fidgeting after about five minutes, tops.

I watch as he clips the mic to his lapel. He's wearing a three-piece navy suit today. It must take his tailor weeks to get it to fit that well. I usually see him late in the day when he always has a five o'clock shadow, but he's clean shaven this morning, and his hair is neatly combed. He looks young and handsome and wealthy. I've already had two teachers ask me for his number. I was very naughty and told them he was taken. I don't know why I did that.

Who am I kidding? I totally know why I did that.

"Morning everyone," he says. "Can you hear me at the back?"

"Yes," everyone calls.

"Cool," he says. "Okay, I'm Alex Winters, and this is Henry West. We run our own company called Kia Kaha with a couple of our friends. Henry and I are computer software engineers, which is a fancy word for a nerd, or a geek. Which do you prefer?" He directs the question at Henry.

Henry gives a mock frown. "I'm not a nerd."

"Geek, then?" Alex looks back at the kids. "He's totally a geek," he tells them, and a ripple of laughter runs through the hall. "We both are," he admits. "We've been into computers since we were kids. I can still remember getting my PlayStation 3 when I was ten…"

"You're showing your age," Henry tells him.

"Yeah, just a bit. I loved that PS3. My favorite game was Ice Age 2 back then."

"Mine was Marvel: Ultimate Alliance, but then I've always been cooler than you," Henry says, and there's another ripple of laughter.

"We both knew we wanted to work with computers," Alex says. "At first, I thought I wanted to develop computer games. Best job in the world, right?" The boys, especially, all murmur their agreement. "People often ask what are the best subjects to take if you want to work with computers. The sciences are great, of course, and maths will always be useful, but the truth is that all subjects are important at school. Maths helps us understand the financial side of running a business. English and history teach us how to communicate and analyze. Art gives us creative skills that are useful in design, and it also gives us a soul." He looks at me then, and smiles, making the hairs rise all over my body.

"We went to university together," Alex continues, gesturing at Henry, "still with the intention of making computer games. But in our final year of university, something happened that changed our minds. One of our best friends was involved in a car accident. His name was Tyson. He damaged his spine, and doctors told him he'd never walk again."

He starts walking up and down in front of the kids as he talks. I glance across the hall, not surprised to see them all mesmerized. There's something about this guy that makes you unable to tear your gaze away.

"Gaming is important," he states. "People who don't game don't get it, right?" The majority of the kids murmur their agreement. "Gaming improves our concentration, and it teaches us creativity, languages, teamwork, and how to overcome challenges. But when your best mate ends up in a wheelchair, suddenly games don't seem so important. And that's when we decided that we were going to use the skills we'd learned to help Tyson."

He walks over to THOR. "This is called an exoskeleton, and yes, we did steal the idea from Transformers. Henry thinks it looks like Optimus Prime, but I think it's more like Ratchet, don't you?" Some of the kids cheer. "He's the Autobots' chief medical officer," he says to the staff sitting to the side. "You wouldn't understand." They all chuckle.

"An exoskeleton is a hard covering that protects the softer body of some animals," Alex continues. "Think about snails and crabs and turtles, and how they have an outer shell. In this sense, an exoskeleton is a wearable structure that supports and assists movement. We called our first Mobility-Aid eXoskeleton MAX. It took us a couple of years to make it perfect. Since then, Tyson has been exercising with it three times a week, and just a few months ago he was able to stand next to his wife at his wedding to say his vows."

Everyone goes *Awww…*

"Yeah," Alex says, "it was pretty cool. Made me bawl like a baby." Henry nods his agreement next to him, and everyone laughs.

"We've talked to a lot of patients with spinal injuries over the years," Alex continues, "as well as people with conditions like Spina Bifida and Cerebral Palsy that cause difficulty walking. And it made me realize what a difference these machines can make to people whose muscles don't work properly. It's the main reason we decided to create a version for children."

He pats the machine next to him. "We nicknamed him The Hands-On Robot," he says, "or THOR for short. He's smaller than MAX, and not as heavy. We brought him in today because a very special guy who goes to this school has offered to show you how he works."

He gestures at Finn. "As many of you will probably know, Finn Taylor was involved in a car accident last December, and he suffered an incomplete spinal cord injury, which means he retains some motor and sensory function, but at the moment he has trouble walking on his own. Finn has been coming into Kia Kaha three times a week, and he's been working super-hard to strengthen his muscles. You want to show them how it works, bro?"

Finn nods and wheels himself forward. Everyone claps politely. I give a small smile as some of the teachers give me a glance and a pitying smile. They all know what we've been through.

"Finn's been having physio since April," he tells everyone. "So just over seven months. Remember that when he came in, the muscles of his hips and legs weren't working properly, and he couldn't walk a step, even with crutches." He looks at Finn. "You ready, dude?"

Finn nods.

I've watched Finn have his therapy a few times, but lately I tend to turn up once they've gone into Alex's office to play with Zelda. I talk about his progress with Alex, but I haven't watched him for a while.

I'm puzzled, therefore, when Alex moves in front of Finn's wheelchair and holds out his hands, palms up. Finn grasps Alex's forearms, and Alex grasps Finn's.

I gasp as, slowly, he lifts Finn to his feet. He's supporting Finn, but there's no doubt that Finn is using his own muscles to push himself up.

Covering my mouth, I watch as Henry brings forward a pair of crutches. He slots them under Finn's arms and, for the first time in eleven months, I watch as my boy walks six feet from Alex to Henry, then carefully turns and walks back again.

His gait is stiff, and his legs obviously can't support his weight yet. But he's walking, which is more than I thought he'd be able to do when the doctor told us he'd never walk again.

Tears sting my eyes, and I fight desperately not to let them fall. Next to me, another teacher moves her chair forward so she can give me a hug, and around us the teachers say *Awww* again.

Everyone in the hall cheers. Alex glances at me, but he doesn't say anything. He does give the biggest smile I've seen him give as he murmurs something to Finn. He holds him while Henry removes the crutches, turns him around, and lowers him onto the seat inside THOR, and then the two of them do up the safety straps.

"There we go," Alex says, and he turns back to the rest of the school. "Finn's been working hard over the past few visits to use the crutches," he says. "The progress he's made is a good indication that he's going to regain a high proportion of his mobility. What does that mean? I'm hoping he'll be able to walk on his own with crutches in a month or two, and hopefully get rid of the crutches altogether next year sometime."

He pats THOR's arm. "Okay, Finn, let's show them how it's done, right?"

Every single person in the audience gasps as the robot springs to life and moves just like one of the Transformers in the movies. They run through a series of exercises, showing how the exoskeleton guides Finn as he bends, stretches, turns, and walks, giving him just enough support to encourage him to use his own muscles.

I watch with everyone else, but inside I'm a roiling mass of emotion. I don't care that Finn had crutches, or that he moved only six feet. My boy walked on his own. I'm so stunned that I can hardly think.

When they've finished with the exercises, Alex helps Finn back into his chair, and Henry takes him back to the side of the hall. Alex concludes with a bit more detail about Kia Kaha, and the jobs that he and Henry do there, and then he asks if there are any questions. A dozen hands shoot up, and he spends the next fifteen minutes answering them, continuing to make everyone laugh with his quips.

Eventually, Emma thanks him for attending and brings the lesson to an end. Everyone gets to their feet, and the teachers lead the kids out for their morning break.

As he and Henry load THOR back onto the trolley and take it out to the van, I turn to go over to Finn and give him a hug but discover he's surrounded by other kids. They all want to talk to him about the robot. Alex has made him into the coolest kid on the block. Tears prick my eyes again. That's almost as much of a present as helping him to walk.

Leaving him to it, I take my class to their playground. I wish I could say goodbye to Alex and Henry. Maybe if I'm quick, I'll be able to catch them?

Leaving the kids in the care of the teacher on duty, I'm about to run back to the office block when I stop and inhale sharply as I see Alex leaning against the wall of my classroom, watching me.

I walk over to him, my pulse racing, and stop just in front of him.

"Thought you could show me your classroom," he says.

"Okay." Tucking a strand of hair behind my ear, I open the door, and we go inside.

He walks along the line of desks, looking up at the colored maps of New Zealand, the posters showing fractions and percentages, the pictures of the solar system. His lips curve up as he stops to look at a display about saving stranded whales and dolphins. Then he stops and turns to look at me.

"I'm sorry to spring that on you," he says. "I should have told you that Finn was practicing walking with crutches, but we thought it would be a nice surprise for you to see him do it."

I just nod.

"You're not angry?" he asks.

I shake my head.

Outside, the kids careen around the playground like ball bearings in a pinball machine, yelling and laughing. The sunlight spills across the desks like melted butter. I can smell whiteboard pens and mown grass and Alex's cologne. I stifle a groan. The classroom is going to smell of him for the rest of the day.

He glances around again. "Nice room," he says. "I like the bird." He gestures to the picture of a fantail that we made in our art lessons. Every child painted a different feather with their own pattern.

"Thank you," I whisper.

He looks back at me.

"For what you've done for Finn," I add. "For THOR, for helping him walk, for Zelda, for everything."

"You're welcome," he says.

"You've gone to so much trouble." I'm unable to stop my mouth moving. "You really shouldn't have."

He slides his hands into his pockets. "It's my job."

Of course it is. I'm reading too much into it.

And now I'm tongue-tied. His gaze is level and calm. I can't tell what he's thinking. Does he like me? Maybe I should just ask him. But the words won't come.

I've been going to Kia Kaha for something like nine months now. All that time ago, Juliette told me he wasn't dating, but is that still the case? It's possible he does like me, but no guy is going to wait nine months or even longer for a woman he hardly knows. We've never discussed whether we're interested in each other. He has no idea that I still dream about him. That my pulse picks up whenever I smell his cologne. Or that one look from those steady dark eyes makes me weak at the knees.

The door opens and a teacher sticks her head in, sees him, and says, "Oh sorry," and goes out again.

"I'd better go," he says.

I nod, disappointed, but I can't think of a reason to ask him to stay.

"I'll see you tomorrow for Finn's physio?" he asks.

"Yes, okay. See you then."

He hesitates. Then he walks across the room and heads back to the office block.

I sit hurriedly on one of the tiny chairs before my legs give way, and fight against the tears that prick my eyes.

Chapter Seven

Alex

Gradually, November slides into December. The weather grows warmer, and Christmas displays dominate the shops. The sliding doors in the offices at Kia Kaha are open most of the time, letting in the aroma of the fresh water of the Avon, the smell of mown grass, and the scent of flowers that reminds me of Missie's perfume.

Zelda gets bigger every day. She's now seven months old, and I've been training her daily, so she's a good girl, and happy to sit in her bed in my office during the day providing she gets regular walks and is allowed to greet anyone who comes in.

Despite the better weather, I'm not keen on this time of year. It holds bad memories for me, and I always feel relieved when New Year arrives with all the promise of a fresh start. It's what earned me the titles of both Scrooge and Oscar the Grouch, because I'm reluctant to join in the festivities. And it usually gets me out of all sorts of social events.

This year, however, the presence of a certain dark-haired minx gets me into all kinds of trouble.

It starts one afternoon early in December when the boardroom telephone rings while we're in the middle of a meeting, and Rebecca announces that Missie's here, and she's wondering whether she can talk to all of us. Surprised, because it's not one of Finn's physio days, I say, "Send her in," and we all exchange puzzled glances as we wait for her to arrive.

I watch her walk along the glass-walled corridors and approach the boardroom. She's wearing navy capri pants and a white tee with a picture of a daisy on the front that has the words 'You are my sunshine' in a semi-circle over the top. It makes me smile even before she reaches the automatic doors.

Juliette glances at me, and her own lips curve up as she sees me smiling. I scowl at her, and she gives a short laugh and looks back at Missie.

She comes through the doors and gives us all a hesitant smile. We're all here—James, Henry, Tyson, Juliette, and Damon's down too from Wellington. Zelda gets up and runs over to greet her, and she bends to give her a kiss and ruffle her ears before straightening.

"Hello," she says brightly. "I'm so sorry to interrupt."

"No worries," James says. "What can we do for you?"

Her gaze skims briefly over me before she addresses the room as a whole. "I was wondering whether one of you kind gentlemen would be able to help me. I made the mistake of volunteering to help out with the school's end of year Christmas fair, and it's my job to organize a replacement Santa for the day because the one we did have organized has had to withdraw. The trouble is that the few guys at the school are all busy doing other things, and any men I know outside the school are also busy. I could put a call out to the parents, but before I did that, I thought I'd ask whether any of you would be available to help. It would be this Saturday, from eleven until about three."

"I'm so sorry," James says, "I would, but I'm off to Australia to visit my dad on Friday."

"I'm going back to Wellington tomorrow," Damon says. "Sorry, or I'd happily do it."

"Gaby and I are going with him," Tyson states. "She's helping Belle with some last-minute wedding stuff." Damon and Belle are getting married just after Christmas.

"Henry?" Juliette asks. "You've done it before haven't you, for one of the department stores?"

"I did," he says, but he sends a hopeful Missie an apologetic look. "But I'm picking my sister up from the airport at eleven and driving her down to see our folks in Queenstown."

"Aw," Juliette says, "I was looking forward to seeing you fat and hairy."

Henry mutters something about not having to dress up to look like that, and I give a wry smile as I tap on my laptop, noting where everyone is at the weekend. I like to keep an eye on staffing just in case there's ever an emergency in the building.

I finish typing and realize the room has fallen quiet. Without lifting my head, I glance up. Missie has obviously gestured at me, and the others are all shaking their heads.

"Never going to happen," Damon says, amused.

"Alex as Santa?" Juliette snorts. "That's like asking Jason Momoa to play Tinkerbell."

Missie giggles, a sound that's so delightful, I immediately decide to do whatever she's asking me. "You're not quite what I had in mind," she admits, eyes sparkling. "You'd need a lot of padding."

"Santas are supposed to be fat, jolly, and laugh a lot," James points out. "He'd be the worst Santa in the whole history of Christmas."

"I can be jolly," I protest. "I know tons of Christmas jokes."

"Like?" Damon asks.

"What do you call Santa's little helpers?" When everyone shrugs, I reply, "Subordinate Clauses."

That makes them all laugh, and James says, "God help the children."

"He used to be a stand-up comedian at uni," Juliette tells Missie.

Her jaw drops. "Seriously?"

"You'd never know it from his grumpy demeanor, but yeah. He was pretty good at it."

"I'm seriously funny," I say.

Missie meets my eyes, and hers are filled with warmth. "Would you do it?" she asks softly. "You'd be saving my bacon."

"I like bacon," I reply. "So yeah, sure."

"Thank you. I really appreciate it." She gives everyone a smile. "See you on Friday for Finn's physio."

"Bye," they all say, and she slips out and jogs back to the lobby.

Everyone looks at me, and they're all grinning.

"What?"

"You playing Santa," Damon says with amusement. "Never thought I'd see the day."

"Might have had something to do with the person asking him," Juliette states.

"I didn't want to let the kids down," I say, helping myself to one of the pastries in the middle of the table.

"I'm sure they'll be rolling in the aisles when they hear your subordinate clauses joke," James points out.

"I have better ones," I reply. "What do you get when you cross Santa with a duck?"

"I don't know," he says.

"A Christmas quacker."

He rolls his eyes as everyone else laughs. "That's my cue to move on," he says, and changes the subject.

I eat the pastry, pretending I'm listening to what he's saying. But it's hard not to think about Missie and what I've just agreed to do.

Me, playing Santa? Jesus, what the hell is the woman doing to me?

*

I arrive at the primary school at ten-thirty, and make my way to the school field, Zelda trotting by my side. Luckily it's a glorious day. The sun is already beaming, and there's hardly any wind.

The field is all ready for the opening of the fair at eleven. Stalls around the edge of the field are selling homemade Christmas crafts and toys and all kinds of food from cakes to sweets to pulled-pork buns. There are donkey rides and pre-loved fashion stalls and tables where you can make your own Christmas decorations, live music, face painting, and a bouncy castle. There are probably summer fairs being held like this all over the country, and it takes me right back to my childhood, and gives me a pang of nostalgia for a more innocent time.

I ask one of the teachers where Missie is, and she directs me to a large tent. I go over and duck under the flap, bringing Zelda with me, and find myself in a Christmas grotto. She's strung fairy lights all the way around and bedecked it in tinsel. A large, dressed tree stands beside Santa's big red chair. A smaller chair nearby is presumably where the kids sit, with a couple of others to one side for parents or caregivers.

I walk up to where she's stringing yet another set of fairy lights around Santa's chair. She's standing on a step, reaching up, and her T-shirt has risen up to reveal the section of pale skin above the line of her shorts.

Another teacher is standing next to her, untangling the lights. She catches my eye and gives me an impish smile, obviously noting the way I was checking Missie out. I give her a wry look and say, "Hello."

Missie's head snaps around and she wobbles on the stool. I stretch out a hand, and she grabs it.

"Oh," she says. "You came!"

I wait for her to steady herself. "You didn't think I would?" I don't bother to hide my indignation that she thought I'd back out when I'd given my word.

She meets my eyes and smiles. "Of course you would. I should have known better." She looks at where I'm still holding her hand. "Thank you, I've got my balance now."

Reluctantly, I release her, and she finishes off pinning up the lights, then gets down to greet Zelda. "Hello girl!" she says, kissing her head. "I'm sure you've grown since the last time I saw you."

"She's eating me out of house and home," I tell her. "I'm sure she's doubling her weight every other day."

She laughs, straightening. "This is Carly. Carly, this is Alex."

"That's Mr. Claus to you," I advise, and she grins as I shake her hand. She's around the same age as Missie, wearing shorts and a blue tee, with blonde hair in a ponytail.

"Look at you, all hot and summery," Missie says, gesturing to my outfit. "It's the first time I've seen you in civvies."

I look down at myself—I'm wearing beige cargo shorts and a plain gray tee. "I thought I might get hot under the costume."

"It's going to be thirty degrees today," Carly says. "You should probably strip everything off so you don't cook."

"Carly," Missie scolds, and her friend grins.

"I think your principal might have something to say if she knew Santa was going commando," I reply, and they both laugh.

"You want to get changed?" Carly asks, gesturing to the screen behind the chair.

"Probably a good idea." I go around the screen with Zelda and discover the red outfit trimmed with white fur resting on a chair. There's also a big, padded belly and a long white beard and mustache.

Missie appears. She's wearing a pair of green Christmas-tree earrings with flashing gold lights, and now she's facing me, I can see that her T-shirt says, 'Is it too late to be good?' I lift my gaze to hers to see her smiling.

"I was looking at your T-shirt," I point out.

"Yeah, yeah," she says. "I'm just relieved I didn't wear the one that has two baubles on the front and says, 'Tits the Season.'"

That makes me laugh. "I've got one that says, 'Stop staring at my package.'"

"Really?"

"No, Missie, God, you're so gullible."

She pushes me playfully. "You love to tease me."

"It's my superpower."

She blushes. "You want help getting ready?"

"Like a five-year-old?"

"Oh, um, yeah, sorry, I slipped into teacher mode then."

"Only I was going to say yeah, totally. There's no way I'm getting into this on my own."

She laughs and picks up the padded belly. "Let's get this on first."

"You think I need it?"

"Alex? You're *skinny as*. You need a good woman to fatten you up."

"Well I'd say I'd found one, but Finn told me you can't cook."

She giggles as she lifts the loop over my neck. "Unfortunately he's right, I'm not great in the kitchen. Can you cook?"

"Yeah, I'm a diva."

"Seriously, Alex."

"I am! I'm like Gordon Ramsay without the swearing."

"I've noticed that you don't use bad language." She holds up the trousers for me, and I step into them. She lifts them up and I tie them, then she helps me on with the long jacket.

"Juliette said she wonders whether you…" She looks up at me and her words trail off. "Nothing," she mumbles.

"What?"

She shakes her head, laughing.

I can guess what Juliette said, and I watch Missie, amused, as she continues to dress me, keeping her gaze lowered. Somewhere along the way, our banter turned into flirting. I've been waiting a long time for it to happen, and the fact that she's finally relaxed enough is the best Christmas present I could have asked for.

She reaches both arms around me to bring the belt around my waist, and glances up as she does so, meeting my eyes again. She doesn't say anything, but I hold her gaze, and her lips curve up.

"Done," she murmurs, moving back. "Now it's just boots, hat, and beard."

I pull on the boots, slide the elastic of the beard over my head, and let her adjust it so the curly beard tumbles down my front. Finally, she adds the hat, and then she stands back to admire the finished product.

SERENITY WOODS

Zelda is sitting staring at me as if she doesn't recognize me. I hold out a hand, and she sniffs it, then licks it as if to say, "Oh it is you."

"Not bad at all," Missie says with some surprise. "You want to try the chair?"

"Carly's right, I'm going to cook in this," I tell her. "I'm already sweating."

"Stop grumbling." She leads me around to the chair. "Go on, sit down."

I lower myself into the chair. "Wow, this is hard."

"What are you, eighty?"

"I'm going to be here for four hours. I don't have a lot of padding."

Carly chuckles. "I'll find you a cushion."

"Don't pamper him," Missie tells her. "He just loves complaining."

"Come and sit on my knee and say that."

They both laugh. "Don't tempt me," Missie says, "I'll squash you."

"Oh, that's it—you're on my naughty list. I'll have to put you *over* my knee instead."

Immediately, she blushes almost the same color as my Santa suit. Carly stares at her and says, "Whoa," laughs, and goes out, hopefully to find a cushion.

"Alex," Missie scolds, tucking her hair behind her ear. "What's got into you?"

"What do you mean?"

"I'm totally going to find all the badly behaved children now and make them come and see Santa."

"Bring it on, girl. I can handle it."

She rolls her eyes and gestures to the pile of wrapped gifts in the box by my side. "Every kid gets one of those, okay? They're just small bits, coloring sets, that kind of thing."

"Sure. Hey, I wanted to ask you something."

She bends and switches on the fairy lights, illuminating the tent. "Ooh, nice. Sorry, yes?"

"Would you like to come to our staff Christmas party? It's on the twenty-first. We're holding it at The Pioneer. It's Christmas trivia night, so we've booked half a dozen tables, and then there'll be drinking and dancing."

She studies me, bemused. "I'm not staff."

"No…"

"Do you invite all your patients?"

"Technically you're not a patient either."

We study each other for about twenty seconds.

"You're going?" she asks eventually. "I wouldn't have thought you were the party type."

"I'm not, normally. But this year…" I shrug. "I thought I'd make an exception."

Still she hesitates. "I'm not sure…"

"I'm still prepared to put you over my knee if you're not a good girl," I tell her.

That makes her laugh. "All right."

"Aw," I say, "I thought you were going to say no on purpose. You're no fun."

She's saved from having to reply by Carly coming back. "For your firm manly butt," Carly says, waving a cushion at me.

"Ah, thanks, I've already lost the feeling in both legs." I take the cushion and sit on it. "That's better."

"Are you ready to get started?" Missie asks. "There's already a queue forming outside."

I sigh. "Might as well get it over with."

"That's the spirit," she says, and goes outside to bring in the kids.

It's the first time I've played Santa, and I haven't spent much time around young children, so I don't really know what to expect. I'm anticipating either spoiled young brats or rude pre-teens like Dudley Dursley from the Harry Potter movies, and I'm sure I'm going to regret offering to help by 11:05.

To my surprise, ninety-nine percent of the kids are a lot of fun. Missie deals adeptly with any who are problematic, scolding them and telling them they won't get any presents if they don't behave. They soon calm down when I tell them that if they're good, they can fuss up Zelda for a few minutes.

I thought they were all going to ask for PlayStations and other expensive gifts, but although some do ask for phones or computers, most of them talk about small toys that hold meaning for them— action figures, LEGO kits, video games, or items for their favorite hobbies.

Carly patrols the doorway, and Missie helps inside with getting the children to sit quietly and handing out the presents. We make a good team, and she spends most of it laughing at my interactions with the kids.

"And what's your name?" I ask a girl as she sits beside me. She looks to be eight or nine.

"Scarlett," she replies.

"I thought you were great in Black Window," I tell her in my deep Santa voice, and she giggles.

"That was Scarlett Johansson," she scolds.

"Oh, I'm sorry. And how is the Tara plantation?"

"That's Scarlett O'Hara," her mother corrects, laughing, and the girl giggles again.

"Stop teasing her, Santa," Missie admonishes, eyes dancing. "Naughty boy," she mouths, and I wink at her.

Missie brings me regular cups of coffee and free samples from all the food stalls throughout the morning. I'm more than happy to try the chocolate brownies, shortbread, and fudge, although the best bit is the pork bun she brings me during our lunch break.

When I start up again, Carly holds the tent flap to one side, and to my surprise Finn comes in, pushed by an older woman with hair that's completely silver and cut in an attractive bob. She looks enough like Missie for me to guess that this is her mother.

"Hello Santa," Finn says, grinning, as Zelda leaps up onto his lap. "I brought my grandma to meet you. Grandma, this is Alex."

"Who is this Alex of whom you speak? My name is Santa," I tell him in my booming voice.

He rolls his eyes. "I stopped believing in Santa two years ago."

Missie and her mum exchange a glance, smiles slipping. Ah. I have a feeling Finn's dad might have been to blame for that.

Keeping in character, I say, "Hello Grandma." I hold out my hand. "How very nice to meet you."

"Hello, Santa, I'm Sandra." Her eyes sparkle, especially when she watches Finn and Zelda playing together.

"And hello young man," I say to Finn. "What do you want for Christmas?"

"A new pair of legs, please," he says. Sandra glances at me, but Missie just laughs. From any other kid, that might have been upsetting or poignant, but she gets that Finn and I know each other well enough now to enjoy the other's slightly twisted sense of humor.

"I'll come down the chimney and leave you a pair of robot pants like in Wallace and Gromit's *The Wrong Trousers*," I tell him, and he giggles.

"What else do you want for Christmas?" I ask.

He rolls his eyes. "I want to finish the Mayachin Shrine on Zelda. I've read the walkthrough, but I can't work out how to attach the lever to the bit that rotates—it won't stick."

"You need to turn one of the stakes and push it through the central device," I tell him in my Santa voice. "Then attach the lever to the stake."

He stares at me. "Oh… I didn't realize that. Wow, thank you."

"You're welcome. Merry Christmas."

Sandra and Missie both chuckle.

"What do you really want?" I ask Finn softly.

He hesitates, and I nod to encourage him. "I'd like to go up in your helicopter," he says eagerly.

I clear my throat. "You mean my sleigh?"

"Oh yes, of course, your sleigh."

I glance at Missie. She's smiling, so I guess she won't mind if I agree. "I'll sprinkle some fairy dust and see what I can do."

He grins. "Thank you, Santa."

"Come on," Sandra says. "There are more kids waiting."

I groan. "Save me, Finn."

"Mum says you need punishing because you were cheeky to her," he points out as Sandra turns him around.

"Slave driver," I tell Missie, and Sandra laughs and wheels him out.

At three o'clock, the fair is coming to an end, and Missie finally declares it's time to wrap up. I take off the Santa suit, then go out the back of the tent into the fresh air and lie on the grass in my tee and shorts, exhausted and soaked with sweat, even lacking the energy to push Zelda away when she licks my face.

A shadow falls across me, and I open my eyes to see an upside-down Missie leaning over me, her hands on her knees. "You did a great job," she says.

"Ho, ho, ho."

She smiles. "You never fail to surprise me, Alexander Winters."

"I've eaten so many brownies, I don't need the padding anymore."

She laughs, walks to my feet, and holds out a hand, and I take it. She tries to pull me up, but it's not easy for her, and she groans.

"Ooh, you're heavy," she complains, pulling back with all her weight.

"I told you, it's all the cake." As I finally get to my feet, I topple forward and bump into her. "Sorry."

We stand there for a moment, surrounded by the sights, sounds, and smells of the school fair. It's a beautiful afternoon. A few kids are still on the bouncy castle, and their laughter floats across the field, along with shimmering bubbles that a little girl is blowing with a wand. Next to Santa's Grotto, a stall is selling homemade Christmas potpourri, and I can smell cinnamon and cranberries and baked orange slices. Missie's long ponytail lifts in the light breeze, and her eyes sparkle like her Christmas-tree earrings. Man, she's gorgeous. I feel like a kid on Christmas Eve, the air between us full of magic and promise of what's to come.

Chapter Eight

Missie

Alex has a large triangle of sweat on his T-shirt, his face is flushed, and his hair is completely soaked, a far cry from the suave, sophisticated image he normally projects. The poor guy has worn a fur coat and thick trousers for four hours, and apart from a brief joke at the beginning, he hasn't complained once.

I'd say he's done it for me, but I can't be sure. Despite his grumpy demeanor, he's obviously altruistic and kind deep down. How do I know what his true feelings for me are?

Carly thought I was mad when I voiced my doubt at lunchtime. "Girl," she said, "he's crazy about you. I can tell by the way he's looking at you. There's no doubt about it."

But I haven't seen it for myself. His face is always impassive. His eyes are a different story—they often seem full of heat when they look at me. But maybe I'm just seeing what I want to see. How can I be certain?

He's prime real estate—young, gorgeous, and a top businessman—incredibly smart, and quite the genius, from what I've heard. Why on earth would he be interested in me?

He's looking at me now with his usual expression that could be affection but could also be utter incomprehension. He's so gorgeous, even though he looks as if he's been caught in the rain. Oh God, is he interested in me or not? I know the year isn't up yet, but it's damnably close, and I'm getting excited about the prospect of being free. And suddenly I need to know how he feels about me more than anything else in the world.

"Alex…"

"Yeah?"

We're standing only a foot apart. I can smell his spicy vanilla cologne, warmed by his body. I'm wearing sandals today rather than my usual high heels because we're on the field, and he's a lot taller than me. He's hot and sweaty and sexy and I wish I could just push him onto the grass and jump him. Oh man, I want to do that so much. His eyes gleam. Does he have any idea what I'm thinking?

I hesitate, then take the plunge. "Are you seeing anyone? Juliette told me you weren't, but it was back in April, and I wondered whether maybe you'd started dating since then because it's been such a long time, and you're gorgeous, and I can't believe you'd be single this long, and it would make sense if you'd found someone…" My voice trails off.

He shakes his head. "No."

"Um, no, you're not seeing anyone? Or no, you're not single?"

"The former."

The former? That's such an Alex answer. He's not smiling, although his eyes sparkle a little.

He's not seeing anyone! Oh. Wow. That's great news! But… even if that is the case, it doesn't mean he's interested in me, right?

I clear my throat. "Do you… you know… like me?"

"Yeah," he says.

"I mean, do you *like* like me?"

"Yeah," he says again, in the same tone as before. He surveys me patiently. I don't think he gets what I'm trying to say.

"I'm not sure you understand," I say carefully. "I'm embarrassed to ask this, but I keep thinking about it, and it's been on my mind practically twenty-four-seven. I'm asking whether you have feelings for—"

"Missie, I get it. And yes. I *like* like you. A lot."

My jaw drops. His lips curve up, just a tiny bit.

He *likes* likes me?

Oh my God.

"I wasn't sure," I admit eventually. "You're a hard guy to read."

"You seriously had no idea?" He sounds half-amused, half-baffled.

I'm genuinely confused. "Why do you like me?"

"Because you're gorgeous and you make me smile, and I want you," he says.

My jaw sags. Slowly, heat blooms in my face. He notices, and this time he gives a proper, naughty smile.

When he speaks, though, his tone is gentle. "I'm not expecting anything. But I guess it's time we had a conversation about where we go from here."

"There are things you don't know," I say desperately. I want to tell him, but I'm ashamed, and I'm afraid he'll look at me differently if he knows.

He tips his head to the side. "All that matters is if you're ready now."

I bite my bottom lip. "I think so."

His eyes meet mine. Then he glances above our heads. I follow his gaze and discover we're standing right underneath a piece of mistletoe that someone's tied to the top pole of the tent.

"It's nearly the twenty-first," he says.

My heart leaps. "You want to kiss me?"

"Unless you'd rather wait another week?"

"No," I whisper. "It's close enough."

"If you'd prefer to postpone it until I've taken a shower, I'll understand. I know I'm disgusting right now." He glances down at himself and his lips twist.

"That's the best kind of dirty," I say before I can think better of it.

His expression turns sultry then, filled with heat.

"See," I say breathlessly, "if you'd looked at me like that, I'd have known how you felt immediately."

He laughs, and then he closes the distance between us and cups my face in his hands.

"I've thought about this a lot," he murmurs, making my heart race. Then he lowers his lips to mine.

I inhale and hold my breath as he kisses me. His hands are warm on my face, and his lips are dry and firm.

A million thoughts race through my head, the main one being *oh my God, Alex Winters is kissing me!* Just the nearness of him and the unexpected intimacy make my face burn. It's been such a long time since someone's done this.

I've thought about this a lot, he said. I wonder why? I'm really not that special. He's going to be so disappointed when he gets to know me. He's young, rich, and handsome; he could have any girl he wants. I'm not old, exactly, but I'm very ordinary, and I'm a mother, for Christ's sake. I can't imagine this suave, sophisticated guy has ever dated a girl with stretch marks before.

Shocked at the way he kisses me, as if the very act of our lips touching is precious to him, I stand frozen as he presses his lips to mine, and eventually he lifts his head.

"You okay?" he asks, brushing my cheeks with his thumbs.

I nod.

"Don't forget to breathe," he teases.

Oh shit, I've messed up. He's going to think I'm a terrible kisser. My breath leaves me in a whoosh, and I moisten my lips with the tip of my tongue.

"Sorry," I mumble, "I'm super nervous."

"Why?"

"Because I haven't kissed anyone for well over a year."

"Me neither."

"Really?"

He shakes his head.

"Why?"

He shrugs. "Haven't met the right girl." He picks up a strand of hair from my ponytail and slides it through his fingers. It's a sensual, sexy gesture, as if he's been waiting to find out how silky it is, and he looks into my eyes as he does it, his holding a lazy heat that makes my heart race.

"Want to try again?" he murmurs, looking at my mouth.

"I'm nothing special," I whisper, fighting back tears.

"I beg to differ."

"I'm not just saying that to provoke a compliment, Alex. When you get to know me, you'll realize you've wasted your time."

"Why don't you let me be the judge of that?" His voice holds a hint of reprimand that makes me shiver. He doesn't like being told what to do.

Moving a bit closer to me, he slides a hand to the back of my neck in a possessive move that sends a thrill through me. "You set me alight," he murmurs, which is so sweet and so sexy that my heart threatens to leap out of my chest and bounce along the ground like a space hopper.

Then he lowers his head and kisses me again.

His lips press across mine with soft butterfly kisses. His thumb strokes my neck, right by the nape. It makes me shiver again, and he obviously feels it, because he tilts his head to the side, changing the angle of the kiss. He slants his lips across mine, and then I feel his tongue brush across my bottom lip. As electricity zaps through me, I open my mouth, and he slides his tongue inside. I inhale, joy flooding through me, and I rise up onto my tiptoes so I can lift my arms around his neck while he lowers his around me.

The fiery kiss fills me with delicious heat. He rests his hands on my waist, then slides them around my back, holding me tightly as I press up against him. Oh man. Alexander the Great kisses like a god. I should have guessed.

Conscious that we're on the school playing field and there might be kids around, I eventually move back before I do the whole pushing him on the grass and doing him there and then thing. Luckily, we're around the back of the tent, and nobody's seen us, except for Zelda, who's lying with her head on her paws, watching us.

"Mmm," I say as Alex lowers his arms.

His eyes are intense. "That was worth waiting for."

"Merry Christmas," I whisper, and his lips curve up.

"Merry Christmas, Missie." He gives me a final kiss, just touching his lips to mine. "I'm in Wellington until the twentieth," he says. "So the next time I'll see you will be at the party."

I nod and move back. I'm disappointed, but at least I'll have something to dream about over the next week. "Thank you again for helping out today," I murmur. "I really appreciate it."

"You're welcome." We smile at each other, and then we walk around to the front of the tent.

"Wow," Carly says, obviously spotting his soaked tee, "that's a lot of sweat."

"It's thirty degrees and I've been wearing a fur coat," he points out, clipping Zelda's leash to her collar.

"Nothing to do with the steamy snog you've just had, then?"

He gives a short laugh and exchanges an amused look with me as I blush. "See you on the twenty-first," he says.

"Bye, Alex."

"Bye," he says, and I watch him go, my heart floating with the bubbles all the way up to the sky.

*

At first I assume the next week is going to go by at a snail's pace, but the days pass quickly, especially once school finishes. December is always an emotional time because the following year I have a whole new class of students, and it always humbles me to think back over the year and see how far the children have come since their first day in my classroom.

Also, it's Finn's last day at primary school as he's starting high school in February, and his graduation is an emotional one for me, as he's my only child, and I'm not sure I'll have any more kids. He's excited to be moving forward, though, especially as his physio is going well, and he's able to move about a lot more on his own with crutches.

There's Christmas shopping to do, and wrapping presents, dressing the tree, buying food, and baking, as well as continuing to take Finn for his physio three times a week, and sometimes taking him to friends' houses. We also travel up to Blenheim for a couple of days to see my aunt and uncle so we can deliver their Christmas presents.

The weather is changeable—warmer than it has been, but with some rainy days that leave the tarmac steaming when the sun comes out. Alex texts me, telling me it's hot in Wellington. I reply that's because he's there. He comes back with a laughing emoji. And that's it—from then on we text continually. Just short messages talking about our day, nothing too intimate, but my heart leaps every time I feel my phone buzz in my pocket.

I feel odd—restless and emotional and scared and excited all rolled into one. It's not surprising, I guess. The memories of last December are still fresh in my mind, even though a whole year has passed.

A whole year. I can hardly believe it. Back in March, when I first met Alex, I knew I wouldn't be ready to start a relationship for a long, long time. I needed to get over the grief and guilt and trauma of Finn's accident, and even though it might seem like an arbitrary number in many ways, it was important to me for Finn's sake, if nobody else's, that I wait until a year passed before I started seeing another man.

And now it's the twenty-first of December, and tonight's the night of the Kia Kaha Christmas party.

Which is why Carly and her husband, Sean, arrive an hour before I'm due to leave, complete with an armful of outfits, a dozen pieces of jewelry, hair curlers and tongs, and a box of makeup, as if we're sixteen years old getting ready for the school ball.

Sean gets stuck into LEGO Star Wars on the PlayStation with Finn, while Carly comes into my bedroom with me.

"You're not wearing that," she states when I show her the black shirt and skinny jeans I'd hung up ready.

"What's wrong with it?" I protest.

"It's *bleugh*."

"I happen to like *bleugh*."

"Missie, you want to stand out tonight. You want Alex to look at you and think holy shit, look at how gorgeous that woman is."

"I hate to break it to you, but there really aren't such things as miracles."

"There totally are, especially at Christmas. Now, try this on." She passes me a white crossover dress of hers with big red flowers. It's bright and bold and perfect for a party.

I pull it on. We're the same height and build, but she's flat chested and I'm… not. The crossover front clings to my breasts and gives me a cleavage like the Grand Canyon.

"Jesus." I try and pull the two sides closer together. "I can't wear that."

"You are absolutely going to wear that. You have gorgeous tits, Missie. Show them off!"

"She's right," Mum says, coming into my room with a glass of wine for us both. "They're one of your best assets."

"You should listen to your mother," Carly advises, giving Mum a wink as she goes out. "If I had a D cup, I'd wear tight tops all the time. He won't be able to take his eyes off you."

"I'd rather he look at my face."

"I'm telling you, he'll be mesmerized. Do you want to get laid or not?"

"I really do. But…" I hesitate. "It's not me, you know?"

"Maybe you should make it the new you."

I consider my reflection. Carly knows what I've been through, and she's begged me to forget Lee and get on with my life. Until now, I've not been able to follow her wishes, but for the first time I feel ready to move on.

"I'll ask the guys," I say, and go out into the living room. When they pause the game, I say, "What do you think? Too much boob?"

Sean gives them a polite appraisal. "Nope."

"He'll never say there's too much," Carly advises, coming into the room behind me. "He's married to an ironing board."

"Aw," he says, "don't say that. I love your figure."

"You're just being polite," she states, kissing the top of his head, "but thank you, sweetheart."

"What do you think, honey?" I ask Finn. "Too much?"

"Men like boobs," he says helpfully, and Sean nods his agreement.

"But I don't look, you know, tarty?"

Sean smiles. "You look lovely, Missie. Young and gorgeous."

"Told you," Carly says triumphantly.

"Plus you've got somewhere to keep your credit card," Sean adds, pointing at my cleavage, and Finn giggles.

Carly glares at them and steers me out of the room. "He's teasing you. You heard what he said—you look young and gorgeous. You're absolutely going to slay this guy. Now come on, let's have a go at your hair. You're wearing it down tonight, and if he doesn't get the urge to run his fingers through it, I'll eat my hat and coat."

*

It takes me longer than I expected to do my hair and makeup, and I end up walking into the bar at 6.45, fifteen minutes later than I'd planned. It's busy and bustling, warm and Christmassy. The long bar is bedecked with tinsel and sprigs of mistletoe. A huge tree stands in one corner, glittering with fairy lights and gold and red baubles. They're offering a special mulled wine, which has filled the air with the smell of cinnamon and oranges. As it's warm, most people are in tees or short-sleeved shirts, and lots of the women are wearing flashing Christmas earrings or sparkly tops.

I spot the guys from Kia Kaha standing by the bar, talking and laughing, and thread my way through the crowd toward them. I'm tempted to pull my jacket close around me, but I take a deep breath and let it slip from my shoulders as I approach. Alex is talking to James and a pretty blonde standing next to him. Alex is wearing jeans and a long-sleeved plum-colored dress shirt with the sleeves rolled back. He's obviously forgotten to use product because his hair is fluffy. Oh, I like it like that. I love the way it flops over his forehead.

He turns as I walk up, spots me, his eyebrows rise, and he stares. Then he turns away and obviously says something to the others because they all laugh. Hopefully he wasn't making fun of me!

"Hello," I say as I reach them.

"Hey," he says, smiling and bending to kiss my cheek. "Glad you came. Can I get you a drink?"

"Um, I'll have a glass of Sav, please."

He nods and walks over to the bar.

Juliette grins at me. "Hello."

"Hey. What did Alex say when I walked up that made you all laugh?"

"He didn't say anything. This is what he did when he saw you." She widens her eyes, inhales, then blows out the breath slowly.

"Oh no. I'm showing too much boob!"

"No, sweetheart, I think you're showing exactly the right amount," Juliette says as all the others try to hide a laugh, and fail. "Let me introduce you to everyone," she says. "You know James, and this is his girlfriend, Cassie."

I shake hands with the blonde. She flicks me a quick smile that rapidly disappears, then she finishes off her drink. "James," she says, holding her glass out to him.

"Alex is at the bar," he says curtly. She meets his gaze, then saunters off to Alex.

"You two all right?" Juliette asks softly.

"Nope," he says. He huffs a sigh and waves a hand, telling her to move on.

Juliette clears her throat. "You obviously know Henry. This is my other half, Cam."

I shake hands with a tall, good-looking blond guy. "Nice to meet you at last."

"Likewise," he says. He rests a hand on Juliette's hip and pulls her toward him. She takes a step to the side, causing his hand to fall. It's subtle, but I catch it. Ooh, it looks as if not everything in the garden is rosy with everyone tonight. What a shame.

"You've met Tyson," Juliette continues.

I smile at the guy perching on the barstool. "Yes, hello!" Tyson is the best advert for Kia Kaha they could have. Also told he'd never walk again, he's worked hard with MAX to strengthen his muscles and now he can walk unaided for short distances, using a walking stick just for balance and security.

"This is his wife, Gaby," Juliette states, gesturing to a pretty young woman with short dark hair.

"I'm Alex's sister, too," Gaby says, shaking my hand.

"Oh." I flush as she gives me an appraising look, and smile at Tyson. "I didn't realize you were married to Alex's sister."

"Gabrielle Audrey Winters-Palmer," he says. "It's a bit of a mouthful."

She chuckles. "I've heard a lot about you," she says to me.

"I haven't told her anything," Alex announces, reappearing at my side with a glass of wine, which he hands to me.

"All right," she says good-naturedly, "I'll stop teasing. Missie, I understand you're a teacher as well, is that right?"

"Yes! You teach?"

"I do!"

"What school?"

"I'm not actually at a school—I run my own company, Hepburn Education—I provide English and Maths tuition for primary and secondary school students, in person and online."

"Oh, I've heard of you! I've had several sets of parents say how you've helped their children. It's so great to meet you at last."

She beams at me. "That's cool to hear. Oh, by the way, this is my friend, Aroha."

I shake hands with a pretty Māori girl. "I'm just making up the numbers," Aroha states. "I'm terrible at trivia."

Gaby leans close to me and whispers, "I was hoping she and Henry might hit if off if they spent some time together."

I watch as James bumps shoulders with Aroha and apologizes, and the two of them hold each other's gazes for a moment before looking away. Oh-ho, I don't think it's Henry she's interested in.

I look at Gaby to see if she's noticed, but she's watching me, clearly curious.

"Don't gawp," Alex scolds her. "You're not at the zoo."

"I wasn't gawping." She grins at me. "I'm intrigued. Alex doesn't date very often."

"This isn't a date," he states. "I wouldn't take a girl on a first date to a trivia night. Give me some credit."

"So where are you going for your first date?" Gaby asks, eyes sparkling.

"None of your business."

"Aw," she says. "Come on, spill the beans. Want some tips? Here you go… When you kiss, try not to knock her teeth with yours."

"We'll bear that in mind, won't we, Alex?" I say. "When we have our first kiss?" I wink at him.

"Ohhh…" Gaby says. "You've already kissed? When was this?"

"Jesus," he replies, and everyone laughs. He takes my hand. "Come on. The quiz is going to start soon."

He leads me over to a table marked Reserved. "Sorry about that," he says. "I'm not sure this was such a good idea."

"I'm having a great time," I tease.

He stops by the table and fixes his gaze on mine. "You're going to be trouble, aren't you?"

"Only the best kind."

His eyelids drop to half-mast. "I knew you'd be a brat the moment you told me off for having windows that were too clean."

My pulse speeds up. "Something tells me you don't mind too much."

His gaze slides to my mouth, and he just murmurs, "Hmm."

My heart gives a little flutter. His dark eyes are full of heat and the promise of a very special Christmas present. The only question is, when will I get to open it?

Chapter Nine

Alex

There are around twenty tables in the bar, all rectangular, some with stools and some, like ours, with one long bench on either side. The staff from Kia Kaha takes up six tables, split into departments, and there's a prize for the department that comes top.

There's only room for three people on each bench, but as I sit and move across it to the partition on the other side and Missie takes off her jacket and joins me, Juliette slots in and bumps Missie with her hip to close the distance so Cam can sit next to her, forcing Missie right up against me.

"Sorry," she says.

"No worries." Turning a little in the seat, I lay my arm along the back, not quite around her, but it means she's pressed up against me, and we're touching all the way down to our hips and thighs.

Not going to complain about that.

Cassie slides in opposite me, then James, then Aroha, and Henry squeezes on the end, which isn't easy because he's huge. Gaby and Tyson take the two chairs at the end of the table, and the trivia team is ready.

As the final people take their seats across the room, the MC welcomes everyone and begins going through the rules of the quiz. I listen, but I'm distracted by the subtle perfume of the woman tucked up against me and the softness of her body. She's wearing her hair down today, and it falls past her shoulders in attractive dark-brown waves. I bend my head closer to hers and inhale.

She looks up at me then, and her lips curve up as she whispers, "Did you just sniff my hair?"

I murmur back, "It smells nice."

"You're supposed to be listening to the rules."

"I am listening."

"Name one."

"Don't cheat."

She laughs. "Fair enough."

"James will remember all the rules," I say, raising my voice. "He always tells everyone what to do anyway."

"Someone has to," James says. "You lot are useless."

"You don't have to be so rude about it," Cassie states tartly.

James gives her a look. "I wasn't talking about you. I was referring to these losers." He gestures at the rest of us.

She gets out her phone and starts scrolling as she finishes off the glass of wine I just bought her.

I lift my eyebrows. They've been bickering a lot lately, but not quite as openly as that. James rolls his eyes and looks away, but the rest of us exchange awkward glances.

"Got a Christmas joke for you all," Missie says. "What do you call a kid who doesn't believe in Santa?"

We all shake our heads.

"A rebel without a Claus," she answers, prompting lots of groaning and laughter. She winks at me, and I know then that she told the joke to diffuse the tension.

"Did you hear about the dyslexic Satanist?" Henry asks, joining in. "He sold his soul to Santa."

That prompts more laughter, although I note that Cam doesn't smile. He just glares at Henry. Hmm... wonder what that's about?

"Go on," Juliette says to me, "you must have another one in your repertoire. He's the best joke teller," she tells Missie.

"I have hundreds," I reply, "but they're not appropriate to tell in public."

"Oh my God, you absolutely have to tell one now," Missie prompts.

"All right. Why does Santa always come down the chimney?"

Juliette grins. "I can guess where this is going, but I don't know."

"Because he knows better than to try the back door."

Missie giggles, and that starts the other girls off, and soon everyone's laughing again, except for Cassie, who just huffs a sigh and continues scrolling on her phone.

There's a pause as one of the staff arrives to give us a sheet of paper and a pen, and then the waiter arrives with a large bowl of mulled wine and a tray of small glasses that Henry apparently ordered. Juliette and

Missie ladle the wine into the glasses and pass them around, and they've just finished when the MC announces it's time to start.

I sip the drink, tasting orange, cloves, cinnamon, and raisins with the red wine, and a feeling of contentment settles over me. I wasn't sure if Missie was going to back out at the last minute, and I felt such a surge of pleasure when I saw her walking across the room. And now I'm sitting here with her on an almost-date, almost-touching her, with my friends, drinking mulled wine, and things are feeling pretty good.

"I forgot to ask," she says, "is Zelda at home on her own tonight?"

"No, she's with my dad. He loves the chance to get his hands on her. I'll pick her up in the morning."

"Does she sleep on your bed?"

"No, I crate-trained her. I didn't want to start her off with bad habits." Plus, I want to make sure the bed isn't too crowded if I ever get to share it again.

She looks into my eyes, and for a moment I wonder if I've said it out loud, but she just smiles and turns her gaze to the small stage.

"Round one," the MC states, "Geography."

Juliette picks up the pen. "Come on guys, let's do this."

We get seventeen out of twenty on Geography, sixteen on History, nineteen on Sports, a dismal twelve on Music—mainly because it's classical music and we're all pretty hopeless at that—eighteen on Food, twenty out of twenty on Science—unsurprising, considering we're a table full of nerds—but more surprisingly we also get full marks on Art and Literature, due mainly to Missie chipping in with her knowledge of artists.

It's a fun evening, marred initially by two events. The first involves James and Cassie. She sulks through the first thirty minutes of the quiz without answering a single question. That obviously pisses James off, and he has a quiet word with her during the halfway break, following which she snaps back at him, then makes everyone get up so she can slide out of the seat, and storms off to the front door. James stands with his hands on hips for a moment, then follows her. They disappear outside, and I assume he's left with her. But then, five minutes later, he reappears at the table, tells everyone to stay where they are, climbs over the back, and slides in beside Aroha.

"All right?" I ask cautiously.

"Hunky dory," he says. He knocks back the rest of his whisky in one go, then he blows out a long breath. "We broke up."

"James!" Juliette exclaims. "Oh my God, I'm so sorry."

"Are you okay?" Aroha asks quietly.

James nods. "It's been coming for a while." He gives us all an apologetic look. "Sorry, I didn't mean to bring the mood down. Would you rather I go?"

"Absolutely not," I say firmly. "Time to drown your sorrows." I gesture to the waiter currently making the rounds and say to the rest of the table, "Consolation whisky, anyone?"

Henry and Tyson both nod, so I ask the waiter for three doubles of Glenlivet on the rocks.

"Cam?" I ask.

He shakes his head. "No, thanks, I've got to shoot off soon."

Juliette stares at him. "You're kidding?"

"I told you, Pete's coming around," he says, naming his brother.

"You promised you'd stay till ten," she whispers, obviously hurt.

He glances across the table in Henry's direction, then back at her and raises an eyebrow. She immediately turns scarlet and glares at him, clearly furious.

Missie clears her throat and looks at Gaby, then Aroha, as she says, "Maybe we should have another bowl of mulled wine, what do you think?"

"Sounds great," they both say, and the waiter nods and goes off to order.

Cam gets up. "Probably best if I go now, too. See ya." He strides off.

"Cam," Juliette snaps, but he doesn't look back. She watches him go, then turns back to the table. "I'm not going after him," she states, lifting her chin.

Henry pushes the remainder of the whisky in his glass over to her. She looks at it, then at him, then drinks the rest of it in one go.

"Euw!" She pulls a face. "I hate whisky." She puts the glass down, then covers her face with her hands. "Oh God. What have I done?"

"You haven't done anything," Missie says firmly. "You're staying with your friends for the evening, that's all. I'm sure he'll calm down after a few hours."

Juliette heaves a shaky breath. She's wearing a sari tonight, and she's outlined her eyes in kohl and looks hauntingly beautiful. She and I clash sometimes because she's not afraid to say what she's thinking, but she's one of my dearest friends. I believe in equality one hundred percent, but I also think women deserve to be worshiped because of everything they have to deal with, including us. Cam never puts her first, though. I'm sure she's not easy to live with, but I hate the way he treats her sometimes.

"Well, this is turning out to be quite the evening," Tyson states. He looks at his wife. "You want a divorce now or do you want to wait until the end of the day?"

Juliette snorts and James gives him the finger, which makes everyone else laugh, and we all start to relax again.

Oddly, despite two of us having lost our partners, the atmosphere improves after Cassie and Cam's departure. The drink continues to flow, and we order a couple of platters of breads, dips, and hot savory nibbles to soak up the alcohol. The bar also delivers a plate of mince pies to each table. Much laughter ensues when Aroha sneezes as she goes to take a bite of hers, sending a shower of icing sugar all over James.

"I should put you over my knee for that," he tells her, dusting it off his hair and sending her an amused look, and she turns scarlet.

"I seem to remember you telling me the same thing," Missie murmurs to me with an impish glint in her eye.

I dip my head so my mouth is close to her ear. "And I'm still planning to."

She lifts her gaze to me, and our eyes lock. All the hairs rise on the back of my neck. She looks amazing tonight. The kiss we shared at the school fair was explosive, and I've barely thought about anything else since. I want to kiss her again. But not here, not in front of everyone. This time I want it quiet and private, so I can concentrate on her and nothing else.

Eventually I tear my gaze away as the MC starts the next round, but from that moment on the atmosphere changes between us. I'm sure we look as if we're acting normally, but I'm conscious of her with every cell in my body, and I know she feels the same from how her breathing changes, and the way she's distracted and only half-listening to everyone else.

At one point, I have to visit the Gents. Rather than make everyone move, I climb over the back of the bench. When I come back though, I discover that Gaby has squeezed on the bench next to Juliette, shoving Missie further along, and there's no room left for me.

I put my hands on my hips and then gesture to Gaby to move back. She gives me the finger.

"Right." I go behind Missie and instruct her to stand up.

"There's no room," she objects, laughing.

I hold her gaze and scold, "Do as you're told." Lips curving, she lifts up and leans forward on the table. I climb over the back and slide onto the bench behind her.

"Where am I going to—"

I pull her onto my lap, and she squeals, then laughs and turns, putting an arm around my neck. The others whistle, and James asks me, "Jesus, how many whiskies have you had?"

He knows I don't normally do this kind of thing in public. But I haven't had that much to drink. The truth is that I feel almost dizzy with desire. Or maybe it's just that it's nearly Christmas, and the very air is filled with excitement, as well as glitter from the balloons above our heads that scatter everything with fairy dust.

Whatever it is, I revel in the feel of Missie so close to me, soft in my arms, her arm around me, and her hair tumbling over my shoulder. I have to fight not to turn and bury my face in it, or pull her head down so I can kiss her. I want to lift the hem of her top, slide my hands beneath, and trace my fingers over her bare skin.

I don't though. I behave myself, as we take the last round of questions, which is on Christmas movies. Juliette and Henry get into an argument about whether the actor who plays Daniel Cleaver in Bridget Jones is Colin Firth or Hugh Grant. I can tell from the glint in Henry's eye that he knows it's Hugh Grant, but he's teasing her on purpose, forcing her to argue with him until she's red-cheeked with earnestness. They've always been like this, and now Cam's not here, something's kicking off between them.

The same thing is going on with Aroha and James—he's resting one arm along the back of the bench, which just happens to be behind her, so she's tucked against him the same way Missie was earlier. That's a little more worrying, as I know he's going to be upset over what's just happened with Cassie, and he's had quite a lot to drink. I know he likes Aroha—he told me that ages ago, when they first met—but I'd hate him to sleep with her on the rebound, because that wouldn't be fair to her and it wouldn't be good for him. But hey, he's a grown man and has to deal with the repercussions of his actions like the rest of us, so I leave him to it and concentrate on the woman in my arms.

Our table comes second overall in the quiz, which we're thrilled with considering how much we've drunk. Gaby goes up to collect our trophy and prize—a giant box of Favourites—and then it's time for the party. They lower the lights and turn up the music, and the smallish wooden floor is soon filled with people dancing to *I Wish it Could Be Christmas Everyday* and *Step Into Christmas*. Behind the DJ they have a projector playing Christmas and party scenes on the wall, and they release balloons and streamers that add to the festive atmosphere.

We all stay where we are for a while, just enjoying being together and relaxing after what's been an intense year. But eventually I hear Justin Bieber's *Mistletoe* start up, and the urge to dance with Missie becomes too much.

"Everyone up," I instruct. They complain, but I say, "I want to dance and I'm not making Missie climb over everyone—up!"

They all grumble, but I have a sneaky feeling that none of them is disappointed to take to the dance floor. Tyson enjoys being able to dance with his wife for the first Christmas in a long time, Aroha and James are soon locked together. And Juliette and Henry, while standing a polite six inches apart and saying nothing, are oozing sexual tension.

But I ignore them all and concentrate on the woman in my arms. Missie is soft and warm, and she smells amazing. I hold her right hand and rest mine in the small of her back, and we move slowly to the music. Glitter sparkles in the air, and some of it has fallen on Missie's skin, so it shines in the flashing fairy lights.

"Thank you for inviting me out," she says. She's wearing a pair of sexy strappy sandals that have exceptionally high heels, making her around five-ten, but she's still smaller than me, and she has to look up into my eyes.

"Thanks for coming. Finn didn't mind you going out?"

She shakes her head. "He was pleased for me. I don't get out much. Carly and I go out sometimes, but we're getting old now, so we're usually home by ten." She smiles.

"Is Carly married?"

"Yes, to Sean. They've been trying for a baby for a couple of years, but she hasn't fallen yet."

"That's tough."

"Yeah. They're young, though. They've got plenty of time."

"What about you?" I ask her. "Do you want more kids?"

She surveys me for a moment, her eyes holding a touch of wariness. "I'm not sure," she says. "I've been lucky enough to have Finn. It would be strange having a baby again, but nice, I guess. But… I don't know." I think she's nervous about committing either way because she's not sure of my opinion. I guess some guys are frightened off by the thought of having a family. "What about you?" she asks cautiously.

"I wouldn't mind my own rugby team."

She gives me a beautiful smile at that, and for the first time I realize her cheeks have a slight dimple.

"Finn's a great kid, though," I add. "I'm looking forward to spending more time with him." I want her to know that although I want to be with her alone, I'm aware he's a very important part of her life.

"He'd like to get to know you better, too. He hero-worships you, you know."

"The poor guy. If I'm what he's aspiring to, he's not aiming very high."

"Oh, you're just being self-deprecating," she scolds, "which is very sweet. But you must know how you appear to him. Older, handsome, suave, and sophisticated. Smart, rich, and successful. And cool, too, because you like gaming."

I'm genuinely flattered, although I say, "You've left out grumpy and grouchy."

"And other dwarves." She giggles, then presses her fingers to her lips. "Sorry, I've had quite a lot to drink."

"If you don't get out much, it must be nice to relax a little."

"Yeah. It is."

The music changes to *Last Christmas*, and even though it's around twenty-five degrees Celsius, or nearly eighty Fahrenheit, the projector shows pictures of snow-covered cabins that adds to the holiday feel.

Missie's gaze drops to my mouth. "I've been thinking about our kiss," she murmurs.

"Me too."

Her eyes return to mine, filled with longing. "Will you kiss me again tonight?"

"If you're a good girl."

"I'm always a good girl."

"I sincerely doubt that."

She gives a short laugh. "Sorry, but I've never been bad."

"Yet. You are on my naughty list, just so you know."

Her eyes flare. She sucks her bottom lip. "I'm glad you kissed me at the fair. I wasn't sure that you liked me."

"I like you, Missie. I've liked you from the first moment I saw you."

"When I walked into your office door? I'm such a dork."

"A beautiful one, though."

She blushes. "That's a nice thing to say."

"I'm sure U2 sang a song about you."

She laughs. "That was *Beautiful Day* not *Beautiful Dork*."

"Ah. My mistake."

She chuckles. Then she drops her gaze to my shirt and fiddles with one of the buttons. "Alex…"

"Yeah…"

"I need to say something."

"Uh-oh."

"I just want you to know that I'm not interested in you because of what you're doing for Finn. I mean, obviously the fact that you've been so good to him, and you're helping him walk again, is going to have an influence. But that's not why I like you. And it's not your money, either."

"Okay."

"I need you to know that."

As the chorus hits, I twirl her in a circle, then bring her back into my arms, and she laughs. "I'm serious," she protests.

"I know. And I appreciate it—it means a lot to me. You know Damon?"

"Yes."

"He was living with a girl for a while, and James overheard her saying to a friend that she only wanted Damon for his money. He broke up with her pretty quickly after that."

"Oh no! What did she do?"

"Cut up all his suits and keyed his E-Type Jag. He wasn't a happy bunny."

"No shit. Aw. Poor guy."

"He's better off with Belle. But anyway, I appreciate you saying that. I'm glad you're with me for my winning personality." We both give a short laugh.

"That first day at your office, Juliette told me you were the grumpiest guy in the history of the universe," she says. "I know you well enough now to understand that you're not deep down."

"I dunno. I earned the nickname of Oscar the Grouch for a reason."

She giggles. "Have you always been grumpy?"

"No. I guess I've just got more cynical as life has thrown things at me."

She tips her head to the side. "Like what?"

One day, maybe I'll confess what turned me into such a curmudgeon. But tonight's not the night for it. I don't know her well enough yet, and it's nearly Christmas, and I don't want to spoil the atmosphere.

So, as the music changes to Mariah Carey's *All I Want for Christmas is You*, I say, "Can you dance properly in those high heels?"

She laughs and says, "I guess we'll find out."

We sing the slow opening lines together, and I don't miss the irony as I sing about wishes coming true. Then, as the beat picks up, I spin her around, and we start to dance for real.

I'm not a great dancer, but Damon's parents used to perform in competitions, and one Christmas when I was eighteen and I stayed with them, his mum taught me a few moves that I use now on Missie, making her laugh as we turn to the music.

We continue to dance as the snow falls on the cabins, while the fairy lights sparkle, filling Missie's eyes with glitter, and making me want to kiss her more than ever.

Chapter Ten

Missie

Alex is such a strange guy, full of conflicting qualities. He can be grumpy, terse, and impossible to read, he's obviously a workaholic and a control freak, and I've heard rumors at Kia Kaha that he pushes the staff hard, although no harder than he works himself. But he's also kind, generous, funny, and sexy, and he can dance! I didn't expect that.

My heart races every time I wonder what he's like in bed. Some of his comments have made me think that maybe his control freakiness extends to the bedroom. Oh my God, I would kill to go to bed with a man like that. Judging by the look in his eyes, though, I won't have to resort to murder. He could melt a chocolate truffle at fifty paces with the heat in his gaze.

I can tell he's thinking about kissing me again. And I'm sure he's thinking about what I look like naked. It's been a long time since I've taken a guy into my bed, and I'm nervous about exposing my body when I'm not as young and tight as I used to be. But I'm also super-excited at the thought of sharing myself with him.

There are things to work out before we get there, though, and that's making me concerned. I don't know if he's fully thought it through. But there's not a lot I can do about it—we'll have to have a conversation, and just see if he feels the same way afterward.

Judy Garland starts singing *Have Yourself a Merry Little Christmas*, and Alex pulls me close to him once more. "James and Aroha are leaving," he says, amused. I glance around and see the back of them disappearing through the crowd. He's holding her hand, and, when she glances back, I can see that her eyes are alight and her face is flushed.

"That was quick," I say with a laugh.

"He's liked her for a long time," he replies. "I hope he doesn't regret it in the morning, though. He doesn't normally do this kind of thing."

"I guess he's hurting and looking for solace. Aroha seems like a smart girl—she'll know that. She saw it happen, and maybe she wants to comfort him."

He looks back at me. "That's very practical."

"Not everything has to end in marriage and forever."

"Some things do." He looks to his right, and his lips curve up.

I follow his gaze and see Tyson and Gaby over by the bar—he's sitting on a bar stool, and she's standing with her arms around him, kissing him while they talk. They seem so in love, it warms my heart.

When I look back at him, though, he's watching the couple in the middle of the dance floor. Juliette is gazing up into Henry's eyes, and the two of them are completely lost in one another.

"More solace?" I query.

"Hmm," is all he murmurs.

"He seems like a nice guy," I say. "I'm sure he wouldn't hurt Juliette."

Alex looks back at me. "It's not her I'm worried about."

That surprises me. "You don't think she's done with Cam?"

"I think she has a very strong sense of right and wrong that's been suppressed by misery and alcohol and a momentary sense of carpe diem, but I think she'll regret it in the morning, and that's a shame, because Henry wants her."

"Should you say something?"

"She wouldn't listen, even if I did. She's a grownup. She can sort out her own mistakes."

We turn slowly to the music, his hand warm around mine.

"You're a big believer in personal responsibility, aren't you?" I ask.

"Yeah."

"Even with Finn. He's told me the speech you gave him about it being his decision whether to give up or not."

"Ah. Well, I don't have kids, so I can see how some parents might not approve of that. They believe children should be told what to think and do until they come of age."

"But you don't agree?"

"I think they need guidance, but I also believe it makes them work harder if they make their own decisions." The song comes to an end, and a faster one begins. "You want to keep dancing?" he asks.

I check my watch. It's nearly ten. "Actually I might get going. Finn's supposed to go to bed at nine, but I have a feeling he'll wait up for me."

"The man of the house, huh?"

I smile. "Yeah, something like that." Even though Alex said this wasn't a date earlier, Finn will want to know how it went.

"Come on." Alex takes my hand and leads me across the dance floor. Henry and Juliette have disappeared. We say goodbye to Gaby and Tyson, collect our jackets, and then go out into the cooler night air. Alex holds my jacket up so I can slip it on, and then he pulls his on.

"I'd better call an Uber," I say.

"Or I could walk you home."

"Through the park?"

"Yeah. It's well-lit at night, and there'll be plenty of people around this close to Christmas."

I smile with pleasure. "Well, if you wouldn't mind."

He holds out his hand again, I slip mine into it. The bars and restaurants are busy tonight, people spilling out to sit at the outside chairs and tables, talking and laughing in the cool early summer night.

"You sure you're okay to walk in those high heels?" Alex asks as we cross the road and head toward Hagley Park

"Oh yeah, I'm used to them."

"I don't know if I said, but you look lovely tonight."

My face warms. "Thank you. So do you."

He chuckles. "You're very kind."

"I notice you didn't use product tonight."

He gives a wry smile and runs his free hand through his hair. "It's gone fluffy."

"I like it fluffy."

"Then I'm glad I left it."

I smile. Down by our sides, he links his fingers with mine, which is an oddly intimate gesture, a premonition of our bodies intertwining, and it warms me through.

"I need to talk to you about something," I say cautiously.

"Okay."

"I… um… don't want to preempt anything, but you said tonight that this wasn't a date…"

"Ah, I was winding Gaby up."

"Yeah, I know. But… I'm guessing there *will* be a date?"

"Yes, Missie, there will be a date. More than one, I'm hoping."

"The thing is… you know that Finn and I live with my mum, right?"

"Yes, he told me."

"I moved up here after the accident. Partly for emotional support, and partly so she could help with Finn."

"Of course."

"But I haven't… you know… dated anyone since."

"Yeah."

I hesitate. I'm not sure how to phrase it. "It's just that I'm not quite sure how it's going to work."

He glances at me. "What do you mean?"

"Well, I'm twenty-eight now, I have an eleven-year-old son, and I don't live alone. It's not very… conducive to a spicy love life, if you get my drift."

He looks puzzled.

"Alex, don't be dense. I mean we can't exactly go at it like rabbits. I'd be too worried my mother might walk in. I'm just not sure you realize what you've signed up for. Not that you've signed up for anything, I mean we haven't even gone on a real date yet, but I'm just saying, maybe you should think a bit more about…"

My words peter out as he stops walking. I turn to face him, surprised.

He fixes me with one of his looks. "Did you think I was hoping you'd ask me in for a quickie on the kitchen table?"

"Oh. Ah… maybe."

"Well, for a start, I don't expect a girl to put out on the first date. What kind of guy do you take me for?"

I can see he's genuinely indignant. I've insulted him by insinuating he's not a gentleman.

I give him a helpless look. "I'm not very good at this."

He moves closer to me and cups my face. "Silly girl," he murmurs.

"You're not angry with me?"

"No, because I don't get angry with my girl."

His girl. His words warm me from the roots of my hair all the way to the tips of my toes. This guy absolutely melts me.

"I'm not averse to a quickie on the kitchen table," I point out hopefully.

He brushes his thumb across my bottom lip, his gaze turning sultry. "Mistletoe Macbeth, when we first have sex, it's going to be *slow as*, and we're going to be alone, so you don't have to worry about anyone listening in when you have all those orgasms I'm going to give you."

My eyes widen and my lips part as I inhale. His assumption that it's definitely going to happen sends heat rushing through me. "Orgasms... plural?"

"Oh yeah." He bends his head and gives me the lightest of kisses. "It's going to be amazing."

My brows draw together. "But—"

He kisses me again, stopping me speaking. "Neither of us is eighteen," he says afterward. "We're adults, and we'll work it out in an adult way. I know you have a family. That's partly what appeals to me. I like your mum, and I think Finn's a great kid. I want the whole package."

I swallow hard. "You don't mind that I'm not... you know... all tight and perky?"

"You look pretty perky to me."

"How do you know? You haven't eye-dipped me once."

He rolls his eyes. "Well, not conspicuously. That would be rude."

"So you have noticed my boobs?"

"I am a man, Missie. Of course I've noticed your boobs."

"They're not bad."

"They're very nice. But the point is, I like that you're a woman. You're smart and beautiful and incredibly brave. And I've waited this long—I'm not going to rush things now. I want to take my time to get to know you."

He waited? I'm not sure what he means by that. But there's no time to ask him, because he dips his head and kisses me again. His lips move across mine, slow and gentle. We're in public, with people walking around us, so it can't get ultra-steamy, but he still manages to send tweety birds flying around my head. When he eventually moves back, I have to be careful not to fall off my high heels.

I clear my throat. "So... no quickies on the kitchen table, then?"

"Well, never say never. I must add that I prefer being in a soft bed, but I think that would make me sound old."

I giggle. "A bit."

"Yeah, well, I'm about a week away from groaning when I get up out of a chair." He takes my hand. "Come on. The kitchen table might be out of the question, but if you'd like to invite me in, I'd love a cup of coffee."

I'm so happy that I have to fight against the tears pricking my eyes as we continue walking.

"Aw," he says as we cross the road and head into the park, and I sniffle and snuffle, "don't cry."

"I can't quite believe you," I say, my voice husky. "I don't know what I've done to deserve you."

"Gaby would say you must've been Attila the Hun in a previous life to be landed with me," he says. "Oh, look at this."

I stare at the scene ahead of us. Wow. I hadn't realized, but the Botanic Gardens are open, and they've been turned into a Christmas grotto. Solar fairy lights have been strung through the trees, and lamps hang from branches that make it look like something out of Narnia. Couples and families, even this late at night, are strolling along, looking at the displays. There are stalls selling all kinds of food and non-alcoholic drinks, while a group of carol singers makes the hairs rise on the back of my neck with their rendition of *O Come All Ye Faithful*. Several groups of teens are hanging around, eating and laughing, but they're all behaving and seem to be enjoying the atmosphere. A couple of police officers sip coffee as they walk along admiring the sights, as they have little to do.

"Did you know this was happening?" I ask Alex.

"Might have."

"You brought me here on purpose?"

"You need some romance in your life, Missie, so you'd better start getting used to it, because I intend to provide as much of it as I can."

I stop walking and turn to him, still feeling emotional. "I don't understand why you want me. I'm nothing special. I'm a horrible person."

He frowns. "What are you talking about? You're the nicest person I know. I've never heard you say a bad thing about anybody. You're kind to kids and puppies *and* you want to save the whales."

My bottom lip trembles. "I like the way you look at me," I whisper, "and you'll stop if I tell you."

His gaze softens. "Nothing you can tell me would change the way I feel about you, honey."

He's only saying that because he doesn't know. My arms are wrapped tightly around me, and I stare at the ground, fighting to keep my composure.

Moving forward, he wraps his arms around me and pulls me close. "I know it's the anniversary of the accident," he murmurs. "I'm amazed you've managed to get through the day as well as you have."

"I didn't realize you knew that."

"It was always going to be a difficult day for you. I thought coming to the party might help you get through it. I hope that wasn't the wrong decision."

I stand stiffly for a moment, shocked that he's known all this time, and that he's made the effort to help me through it. Then, as he continues to hold me, murmuring gentle words of encouragement, my muscles loosen, and I relax into his embrace. Turning my head, I rest my cheek on his shoulder, and he strokes my hair.

"No," I say softly, "you weren't wrong."

He sighs. "We all say things we don't mean at times. We all have our limits. People who are close to us know what those limits are, and they like to test them. It's not surprising when we react."

He's obviously guessed it's something to do with Lee. I inhale a deep, shaky breath and, as I exhale, I feel as if I'm releasing all the tension I've held inside me over the past year.

Coming toward us is an older couple, walking hand in hand. The woman, with gray hair cut in an attractive bob, glances at us and smiles as she sees us cuddled up. I give her a small smile, knowing I should move, but not wanting to. It's been so long since someone held me like this. His subtle cologne rises to ensnare me, welcome and familiar. His jacket is open at the front, and I can feel the warmth of his body through his shirt.

Unfolding my arms, I slide them around him beneath his jacket.

"That's better," he murmurs.

We stand there like that for a while, listening to the choir sing *The First Noel*, the music spiraling to the tops of the trees and up into the night sky, where the stars are popping out on the black velvet. It's a beautiful evening, made for lovers.

Turning my head to rest my other cheek on his shoulder, I study his collar, and the V of skin that's visible where the top two buttons are open. I can see his Adam's apple and the slight hollow beneath it.

Leaning forward, I place a light kiss there, and I'm rewarded with his answering shiver.

I move back and look up at him. He's so gorgeous. Now I know him better, I can recognize his subtle expressions, and there's tenderness in his eyes as he lowers his head and kisses me.

"Come on," he murmurs. "Let's get you home."

He holds my hand, and we continue walking through the park. More lights guide our way, and halfway along there's a wonderful display of Santa on his sleigh with his reindeer pulling him along.

Not far after that, Alex leads me away from the main pathway, and we enter a pavilion lit by solar lamps. In the midst of all the greenery is a large structure, the concave roof of which seems suspended in mid-air until we get closer, and I realized it's supported by stainless-steel columns. In the middle, hanging above a pond, is a large bell.

"Have you been here before?" Alex asks.

I shake my head. I've only lived in Christchurch less than a year, and although I walk through the park often, I haven't seen every nook and cranny.

"It's a World Peace Bell," he says. "After the Second World War, a Japanese mayor presented the United Nations with a bell as a token of world peace. There are twenty-two replicas around the world now, and Christchurch is the Peace City in New Zealand."

"I didn't know that."

"Ngāi Tahu blessed the site and gifted a piece of *pounamu*, which was placed in the pond." He gestures to the water beneath the bell. I know that Ngāi Tahu is the principal *iwi* or Māori tribe in the South Island, and *pounamu* is the Māori word for greenstone. "A sister piece was placed under the Cloak of Peace sculpture which New Zealand gifted to the Nagasaki Peace Park. So when the bell here is rung, the *pounamu* resonates between New Zealand and Japan."

"Oh, what a lovely story."

"Henry's a member of the *iwi*," he says. "He was only young, but he was there at the unveiling in 2006. He taught me a saying. '*Āio ki te rangi, Āio ki te whenua, Āio ki ngā mea katoa, Tihei mauri ora.*'"

"That's beautiful. What does it mean?"

"Peace to the sky. Peace to the land. Peace to everything. I am alive." He smiles and cups my face. "You're alive. You made it through. You're going to be okay, Missie."

I bite my bottom lip as tears prick my eyes again. This guy is determined to make me cry tonight.

"Don't do that," he murmurs. "It makes me want to kiss you."

My gaze drops to his mouth. God, I've never wanted anything so much in my life.

Lifting onto my tiptoes, I raise my arms around his neck and crush my lips to his.

We're not alone—other people are here, looking at the bell—but we're off to one side, in the shadows, and anyway, I don't care. I open my mouth to him, and he sweeps his tongue inside, and we exchange a long, luscious kiss that soon has me filled with yearning. Our tongues tangle, and for a moment heat flares between us, causing a growl to rise deep in his throat that gives me tingles all the way through.

He lifts his head, and his eyes are very dark. "You drive me insane," he says gruffly. Sliding a hand into my hair, he wraps the strands around it and pulls gently to make me tip my head back. Then he bends his head and kisses my neck, just beneath my jawline.

I shiver, and he straightens and sighs, releasing my hair. "Come on." He takes my hand again. "I think we could both do with a strong coffee."

His hand curls around mine as we cross the park and then we walk the short distance through Riccarton to where I live. "You're sure about this?" I ask as we go up the short drive to the front door. "Finn's going to be over-excited to have you in the house."

He chuckles. "I'm sure I can manage."

I'm not so certain, and I'm also conscious that our house is probably very small compared to what I'm sure he's used to. But I slide my key into the lock, open the door, and lead the way in. "Stay here a sec," I tell him, and I go through to the living room. Mum and Finn are sitting watching an episode of *Stranger Things*, but Finn pauses it as I enter, and they both look over eagerly. Finn's in his pajamas but Mum's still dressed.

"Hey," Finn says, "how did it go?"

"Um, Alex wants to come in for a coffee," I tell them. "Are you both okay with that?"

"Oh, of course!" Mum springs to her feet.

"Yeah!" Finn says enthusiastically.

"Think calm thoughts," I tell him, and he rolls his eyes.

I go back to the hallway. "You can come in," I say to Alex. He's taken off his jacket and hung it on the peg by the door. "You don't have to do that," I say as he toes off his Converses, but even as the words leave my mouth, I realize he's obviously been brought up to do that, and there's no way he'd go into someone's house without removing his shoes.

He follows me into the living room and says, "Hey, dude!" to Finn, holding out his fist. Finn bumps it, beaming at the manly interaction.

"Where's Zelda?" Finn asks.

"With my folks. She didn't want to go to the party. Hello, Sandra," Alex says to Mum, "it's good to see you again."

"Likewise," she says. "Did you have a nice time this evening?"

"We had a great time," he replies.

"Oh, I'm glad. I'll go to bed now, then," she says, "leave you two alone."

"What?" He frowns. "No, come on, have a drink with us, at least. Missie told me you're a Science teacher, and I wanted to ask your opinion on the new Science curriculum."

She glances at me, face flushing. "Oh, er…"

I smile. "I'll put the kettle on." I gesture for Alex to sit, and then go into the kitchen and fill the kettle with water. As I switch it on, I can hear Alex asking Finn whether he enjoys Physics at school, and it fills me with a warm glow.

I feel as if I'm setting out on an adventure, like Pooh Bear, with all his worldly belongings in a handkerchief tied to a stick. I don't know where this path is going to lead me. I'm excited and nervous in equal measure, especially because we've so much to discover about each other, and I'm still not convinced he's going to like everything he finds. But every journey begins with a single step, right?

This year has been hard, but at last I've found the courage to begin, and that's all that matters.

Chapter Eleven

Missie

I make Alex and myself a coffee and Mum a cup of tea, and we chat while we drink them, with Finn interjecting, clearly excited at being up so late and having Alex in his home.

I sit and listen to them talking, while the lights on the Christmas tree by the window blink on and off, making the gold and red tinsel and the baubles glitter. Mum's switched on the lights of the gas fire too, adding to the cozy atmosphere. I feel excited, the way you do before a driving test or an interview. I'm so thrilled he's here, and that he wanted to come in. I just like being with him, even if we can't exchange more than a glance. It's good for Finn to spend time with a guy. Most of his teachers are women, and now it's just me and Mum, it's strange to have a man in the house again.

Eventually, though, as it nears eleven and Finn's eyelids start to droop, I say to him, "Time for bed, I think."

"No," he protests, "I'm enjoying myself."

"Finn," Mum says firmly. "Time for bed."

"I don't want to go to bed," he protests in an uncharacteristic display of temper that shows how tired he is. "I want to stay up, too. It's not fair."

"Finn," I scold, embarrassed that he's not doing as he's told.

But Alex just says, "I bet you have some cool stuff in your room. Transformers and LEGO?"

Finn nods sulkily.

"Can I come and have a look?" Alex asks. "When you're in bed?"

Finn brightens. "Okay." He gets his crutches. Alex rises and helps pull him up and holds him steady until the crutches are in place, and Finn makes his way down to his room.

"That was sweet," I say softly once Finn has gone. "But you don't have to do that."

"All guys are eleven years old at heart," he replies. "I love LEGO."

Mum chuckles and holds out her hand. "Goodnight, Alex. I hope we'll see you again soon."

"You can count on it."

She smiles, winks at me, then leaves.

"I'll just check on Finn," I tell him, and follow her along the corridor.

She stops outside the bathroom and turns, eyes shining. "So you had a good evening?"

"Wonderful," I admit. "But you don't have to go to bed. We won't... you know... get up to anything..." I blush.

"Missie," she says, "You know how much I appreciate you coming to live here. But you're still very young. Look, I've been thinking about converting the spare bedroom into another living area for myself."

My jaw drops. "You don't have to—"

"I know. But I kinda like the idea. It would be good for us both to have our own space. You have Alex now, and..." She hesitates. "You never know, there might come a day when..." Her voice trails off, and she bites her lip.

My eyebrows lift. She lowers her gaze. "Mum," I say softly. "Have you met someone?"

She clears her throat. "Sort of."

"What's his name?"

"Mike. He's a widower—his wife passed away from breast cancer a few years ago. He has a couple of grownup kids. He teaches at the high school as well. Nothing's happened," she says hastily, "we've just met for coffee a few times, but..." Her brows draw together.

My throat tightens. "Mum, you know I don't mind if you date another man, right?"

Her eyes glisten. "I don't want you to think I don't still love your dad..."

"I know you still love him, but it's been three years, and you're not even sixty yet. You're going to live until you're a hundred! You don't want to be on your own for forty years."

She presses her fingers to her lips, and I go up to her and put my arms around her. We have a big hug, until the bathroom door opens and Finn comes out on his crutches, eyebrows rising to see us both there.

We break apart, laughing and sniffing. "Good night, love," Mum says, kissing Finn's forehead. She goes into the bathroom.

Finn gives me an amused look. "What was that about?"

"We're being soppy."

"Well, duh."

"Come on, you. Bedtime." I usher him into his room.

"You just want to be alone with Alex," he says.

"Absolutely, I do, so I'd be grateful if you got a move on."

He leans his crutches up against the wall. "Have you kissed him yet?"

"Yes."

His face lights up. "Really? Excellent."

"I'm glad you approve. Now, will you get in bed?"

He slides under the covers. "Are you going to make out?"

I stare at him.

He rolls his eyes. "You know I know about sex, right?"

"No, Finn…" I can hardly breathe. "You walked over to the bed."

He blinks, then looks down at the duvet. "Oh." A smile breaks out on his face. "Yeah, I guess I did."

We stare at each other with growing delight.

"Have you done that before?" I ask, my voice just a whisper.

"We've been doing some different exercises, but no. That's my first time without the crutches."

I sit on the side of his bed and take his hand in mine. "That's the best Christmas present I could ever have."

"I don't know," he says mischievously, "I'll be interested to see what Alex gives you."

"Finn!"

He looks confused. "I mean he's probably bought you some jewelry or something, right?"

"Oh, yes, I mean I don't know. Maybe." Blushing, I lean forward and give him a big hug. My eyes prick with tears. He walked, on his own, without crutches. Oh my God. I feel as if someone's handed me a million dollars.

"Tell him I'm in bed," he says.

I give him a final squeeze and move back, trying to hold in my emotion. "All right, but the poor guy didn't come here to have you monopolize him." I cup his face. "You're doing so well and working so hard. I'm so proud of you. You know that, right?"

"Aw, Mum."

I laugh and ruffle his hair. "All right."

"Can you move the chair closer?"

Smiling, I pull the chair in the corner over to the bed. "See you in the morning."

"'Night."

I return to the living room to find Alex standing looking at our Christmas tree. I pause and lean against the doorway for a moment, studying him. His hands are in the pockets of his jeans, but as I watch, he reaches out to examine a Rudolph decoration whose red nose is on a wobbly spring. I wouldn't be surprised if he was trying to apply Hooke's Law to it. I know his brain is constantly working.

His hair is almost shaved at the base of his neck, but grows longer until it flops over his forehead, which bears a slight frown. He's so serious, and so in control. I want to sink my hands into his hair and kiss him until his frown disappears. And I want to have sex with him… oh, so much. He's like a big red bow on a sparkling Christmas present, and I want to pull him undone.

He looks over at me at that moment. "Finn in bed?"

"Yeah."

He crosses the living room to stand before me. "Everything all right?"

"He just walked a few steps to his bed without his crutches."

His eyebrows rise, and then he gives me a beautiful smile.

"See, why don't you do that more often?" I scold, lifting a hand to cup his face. "You're so gorgeous."

He gives me a quick, fierce kiss. Then he strides away, clearly wanting to talk to Finn.

I don't know how many different emotions I can feel today. All mixed up and still a tad tearful, I collect the empty coffee cups, take them into the kitchen, and stack them in the dishwasher. I wipe a cloth around, then spend five minutes writing out a shopping list for tomorrow for some last-minute food. Carly and Sean are coming over on Christmas Day this year, so I want to make sure I have everything ready for a top-notch dinner.

When I'm done, I go back into the living room. Alex still hasn't returned. Oh God, has Finn captured him? Maybe Alex is too polite to say he's had enough?

I walk quietly along the corridor. The bathroom door is ajar now, so Mum must be in her room. I stop just before Finn's door and listen. The two of them are talking.

I should go in. But I know Finn loves talking to Alex, and to be fair, Alex doesn't sound as if he's trying to escape.

"…go to high school," Finn is saying, "especially because you get to go to other classrooms for different lessons."

"Yeah, it's much better than staying in one classroom all day, right?"

"It's a bit scary," Finn admits. "There are over a thousand kids there, and I'll be one of the youngest."

"That's true. But you're a good-looking lad, and you're intelligent and funny. I don't think you'll have any trouble making friends."

"It's going to be weird not having any girls there." He's going to an all-boys school, mainly because it's the closest to us.

"You get used to it. I went to an all-boys school, too. It's easier to concentrate when there aren't any girls in the class."

"Yeah, I guess. Robbie—my best mate—is going to be in my new class. He's cool, you'd like him. He's like me. He's got an older brother called Mark. He smokes. Have you ever smoked?"

"No."

"Mark says it's cool."

"If being cool means making your clothes and breath smell and dying from lung cancer. Girls don't normally find that attractive."

"What about, you know, drugs? Mark smokes weed."

"Someone at uni used to make muffins with it," Alex says. "Look, I play a bit of rugby and cricket, but I'm not great at sport. I can't draw or paint. And I'm not great at singing. But I'm pretty smart. I like my brain and the way it works, and I don't like taking things that interfere with it."

"Mum says you like whisky."

"Ah, yeah, well. Whisky's a man's drink."

"Do you get drunk much?"

"Nah. I don't have enough. Not often, anyway. When you're an adult, a glass of Islay malt is one of life's little pleasures. But when you're young, drugs and alcohol change the way your brain works. I wanted a healthy brain, and I was determined I wasn't going to damage it."

There's a short silence. I can imagine Finn thinking about his words. Alex hasn't laid down the law. He's given his honest opinion, and Finn will trust that more than anything.

"Can I tell you something?" Finn asks eventually.

"Sure."

"I haven't told Mum."

My eyebrows rise.

"Okay…" Alex says.

"There's someone in my class that I quite like."

"What's their name?" I'm sure Alex has chosen the neutral pronoun on purpose, his voice non-judgmental, and I close my eyes. God, I adore this guy.

"She's called Josie," Finn says.

"Blonde or brunette?"

That makes me stifle a laugh. At least he didn't ask what her boobs were like.

"What does brunette mean?" Finn asks.

"Dark-haired, like your mum."

"Oh, it's sort of fair and reddish, but not, like, ginger. Mum calls it strawberry blonde."

"Nice."

"She's finished Zelda as well."

"Wow. I think you should ask her to marry you."

Finn giggles, and my lips curve up.

"Does she like you?" Alex asks.

"Dunno. She's taller than me."

"She won't be for long. We measured you the other day, remember? You've grown, like, five centimeters since we first met."

"Mum says my voice might break soon."

"Yeah, that's right."

"How old were you?"

"Twelve, I think. Your Adam's apple gets bigger. See?" I guess he's pointing to his own.

"How long does it take?" Finn asks.

"It can happen overnight. But it's usually a gradual thing over a few weeks or months. Your voice gets a bit croaky and squeaky, and then it just goes deep."

"And… um… you get hair, right?"

Oh God, poor Alex. He didn't bank on this. I really should intervene.

But he continues talking as if it's the most natural thing in the world, and I'm so touched that in the end I slide down the wall and sit on the carpet, my arms around my knees, listening to this man talking to my boy, afraid to break the spell.

*

Alex

Finn is sitting up in bed, in his PJs, his back against the headboard and the duvet pulled up to his waist. I'm leaning back in the chair next to him, my feet propped on his bed. It's a cool room, with Transformers posters, completed LEGO models on the shelves, and several big boxes of LEGO blocks against the wall. The small bookcase contains the Harry Potter series, the Alex Rider collection, and lots of other fantasy authors like Rick Riordan and Neil Gaiman. This could so easily have been my room when I was a kid.

"Yeah," I reply to his question. "It takes a while for the chest hair to come through. But you'll get it elsewhere pretty fast." I make a downward gesture.

His lips twist. "I've already got a few. Not many though."

"They'll come. At least yours will be dark. Mine are going silver already."

He giggles. "Old man."

"Yeah, I know. Don't mock the afflicted."

"When did you start shaving?"

"Ah… when I was about fourteen, I guess."

"Did your dad show you how to do it?"

"Yeah."

He looks at where his hands are resting in his lap.

Conscious that it's the anniversary of his father's death, I say gently, "Mums can do it too, though. Women are used to shaving under their arms and stuff."

He just nods.

"I know your grandfather on your mum's side passed away," I say. "What about your dad's side?"

"He lives in Auckland. We don't see him much."

"Are you close to any other guys? Your uncle?"

He shrugs. "He's okay."

"What about Carly's husband?"

"Sean's cool. But I wouldn't talk to him about… you know… stuff like this."

And yet he'd talk to me. I'm quite touched by that. I feel for the kid. He's not about to go up to a male teacher at school—if he has any—and ask questions about puberty. And although I know Missie is a great mum and she's obviously talked to him about what happens, I can remember being that age and being excruciatingly embarrassed when my mother tried to talk to me about the facts of life.

"Well," I tell him, "in that case you'll have to talk to me. I'll show you how to shave when the time comes."

He looks up at me then. "Even if I'm fourteen?"

"Yeah."

"Do you think you'll still be around?"

I think he means will I still be dating his mum. "I'm not planning on going anywhere," I tell him. "When you finish your treatment, we can stay friends, right? Whatever else happens."

His face brightens, and he nods.

"I'm glad Mum went to the party," he says. "She's been very sad."

"Yeah, I know. I'm sure you have been, too. It's a sad day."

He brings his knees up under the covers and hugs them. "Not really," he says. He looks at me, challenging me to scold him.

"Fair enough," I say. "There's no law that says you have to be sad. But it's okay to have more than one emotion. You can be angry and sad at the same time."

He rests his chin on his knees. He's quiet for a while.

"Are you looking forward to Christmas?" I ask. "Do you know what Santa's bringing you?"

He blows a raspberry. "I know he doesn't exist. Christmas is something grownups invented for kids."

I think about it. "I don't know. Christmas is the time that families think about each other. We write messages in cards and think about what our friends and family might like to have for a gift. It's often a time when people give more to charity. What's Christmas spirit, if it's not thinking about others?"

He studies me for a moment. "Juliette calls you Oscar the Grouch, but you're not really grumpy, are you? You're just griff."

"I think you mean gruff. Although I'm sure I can be griff, too, at times."

He giggles. Then he chews a fingernail. I think he's fighting with himself as to whether he should say something.

"You can talk to me about anything," I prompt him. "I won't judge, and I won't tell anyone."

"Not even Mum?"

"Well, that depends. She's your mum, and if it was about your health or wellbeing, I wouldn't want to keep it from her. But otherwise, I can keep a secret."

He picks at his fingernails. "I told Mum I don't remember the day of the accident. But I do."

My lips part, but no words come out. I wasn't prepared for that. I feel a stab of guilt that he's confessing to me and not his mother. But he obviously wants to talk. I decide I'll worry about what to do with the information later. "What do you remember?"

"Dad picked me up from school, and he said he had to take a client around a property. He did that sometimes after school. I just stayed in the car and played on my Switch."

"Okay."

"He went to his office, and when he came back, he had a woman with him. She got in the car, in the passenger side, and he got in the driver's side. He said her name was Sarah, and she turned around and shook my hand."

I nod, wondering where this is going. Why did he lie about remembering?

"He started driving. They were talking in low voices. I wasn't really listening—I was on that part in Zelda where you fight the troll crossing the bridge."

"Yeah, that's tricky."

"I kept dying, so I was concentrating. But then I realized they were arguing. I pretended I wasn't, but I started to listen. He asked her when she was going to leave. I didn't know what he meant. She said after Christmas. He said he wanted her to leave now, and she said she couldn't because of her kids."

I stare at him, aghast. Oh Jesus. They were having an affair?

"He looked at me in the mirror," Finn continues, "and he saw I was listening. He yelled at me to put my headphones on. I did, but I didn't turn them on, so I could still hear them. She said he needed to be patient, but he said he'd had enough, and if she loved him she'd leave today. She got angry and said he didn't understand, and told him to stop and pull over, but he wouldn't. He was on the state highway, going quite fast. She yanked at his arm, and the car swerved. I told them to stop, but she kept doing it. Then she caught the wheel and pulled it, and the car went onto the other side of the road. That's when it hit the lorry."

He falls quiet. We stare at each other for a long moment.

"Your mum doesn't know?" I confirm.

He shakes his head.

Fuck.

"Did you know they broke up for a bit?" he says.

"Who?"

"Mum and Dad. A few months before the accident."

My eyebrows rise. "No, I didn't."

"They were arguing a lot. I don't know what about. They'd always do it after I went to bed, but I could hear them. And sometimes there'd be a crash or something, and later Mum would come into my room and get into bed with me, and she'd cry. She always thought I was asleep, but I was always awake."

"I'm sorry, Finn."

"One night, the September before the accident, she came into my room and woke me up. She'd already packed a bag, and she took me out to the car, and we drove all the way here in the dark."

"Jesus." It's nearly a five-hour drive from Dunedin to Christchurch. "Did she tell you what had happened?"

"No. I knew, though. She had a bruise on her face."

I tip my head back and look up at the ceiling. I study the glow-in-the-dark stars that are stuck there in the shape of the Southern Cross for a moment, then drop my head and look back at him. "How long did she stay here?"

"Dad drove up a few days later and begged her to go back. I said I didn't want to, and Grandma told her not to, but she said a boy needs his father, so we went back."

I lower my feet to the floor and sit forward, elbows on my knees, hands clasped. "Do you think your dad was seeing Sarah before the accident? Is that why he and your mum argued?"

"I don't know. She doesn't like talking about it."

There's a sound outside the room. Finn's reaching over to get the glass of water he has on the nightstand, so I don't think he heard it, but I glance at the door and see a shadow move before light footsteps echo along the hall into the living room. Oh shit, I think Missie was outside, listening.

I look back at Finn, who sips the water and replaces the glass on the nightstand. "I'm glad you told me," I say.

"You won't tell the police?" he says.

"The police?"

"They don't know how the car came off the road. They asked me lots of questions, but I didn't want Mum to know what they were arguing about, so I said I didn't remember."

My heart goes out to him. Not only has he carried this burden for a whole year, he's done it believing he's breaking the law in doing so.

"I think you're an incredibly brave lad," I tell him sincerely, "and admirable for wanting to protect your mum."

"She doesn't have anyone else. She needs me to be the man of the house."

"And you're doing a great job. Look, it's late, and you need your sleep, because your body heals itself when you're sleeping. Don't worry about it, okay? I'm here now, and I'm planning to do my best to look after you both."

He meets my eyes then, and his lips curve up. "I'm glad we met you."

"I'm glad I met you, too." I get up, and then, as he looks up at me hopefully, I bend and give him a hug. "Sleep tight," I say gruffly.

"Don't mention bedbugs," he says, moving down under the covers.

"Jeez, no. See you soon." I go out of the room and close the door.

The corridor's empty. I walk along it and into the living room, and close the door behind me. That's empty, too.

I go through to the kitchen and discover Missie standing by the sink, looking out at the small garden. She's holding a glass, and a bottle of vodka stands on the counter with the top off.

She didn't know Lee was having an affair. Ah, Jesus. What a thing to find out on the anniversary of the day he died.

I walk up to her, wondering if she'll let me comfort her. But as I get near, I realize with some surprise that her cheeks are dry. And when she glances at me, I see it's not sadness in her eyes, but anger. Her eyes are blazing. She's furious.

Whoa, if that isn't the sexiest thing I've ever seen.

Chapter Twelve

Missie

"Are you mad at me?" Alex says.

I blink. "For what?"

"For talking to Finn. I know you overhead us."

I bristle. "I'm not going to apologize for listening. This is my house."

"I'm not expecting you to." His gaze is direct, a tad admonishing.

I bite my lip. "I'm sorry."

"It's okay."

"No, it's not. You've just been incredibly sweet to my son. I'm angry and resentful, but not at you."

"Missie, it's okay. You've had a hell of a day. And after that revelation, I'm not surprised you're furious." He tips his head to the side. "You're very beautiful when you're angry, by the way."

I stare at him.

After a moment, his lips twist. "Sorry. That was probably inappropriate timing."

But in a single second, all my frustration dissipates, and the iron frame holding up my skeleton vanishes. I lean back against the counter and study the man I've been keeping at arm's length for so long.

"No, it was perfect timing," I say softly.

He continues to look at me, his gaze brushing down me, soft as a feather, then coming back to rest on my mouth before returning to my eyes.

Lee never called me beautiful. My eyes prick with tears, and I look away and finish off my vodka.

"If you want to leave, I'll understand," I whisper, placing my glass on the counter.

In answer, he opens the cupboard doors one by one until he finds the glasses, takes one out, and picks up the vodka bottle. He doesn't want to leave. My heart swells.

"No." I open the cabinet where we keep the alcohol. "You'll prefer this." I take out the bottle of whisky and pass it to him. "It's only a cheap blend," I admit, a tad embarrassed, as he, James, and Henry have joked about enjoying the most expensive single malts.

But, ever the gentleman, he just says, "Thanks," and pours himself a shot before tipping more vodka into my glass. I get some ice from the freezer and add it to both tumblers, then add a splash of tonic to mine from the bottle in the fridge. "Come on," he says when I'm done, and he takes my hand and leads me into the living room.

We both sit on the sofa, a few feet apart, turned toward each other, not quite touching. He swirls the whisky over the ice and takes a mouthful.

"I'm guessing you didn't know," he says.

I blow out a long breath and tip my head back on the sofa. "It's a long story."

"I'm not going anywhere."

I glance at the Christmas tree. Last Christmas, Finn was in hospital. After the doctor told us his spine was irreparably damaged, I was convinced he'd never be able to dress the tree again, but this year he was able to stand on crutches long enough to put the star at the top. Next year, judging by the few steps he just took, he probably won't need the crutches. Part of that is down to Juliette and her hard work, and of course the others at Kia Kaha who helped create THOR. But the main reason Finn can walk is sitting next to me.

I look back at him. I've made him wait because of my guilt. I feel so goddamn bitter about that, I feel as if I've eaten a dozen lemons, peel and all.

"Finn told me you had a short separation before the accident," he says.

I nod and sip my vodka, welcoming the way the alcohol sears down inside me, rushing through my veins. I exhale, trying to let go of all the tension that's been building up over the past year.

"It was never a great marriage," I begin. "He was three years older than me, and I was a virgin when we first slept together. I was seventeen and still at school. He was twenty and already working. He charmed me, and he talked me into bed. Don't get me wrong—I went willingly. But I was clueless. He told me I couldn't get pregnant the first time, and I believed him."

"He didn't use a condom?" I'm sure Alex's tone would hold similar disapproval if I told him that Lee didn't give me an orgasm until we were two years into our relationship. I decide not to confess that bit.

Instead, I just give a humorless smile. "No, he didn't. His father was very old-fashioned, and when he found out, he told Lee he was going to marry me so the child wouldn't be born a bastard. Lee agreed, which pleased my parents, especially my dad. I went along with it because I was scared about bringing a baby up on my own. We got married, and Finn was born soon after."

I have another mouthful of vodka. "Lee's parents moved to Auckland a year later because of his dad's job, but my parents were great. Lee wanted me to get a job, but Mum and Dad encouraged me to go to university and get my teaching degree. They paid for a nanny to look after Finn during the day. Money was tight, but it got better once I was qualified. Lee hated that I had a degree and he didn't, though. I had to work so hard in the evenings those first few years, preparing lessons and writing reports, and he made such a fuss when it meant he had to look after Finn. It was a difficult time."

"You stayed together, though?"

I shrug. "He was my husband, and I didn't want to have a failed marriage. I was realistic. I didn't believe in fairy tales. Mum has always said that a successful relationship takes hard work, and I was determined not to be the one who backed out."

"Did you love him?"

It's a difficult question to answer. "I did. I think. I don't know. We were never crazy about each other like you see in romantic movies. Lee liked to be admired, and when I was seventeen he charmed me, and I looked up to him. After a couple of years, that wore off, and I saw him for what he was. He didn't like that. But money wise, it got a bit easier as I settled into teaching. Lee was working in real estate, and he was pretty good at it. Finn started primary school. We had friends, and a bit of money. Things weren't too bad. Then his firm closed, and he got a job in Dunedin, so we had to move."

"You got a new teaching job down there?"

"Yeah. I liked my old school, which was tiny, and you felt like part of a family, you know? The new one was bigger, less friendly. Finn went there and he didn't like it either. Both of us struggled to make friends. I didn't have my parents around for support, which made childcare more difficult. Lee was happy though—he was enjoying his job, and he wouldn't talk about moving back. Things were tough. We argued a lot about… this and that." I drop my gaze, not sure whether to broach that subject.

Alex has a mouthful of his whisky. "Finn told me some time ago that Lee had a temper."

My eyebrows rise. I hadn't realized they'd talked about it. "What did he say?"

"That Lee shouted and threw things. He punched a hole in the wall once. And…" He frowns. "That he got physical with you."

I close my eyes for a moment.

"Is that why you walked out?" Alex asks.

"Partly. He'd been different. Distracted. Secretive. I suspected he was seeing someone else. It seemed ridiculous, because… well… just because, but I couldn't shake the feeling. I confronted him and he denied it, then gave me a black eye. I bundled Finn in the car and drove up to my parents. He came up and talked me into going back. It was a stupid thing to do, but…" I trail off. "I don't know why I did," I say eventually, rubbing my forehead. "You see women talk about their man being violent, and you tell yourself they're ridiculous for staying, and that you'd be straight out of the door if it ever happened to you. But he told me he missed Finn, and that he'd changed. He begged me to come back, and promised he'd try harder."

I glare at my glass, then have a large mouthful of vodka.

"Did he?" Alex asks.

"For, like, a week. Then things went back to normal. Well, no, not quite normal. I was sure he was still seeing someone. We had a huge row about it on the twentieth of December. He slept in the spare room that night. Then, on the morning of the twenty-first, after Finn had left for school, we argued about it again. I couldn't let it rest. I was so sure he was cheating. I told him that I knew he was having an affair. He said I was fucking crazy. We had another bad argument. I mean, really bad. In the end, I told him not to bother coming home that night. I said I hated him, and…" Oh God. "I said I wished he was dead."

Alex just sighs.

"He walked out," I whisper. "I had to go to work too, but it was a horrible day. I didn't know what I was doing, and I had a parents' evening, too. I was there when the police came and told me there'd been an accident. They said Lee was killed outright, but Finn had been injured and was in hospital. They told me Lee had been taking a client to a property. He did that a lot. I didn't think anything of it, even when they said it was a woman, because Finn was with him."

I lean forward, put my glass on the coffee table, and sink my hands into my hair. "I'm so fucking stupid. All this time, this whole year, I've been wracked with guilt because of what I said to him. I felt as if I'd caused the accident. I've tortured myself with thinking that maybe he wasn't having an affair, and I'd upset him so much it had made him lose control at the wheel. And all this time, I was right…"

Tears prick my eyes, and this time they tip over my lashes. I dissolve into sobs, as unable to stop them as I would be to force a river to flow uphill.

"Hey." Alex moves forward and rests his glass beside mine, then puts his arm around me. "Come here," he says, trying to move me back.

I stay where I am, my back rigid, full of whirling emotions: resentment, anger, guilt, and bitterness. "Don't," I sob. "You don't want to get involved with me. I'm evil."

"Yeah, you're practically Hitler."

I give a half-laugh, in spite of my misery. "I am. I don't deserve you."

"I'm hardly a saint, Missie. Come here."

"You should go…"

"Come here," he scolds. "Do as you're told."

He speaks so firmly that I let him pull me back. He turns me so I can bury my face in his neck and wraps me in his arms. "There, there," he soothes, rubbing my back. "Everything's going to be okay."

"It's not. I'm going to hell."

"You're far too pretty for that."

"Don't make me laugh. I'm a horrible person."

He sighs again. "Missie, you're hardly the first person to say something you regret in the middle of an argument. He provoked you, and you lashed out. You didn't cause the accident. It's natural to feel conflicting emotions. He was violent toward you, and it doesn't sound as if he put you first at any point. He cheated on you, and he gaslighted you, which is unforgivable. But he was your husband, and Finn's father, and you must have loved him, or why would you have stayed with him so long?"

His shirt is soaked now, but still the tears flow. "I'm so angry," I say in between sobs.

"Of course you are."

"I waited for a year because I felt so guilty."

He kisses my hair.

"I'm sorry," I whisper.

"You've nothing to feel sorry about. You've done nothing wrong, sweetheart."

His endearment warms me. I fall quiet then, taking big, shivery breaths as my sobs die away. He holds me, propping his feet on the coffee table, and strokes my back and hair.

It's dark outside now. The only light comes from the gas fire and the fairy lights on the tree. I can smell Alex's cologne mixed with the warm natural scent of his skin that sends the hairs prickling on my neck.

Gradually, my whirling emotions settle like snow.

Alex is right. People often say things they regret when they argue. You want to hurt the other person the way they're hurting you, and you lash out. I didn't mean that I wished Lee was dead, of course I didn't. And I didn't cause the accident. It's not my fault that he died, or that Finn was injured.

In a way, learning that Lee was having an affair has lifted a huge weight off me. I wasn't going mad. Even though it spiraled out of control, I was right to question him. He should have been honest with me and admitted it—it was wrong of him to deny it and make me feel as if I was crazy. He was going to leave me for the woman in the car. Sarah Pickford, that was her name. The police told me she was married and had two young children. From what Finn says, she didn't want to leave her family before Christmas. Would she have left afterward? I guess I'll never know.

I do feel resentful that I've felt so guilty this year. It's definitely made me hold back from Alex. But in a way, I've enjoyed getting to know him slowly. I lift my head and turn to look at him. He surveys me, patient and calm, his gaze gently caressing my face.

"Panda eyes?" I query.

He tips his head from side to side and smiles. "A beautiful panda."

"Lee never called me beautiful."

He frowns at that. "His behavior left a lot to be desired." It's such an Alex thing to say that it makes me giggle, and his expression turns wry. "What?" he asks.

"Nothing."

He strokes my face. "Do you feel better now?"

"Maybe a bit."

"I'm glad. You've been through such a lot. And you've coped so well. You shouldn't feel bad."

"I did try to make it work."

"I know."

"And I have mourned him."

"Even though he didn't deserve it."

I lift up and kiss him for that.

I press my lips against his, intending to just give him a peck, but his hand rises and slides into my hair, and he holds me there while he kisses me a second time, then a longer third. No tongues, but it still turns up my thermostat by a few degrees.

When he eventually lets me go, he says, "I have a question."

"Okay."

"I asked if the reason you walked out was because Lee got violent, and you said partly. And you said you argued about this and that." He tucks a strand of my hair behind my ear. "What's the 'that'?"

I fiddle with the top button of his shirt. "We argued about sex mainly."

"Oh?"

"About not having it often enough," I admit, embarrassed.

He's quiet for a long moment. I continue to fiddle with his button, not looking at him.

Eventually, he says, "He was too demanding?"

I hesitate. Then I lift my gaze to his. "No. I was the one who wanted it more."

His eyebrows rise.

I glare at him. "Don't laugh at me."

"I'm not laughing."

"I know you, Alex. You're laughing inside."

That makes his lips curve up. "A bit."

"You find my misery amusing?"

"Only because I've had the same problem."

I stare at him. "Seriously?"

"Yeah. A couple of times."

He's never mentioned his exes before. What was it Juliette said? He's had two, maybe three, longish-term relationships that have ended quietly, without drama. "You broke up because you wanted it more?"

"It's no fun when you have a high libido and your partner doesn't."

We study each other as we think about this new revelation.

"You've been single for a whole year," I point out.

"So have you."

"Yeah, well, I have Mr. Buzz to help me out."

Now he's definitely amused. "You name your vibrator?"

"Of course. We've got to know each other very well over the past twelve months."

He gives a short laugh.

I lean my chin on my hand. "I'm guessing you've been developing the muscles in your right wrist?"

He doesn't confirm it, but his wry smile tells me I'm right.

I study his mouth. "That's so fucking hot."

"So's the thought of Mr. Buzz doing his job."

I giggle.

In answer, he slides his hands under my upper arms and lifts me easily up his body, turning and stretching out so we're half-lying on the sofa with me on top. Then he slips his hand behind my head and brings my head down to kiss me.

When he touches his tongue to my bottom lip, I open my mouth, and he slides his tongue inside.

Mmm… this is bliss. It's warm and cozy, and the flickering lights cover us in a Christmassy glow.

We're only about ten seconds in, though, when he moves his head back and says, "Wait a minute."

Surprised, I watch as he picks up his phone from the coffee table. He taps on the screen a few times, then scrolls down. Is he checking his messages? That doesn't say much for my kissing technique.

But then music starts playing—it's Nat King Cole singing *The Christmas Song*. Alex puts the phone back on the table and smirks before he returns his hand to my hair and resumes kissing me.

Oh, okay, yeah that's nice.

We kiss for ages, taking our time, unhurried and sensual, while the music changes to *White Christmas*, and then *O Tannenbaum*. Occasionally I lift my head to look at him, and he slides a strand of my hair through his fingers while we study each other's faces. I discover he has a chickenpox scar on his temple, and I brush my fingers across the stubble that's just starting to show on his jaw. He presses his lips to the mole on my cheekbone, and then kisses back to my mouth again.

At one point I move back and say, "Finn asked if we were going to make out."

"Smart lad."

I stroke his cheek. "Thank you for being so cool with him. He asked you some pretty embarrassing questions."

"I don't get embarrassed about the human body. He can always talk to me about anything."

I frown, puzzled, scraping my nail against his bristles. "You're such an unusual guy. So quiet and unassuming, but smart, and gorgeous, and incredibly generous."

"If you're trying to get in my boxers, you should know I'm a sure thing."

I giggle. "Really?"

"Oh yeah. I've waited a long time to get you into bed, so when we're ready, you're not going to be able to stop me."

My heart gives a little leap. "You really have a high libido?"

"Yep." His eyes crease at the corners as he smiles.

"Ooh." I moisten my lips with the tip of my tongue. "How often do you like to have sex?"

"As often as I can get it."

"So more than once a week, then?"

He laughs. "Yes, Missie. More than once a week would be cool."

"Twice a week?"

"Twice a night, if you're up for it."

"Seriously?" Delight fills me.

His eyes are hot enough to turn sand into glass. "That appeals to you?"

"Oh my God, I've died and gone to heaven. I'd *kill* to have sex more than once a week."

"I intend to wear you out."

"I want you to fuck me until I can't walk."

"Okay."

"Oh my God, really?"

He just laughs.

"I want you now," I whisper.

"Plenty of time," he scolds.

"When?"

"I was thinking maybe after Christmas we could go away somewhere and—"

"Oh jeez, Alex! I can't wait until after Christmas!"

"You'll have to develop some self-discipline."

"No! Aw. You can't tease me with promises of twice a night and then make me wait."

He smiles, stroking his hands down my back, then up my ribs, making me squirm. "Well, I was going to ask you whether you'd like to go to dinner on your birthday for our first date?"

"Dinner and sex?"

He gives me a helpless look. "I was going to be a gentleman and wait until a few dates in."

"Alex!" I rest my forehead on his shoulder. "I honestly think I'll die from frustration."

He sighs. "All right. How about I cook us dinner at my place? Then afterward we can make love to our hearts' content?" I stifle a laugh, and he lifts an eyebrow. "What?"

"Make *luuurv*," I tease.

"Are you mocking me?"

"You old romantic."

"What's wrong with that?"

I touch my lips to his. "Don't you want to fuck me senseless, Alex Winters?"

His eyes flare, and then, holding me tightly, he twists on the sofa so I'm pinned beneath him. My hair is caught beneath his arm, our legs are tangled, and I discover that I can't move.

"Don't tell me what I want," he scolds. "The first time we sleep together, I want to take it as slow as possible."

"Aw…"

"I want to make it last," he says, kissing my cheek, over my jaw, and down my neck.

I sigh.

"I want to kiss every inch of you," he murmurs. He pulls the sleeve of my dress over my shoulder and touches his lips to the bare skin.

It's impossible to stifle a shiver.

"You're going to beg me to let you come," he says, kissing back up to my mouth and then looking down at me. "And then I'm going to give you so many orgasms, you're going to pass out from all the pleasure."

Looking up at him, I feel so overwhelmed that I want to cry again.

"All right?" he asks.

I nod.

"Good. And bring your toothbrush. I don't want you dashing off afterward."

He wants me to stay the night. I swell with pleasure, but cover it with a mischievous smile. "So tell me, was Juliette right? Do you swear in the sack?"

"You'll have to wait and find out."

"She reckons you're a tiger when you're let loose."

"I fully intend to devour you," he says, eyelids lowering to half-mast.

My lips part, and my voice is just a squeak. "Oh…" I swallow hard.

Alex strokes my cheek. "What's the matter?"

"It's just… By the end of my marriage, Lee and I hardly ever slept together. But he was having an affair. Which must have meant that it was me he had the problem with." My voice turns husky. "What if there's something wrong with me?"

Alex rolls his eyes. "There's nothing wrong with you."

"You don't know that."

"I do. I'm an expert."

"In what?"

"Everything. You're young, smart, sexy, funny, and beautiful. And you're going to absolutely kill me in bed, I know it already."

My lips gradually curve up. "I'll do my best."

He blows out a breath. "I need to start eating steak."

That makes me laugh. "I can't wait."

He kisses my nose, then my lips, for a long, long time.

Eventually, though, he lifts his head and sighs. "It's late. I should go and let you get some sleep."

I don't want him to, but his promise of a birthday treat has cheered me up. "Okay."

He doesn't move, though. "Is it going to be all right for you to come over on your birthday?"

"Yes, Finn will be thrilled. I'll see whether he can stay with Robbie for a night."

"And your mum won't mind?"

"Not at all. She told me tonight she's been seeing someone. Maybe she'll invite him over for dinner or… something."

He tips his head to the side. "How do you feel about that?"

"It's weird. I miss my dad so much. But she's been single for three years. She deserves to have someone of her own."

He smiles and kisses me again. "Good girl," he murmurs.

I shiver. "If you keep calling me good girl, I'll do anything you want."

He runs his tongue over his top teeth. "I'll bear that in mind. Now, I'd better get up."

But he doesn't. He kisses me again. And then he continues kissing me for a long time, while the fairy lights flicker, and the flames in the gas fire dance to the Christmas music.

Chapter Thirteen

Alex

The twenty-second is the last official day the office is open, and therefore also party day. Henry, James, and I are usually in and out over the Christmas period, but the rest of the staff are looking forward to the break, and everyone's in a festive mood.

I work in the morning, finalizing anything urgent that needs doing before the country goes on summer vacation. It's normal for businesses to be closed for several weeks through Christmas and January in New Zealand, and even if I'm in the office, it'll be tough to get hold of anyone for a while.

At one p.m., Juliette comes in, closes my laptop, grabs my tie, and drags me out and into the main office. I give in, more than happy to help devour the lunch the caterers have put on. The tables are groaning with sandwiches, hot savories like pies and sausage rolls, sushi, mince pies, Christmas cake, and a hundred other things. Someone sets Christmas music playing, bottles of bubbly are popped and poured, and soon people are singing and dancing and generally having a good time.

I circulate for a while, thanking everyone for their hard work during the year, asking after their families and where they're going for Christmas. I get hugs and kisses on the cheek, and lots of people saying how much they love working here, which pleases me no end.

Juliette's organized a Secret Santa, and it's Henry's turn to come in with the suit and hand out the presents. Everyone had a twenty-dollar limit, and I know the person I picked—Robyn in Accounts—makes her own jewelry, so I bought her a small box with six compartments containing different color sparkly beads, and she squeals with delight when she opens it.

My present turns out to be a pair of boxers with a picture of a wrapped present over the crotch area and the slogan 'I have a huge present for you' on one side. Everyone erupts into laughter as I open it, and I cast a wry glance over to the group of interns we have working for us and say, "I know this is from one of you, and you're all fired," and they giggle.

"You'll have to wear them tomorrow," James murmurs next to me. He knows that Missie is coming over for dinner.

"I'm sure she'll appreciate them," I reply, and he laughs. As Henry moves on to Rebecca from reception and hands her a present, I say to James, "So… are you seeing Aroha over Christmas?"

"No."

"Why not?"

"I fucked up. She's not talking to me."

I give him an amused look. "What did you do?"

"I don't want to talk about it." He looks embarrassed.

"Oh dear."

"Plenty more fish in the… you know."

"Sure."

He huffs a sigh, and I hide a smile.

"Are you getting back with Cassie?" I ask.

"Nope. I'm done with women."

"For the next five minutes."

"I'm serious." He rubs his forehead. "They do my head in."

"What the hell happened?"

"I told you, I don't want to talk about it." He walks off.

I frown, puzzled. At that moment, Henry walks past me, over to Juliette, and hands her a present. "Here you go," he says softly.

She doesn't look at him. "Thank you."

I don't know what happened between them either, but he hesitates, waiting for her to say something. She keeps her gaze on the gift as she unwraps it, though, and in the end he walks away, over to the next person.

I walk over to her as she examines her gift—a book about the New Zealand national netball team, the Silver Ferns. "Nice," she says. "Haven't read this."

"How are you doing?" I ask.

"Great." She balls up the paper and tosses it into one of the nearby black rubbish bags.

"Everything all right between you and Henry?" I ask.

"Mind your own business."

I fix her with a steady gaze, and she flushes. Today she's wearing a red sari, and the color is a little too harsh for her pale skin. She's incredibly beautiful, but she's lost weight recently, and she has hollows in her cheeks and shadows beneath her eyes.

"If you want to know if it'll affect our working relationship, it won't," she snaps.

"Hey, give me some credit. I'm worried about you." I dip my head to try and catch her eye. "Are you still with Cam?"

She swallows hard. "Yes."

So whatever happened with Henry last night wasn't enough to convince her to leave Cam for him. I feel a wave of sadness. "Aw, Juliette…"

"Don't…" Fighting back tears, she takes her present and walks away.

A little depressed, I leave the rest of the staff to the music and food and go back to my office. Zelda is waiting there for me, and she wags her tail as I go in and comes up to lick my hand.

"This should be a time for miracles," I murmur, lifting her up onto my lap as I sit in my chair. She stands on my chest and wags, then gives a high girlie yap. "Yeah, I know," I reply. "I've got to let them sort themselves out."

She sniffs my shirt, then sneezes.

"Bless you. I hope there's enough Christmas magic for me, anyway."

She licks my chin. I kiss her head, and she sighs and collapses onto me, looking up at me with her big puppy eyes. At that moment, my phone buzzes on my desk, and I look at the screen to see a text from Missie. Zelda gives me a reproachful look.

"Aw," I say, "come on, you know you'll always be my number one girl." I give her another kiss, then bring up the text.

Missie: *How's your party going? Miss you!*

I smile, my spirits lifting.

Me: *I miss you too. It's going okay, but I'd rather be with you!*

Missie: *Aw, not long now!*

Me: *What are you up to today?*

Missie: *Getting ready.*

Me: *For Christmas?*

Missie: *For you.* <smiley emoji>

Me: *Sounds promising!*

Missie: *Carly's come over with a load of torture implements. She's waxing me within an inch of my life.*

Me: *LOL! So I can expect some smooth skin tomorrow, can I?*

Missie: *Oh yeah. Like a baby's bum.*

Me: *Well I'm debating whether to wear my Secret Santa gift. A pair of boxers with a picture of a gift and the slogan 'I have a huge present for you.'*

Missie: *Love it!*

Me: *Ah jeez I've just realized there's another pair attached to the first.*

Missie: *What do they say?*

Me: *Jingle my bells and I'll guarantee a white Christmas.*

Missie: *OMG I swear coffee just came out of my nose!*

Me: *I'm not wearing those.*

Missie: *I'll be very disappointed if you don't. And now Carly's wondering what's going on because I've got the giggles.*

Me: *LOL*

Missie: *I can't wait to see you tomorrow.*

Me: *You sure you don't want me to pick you up?*

Missie: *No, I'll Uber. I'll see you at six?*

Me: *I'm looking forward to it. Xxx*

Missie: *xxxxxxxxxx*

I put the phone down and look at Zelda. "She's one in a billion," I say, scratching her ear. "You'll help me get the girl, right?"

She licks my hand and nibbles a finger with her tiny pointy teeth. I sigh. God, it's going to be a long twenty-four hours.

*

I spend most of the next day in a feverish haze. I go to the supermarket in the morning to get the ingredients for dinner, then spend a couple of hours on the phone, checking on last-minute details for Damon's wedding and stag night. It's going to be a big do, and he has people coming from all over New Zealand, including the guys we often deal with in Auckland—Mack and Huxley, and Titus has flown back from the UK for Christmas and the wedding. I'm organizing something special for the stag night, and I check up on people to make sure everyone's on the same page.

I tidy and decorate the house. As I rarely have visitors, my one concession to it being Christmas is a small fiber-optic tree beside my TV, but I splash out on several strands of fairy lights because I know Missie likes them, and take a while to string them around the living room and bedroom.

After that, Zelda and I go for a long walk through Hagley Park, and I run her ragged chasing balls, knowing it'll zonk her out for the rest of the day. I'm halfway around when I get an interesting text, and I muse on that as we walk back, the air filled with the smell of freshly mown grass.

When we get home, I lay the table, set a Christmas playlist going on my phone through the speakers, then start preparing dinner. First I make the dessert and put it in the fridge to set. For the main course, I've bought an eye-filet steak each, and I'm going to serve it with chunky fries and a fresh green salad, and her choice of a blue-cheese or peppercorn sauce.

I've just finished making the blue-cheese sauce when, a few minutes past six, I hear a knock at the door. Zelda barks, and I tell her that it's Missie and it's okay. Flinging the tea towel over my shoulder, I go to the door and open it.

It's only been two days since I saw her, but the sight of her still takes my breath away. She's wearing a long, blue, sleeveless maxi dress that clings to her bust then falls to the ground in folds. Her hair is pinned up in a loose bun, and tendrils curl around her face. Her makeup is immaculate, her eyes sultry, her lips glistening with gloss. She's so fucking beautiful that for a second I can only stare, mesmerized.

"You didn't tell me you lived in a mansion," she says, eyes wide, bending to say hello to Zelda as she bounds around her. "Hello Miss Zee! Wow, you've grown!"

"You want to come in?" I step back and hold out my hand. "I'll take your bag. The butler's got the day off."

She gives me a wry look as she hands me the small case, then picks up Zelda and carries her into the house, leaving behind the faint scent of her perfume. It wraps around me like silk ribbons, and my pulse picks up speed.

Still holding the puppy, she takes off her sandals, then walks barefoot into the main room. She looks like a Greek goddess. As I watch, she nuzzles the puppy's ear and says, "Nom, nom, nom, are we having you for dinner?"

Muttering under my breath, I close the door and follow her. It's all open plan, the kitchen fronted by a long breakfast bar, a large living room that overlooks the lawn, and beyond it the Avon and Hagley Park.

"Oh, Alex," she says, putting Zelda down, "it's amazing."

"It's not bad," I admit modestly.

"How long have you been here?"

I go into the kitchen and get the bag of salad leaves out of the fridge. "I moved in just after Christmas last year. I'd been living in an apartment, but I wanted something bigger."

She glances over her shoulder as she walks around, inspecting the place. "So… your ex didn't live here?"

"No. You're the only girl who's set foot in this house, apart from Belle and Gaby."

She gives me a happy smile and carries on walking around. Lips curving up, I retrieve a lemon and a bottle of olive oil for the dressing.

"It's very tidy," she teases. "I should have guessed."

I just send her a wry look.

She looks at the art on the walls, admires the view, then comes back to the kitchen. "Something smells nice," she says.

"Chunky chips. They're nearly done." I shake the dressing and put it to one side, ready to pour over the leaves when I'm ready.

"Zelda looks tired," she says, watching the puppy get in her bed, walk in a circle half a dozen times, then flop down.

"We spent an hour in the park this afternoon. There's a bridge over the river just down from here, so it's an easy walk."

"It's a lovely place, Alex."

"I'm glad you like it."

She leans a hip on the counter. "Shall we go to bed now?"

"Behave," I scold, turning away to pour some olive oil in the pan. "Food first. We need to keep our strength up. We're having steak so we'll have plenty of iron."

"Are you sure you don't want to have sex now?"

I retrieve a spatula from the drawer. "Stop badgering me. I told you we're going to wait." I turn… and then I stop dead. She's taken off her dress, and she's leaning against the counter, hands resting on the edge,

SERENITY WOODS

waiting for my reaction. She's wearing a white, stretchy lace teddy, and nothing else.

"Holy fuck." The end of the spatula in my hand slowly rises a few inches. She notices and giggles.

I meet her eyes. They're full of longing and a smidgeon of embarrassment and fear that I'm going to turn her down. Aw. It must have taken some courage to do that.

I stare at the oven for a second. Then I place the spatula on the counter. Rest a plate on top of the salad bowl. Turn off the hob, and lower the temperature on the oven. Remove the tea towel from my shoulder and toss it onto the counter.

Then I walk over to her and stand before her.

She moistens her lips with the tip of her tongue, her eyes wide. She's actually trembling, but whether it's from nerves or desire, I'm not sure. Maybe both.

"Um," she says, "I'm sorry, I'm not sure what made me do that. I don't want to spoil dinner. If you'd rather—"

Lifting my hands to cup her face, I crush my lips to hers.

"Mmm…" She rests her hands on my chest, then lifts them around my neck as I tilt my head to the side and plunge my tongue into her mouth. Aaahhh… she tastes sweet, and her answering half-sigh, half-moan sends the hairs rising all over my body.

"Alex," she whispers when I eventually leave her lips and kiss around her jaw to her ear. "I want you so badly…"

"If my girl needs me, I'm not going to complain," I reply, my voice husky. As I nibble her earlobe, I rest my hands on the outside of her smooth thighs, then draw my fingers up over her hips, into the dip of her waist, and up her ribs, and she shivers.

"I've been thinking about you all day," she says.

"What have you been thinking about?" Finally, I cup her breasts, and she trembles again.

"This. You kissing me. Touching me." She tips her head to the side, her breasts rising and falling rapidly. "Fucking me."

I lift my head and raise an eyebrow.

"Having sex," she amends.

I rest my hands on the counter on either side of hers and glare at her.

She presses her lips together, then murmurs, "Making love to me."

"That's better."

"You're such a nice boy."

I move closer to her. "Not all the time."

"I certainly hope not." She's quite a bit shorter than me. I look down at her, then cup her breasts again and slowly stroke my thumbs across her nipples. She has beautiful, generous breasts, and her nipples are large and swollen, although they contract as I tease them into tight buds.

"Why are you shaking?" I ask, amused. "Are you cold?"

She shakes her head.

"Nervous?"

She swallows. "A little." Her voice comes out as a squeak.

"Why?" I continue to stroke her, and her eyelids close in slow motion, then open to reveal her hazy blue eyes.

"It's been a long time," she whispers.

"Same for me. I understand it's like riding a bike."

She tries not to laugh. "And I've only ever slept with one guy."

"Well I haven't slept with any guys…" I take the straps of her teddy in my fingers and begin to peel them down her arms.

"Alex!" She catches them and pulls them back up.

"What? You're beautiful and I want to look at you."

"It's daylight."

"If you think I'm a bedroom only, lights out kind of guy, you're going to be severely disappointed."

"I… have stretch marks." She bites her lip.

"I'm sure I've got a few."

She nudges me. "Can I keep it on?"

I lift her chin so I can look into her eyes. "Just this one time. But later, I'm going to want you naked, okay?"

She nods, her expression lighting with relief.

"Silly girl," I say, and kiss her again.

This time, I kiss her for ages, delving my tongue into her mouth, and continuing to stroke her, enjoying the feel of her trembling in my arms.

"Can I take off your shirt?" she asks at one point, and when I nod, she undoes the buttons and pushes it over my shoulders. I let it drop to the floor, and she moves back so she can look at me, lifting her hands to trace her fingers over my pecs and down to my abs. "You work out," she whispers.

"I've got a mini-gym here. I try to stay in shape."

"Me too," she says. "Round is a shape."

I rest my hands in the dip of her waist. "You have an hourglass figure. It's amazing."

She shivers as I stroke her ribs. "Alex…"

"Turn around." I guide her until she's facing away from me. Then I move up against her, pushing her forward so she bumps into the counter. She leans on it and tips her head back so it's resting on my shoulder. I brush up her body and cup her breasts.

"I'm going to make you come now," I murmur, squeezing her breasts, then tugging gently on her nipples. "Okay?"

She blinks. "Here?"

"Yes."

"Don't you want to—"

"Not yet."

She looks over her shoulder at me, her eyes huge, the pupils dilated. I watch her as I play with her breasts, giving a smug smile as her gaze turns hazy again.

"Oh…" She bites her bottom lip and closes her eyes.

Slowly, I slide my right hand down, over her ribs, her tummy, her hip, then tuck my fingers beneath the elastic of the teddy and slip them further south. Her skin there is hairless and soft as satin, and I groan, nudging her legs apart with my knee so I can stroke all the way down her mound and into the heart of her. As I suspected, she's swollen and moist. Her head falls forward, and she moans as I slip my fingers into her folds.

"Look at you," I murmur. "All ready for me like a good girl."

She groans and tilts up her pelvis, making my fingers move deeper into her. "Ah God," she whispers, "Alex…"

I dip my fingers down to collect her moisture, then use my middle finger to swirl over her clit. Using my other hand to move her hair aside, I kiss her neck, trailing my tongue across her skin. "You're so fucking beautiful."

She shudders. "I knew you'd swear during sex."

"You bring out the devil in me." I circle my fingers faster, encouraged by her ragged breaths and moans. She's not going to take long. Clearly, my Missie likes her orgasms medium-rare.

She turns her head so she can kiss me, and I delve my tongue into her mouth, plucking her nipple with my left hand and arousing her with my right. Her hips rock against my hand, and her gasps grow deeper and more uneven.

"Come on baby," I tell her, kissing her in between phrases. "I want to hear you say my name as you come. I want to watch you."

Her lips part, she holds her breath, and I tighten my arms around her, supporting her as her orgasm hits. She clamps around my fingers, and wails, "Ah, Alex!" as she comes, her body jerking with each pulse. Five, six, seven… she groans, and then finally exhales, releasing all the tension that's been building up inside her.

"Aw, baby…" I hug her as she goes limp against me. "Is that better?"

"Oh God…" Still trembling, she looks over her shoulder at me, eyes dazed.

As she watches, I lift my hand and lick my fingers one by one, as if I've just eaten fried chicken.

"Alex!" She looks mortified.

"What? Seems a shame to waste it. You taste nice."

"Oh my God."

I release her, make sure she's not going to fall over, then say, "Wait here."

She leans on her elbows on the counter, sinking her hands into her hair, mumbling something.

I take a moment to admire the way the lacy teddy clings to her shapely figure.

Then I pick up the spatula and flick the end. It meets her butt with a loud thwack that's more noise than anything, but it makes her jump.

"Ow!" She leaps up and spins around, laughing. "What was that for?"

I point the spatula at her as I walk backward to the hob. "For misbehaving. I said: food first, then sex. I want to make sure you've eaten before we engage in serious exercise." I switch the hob on, and turn the oven back up. I walk over to the fridge and retrieve the steaks, then close the door and glance at her. She's staring at me, mouth open.

"I told you to behave yourself," I tell her. "Now pass me the salt and pepper. I'm going to cook you the best steak you've ever had in your life."

Chapter Fourteen

Missie

Oh my God, the man's serious. He's just brought me to an earth-shattering climax, and now he wants to stop and have dinner.

Somewhat sulkily, I pass the salt and pepper grinders to him.

"Don't pout," he says.

"I'm not pouting."

"Yes, you are. You've had an orgasm. What more do you want?" His tone is teasing as he turns back to his cooking.

I want you. I don't say it, but I think it.

He seasons the steaks, then put them in the pan and sets a timer on his watch. While they're cooking, and while he hums along to *Baby It's Cold Outside*, he stirs whatever is in two small saucepans on the back of the hob, then goes over to the bowl of salad, removes the plate on top, adds the dressing, and tosses it with the salad servers.

Then he glances at me and gives a short laugh. "What's up? Your eyes are like saucers."

How can they not be? He's naked from the waist up, and while he doesn't quite have a six-pack, he's toned and muscular. His old, faded jeans hang low on his hips, and he's barefoot. He wears his innate sexiness with ease. His hair is messy and damp at the temples, flopping over his forehead, and he's clean shaven. He showered for me. That makes me melt.

I'm puzzled, though, and I don't quite know how to handle him. He's almost the exact opposite of Lee, who had no subtlety to him at all, no discipline, no wit, just empty charm, like a Pavlova dessert that looks great, but once you take a bite it's nothing but air. Alex is a chocolate torte—rich, dark, and complicated.

"I guess my powers of seduction aren't quite as good as I hoped," I joke, a little embarrassed that I stripped off in front of him. Most men would have dropped everything to take advantage of that, but he obviously wasn't turned on enough for his desire to overcome his urge for food.

He studies me, and then he stretches out a hand toward me. "Come here."

I don't move, still pouting.

He raises an eyebrow and gives me a look that says, *You really want to test me?* Conscious of the spatula lying on the counter, my lips twist, and I walk toward him.

He puts his arm around me. Then he says, "Give me your hand." When I hold it out, he takes it and moves it to the front of his jeans. Oh! He has a hard on. I didn't expect that. My face flames.

"Can't fake that," he says, amused. He kisses my forehead. "If you must know, Finn texted me earlier to say you were nervous and hadn't eaten all day."

My jaw drops. "Seriously?"

"Yeah. He was worried about you passing out in the heat of passion."

"He did not say that!"

"Well, no. Words to that effect. So despite the incredible urge I have to hoist you over my shoulder in a firefighter's lift, carry you off to the bedroom, and spend all evening making love to you, I'm going to wait until you've eaten the steak and chips and the magnificent dessert I've prepared." He kisses my lips. "Then I'm going to screw you senseless."

"Oh, thank God." I slide my arms around him, and he laughs and hugs me. "Finn really texted you?" I ask, still astounded.

"Yeah. He's worried about you. He said you don't get out much, and he wants you to have a good time. I think he meant generally rather than in the sack." He moves across to the pan as his alarm goes, taking me with him, then flips the steak, filling the air with the aroma of cooked meat.

"You sound like you had quite the conversation." I'm not sure how I feel about Finn contacting him without me knowing. Poor Alex. I'm sure he didn't sign up for all this trouble.

But he says, "We text each other quite a lot." He sets the timer again.

"I didn't know that."

"Just stuff about gaming mostly. And I send him photos of Zelda on Snapchat." He glances at me. "I'm sorry, I thought you knew."

"I don't mind," I say softly, touched that he doesn't seem to mind. "It's so good of you to take him under your wing."

"I like the kid. He reminds me of myself at that age."

"Devilishly handsome?"

He chuckles. "All elbows and knees with a squeaky voice. But yeah, nah, I mean a little shy, passionate about computers and gaming, half geek, half nerd. A bit serious. Same floppy hair."

"I bet you were a gorgeous young man."

He just smiles.

I like being so close to him. I rest my lips on his warm skin, then do what I've wanted to do for months, and reach up so I can kiss the hollow beneath his Adam's apple.

He sighs. "You're not making it easy for me."

"I'm so relieved. I thought you didn't fancy me."

He gives me an exasperated look. "You're kidding me?"

"Um, no."

He rolls his eyes. "Missie, I've thought about having sex with you for over a year."

"You've only known me for nine months," I point out, to cover the fact that my head is spinning.

"I was rounding up. I've thought about it every day. In great detail. So please don't accuse me of not fancying you. It makes my heart hurt."

"Aw." I press my lips to his cheek, and he turns his head and gives me a long, luscious kiss.

Eventually he sighs and turns back to the steak. "You can't go all day without eating."

"Yes, Dad."

"Don't be a brat. I'm serious."

"I was nervous, as Finn pointed out."

"Why? Because it's been a while?"

"Yes. And because of you."

"What do you mean?"

"You really have no idea?"

"No."

"You're pretty intimidating."

His eyebrows rise.

"Don't tell me you're not aware," I scoff. "With all the 'I told you to behave yourself' comments and the spatula action."

He frowns, though. "I know I can be terse, but I wouldn't have said I was intimidating."

"Oddly, I'm sure Finn would agree. He doesn't find you scary."

That earns me an amused look. "You do not find me scary."

"A little bit."

"Missie…"

"I've not met a man like you before."

"Uh… not sure whether that's a compliment or not."

"It's definitely a compliment."

"Are you sure?"

"Oh yes. I've waited my whole life for a man like you to boss me around."

He gives a short laugh and turns off the hob. Then he faces me, pushes me up against the counter, and nuzzles my neck. "So you do like being bossed around?"

I shiver. "I love it." Then, as he nips my earlobe, I add, "Ow!"

"That's for not eating today."

"So every time I do something you don't like, you're going to punish me for it?"

"Yep." He kisses back along my jaw to my mouth.

"You realize I'm going to misbehave on purpose now."

He moves back a little to look at me, and we study each other for a moment. His eyes are hot and amused. My heart's racing. Does he understand how much I want him?

He steps back, puts his hands on his hips, and blows out a long breath. "Food first," he scolds. "Stop tempting me."

"I'm just standing here."

He huffs a sigh and turns to switch off the oven.

Trying to keep my frustration under control, I pick up my dress and go to put it on. I'm just about to put it over my head when he lifts it out of my hands with a clean wooden spoon and tosses it over one of the stools by the breakfast bar.

"You want me to eat dinner like this?" I ask.

"You took it off." He puts two plates on the counter and serves up the steak. "Can you take the salad to the table?"

Muttering under my breath, wearing just the teddy, I carry the salad through to the dining area.

It's a beautiful house. God knows how much it cost—it would have been several million, I would think. There are eight properties in this private country estate, and you need a code to get through the gate. A long deck runs the width of the house, overlooking the large lawn, and at the bottom a gate leads to a path that crosses the Avon to Hagley Park. To the right I can also see a pool glittering dark blue in the evening sunshine. Imagine having your own pool! Jesus.

This open-plan room has polished kauri-wood floorboards, with a big fluffy cream rug in front of the leather sofa. The dining area contains an eight-seater glass table and black chairs. A huge flat-screen TV hangs on the wall of the living room, with a PlayStation and an Xbox underneath. On the other side of the room is a work area—a computer sits on the table with two monitors and a host of accessories, and another table set at right angles to it is covered in paperwork, folders, pens, two tablets, and another phone, as his normal one is in the back pocket of his jeans. The leather gaming chair is the most worn piece of furniture in the room, so I can guess where he spends most of his time.

A smallish fiber-optic tree that looks brand new sits beside his TV, and a few strings of fairy lights are his only decorations, although Zelda's big bed does have a Christmas blanket in it with pictures of Rudolph. The puppy hooks her head over the edge of the bed, watching me as I walk around.

He's already put two placemats and cutlery opposite each other at one end of the table, so I put the salad bowl in the middle, then go back to the kitchen.

"Anything else I can do?" I ask him.

He gestures to two wine glasses and a bottle of Pinot Noir. "You could take that in."

"Jules Taylor," I comment, picking it up. "That must have cost you a pretty penny."

"A hundred and eighty-five bucks, from memory."

I blink. "For a case?"

"For one bottle."

I nearly drop it. "What the fuck?"

Picking up the plates, he kisses me on the forehead before taking them over to the dining table. "Only the best for my girl."

"I don't know whether to drink it or frame it."

He goes back to the kitchen to retrieve two small jugs and brings them back. "Missie, you know I'm rich, right? I can't imagine that comes as a surprise."

"Um, no, I guess… I don't tend to think about it."

"Well, I am, so you can expect to be spoiled. I hope you don't mind."

"I'd rather you didn't."

His eyebrows rise. "Seriously?"

"No, Alex. You're so gullible. You can spoil me all you want."

He gives a short laugh, and we take our seats. "I guess I asked for that," he says.

I chuckle. Luckily he hasn't put his shirt back on, so I don't feel quite so bad sitting there in my underwear.

I study my plate. The filet steak smells amazing. "I love thick-cut chips."

"I know."

"How… oh, don't tell me. Finn. Has he told you all my secrets?"

"Pretty much." He gestures to the two jugs. "Blue cheese or peppercorn sauce?"

"Can I have both?"

That makes him smile. "Of course." He opens the wine bottle and pours us both a glass.

I tip a generous amount of both sauces over the steak, then help myself to the salad. "This looks lovely, thank you."

"Happy birthday." He passes me my glass, then holds his up.

I tap mine to it. "Thank you so much for this."

"Let's hope your next year is better than your last," he says gently.

I nod, and we both sip the wine. Cherry and plum flavors flood my mouth, and I sigh. "That's amazing."

"Please eat something before you fall over."

I cut off a big chunk of steak, cram it in my mouth, and cross my eyes as I mumble, "Happy now?" Immediately, though, I taste the flavor of the steak, and I close my eyes. "Oh my God." I chew slowly, then swallow. "Oh wow. That's amazing."

I open my mouth to discover him watching me. Conscious that I might have peppercorn sauce around my mouth, I wipe it surreptitiously and admit, "It's a good steak."

"I'm glad." Clearly amused, he cuts into his and starts eating.

"I didn't realize how hungry I was." I eat one of the chunky chips. It has just the right amount of crunch on the outside while being nicely fluffy inside. "You like cooking?"

"Yeah. I find it relaxing."

"What's your favorite dish?"

We talk about cooking while we eat, while Kirsty MacColl sings *Fairytale of New York*, and then Eartha Kitt sings *Santa Baby*. I drink my wine, and Alex pours me another glass. Slowly the food fills my stomach and the alcohol filters through me, and I start to relax.

When we've finished our main, Alex clears the table and brings out the dessert. "It's something I invented just for you," he tells me, placing one of the individual dishes before me. It looks like a trifle, with layers of cream and chocolate visible through the glass. "It's a Jaffa Cake Tiramisu."

I inhale with pleasure. "I love Jaffa Cakes! How…" I roll my eyes. "Finn?"

"Yep." He sits opposite me with a grin.

I dip my spoon into it, scoop some up, and eat it. "Oh my God," I mumble through a mouthful of mascarpone, orange liqueur, softened Jaffa Cakes, and chocolate. "Oh that's amazing."

He has a spoonful. "Oh yeah, that's pretty good."

"Pretty good? It's orgasmic."

He chuckles. "You're easy to please."

"I really am."

He meets my eyes, and I wink at him.

He smiles. Then he reaches into his pocket, extracts a box, and slides it across the table to me. "Happy birthday."

My eyebrows lift. It's a velvet jewelry box. I lift my gaze to him. He returns it levelly, leaning back in his chair.

Heart racing, I look back at the box. I have another spoonful of the dessert, then, as I lick my lips, I open the box with shaking hands and study the contents.

It's not a ring. Of course it's not a ring. I feel stupid for even thinking that. But it is a beautiful piece of jewelry. It's a silver chain with a pendant in the shape of an artist's palette, complete with a tiny brush. The five hollows holding paint are each filled with a colored stone. I take it out and rest it on my fingers. I wonder where he got it? I haven't seen anything like it in the local jewelers.

Then I frown and look a little more closely. In the center of the palette is the engraving of a plant—it's a sprig of mistletoe.

"Turn it over," he says.

I do as he says, and on the back is an inscription, 'To M,' a heart shape, and 'from A.'

I lift my gaze to his.

"I had it made," he says.

I look back at it. "Is it... silver?"

"Platinum."

Oh fuck. "And the stones... are glass?"

"No, Missie." He leans forward and points to each in turn. "Emerald, sapphire, ruby, yellow diamond, white diamond." For once, he looks unsure. "Do you like it?"

My mouth has gone dry. "Oh, Alex. It's beautiful."

Relief lights his features. "I'm so glad."

"I can't believe you had it made for me."

"I wanted something original, that nobody else would have. And something personal to you."

I turn it over and look at the inscription again. To M, love from A. My eyes prick with tears.

"Aw," he says, "it wasn't supposed to have that effect."

"I've never had anything like it. I don't just mean that it's obviously expensive. Lee never bought me anything romantic like this."

"Then he was a fool." His voice is hard.

I turn it back over. The gemstones glitter in the glow from the sparkling fairy lights. Carefully, I put it back in the box.

"Would you like me to help you put it on?" he asks.

I clear my throat. "Later. I don't want it to get damaged while we're... you know." I give him a mischievous look, trying to cover up my emotion. The obvious cost of the present has taken me aback, but that's not the most overwhelming thing about it. It's an incredibly thoughtful gift, and I'm so touched by the fact that he went to the trouble of having it specially made. "It's the most beautiful thing I've ever seen. Thank you so much."

He has a mouthful of dessert while he studies me thoughtfully. Turning his spoon over, he sucks it, licking it clean, then points it at me and says, "Pineapple."

I look at the dish in surprise. "There's pineapple in it?"

"No." He has another spoonful. "That's your safe word."

I stare at him. "My what?"

He licks his lips free of chocolate. "Just in case."

My lips curve up. "Can it be any fruit or does it have to be tropical?"

He laughs. "That's exactly what I said when Juliette suggested it."

"Wait, what?"

"Long story. She was talking to all of us, not just me."

I have another spoonful of the dessert. "Am I going to need a safe word?"

His eyes gleam. "Best to be prepared."

We study each other while we finish the tiramisu. George Michael is singing *Last Christmas* again, reminding me of the night of the party, when we lay on my sofa and made out for over an hour. I think about what just happened in the kitchen, how he turned me around, slid his fingers down into me, and made me come within minutes. Okay, that was partly due to the fact that I was begging for it, I acknowledge that. But he obviously knows his way around a woman's body.

"Penny for them," he says.

"I was thinking that sex with you is going to be splendiferous."

He laughs. "Good word."

"I know it's going to be apt."

"I might be rubbish. It's been so long, it might all be over in seconds."

I giggle, finish off my glass of wine, and hold the glass out for him to fill. He finishes off the bottle, half in his glass, half in mine. "Feeling better?" he asks.

"Much. Thank you. For being patient with me. For waiting. For being so good with Finn. For the orgasm. The steak. For everything."

He smiles. "You're welcome."

"I mean it, Alex. I don't know what I've done to deserve you. I really am nothing special. I just hope... you're not disappointed in me."

His brow creases.

The song changes to *Have Yourself a Merry Little Christmas*. He gets up, comes around the table, and holds out his hand.

Lips curving, I slide mine into his, and I let him pull me to my feet. He leads me to the space between the dining and living area, and pulls me into his arms. Slowly, we begin to dance.

Mmm...

This is kind of heavenly. I feel pleasantly sated, and nicely mellow from the wine. Alex smells nice, and his skin is warm and smooth beneath my fingertips. I stroke them across his chest, from shoulder to shoulder, following the line of his collarbone, feeling the muscles above and below. They linger on a scar on his left shoulder.

"Where did you get this?" I ask.

"Playing rugby."

"I thought you were a nerd."

"I didn't say I was any good at it."

I smile, continuing to explore. He has a scattering of brown hair on his arms and curly hairs on his chest. His flat nipples are light brown, and he twitches when I stroke a thumb over them. I trail my hand down his abs to his belly button, then follow the line of hair to where it disappears beneath the waistband of his jeans. He shivers, and I feel a thrill of pleasure. My touch affects him as much as the other way around.

I look up at him, and he pulls me closer to him and lowers his mouth to mine.

He kisses me slowly, softly. Just pressing his lips to mine for a while, teasing me, until he finally touches his tongue to my bottom lip. I sigh and open my mouth, and he slides his tongue inside. I lift my arms around his neck and tilt my head to the side to change the angle. We deepen the kiss, while I sink my hands into his hair, and he drops his hands to my hips, then down onto my butt.

Ooh, this is nice. It's warm and sultry in the room—he hasn't put the aircon on—and although it won't be dark until about nine, the light is fading, and the fairy lights cast glitter across the carpet.

It's so different from last year that I can barely believe I'm the same person. Last Christmas felt like the end. This year it feels like a beginning. It's already a billion times better, and we haven't even really started yet.

Chapter Fifteen

Alex

Missie is all soft surfaces—satin skin, silky hair, velvet lips, rounded breasts, and the wonderful pliable muscles of her bottom. My fingers slide over her teddy, exploring her curves, while I kiss her mouth, enjoying her sighs and occasional sexy moans low in her throat.

I lift my head and study her dark, expressive eyes. "Can you let your hair down?" I murmur.

Her lips curve up, and she lifts her hands to remove the clips in her hair, letting it tumble around her shoulders. She tosses the clips onto the nearby table, and I sink my hands into the long brown locks that slip through my fingers like silk ribbons.

"Do you really have silver hairs down below?" she teases.

I remember that she overheard my conversation with Finn. "You'll have to find out for yourself."

"I intend to." She gives me a mischievous smile.

Feeling a surge of happiness, I slide my hands beneath her butt, lift her, and wrap her legs around my waist. She squeals and laughs, then kisses me, and I walk through to the bedroom, trying not to bump into the furniture as I go. My pulse has picked up speed, and my blood is racing through my veins. I want this girl so much it hurts. I just hope I manage to last five minutes and don't embarrass myself.

She brushes her fingers up the short hair on the back of my head and delves her tongue into my mouth. "Mmm," she says. "You taste good."

"Not as good as you're going to taste in a minute."

She lifts her head to look at me, and her eyes are wide with excitement.

"Have you been a good girl this Christmas?" I murmur, taking her into my bedroom and over to the bed.

"If I say no, do I get a spanking?" Her eyes dance.

I pull the duvet back, climb onto the bed, and tip her onto her back. Then I lean over and look down at her. For a moment, I can't reply, speechless as I look at the way her hair is spread over my pillow. I've waited so long, I can't believe she's finally here, in my house, my bed, my arms.

"More lights," she says, looking around at the fairy lights that are casting jewels across the duvet. "Don't tell me... Finn?"

"He did mention you liked them." I glance down as Zelda follows us into the room and stands there with a wagging tail. "Go and lie down, good girl," I tell her, and she goes over to her bed and flops in it obediently.

"I thought you were talking to me," Missie teases. She trails her fingers down my neck, over my collarbone, and down to my nipples. Then she tweaks them, only lightly, but enough to send an uncomfortable zap through me.

"Ow!" I take her wrists and pin them above her head. "You're definitely on the naughty list."

She laughs, a high female giggle, and it's the most beautiful sound, as alien to this house as the cleansing lotion and tampons and lip gloss I know she'll leave in the bathroom, the diet soda and low-fat cheese she'll insist on keeping in the fridge, the scent of her perfume I'll be able to smell on my clothes. I've been on my own far too long.

When she first told me that she used to argue with her husband about not having sex often enough, I assumed it was Lee who was pressing her for more. My heart sank briefly at the thought that her libido might not be as high as mine, as it's been a problem in the past.

Having a high sex drive sounds great, but it can be a curse. It can cause all sorts of problems in a relationship if your partner is happy with once a week, or even less than that. I've yet to be with a girl who's happy with having sex as often as I am. It always starts off well, then gradually tapers off. There's nothing worse than lying there at night staring up at the ceiling, trying to will your hard-on to go down once your partner has rolled over, making it clear they're not interested. I'd never press a girl to have sex with me, and I've never blamed someone else for not having a high sex drive, but I'd rather be alone than face that constant rejection. I guess Tinder is an answer, but I'm not a fan of one-night stands, and much prefer a long-term relationship.

But Missie's comment, *I was the one who wanted it more*, fills me with hope that it's not going to happen this time.

I crush my lips to hers, and she moans and pushes up her hips against mine. Releasing her wrists, I leave her mouth and begin to kiss down her neck. I've left off the main lights, as the fairy lights are more than enough to see by. This time, when I pull the straps of her teddy down her arms, she doesn't complain but slides her arms out, then watches as I peel the triangular cups down over her breasts.

"Jesus," I mumble as the lacy fabric reveals her plump, light-brown nipples, "you're perfect."

She sighs as I kiss her breasts, then moans when I trace the tip of my tongue around a nipple. I do it until the soft skin tightens to a bead, at which point I transfer to the other one. When they're both puckered and hard, I cover one with my mouth and suck.

"Oh God…" She sinks her hands into my hair and arches her back. Relieved that she doesn't mind her breasts being touched, because not all girls are into it, I kiss them for a while, until she's groaning and writhing beneath me, and only then do I give in and pull the teddy down over her hips and legs before tossing it away.

I move between her legs and kiss down over her belly.

"Don't kiss my stretch marks," she complains as I linger there.

"They're practically invisible."

"*I* know they're there."

"They're beautiful."

"Bullshit. Don't you want some tight young virgin with a concave stomach?"

Exasperated, I lift up and glare at her. "Why would I want a virgin?"

"I thought men liked girls to be young and innocent."

"Well, I don't. I have no interest in teaching someone how to have sex. I want a girl who knows what she's doing."

Her brows draw together. "I know where everything goes, if that's what you mean."

"That's a start."

"But I'm really not that experienced, if you're looking for something fancy."

"I'm not. I just want you, Missie." I kiss her hip, then down to her mound. Wow, her skin here is silky-smooth, and I'm now so hard it's almost painful. I'm not going to give in yet, though. I want her to come first. It is her birthday, after all.

Lowering down, I push her thighs wide, smiling as she covers her face with her hands. Then I part her with my fingers and just study her for a moment.

"Jesus," she says after about ten seconds. "What are you doing?"

"Admiring the view."

"Oh my God."

"You smell amazing."

"Oh. My. God. Kill me now."

I chuckle and brush my thumb up through her folds. She's already swollen, and I spread her moisture up and over her clit, loving the way she groans when I touch it. I stroke her a few times, and then finally slide my tongue into the heart of her.

She gives a long, delightful moan, and continues to sigh and groan as I arouse her, which pleases me no end. It's always easier when your partner tells you what she likes. I try different speeds, and varying pressures, and when she says, "Holy fuck," as I swirl my tongue up her core and then over her clit, I settle on long slow licks that soon have her breaths coming in deep, ragged gasps.

"Alex," she whispers as I add two fingers to the action and slip them inside her. When I turn my hand palm up and press lightly upward, she just says, "Oh!" as if surprised at the sensation.

"You're going to come for me now," I say, massaging her while I continue to lick, and sure enough, it only takes another twenty seconds or so before I feel her clutching my hair, and then she holds her breath, and all her muscles start to tighten.

She clenches around my fingers, her clit pulsing on my tongue as she cries out my name. Oh man… I've waited a long time for this, and it's even better than the thousand times I imagined it. She tastes sweet, and the satisfaction I feel at giving her such pleasure is something that no amount of dollars in the bank could ever buy.

When she's done, I lift up and move over her so I can lean down and kiss her. She sighs, wrapping her arms around my neck as I lower on top of her.

"Mmm," she murmurs, moving against me as I give slow, gentle thrusts, still wearing my boxers, so I'm just rubbing against her.

"Sexy girl." I kiss her jaw, her ear, her neck, and then back up to her mouth. "Do you want me inside you now, baby?"

"Oh God, a million times yes."

I push up and rid myself of the boxers, then go to reach over to the nightstand.

To my surprise, though, she stops me. "Um, Alex?"

"Yeah?"

"I have a Mirena coil fitted, so you don't have to use a condom."

I look down at her. "You're sure?"

"You can if you want to. If you'd rather. But I don't mind if you don't."

Our gazes lock. She trusts me, and I trust her. It's no small thing in this day and age.

"Okay," I say softly. I'm not going to turn down the chance to be inside her without barriers. Just the thought makes me swell.

She looks down at my erection, then gives me a mischievous look. "Wow."

I sit back on my heels and brush the tip through her folds a few times. "I've thought about this a lot." Pushing down so I'm pressing against her entrance, I lift up, lean either side of her shoulders, and look into her eyes as I slide inside her. "Ah… fuck…" My eyes won't stay open, and they close at the sensation of being encased in hot, wet velvet.

"Mmm…" She wraps her legs around my waist. "Oh, that feels good."

I force my eyelids open and look at her with hazy eyes. Hers sparkle in the fairy lights, full of something close to adoration.

"You're so fucking beautiful," I tell her, beginning to move with purpose.

"Santa has a dirty mouth," she teases, her eyelids dropping to half-mast. "I knew it."

"Time and a place." I plunge into her, groaning at the sensation. "Oh, man."

"Now you're talking." She meets me thrust for thrust, in perfect unison. Jesus, I must have drunk more than I thought, but this feels more than perfect, it's like she was made for me, as if I've spent my whole life searching for her, and now that I've found her, it feels as if everything's coming together.

While I move, she's exploring with her hands, tracing the muscles on my chest and shoulders, skating her fingers up my ribs and around to my back, and drawing her nails lightly down either side of my spine.

"You have a fantastic body," she murmurs. "I thought I had a good imagination, but you're even better than I thought you'd be."

I lower onto my elbows so I can kiss her, still moving inside her.

"I'm just sorry it's taken us so long to do this," she whispers.

I kiss her. "Things happen when they're supposed to happen."

"I guess." She looks doubtful, though.

I don't want her to think about it now. I tease her lips with mine, then slide my tongue into her mouth and kiss her deeply, and she moans and sinks her hands into my hair.

I begin to spiral out of control, carried away on a wave of longing and desire so intense that I know there's no coming back from it. This was always going to happen, though. I was never going to last long on our first time, after being celibate for, what, nearly eighteen months, and then having sex with the one girl I've been dreaming about for so long. No man's willpower is that strong.

I lift up again and start moving faster, plunging down into her soft body. It's warm in the room—I haven't switched on the air con. Missie's face is flushed, and her skin is glowing. She's so goddamn beautiful. I'm going to make her come again and again. But first things first.

I close my eyes, concentrating on the growing sensations inside me. Missie says, "Oh, baby," and I feel her cup my face, but I can't do anything but thrust as my muscles contract and heat rushes up from my balls. I shudder and groan as I come inside her, frozen in position, turned to rock for ten long seconds, until my body releases me, and I let out my breath in a rush.

Opening my eyes, I look into hers, which are filled with delight. "At long last," she teases. "Alex Winters, out of control."

Giving her a wry look, I sit back on my heels and ease out of her. I stroke a hand down, dipping my thumb inside her and stroking my release through her folds. That's fucking hot.

As I touch her clit, she sighs. She wasn't far away from coming. Nice. Kind of like a head start.

*

Missie

I drift on a cloud of hazy pleasure as Alex strokes me lazily. Unfortunately I was only minutes away from another orgasm, but I know he hasn't had sex in a while, so it was unfair to expect him to last too long. Shame, though. I wonder if he'll mind if I finish myself off?

He hasn't moved, and when I glance down, I see him give himself a couple of strokes before he presses the tip back against my entrance. Once again, he lifts up and leans over me, and then he slides inside me again.

"You're still hard," I observe, amused.

He just smirks and gives long, slow thrusts.

I blink, realizing it's not going down. "Is that normal?"

"Normal for me." He slides a hand underneath me and then, without warning, rolls over, pulling me with him so I'm on top.

"Ooh!" I sit up astride him, clenching and feeling him inside me, all the way up. "Oh my God, you really are a Christmas miracle."

He laughs, his eyes creasing at the edges, showing me his beautiful white teeth, and then he pulls me down and gives me a fierce kiss. "Make yourself come for me," he murmurs as he releases me. "I want to watch you."

I rock my hips, feeling a tad shy, but he's looking at me with such admiration that it's impossible not to feel like a priceless work of art. I lower a hand between my legs, and he gives a satisfied sigh, lifting his hands to my breasts while I swirl my fingers over my clit.

Mmm… this is fantastic—a guy who actually cares about my pleasure, and, even better, who seems able to keep going long enough to let me get there more than once. He's as hard as he was before, and clearly up for another round.

I think I've died and gone to heaven.

I was close before, and it doesn't take long for me to cover any lost ground. Within minutes, I feel the pleasurable sensations begin, and Alex must feel them too, because he says, "Oh yeah," and tucks his hands behind his head, obviously wanting to watch the performance.

I have a few seconds of feeling self-conscious, and then I think oh fuck it, he's given me enough compliments to suggest he doesn't care that I'm not skinny and perfect, and I abandon my shyness and give myself over to the amazing feelings deep inside me.

Ohhh… there's nothing like an orgasm, so sweet and overwhelming, so intense that for a millisecond you think you're not going to survive it, and it's actually going to kill you, and you cry out and your hand and toes curl, and you lose any ability to control your voice or your body, and it's all just pleasure and fireworks, and you want to cry or scream or say every swear word in your vocabulary.

And then seconds later it's gone, and you're left with this amazing warm glow, and a feeling of it being your birthday and Christmas all rolled into one.

"Fuck yeah," he says, and then he rears up and twists, and I'm on my back again, tossed across the bed like I'm one of the pillows and weigh nothing at all.

As he plunges down into me, kissing me like there's no tomorrow, I feel a moment of realization, a revelation that's almost alarm, as true understanding finally sinks in. Oh man, this guy really does want to wear me out. If he can keep going, oh my God, I'm going to be a shadow of my former self.

"Can you put the aircon on?" I whisper. But he just shakes his head. "Please?"

"Nope."

"But I'm hot."

He smirks.

"Alex…" God, it's hard to catch my breath. "I'm sweating!"

He just laughs though and increases his pace.

Oh, man. My hair's sticking to my forehead, and his skin is sliding against mine. He kisses me again, deeply, so it's hard to catch my breath, and then he nips my bottom lip.

"Ow!" I lift my hands to his nipples and flick them. In response, he catches my hands and pins them above my head. Ah, jeez, he's too strong for me to wriggle out of his grip. All I can do is lie there and watch as he pounds into me.

His hair has flopped over his forehead, and his eyes are very intense. Ooh, I think another orgasm might be on the way. Wow, I didn't expect that. Ahhh… I think I'm in love…

He lifts up then, and to my surprise he sits back and withdraws. Euw, I'm all hot and sticky down there, but his lips curve up, and he twirls a finger in the air. "Up you get," he says.

I sit up and turn onto all fours. He positions himself behind me, and then I feel him slowly fill me up again.

Well, he did say he was going to screw me senseless. Always be careful what you wish for…

He thrusts into me like that for a while, until pleasure begins to build inside me again, and right at that moment, almost as if he can sense it, he withdraws. Before I can move a muscle, he puts a hand between my shoulder blades and pushes me forward, so I collapse onto the bed with an "Oof!" Then he somehow flips me onto my back and pulls me down a few inches before sliding inside me again. Holy shit, I have no idea how he did that. I'm impressed.

I'm lying across the bed now, and he's banging me so hard, he's moving me up with each push of his hips, so I can feel the side of the mattress against the back of my head. He's going to thrust me right over the edge…

Ahhh… and I'm going to come again, if he keeps going like this… ohhh… I'm so close…

"Jesus, Missie," he says, slamming into me, "please come before we fall off."

I almost laugh, but the orgasm hits me, and I squeal and come hard. He rides me all the way through it, grinding against me and almost making me see stars, before he stops and shudders, his beautiful body turning to rock again beneath my fingertips. He gives a helpless groan, and all I can do is lie there and watch, exhausted, as he twitches inside me, filling me up yet again. I'm going to be so sticky after all this, I'll need a shower.

He sighs, and I know what he's feeling because I'm feeling it too. The thought is so beautiful, so amazing, that without meaning to, my eyes fill with tears, and even before we both drift down to earth, the tears spill over and trickle down my cheeks.

Chapter Sixteen

Alex

"Ah," I say as Missie covers her mouth with a hand. "Sweetheart."

I'm still inside her, and I have to wait a few seconds for the aftershocks of my climax to finish rippling through me before I can move. She's fighting her emotion, but losing the battle, and as I finally withdraw and pull her with me over to the pillows, she gives in and starts sobbing.

I sigh, bring the duvet with us, tuck it around her, then lie back and wrap my arms around her. She curls up next to me, and I hold her like that for a while, until her trembling dies down, and she gives a big, shivery sigh.

Out of the blue, Zelda jumps up onto the bed, maybe disturbed by the fact that Missie's crying.

"Hey," I protest, because although she sometimes comes up on the bed, she has to be invited. But as she curls up in the crook of Missie's legs, Missie says, "It's all right," and reaches down to stroke her.

Reaching over to the nightstand, I pull a couple of tissues out of the box there and pass them to her. She blows her nose and wipes her eyes, then cuddles up to me again.

"I'm so sorry," she whispers. "I don't know what happened there."

"It's okay." I brush my fingers across her shoulders and down her back.

"I know you're not going to believe this, but I don't actually cry very often. And I think I've cried, like, at least three times in front of you already."

"Hopefully it means you feel comfortable enough with me to let go."

"Maybe." She turns, resting her hand on my chest and her chin on her hand, looking up at me. "I feel as if I've been locked shut for so long. I've had all these padlocks around my heart, and you've found the key."

"I see it as if you're a rosebud that's been kept in the dark. Flowers need sunshine and rain to thrive."

She gives me a puzzled smile. "That's very poetic."

"I do write poetry, as it happens."

Her smile spreads. "Seriously?"

"Yeah. Not as much as I used to. But I live in a world of science, of physics and technology. I don't do many creative things. Poetry is my one outlet, I suppose."

"I didn't know," she murmurs. The fairy lights behind the bed flicker, making her eyes shimmer. "Can you remember any you've written?"

I lift a strand of her hair and run it through my fingers as I recite.

"Your eyes, your eyes
As dark as stormy gray November skies
Unwrap me like a sweet birthday surprise

Your mouth, your mouth
Plants kisses down my body, heading south
Whisky-warm, as sensual as earth

Your hands, your hands
Communicate your tender thoughts and plans
A language that my body understands

Your voice, your voice
A plangent chime, the resonance of choice
Ties me up in knots with every phrase

You, you
A lighthouse that illuminates the room
Bright as the sun, exotic as the moon."

She stares at me, mouth open. "You wrote that?"

"I did."

"Oh my God. It's beautiful. Who is it about?"

"You, Missie." I cup her face. "Who else has stormy eyes like you?"

"Me?" She blinks. "When did you write it?"

I debate what to say for a moment. Then eventually I tell her, "A while ago."

"But you said about her kissing down your body. We hadn't slept together then."

"Artistic license."

Her lips slowly curve up. "You really wrote it about me?"

"You inspire me." I kiss her. "You're my muse."

"I think that's the nicest thing anyone's ever said to me."

I kiss her again, this time for longer, and she melts against me, giving a long sigh when I eventually lift my head.

"I'm glad you were able to escape for a night," I tell her.

"Me too." She draws circles on my chest, then stops and gives me a mischievous smile. "Oh yeah, I promised myself I'd check." She peels the duvet back, all the way down to our thighs, and runs her fingers lightly through the curly hairs in my groin. "Silver!" she announces. "You weren't kidding!"

"Unfortunately not. One of the drawbacks of being dark haired."

"Tell me about it." She gestures to her head. "I've got the odd gray hair popping out. I have to dye them."

I chuckle and kiss the top of her head. "You'd never know."

"We're both so sticky," she comments. "That's your fault."

"You weren't exactly dry as a desert, Mistletoe."

"Yeah, but you're the one who filled me up. Twice. What's that about?"

"I have a very short refractory period."

"Non-existent, more like."

"Is that a complaint?"

"Fuck, no." We both laugh at her vehement tone.

"Would you like a bath?" I ask. "Or we could get in the spa pool."

"You have a spa pool? As well as an ordinary pool?"

"I do."

"You don't mind getting bodily fluids in it?"

"I'll add extra chlorine."

She giggles. Then she says, "Oh, I didn't bring a costume."

"Nobody will be able to see you. I don't normally wear anything. But if you're worried about it, you can wear one of my T-shirts."

"No that's okay, if you don't mind."

"Would I mind having a naked Mistletoe Macbeth in my spa pool, with her warm, shiny skin? Hmm, let me think…?"

She pushes me. "Come on. There's already a wet patch on the mattress, and I don't want to make it worse."

"It's on your side."

"Of course it is."

I grin, get up, and retrieve two toweling bathrobes from the wardrobe. "Here." I hold it up for her to slide her arms into, don mine, and then take her hand and lead her out to the kitchen, Zelda springing into life and following us. "Want a drink while you're soaking?"

She clips up her hair again. "I've already had two glasses of wine."

"Oh yeah. I forgot about New Zealand's Two-Glass Law." I roll my eyes and take out two heavy-bottomed glasses.

"It's recommended to have only two units a night," she scolds.

"Everything in moderation, right? Including moderation." She looks doubtful. "Jesus, woman, you're only twenty-eight and you've had a hell of a year. You don't have to worry about Finn tonight. Don't you think you deserve to have a few drinks on your birthday?" I take out a bottle of whisky and wave it at her.

Her lips curve up. "Yes," she says confidently, "I do!"

"Great. Would you prefer vodka?"

"Whisky's fine."

I pour us both a shot and add some ice and water. "Grab the chocolates as well."

She finds the box of truffles in the fridge, I decide to bring the bottle, and we take it all out through the sliding doors onto the deck.

The spa pool is cleverly placed just off the deck facing the garden with fencing on either side, so it's nice and private. We leave our robes on the bench to the side, put our drinks and the chocolate on the shelf, and slide into the hot, bubbling water. Zelda puts her paws up and wags for a bit until I splash her, then loses interest and runs off to explore the bushes.

Behind us through the window, the fairy lights on the Christmas tree cast colored light across the spa. It's warm, and the air smells of oranges from the trees over by the fence, and jasmine from the white flowers growing by the deck.

"Ohhh…" Missie gives a sexy groan and slips further down until she's up to her neck. She's pinned up her hair, and tendrils curl in the steam around her face. "That's heavenly."

I pick up my drink and lean back, smiling to see her looking so happy. "What would you like to drink to?"

She picks up her glass. "To a much better New Year than the last."

I clink my glass against hers and repeat the toast, and we both take a sip. I pick up a truffle and hold it out for her, and she closes her lips around my fingers and takes it into her mouth.

"You're going to lead me astray, aren't you?" she asks.

"I'll do my best."

She gives a short laugh. "Do I seem staid to you?"

"Not at all. You're a mother, and a teacher. You have responsibilities. But everyone needs to let their hair down once in a while."

"I guess."

"Do you have a night out with your friends very often?"

"I don't have many friends here. Carly's the only person I see out of work. She tends to come to the house with Sean. We don't go out much on our own." She looks into her glass. "I didn't used to be like this. I used to be fun."

"You were lots of fun tonight."

"You know what I mean. When I was much younger, I used to love parties and dancing. But I suppose getting pregnant so young put paid to all that. I didn't want to go out and leave Finn, and anyway Lee wouldn't have liked it if he'd had to stay in with the baby while I went out and had a good time. We grew up too fast."

"All the more reason to enjoy yourself when you can."

She nods. "I think we should get drunk tonight."

"All right."

She gives me an impish smile, her cheeks dimpling. "I like the way you look at the world. As if you're in charge, and it's going to do as it's told."

"Sounds about right."

"Do you think that comes from having money?"

"Probably. It certainly doesn't hurt."

"Juliette said your mother is Kaitlyn Cross?"

"Yeah."

"She lives in LA, doesn't she?"

"Yeah. I don't see her much."

"How old were you when she moved?"

"Eighteen."

"Did you miss her a lot?"

"It's complicated."

"Are you close?"

"No, not really. Kait doesn't have much time for anyone but herself."

Her blue eyes study me curiously. "You call her Kait? Not Mum?"

"Yeah."

"Why?"

"It's complicated," I say again. I'm crazy about Missie, but I'm not ready to talk about my mother to her yet.

"You've got two sisters, right? Gaby and Michelle?"

"Yeah. We call her Belle."

"Like the Beatles' song?"

"Yeah. It's Damon's fault. He called her it when he first met her, and it stuck. She was only six. I should have known they'd end up together."

She smiles. "She's younger than Gaby?"

"Mmm, she's twenty-two. Gaby's twenty-five."

"I'd like to meet her."

I have a mouthful of whisky. "I was thinking about that. What are you doing next week?"

"We're going up to Blenheim for few days. My aunt—my mum's older sister—and uncle live there, and we stay with them quite often."

"Hmm."

"Why?"

"Damon's getting married. I said I'd fly up on Boxing Day for a couple of days to help organize some of the final bits and pieces. His stag night's on the twenty-eighth. On the twenty-ninth it's the wedding rehearsal, and the thirtieth is his big day. I'm his best man."

"Oh!" She smiles. "You'll be fantastic."

"Well, thank you. I was wondering whether you and Finn would like to come with me? My invitation was a plus-one, and I know Damon wouldn't mind if Finn came, too." Her expression softens, and I add, "What did I say?"

"'You and Finn.' You didn't have to say that."

"Of course I did. I know you're a package. I'm sure your mum's welcome too, except I didn't think she'd want to go to the wedding of someone she doesn't know. But if you have other plans, that's fine."

She nibbles her bottom lip, thinking. Then she says, "What are you doing with Zelda? Is she going to your dad's?"

"No, because they'll be at the wedding."

"Oh, of course, he's the father of the bride."

"I've booked Zelda into the kennels."

"Aw. Look, I have an idea. What about if Finn and Mum take Zelda to Blenheim? My aunt and uncle run a vineyard. They've got a large house and a lot of land. They have three dogs and two kids and grandkids. Zelda will love it, and Finn will be in seventh heaven. Then we can have some time on our own."

I smile at the thought of having her to myself. "Are you sure? I don't expect that."

She puts her arms around her knees. "You're right—everyone needs to let their hair down once in a while. I haven't had a holiday since the accident, and I've hardly done anything for myself. I love Finn with all my heart, and I've devoted the whole of the past year to his recovery. But maybe I've earned a few days off?" She holds out her hand, and I close mine around it. "We need to get to know one another," she says.

"That's true."

"And to have some serious sex."

"Also true."

We both smile.

"We need time, don't we?" she says. "To see whether there's something worth exploring here."

"Yeah. We gotta be sure."

She studies me, then narrows her eyes. "You're making fun of me."

"A little bit."

"What's funny about that?"

"Nothing at all. If you need time to make sure you like me, I understand perfectly."

She splashes me. "That's not what I'm saying at all."

"No, I get it. I'm an acquired taste."

"Alex! You're the one who needs time. You're mega-rich and mega-gorgeous—you could have anyone you want."

"Well, sure, I've got an Oscar-winning actress on speed dial…"

"Stop teasing me!"

"See, this is what I mean, I obviously drive you mad. I give you a week before you decide you want to strangle me."

She narrows her eyes. "Juliette said I needed to get some alcohol in you to loosen you up. She said you were different when you were drunk."

"What do you mean? I'm always witty and charming."

She picks up her glass, finds it empty, and holds it out to me. I finish mine off, then pour us both another. A little splashes over the edge of her glass as she moves it, and she giggles.

"I'm tipsy," she says.

"Glad to hear it."

She has a mouthful, then rests her glass on her lips as she studies me. "I was convinced you thought I was crazy when we first met."

"The jury's still out on that."

She giggles. Then she says, "I was kinda scared of you."

"It's true, I do instill fear."

"You really don't. You're a pussy cat underneath it all."

"I still have the spatula. I'm just saying."

Her eyes dance. "You are quite bossy though."

"I'm a CEO. It's my job."

"I like that."

"Well that's a bit of luck."

Her gaze lingers on my mouth. "And I love that you like sex."

I don't reply to that. Instead, I let my gaze slide down her, over her damp skin, to beneath the surface of the bubbling water. She's naked and wet and flushed and shiny. Ahhh… This girl…

"Alex…" she scolds. "Don't look at me like that."

"Like what?"

"Like you want to be inside me again." She sips her whisky, her gaze locking on mine.

I blow out a breath. "You're going to be a danger to my health."

"What do you mean?"

"I suffer from priapism whenever you're around."

"What's that?"

"A permanent erection."

Her lips curve up. Then she moves toward me, sending the water swirling. She slides a hand down my chest, then continues south.

"Oh yes," she whispers. Her fingers close around me, and she gives me a couple of strokes.

I sigh.

She finishes off her whisky. Places the glass on the shelf behind us. Then lifts up so she's straddling me. She moves until the tip of my erection parts her folds. Then, ever so slowly, she sinks down and impales herself on me.

I groan and let my head fall back onto the edge of the spa.

"Aw," she murmurs, kissing my neck and around to my ear. "Poor baby. Are you worn out, Alexander? Do you need some time to recover?" She nips my earlobe. "Maybe you've met your match," she whispers in my ear.

I empty my glass and put it aside, then slide my arms around her. "We'll see. I'm betting you'll beg me to stop first."

She inhales with excitement. "Challenge accepted." She rocks her hips, riding me slowly, and kisses my lips, dipping her tongue into my mouth.

"You're sure?" I slide my hands over her silky skin. "I intend to fuck you senseless."

"Oh? What happened to making *luuurv*?"

"That fell by the wayside when you told me I've met my match."

"Oh, thank God," she says with feeling, and we both laugh.

I couldn't have asked for a better Christmas present. The colored fairy lights play over her skin as she moves. I can taste chocolate and whisky, and the scent of the jasmine is exotic and sultry. The sun has nearly set now, and the garden is full of orange light. The trees are casting long shadows, but it's still warm. Zelda is lying on her side on the deck, snoring, unbothered by what we're doing.

Missie moves on top of me slowly, sending the water swirling around us, which adds to the sensation of her stroking my skin. She slides her hands up my chest and neck, cups my face, then slips her hands into my hair.

Resting on the back of the spa, she lifts up and gives small thrusts so I'm just moving in and out of her, teasing the tip. At the same time, she lowers her lips to mine, but as I reach for the kiss, she moves back, making me wait.

My eyelids lower to half-mast as she plays with me. She taunts me with brief touches of her tongue, moving out of range each time I try to return it.

"You're skating on thin ice," I tell her with a growl.

"Ooh." She flares her eyes, then takes my face in her hands and kisses me deeply. "I want to drive you crazy," she whispers, nibbling my bottom lip. "Until you can't think of anything else. Until the only thing in your thoughts is me."

She's already done that, but I can't point that out, because she's kissing me again, claiming my lips, and plunging her tongue into my mouth until I'm breathless with need. Ahhh…

"Mmm." I move my head back. "Come on, out, now."

"Aw…"

"Missie…" I lift her off me and deposit her onto the seat with an unceremonious splash.

"Eek! I was enjoying that."

I pull on my robe. "Inside, now."

Her lips curve up. "Yes, sir."

I give her a wry look, pick up the glasses and bottle, and wait for her to get out before following her through the sliding doors. I take the glasses up to the kitchen, splash a last double in each one, then bring them back to the living room.

I find her sitting in one of the armchairs. She's wearing the robe, but it's undone, revealing her pale, damp skin from neck to toe. I pass her the glass, and she accepts it.

Zelda has come in, too, and I close the sliding doors, then fetch a dog biscuit from the box on the side and give it to Zelda. She takes it over to her bed and goes round in it three times before flopping down to crunch it contentedly.

Missie watches me as I sit in the other armchair opposite her. I let my robe fall apart too, and don't bother hiding my erection as I have a drink.

She has a mouthful of whisky, then licks her lips. "I want to taste you."

My heart skips a beat, but I don't move. "Crawl over here on your hands and knees and you can do anything to me you like."

She laughs, her beautiful girlish giggle, has one more drink, then puts down her glass. She slides her arms out of her robe, then slips off her chair onto the carpet. Lifting a hand, she releases the clip holding up her hair, and uncurls it so it tumbles over one shoulder.

Then she tips forward so she's on her hands and knees, fixes her gaze on me, and crawls slowly forward like a cat, right up to me.

I part my legs, and she moves before them and slides her hands up my thighs. She licks her lips, her gaze still locked to mine. And then she lowers her head and closes her mouth over the tip of my erection.

Ahhh… I tip my head back and close my eyes. Merry Christmas, Alex.

Chapter Seventeen

Missie

Alex's long groan sends a shiver of pleasure all the way through me. Holy shit, unraveling this guy is just the best thing in the world. He's normally so in control, and shows so little emotion, that watching him do this is almost erotic enough to make me come on its own.

Making sure he's well lubricated, I stroke him firmly with one hand while I explore him with my tongue. He tastes amazing, and as he sinks a hand into my hair, I know I'm getting to him. I don't think he was far from coming in the spa, so this isn't going to take long. If it truly has been over a year since he had sex, it's no wonder he's struggling to hang onto reality now. Hmm, I wonder if he'll be ready to go again afterward? It doesn't matter if he isn't—I'm pretty sure he'll go down on me again. Ooh. I don't know what I'd prefer.

Oh, man, doing this is making me ache inside. He's applying gentle pressure to my head, encouraging me to go deeper, and I slide my lips down as far as I can, taking him deep inside my mouth, and suck.

"Ahhh…"

I look up and meet his gaze, and let him watch me as I continue to arouse him. His eyes are turning hazy. After lifting my head briefly to lick my fingers, I return to kissing him as I cup his balls, then explore further down.

"Ah, shit," he says, giving a short laugh, his hand tightening in my hair. "Missie…" Gently, I tease the tight muscle there with a finger, and he closes his eyes. "Shit, I'm going to…" He can't finish the sentence, and I watch him as he comes, loving his deep groans, and swallowing down everything he has to give me.

When he's done, I sit back and wait for him to recover.

He stares up at the ceiling for a moment, then drops his head and studies me.

"Yum," I say.

He narrows his eyes. I lick my lips. He huffs a sigh. Then he looks down at his erection, which is still a good seven out of ten, takes himself in hand, and gives himself a few strokes until it returns to a solid ten out of ten. I hide a giggle at the pun. Ooh, I haven't been this tipsy for a while. I'm having the time of my life. I probably won't be able to walk tomorrow, but it'll have been worth it.

"Sofa," he says.

I go to get up, but he says, "Stay on your hands and knees, smart arse."

I bat my lashes. "Did I do something wrong?"

"Don't think I'm letting you get away with what you did with your finger, without warning, I hasten to add."

"You said I could do anything I wanted if I crawled over to you."

"That didn't include a surprise insertion."

"Then you should have made the rules clearer."

He glares at me. "Stop being a brat. Sofa. Now."

I crawl to the sofa, knowing he's admiring my butt as I go. "If you didn't like it, you could have just said."

He tosses his robe away, gets down to his knees behind me, and knocks my knees apart. "As long as you understand that any transgression gets returned tenfold."

That gives me uncontrollable giggles. "That's so you," I tell him as he positions himself behind me.

"You're sure you want to mock me right now?" He presses the tip of his erection into me.

I copy his tone. "'As long as you understand any transgr'—oh!" I stop with a squeal as he plunges into me in one thrust, so deep it takes my breath away.

He sets up a fast pace, pushing me up against the sofa, and I groan and pull a cushion down so I can bury my face in it. He doesn't stop, filling the air with the slick sound of him inside me, and the smack of his hips against my thighs and butt. Oh holy shit… I lower my hand beneath me to try and help myself along, but he takes it and moves it behind my back. Now all I can do is lie there and let him go at it. That's so fucking hot…

If it had only taken a minute, I might have been okay, but I think Alex could screw for New Zealand. The man goes on for an eternity.

Eventually I can't hold my exclamation in any longer and mutter, "Ouch!"

He stops immediately. "Are you okay?"

"Yeah. You're giving me carpet burn on my knees, that's all."

He laughs, but he says, "You want me to stop?"

"Ah, no…"

"All right, sweetheart." Instead, he lifts me up and forward so I'm lying on the sofa, then gets on top of me. He slides inside me again, then lowers down. "Sorry, baby," he murmurs, kissing my neck while he continues to move.

"Mmm… you're forgiven."

He slips his hand under my shoulder to find my hand and interlink our fingers, which seems like such a romantic gesture that I have to fight against emotion again. What is it with me and crying lately? It's this man, who's hot and sexy and yet strangely tender all at the same time.

"You feel so good," he murmurs, kissing my ear, my neck, and my back as I pull another cushion down to rest my forehead on. "Are you going to come for me, baby?"

"Mmm… I don't know… I'm pretty drunk…"

"Aw, baby girl, come on… just relax… let me do all the work…" With his other hand he tugs at my nipple for a while, then slides his hand down under me and finds my clit. "Ah, yeah," he whispers, "so ready for me."

His deep voice in my ear makes me shiver. I feel like a woolen sweater that he's unpicking stitch by stitch. I'm coming apart at the seams, and there's nothing I can do about it.

"Alex…" I can feel it approaching, tiny muscles tightening deep inside me.

"Good girl…"

I squeal as the powerful contractions take over, clenching around him. Oh… it's exquisite, and my pleasure is doubled as he continues to thrust, harder and faster, then stiffens and holds me tightly as he comes, hips jerking, twitching inside me, filling me up, joining us together in a blissful union that's so amazing I feel as if I'm floating up to the night sky, and oh my God I'm so fucking drunk…

He stops and rests his forehead on my shoulder, and I collapse into the cushions.

We stay there like that for a whole minute, catching our breath, as we slowly float back down to earth.

Eventually, he eases out of me, then gets up off the sofa. "Stay there," he says, and I hear him pull on his boxers, then walk away.

"Okay," I mumble. There wasn't much hope of me moving. I wait, listening to him moving around, watching the flickering fairy lights on the tree. Zelda's lying next to it, feet hanging over the edge of her bed, twitching as she chases rabbits in her dreams. Music is still playing, carols now, and a choir is singing *Silent Night*.

I feel exhausted and happy and relaxed and uncaring and loved.

I might never be able to close my legs again, but it'll be worth it.

Footsteps sound again, and he returns and kneels down beside me. "Turn over," he says. I flip onto my back and look up at him with sleepy eyes. "We'll go to bed in a minute," he promises. He's holding a tube of cream in one hand, and he squeezes a bit onto his fingers, then rubs it on my knees. "I'm so sorry about that."

I watch him, swallowing down my emotion. "They're okay."

"They're red. It was very bad of me."

My lips curve up. "Naughty boy."

He throws me a wry look. "This time, I agree with you." He finishes rubbing the cream in and puts the top back on the tube. Then he leans on the side of the sofa and looks down at me. "You're incredibly beautiful."

"Are you trying to make me cry?"

"Maybe." He smiles. "You want to go to bed?"

"Mmm."

"I've put your bag in the bedroom. Come on." He takes my hand and pulls me to my feet. Then he slides his arm beneath my knees and lifts me up.

I loop my arms around his neck and rest my head on his shoulder as he carries me through to the bedroom. He kisses the top of my hair, then lowers me down outside the bathroom. "Go on," he says. "You first."

I retrieve my washbag and the pretty nightdress I've brought, go into the bathroom, and close the door. Taking the washbag over to the sink, I lean on it and stare at my reflection. My hair looks like Sideshow Bob's from *The Simpsons*—completely wild. My face and neck are still flushed. My lips are bruised. I look like I've just had mad monkey sex. Funny that.

A little shocked, I wrestle my hair into an elastic, remove my makeup, wash my face, and brush my teeth. I'm having trouble keeping my eyes open. Alcohol always makes me sleepy. Finally I pull on the nightdress—it's midnight-blue and satin, with shoestring straps and lace over the breasts, and it falls to my mid-thigh. I bought it especially. I hope he likes it.

When I'm done, I go back out and discover him folding up his clothes neatly, wearing just his boxers.

"Hey," I say shyly, tucking a strand of hair behind my ear. "All yours."

He closes the wardrobe door, then comes and stands before me and takes my hands. "You okay?" he asks.

I nod and look down at the nightdress. "I bought this for you."

He runs a hand down it, then slides his hand around to the middle of my back and pulls me against him. "You're so thoughtful." He nuzzles my ear.

"Mmm." I lean against him, and he chuckles.

"You look like you're about to doze off any moment."

"Someone wore me out, not mentioning any names."

He grins and leads me over to the bed. "In you get. I won't be long."

I climb under the duvet, rolling onto my side as he disappears into the bathroom, and prop my head on a hand. The room is neat and tidy, as I'd expect. The duvet is plain light blue, and like the rest of the house, the furnishings look expensive but neutral—it wouldn't surprise me if he hired a firm to decorate. But there are touches of him around. A photo on the wall of some far-off galaxy that looks like it's from the Hubble telescope—that's got to be him. Zelda's bed says "I'm specced into Beast Mastery"—that's a World of Warcraft joke.

On the nightstand are his Apple watch, his large, top-of-the-range iPhone, and half a dozen books in a stack: a biography of rugby player Jonah Lomu, another about Sir Peter Jackson, and one about Oppenheimer, a history book about James Cook, a book about gravity, and Stephen Hawking's *A Brief History of Time*, which looks very well thumbed.

He comes out then, and I say, "You're reading about gravity?"

He glances at the book. "Yeah."

"Did you know that if you break the law of gravity, you get a suspended sentence?"

That makes him laugh. "Jesus."

"Thank you very much, I'm here all week."

"Just how drunk are you?"

"I'm pretty wasted. Hey, could you do something for me?"

"Of course."

"Could you get my necklace?"

He smiles then, and leaves the room, reappearing a few seconds later with the jewelry box. I take it and open the lid, curling up as I study it, turning it in my fingers. It's so beautiful, and it looks so expensive. I still can't believe he bought it for me. Technically, this is our first date. But of course it isn't, not really. Now I look back, I realize he's been seducing me from the moment I met him.

He closes the bedroom door, then bends to give Zelda a last kiss on the head and a fuss before he gets into bed. "Want me to put it on for you?"

"No, I don't want to damage it. I'll wear it tomorrow, though." I leave it open on the bedside table.

"Come here," he says, and he pulls me into his arms. We nestle down beneath the duvet, and he pulls it up and tucks it around us.

"Did you really like me from the first time we met?" I whisper.

"I did."

"Even though I walked into your door?"

"Because you walked into my door."

"You like that I'm ditzy?"

He kisses my nose. "I like that you're you."

"Oh, I'm very me."

"Don't ever be anybody else, Missie. You're perfect." His lips curve up as I frown. "What?"

"It's just… I feel baffled. I'm so far from perfect, it's not funny. I accept that I'm a glass half full kind of person, but that doesn't mean I'm an angel."

"I should hope not."

I push him. "I mean I'm not cheerful all the time. I have grumpy days too."

He strokes my fringe away from my forehead. "I can't imagine you grumpy."

"Well, I am, sometimes. And I'm not a great cook."

"Good job I'm okay, then. I'll make sure we don't starve."

"Alex! I'm trying to explain that I don't understand why you have this view of me. You're going to be so disappointed when you find out I'm not who you think I am."

"Sweetheart, you're gentle, and kind, and you have a heart of gold. You love your son and all the kids in your class. You're fun to be with, and you're sexy as. I can't think of a single thing I don't love about you."

I blink and look into his eyes. That was a throwaway comment, the way you say 'I love chocolate ice cream.' He wasn't declaring that he loved me.

"Alex, you mocked me earlier when I said we need time to see whether there's something worth exploring here."

"Doesn't sound like me."

"Well, you did. But I was serious. I mean, I like you…"

"I'm glad about that."

I ignore him and carry on. "…and I think you like me…"

"Understatement of the year."

"…but just because two people like having sex, it doesn't mean they're compatible, does it…"

"Not in the slightest."

"…I mean, I have an eleven-year-old son…"

"Who's a right pain in the ass. Can't stand the kid."

"…and I have to put him first…"

"I thought we could lock him up in the basement."

"…because he's had such a lot of instability this year…"

"Actually, we could send him to boarding school."

"…and the last thing I want is for him to lock onto you…"

"Like a heat-seeking missile?"

"…and then you realize I'm just an ordinary girl, and you get bored with me…"

"Sounds very likely."

"…and call the actress you have on speed dial…"

"She's always waiting. She's getting pretty insistent."

"Alex! We're having a serious conversation."

He sighs. "Have you told Finn that you overheard him the other night?"

"No. I don't know how to broach it. His dad's not here to defend himself, so he'll only get one side of the story, and that doesn't seem fair, because I know I'm going to sound resentful and angry."

"He's eleven, Missie. He's closer to being an adult than you think. Why do you think he didn't admit that he remembered the accident? Because he wants to protect you. He thinks of himself as the man of the house. He's kept it secret all this time because he didn't want to hurt you, but he'll be relieved that you suspected the truth. It might be the final step he needs in his healing."

My throat tightens with unexpected emotion. "You think so?"

"I do. I'm a man of science, but I believe there's a lot about the world we don't yet understand. One of them is the way the body heals itself. I'm not sure I believe we have physical, mental, and emotional bodies in a New Age sense, but I do think our mental and emotional health impinges on our physical wellbeing. They're inextricably linked in a way we don't yet fully understand. I think Finn has a certain amount of fear that's possibly holding back his complete recovery."

I stare at him in wonder. "I'll talk to him."

He nuzzles my neck. "Your skin is so soft…"

"How can you say something so deep and intense and then go straight back to sex?"

"Quite easily, actually. You smell so good…"

"We were talking about… what were we talking about?"

"Ah, Missie…" He strokes his hands down my back and sighs. "For God's sake, go to sleep or I'm going to make love to you all over again."

"I can't walk as it is."

"Aw. Want me to kiss it better?"

I give up. I'm so fuzzy, I can't remember what we were talking about anyway. "Thank you for a wonderful day."

"You're welcome." He kisses my nose. Then my mouth. Then my mouth again, longer this time.

The tender press of his lips on mine is the last thing I remember before I fall asleep.

Chapter Eighteen

Missie

The next morning it's Christmas Eve. Alex insists on driving me home, and I don't argue, enjoying the trip in his flash Audi sports car with Zelda sitting on my lap.

As he drives, I can't help but cast surreptitious glances across at him. His cheeks and jaw are smooth because he shaved this morning while I watched. The manly act got me all hot and bothered, so we ended up showering together. I was never going to survive being closeted in a cubicle with a naked, wet, and slippery Alex without something naughty happening, but luckily, he didn't seem to mind.

It all feels a bit like a dream. My body is still tingling and tender from our lovemaking. He's so damn good at it. I've had more orgasms over the past twelve hours, I'm sure, than I had in all the time I was with Lee.

Alex is such an enigma. Last night, in bed, he was much more relaxed, teasing me and playing with me all night long. Right now, he's concentrating on the road, an elbow on the sill and his fingers on his lips, lost in thought, and he looks stern and unapproachable. I'm not a hundred percent sure how he feels about me. I have no doubt that he enjoyed the sex, but perhaps that's all it was. Is he regretting inviting me to the wedding with him?

However, when we arrive home, he surprises me by producing a present each for me, Finn, and Mum, and asks if he can come in for a coffee so Finn can play with Zelda for half an hour. He wouldn't do that if he didn't enjoy being with me, right?

And it's him, not me, who brings up the idea of Finn looking after Zelda while I go with him to Damon's wedding. Finn, of course, is thrilled at the notion of having Zelda to himself, and Mum winks at me and says it's no problem at all and she's happy to drive there.

"Or I could fly you there in the helicopter?" Alex asks casually, glancing at me. Last time he suggested it, I refused, but that was before we slept together.

Finn lights up like the Christmas tree. "Mum! Can we?"

I know I still have to be careful with Finn's heart, but equally I can't keep Alex at arm's length after how he was last night. "I guess that would save the long journey. But what about your folks? I assumed you'd be traveling with them?"

"No, they're flying up the day after me. So it's sorted? Ten a.m. on the twenty-eighth at the airport, okay?" He clips Zelda's lead on. "I'd better go. I'm sure you've got lots to do, and Zelda and I are calling in at the office."

"Workaholic," I tease.

"Just making sure there's nothing that needs doing before the Christmas break." He gives Finn a manly bearhug, which brings a lump to my throat, and Mum a kiss on the cheek. "Merry Christmas. See you on Boxing Day."

I go with him and Zelda to the front door, and he makes the puppy sit, then pulls me into his arms.

"Thank you," I murmur. "For suggesting the helicopter."

"I promised him a trip."

"Even so. You're a good man."

"You sure about that?" He nips my earlobe.

"Ouch! On second thought, no." But I temper my words by producing a parcel and handing it to him shyly. "It's only something small," I say awkwardly.

"Aw, thank you." He looks genuinely touched. "I'll save it till tomorrow."

I touch a hand to the pendant I'm wearing today. "Thank you so much for my birthday gift."

"You're very welcome. I'm glad you like it."

"I love it. It was incredibly generous."

"You're worth it."

I give him a peck on the cheek then go to draw back, but he slides his hand into my hair and holds me there, and the peck turns into a smooch. Man, this guy can kiss. He's making me tingle again.

"Mmm," I murmur when he eventually moves back. "See you soon."

He gives me one last kiss, then goes out to his car. He clips Zelda into the passenger seat, then waves at me before getting in the driver's side.

I watch him drive away, close the door, and go back into the living room. Finn and Mum are waiting for me, and they both give me mischievous glances as I walk in.

"So it went well?" Mum asks.

I blush. "Very well. Are you sure you don't mind if I don't come to Pippa's with you?"

"Of course not," Mum says. "I can't remember the last time you had a holiday, and it's important that the two of you spend some time together."

I go over to Finn and kiss the top of his head. "What about you?"

"No, it's cool, especially if I get Zelda!" He grins. "She can sleep on my bed."

"Don't tell Alex," I scold, "she's supposed to sleep in her own bed."

"He won't care," Finn scoffs. He's so sure of Alex's feelings for him. I wish I could be that confident.

I sit on the sofa next to him, remembering what Alex said about the final step in Finn's healing. "I need to talk to you about something, sweetheart." I glance at Mum. "Do you mind giving us a few minutes?"

"Of course not," she says. "I need to give Mike a ring." She gets up and goes out.

Finn's eyebrows rise. "What have I done?"

"You haven't done anything. It's about the other night. When you told Alex that you remembered the accident."

His jaw drops. "He told you?"

"No. He wouldn't betray your confidence. I… um… was listening outside the door."

He glares at me. "That was a private conversation."

"I know, and I'm embarrassed that I listened. I suppose part of me wanted to know what he was saying to you—he's a stranger, and you're my son, and I have to be careful."

"He's not a stranger. I've known him since March. And he's cool. You don't have to worry about him."

"I know. And I am sorry I intruded." I hesitate. "Can we be honest? I like him, Finn. A lot. But you're the most important thing in my life, and if Alex and I have a relationship, I need to know that he's going to treat you well. I didn't mean to listen for as long as I did, but I was touched that he was so good with you."

"We're friends," he says defensively.

"I know."

"And I told him about the accident in confidence. I didn't want you to hear."

"I know." I reach out and take his hand, relieved when he doesn't snatch it away. "The thing is… Finn, it's difficult for me to talk to you about this because Dad isn't here, and it's not fair that he can't defend himself, but we *have* to talk about it. I suspected Dad was having an affair. That's why we separated before last Christmas."

His mouth forms an O. "I didn't realize," he says eventually. "I thought it was because… he hit you."

"It was, partly. I confronted him, and he denied it and lashed out. That's why I left. He talked me into coming home, but I'd only been back a few days when I was sure he was still seeing someone. We argued about it on the morning of the accident, once you'd left for school. It was a bad argument, and we both said some horrible things to each other. He said why had he driven up to Christchurch to beg me to come home if he was having an affair? And I couldn't answer that. It's haunted me ever since. I thought maybe it was my fault he crashed because he was upset by what I said, and it made him lose concentration." My eyes fill with tears.

Finn's bottom lip trembles. "I should have told you. I'm so sorry."

"No, it's not your fault at all. It's just that I was right, and I feel relieved and angry at the same time. I don't know why he wanted me back. I mean, he wanted you at home, and I guess he thought he wouldn't win custody. But he didn't want me." I stop, fighting emotion.

Finn studies me, eyes blazing. "She wore bright red lipstick," he says. "And when we crashed, her face was covered in glass, and I couldn't tell what was blood and what was lipstick…"

I cover my mouth with a hand. He moves closer to me and puts his arms around my neck, and we hug each other tightly.

"She was horrible," he whispers fiercely. "I hate her, and I hate Dad for having an affair."

I bite my lip hard. "Don't say that. Don't be ruled by hate, sweetheart."

"You're such a good person. He shouldn't have treated you like that."

"Oh Finn, I'm not perfect."

"Alex says you're pretty, so that makes up for it."

I give a half-laugh, half-sob. "I'm so sorry."

"You don't have anything to be sorry for, Mum. I should have told you. Maybe you'd have gone out with Alex earlier if you'd known."

I take a deep, shaky breath, and let it out slowly. "No. I had to wait. It was important. Even if I'd known, I would still have had to grieve. You can be angry with someone and still love them."

"Alex said the same thing. He said it's okay to have mixed feelings about someone."

"He's very wise."

"I like him a lot," he says.

"So do I."

He moves back and looks at me, wiping his eyes. "So is he, like, your boyfriend now?"

"Um… I'm not sure. I think he'd laugh if I called him my boyfriend."

"But you're… you know… dating?"

"Kind of. It's complicated."

"Why?"

"I have no idea. Don't grow up, Finn. Adulting sucks."

"Grandma says he's crazy about you. She said she knows these things."

That makes me smile. "Well, that's nice. I hope she's right." I cup his face. "So are we okay? You've forgiven me?"

"Yeah, I guess. I'm not stupid. I know he probably wants me to like him because he likes you."

I frown. "I don't think so, actually. He told you, didn't he, that he would still be your friend, whatever else happens."

"That's true," he admits.

"And I believe him. I don't think he lies. He said you remind him of himself."

He brightens at that. "Really?"

"Yeah. He said you have the same floppy hair."

Finn laughs and runs his hand through it. When he was younger, he couldn't even be bothered to brush it, but now he has it cut at the barber's regularly, and he styles it every morning. My baby's growing up. I get a lump in my throat at the thought that Alex has promised he'll show him how to shave. Will he still be around when Finn's a teenager and growing hair everywhere and getting moody and having girlfriends of his own?

I guess only time will tell.

*

We have a quiet Christmas Eve, then get up on Christmas morning and open our presents together. Gone are the days when Finn used to wake me up at six—this time he comes out on his crutches at ten a.m. looking bleary-eyed, but he's still as excited as usual to open his presents.

Especially the parcel from Alex. I have no idea what Alex has brought him, and I watch Finn open the present with interest. I smile as he peels off the paper. It's a box of LEGO, aged thirteen plus, so it'll be a challenge for him, but it's a kit that makes a golden retriever puppy that looks exactly like Zelda, and Finn's thrilled with it.

Alex has bought Mum a pair of earrings that are the shape of Pohutukawa flowers, which she adores and announces she's going to wear today.

I open my present, a little nervous. It feels like clothing. Oh jeez, is it sexy underwear or something? Should I open it in front of Finn?

I take off the wrapping to reveal a T-shirt with a slogan. Lips curving, I lift it up and read it. It says 'On the naughty list and I regret nothing.' I laugh and show Mum and Finn, and they both chuckle.

"He understands you well," Mum teases, and I smile.

I retrieve a tray from the kitchen and set Finn up on the sofa so he can start his LEGO. Then Mum and I start collecting the discarded paper, doing our best to fold it for recycling.

"What's Mike up to today?" I ask. "Seeing family?"

But she says, "No, actually. He's having a quiet day on his own, then he's heading to the North Island on Boxing Day to spend some time with his kids."

"He's on his own?" I give her a startled look. "Oh Mum. Why didn't you invite him around?"

She looks embarrassed. "It didn't seem right on Christmas Day. It should be spent with family."

"Aw. Mum, call him and tell him to come."

She hesitates. "He did say he's only having a microwave meal for lunch."

"Oh God! Ring him, now!"

She laughs, flushing. "As long as you're sure."

"I'd love to meet him, and I'm sure Finn would too." He looks up and nods.

"Okay," she says, and she picks up her phone and goes outside. Within a minute, she's back, smiling. "He said yes. I said to come around at one p.m., is that okay?"

"Of course! Let's get going!"

The next few hours are busy as we prepare the Christmas dinner, tidy the house, then shower and change. Mum's nervous, which I think is sweet. I don't know how far their relationship has progressed. As far as I know, they've only met for coffee a few times outside of work.

I feel strange meeting him, although I wouldn't say that to her. I think of my dad, who loved Christmas. Is he somewhere watching over us, wondering what on earth we're doing inviting another man into the house at this time of year? And that makes me think about Lee, and whether he's doing the same. If there is an afterlife, I presume he's watching over his son. He wasn't a great father, but I'm sure he loved Finn, although he was a tough love kind of father, and he didn't show affection the same way Alex does to Finn. Odd, that.

I get the turkey out of the oven to rest it and slide the trays of potatoes, roasted vegetables, and chipolatas wrapped in bacon into the oven. I'm just getting the placemats out when my phone buzzes, announcing a text. I take it out, see Alex's name, and smile.

Alex: *Miss you* <heart> emoji

Me: *Aw. Miss you too! Thank you for your present. I'm wearing it now* <smile> emoji

Alex: *Glad you like it. Seemed appropriate. And thank you for your gift. I love it.*

I painted a picture of Zelda for him—just a small canvas, but I was quite pleased with the likeness.

Me: *Oh I'm so glad you liked it!*

Alex: *It has pride of place on the wall by the front door so you see it as soon as you come in.*

Me: *Aw.* <blush> emoji

Alex: *Are you having a nice Christmas Day?*

Me: *Yes! Mum's friend Mike is coming around for dinner. He was spending the day alone so I said to invite him.*

Alex: *How do you feel about that?*

My lips twist at his astuteness.

Me: *Yeah, a bit odd, I have to admit. Does that make me a small person?*

Alex: *Of course not. I know your dad loved Christmas. It's cool that you asked Mike for your mum, though.*

I flush at his praise. Is it weird that it makes me feel good?

Me: *Thank you.* <smile> emoji

After a beat, he comes back.

Alex: *I'm proud of you.*

Me: <blush> emoji

Alex: *You're a good girl.*

Me: *OMG. Stop it. I'm getting all hot and bothered.*

Alex: *Only a few more days and then you can have a reward.*

Me: *Alex!!!!! I thought you might need a fortnight to recover!*

Alex: *You want me to wait?*

Me: *Noooooooo!*

Alex: *LOL. I was worried for a minute.*

Me: *Do you realize you don't use exclamation marks like normal people?!*

Alex: *Really?*

Me: *Even in your texts you're hard to read!*

Alex: *I'm very easy. Just assume I'm thinking about sex whenever you're around and you'll be spot on.*

Me: *Jesus, will you stop? I'm the color of Rudolph's nose!*

Alex: *My work here is done* <devil> emoji

Me: *Gotta go carve the turkey. Are you a breast or leg man?*

Alex: *Definitely breast.*

Me: *I'll save you a bit* <wink> emoji

Alex: *Aw. Now I'm hot and bothered.*

Me: *LOL. See you soon xxxxxxxx*

Alex: *Have a great day, baby girl x*

I slide the phone into my back pocket, heating through at the memory of him calling me that as he slid inside me. Wandering over to the kitchen window, I stare out, trying to focus on the summer sunshine and not the clouds I can see on the horizon.

This is all so new and exciting and scary. I want to be joyful and live in the moment, and not think negative emotions. I'm Miss Sunshine, aren't I? I'm supposed to be the glass-half-full girl. So why am I focusing on the bit that's half-empty?

I didn't really have to make a choice of whether to get involved with Lee—at the risk of sounding as if I was born in the nineteen-forties, I had to marry him. I wish I was a teenager again, and I had no idea of all the things that could go wrong in a relationship, and in life. When you're older, you realize how vulnerable love makes you. Falling in love is like opening up your ribcage and letting someone else reach in and grab your heart. And I think I am falling in love with him. Actually, I think I fell some time ago, but I just didn't admit it to myself.

I might have known Alex for nine months, but I don't know him well. I don't know what he wants out of a relationship. Does he just want sex? Or something more? And if he does want more, what would that involve? He's clearly ambitious—what if he wants to move to Australia or the States for his work? I wouldn't want Finn to have to move schools. He implied he wants kids, but do I want to go back to nappies and breastfeeding in the middle of the night? Do I want to get involved with someone who's obviously very driven and a workaholic? At the moment it's all new and exciting and he's keen to be with me, but what about after the novelty wears off?

I know that this is what dating is about—getting to know one another, trying each other on for size, and finding out what you want from a relationship. But I'm scared about the process. I'm frightened of falling for him too fast and too heavily, and then discovering I'm in quicksand and I can't get out.

But what's the alternative? I back away from something that has the potential to be amazing because I'm afraid of what might happen? That's cowardly, and I refuse to be a coward.

I need to stop worrying. I'm going to Wellington to spend a few days with him, and hopefully over that time I'll be able to gauge a bit better exactly where he hopes this is going.

The next few days are for family—for Mum, and Finn, and to welcome Mike, because I have a feeling he's going to be around a lot more from now on. Later, while we're watching a movie, I'll let myself daydream about Alex and remember how good yesterday was, but I'm not going to worry about the future, or about where this is going. He likes me, and he wants to be with me, and that's the only important thing right now.

Chapter Nineteen

Alex

A few minutes after ten a.m. on the twenty-eighth, an Uber pulls up out the front of Christchurch airport with Missie, Sandra, and Finn.

I go forward to greet them and help Finn get out, holding his crutches until he's steady, then I turn and pull Missie toward me with one arm. She's wearing cut-down jeans and a pretty white vest today, and she looks young and stunning. I've thought about little else except her since we parted, and I spent most of yesterday talking about her, to the extent that I had to stop myself when I saw Gaby and Sherry exchanging amused glances as I extolled Missie's virtues. I thought I'd exaggerated how gorgeous she is, but seeing her now, standing there before me with her shy smile and big blue eyes, I know I severely underestimated her beauty.

I press my lips to hers for a long smooch. Too late, I forget that I haven't yet kissed her in front of her son, only realizing when she returns the kiss briefly, then stiffens in my arms when I don't release her.

Finn smirks. "You've gone red," he points out to his mother as he lowers himself into his wheelchair.

"Jeez," Missie says, flustered, straightening her top as I release her.

"I'm sorry." I wink at Finn and mouth 'Not really,' and he grins.

"I'll get a trolley," she says, and walks off to retrieve one to cover her embarrassment.

Sandra laughs. "She loves it, really." She accepts my kiss on the cheek. "Thank you so much for taking us to Blenheim."

"Oh, you're welcome."

"Where's Zelda?" Finn asks.

"She's in her crate on the helicopter. She's flown before. She's not super-keen, but she'll be okay. It's kind of your sister to have Zelda," I say to Sandra.

"It's a very dog-friendly place, and she loves Finn to bits so she'll do anything to make him happy."

"Did you have a nice Christmas Day?" I ask. "Missie told me that your friend came for dinner."

"Yes, we had a really good time. We were both nervous to start with," she admits. "It's very odd, dating at our age. Neither of us expected to be doing it, and the thought of meeting each other's families made us both anxious. I honestly didn't think he'd come for dinner, so I was thrilled when he turned up."

"And it went okay?"

She nods and leans forward conspiratorially. "I wasn't sure how Missie would be. Her father loved Christmas, and it must have been hard for her. But you know what she's like—she's such a sweetheart. She made Mike feel so welcome. I love her for that."

"Hmm," I murmur, watching her return with the trolley. It doesn't surprise me that Miss Sunshine was able to hide any reluctance she felt. She has the heart of an angel, even though she doesn't always act like one…

"Don't look at me like that," Missie whispers as we turn to pile on their luggage. "You're giving me goosebumps."

"That's not all I'll be giving you today."

"Alex!"

I chuckle. "I meant a kiss. You've got a dirty mind."

"I know you well enough to know exactly what you meant, and it wasn't a kiss."

"Yeah, all right. Can you blame me, turning up looking practically edible in that outfit."

"What do you mean? It's not like I've got my boobs out or anything."

"More's the pity."

"Alex!"

I laugh. I have a feeling she's going to be scolding me a lot over the next few days. "Come on. The heli's waiting."

I push the trolley and Missie pushes Finn through the airport to the gate that takes us out to the charter flights, and I lead the way over to where my helicopter is waiting for us on the TLOF—the touchdown and lift-off area. "Sorry, Finn called shotgun," I tell the two women. "You'll have to sit with Zelda."

Roy, who works at the airport, loads Finn's chair and their cases in the back while I help the boy into the front seat. Zelda's travel crate is already strapped into one of the back seats, and once Finn is secured, I help Missie and Sandra into a seat on either side of her. I make sure they're both buckled in and give them a set of headphones, close and secure the doors, then run the last checks with Roy before getting in beside Finn.

He's already wearing his headphones, and I put mine on and say to them all, "Ready, guys?" I test their microphones and make sure they're comfortable.

They declare they're all ready. Talking to Finn and showing him what I'm doing as I do it, I open the throttle to increase the speed of the rotor, pull up on the collective, and depress the left foot pedal to counteract the torque as the pitch of the blades changes. When it gets light on its skids, I grip the cyclic and nudge the helicopter forward, and we rise slowly.

"Wow…" Finn's eyes are already alight with excitement, and we're only ten feet off the ground.

His delight grows as I head across Pegasus Bay. Keeping the Southern Alps to our left, I follow the State Highway along the coast, pointing out landmarks as we go. The best bit is when we pass over Kaikoura, the old whaling town. I point out Fyffe House, which is built on a foundation of whalebones, and then, as we pass over the point where the seabed of the Hikurangi Trench rises sharply, we see the flukes of two sperm whales, attracted by the abundance of marine life brought in by the prevailing winds and tides of the area.

We stay over the coast for a bit longer, then as we pass from the Canterbury region into the Marlborough District, I turn inland. We fly over the Awatere River and the northernmost tip of the Kaikoura Ranges, then head across the wide plains of the Marlborough wine region toward the town of Blenheim.

I've already spoken to Missie's uncle, John, and he's directed me to a paddock behind his house that will be suitable to land. Sure enough, as I close on the coordinates, I can see the H he's sprayed on the grass, and I bring the helicopter down on top of it.

They're waiting for us, and after I've switched the vehicle off and the blades have stopped, John and Pippa come up to greet us. I jump down and shake hands with them, and they help Missie and Sandra out while I go around to get Finn. He wants to show them how he can walk with his crutches, so I get them for him and make sure he's steady, then walk beside him, carrying Zelda in her crate, while John and the others bring in their luggage.

"Have you got time to stay for a coffee?" Pippa asks.

"Of course," I say, knowing it's the least I can do after they've agreed to look after Zelda for a few days.

Missie slides her hand into mine. "Are you sure?" she asks. "I know you've got things to organize."

"There's no rush, and I'd love to see the house, it looks gorgeous."

Pippa flushes. "It is nice. I'll show you around if you like."

Missie's lips curve up, and she squeezes my hand, but she doesn't say anything.

As we walk the short distance to the house, John explains how the terroir—the warm, relatively dry summers and cool crisp winters, and the fertile soil—are so good to the Sauvignon Blanc grapes growing in the vineyards to the west of the house. "Our cellar is one of the best in the region," he says proudly. "It's a shame you're flying out or you could have sampled some of our vintages."

"We'll give you a couple of bottles to take with you," Pippa states. Again, Missie squeezes my hand. I think she takes their comments as a gesture of approval.

We pass through the gate into the gardens of the house, and three dogs run up to us—a Dalmatian, a Boxer, and a German Shepherd.

"They're all rescue dogs," John says as Finn bends to fuss them up.

I take Zelda out of her crate and hold her as they come up to sniff her. "She's had her first season and she's been spayed," I explain, letting the dogs explore her and me. "She's coming along pretty well with her training. Finn's been working hard on her recall, haven't you?"

He nods, cheeks flushed with the excitement of the day. "She mostly comes when she's called. She's a good girl."

She's struggling to get down, so I put her on the grass. She stands like a statue for about thirty seconds while the others sniff and nuzzle her, and then all of a sudden she bolts away, tearing around the lawn, the others in hot pursuit. I grin and get up, knowing she's going to love it here.

"You okay?" I say to Finn. He's walked quite a distance on his crutches. "You want a piggyback?"

He laughs and says, "No, I'm good," but I can see he's flagging.

"Come on." John puts an arm around him. "Let's get you sitting down. We've got some homemade lemonade, and Pippa's made some mince pies this morning. Teddy and Iris will be here soon." I know they're John and Pippa's grandchildren, and Teddy is only a year younger than Finn, so he'll have someone to play with.

We approach the house, entering a large area with flagstones and an impressive wrought-iron table and chairs. Vines grow up the wooden trellises, and ripening grapes hanging in bunches above our heads. Missie helps Finn into a chair, and Pippa makes him comfortable with cushions and pours him a drink.

John hangs back, and I slow with him, seeing that he wants to talk. "We really appreciate how you've helped him," he says. "There was a point when we were all convinced he wouldn't walk again. But she never gave up." He gives Missie a fond glance. "Right from the start, she was determined to find a solution. She was so excited when she heard about your project, and terrified you wouldn't accept her."

"That was never an issue." I watch her take Finn's crutches as he lowers into a chair, and she kisses the top of his head. "Her commitment was obvious from the start. It's clear she's devoted to him. I was only worried she'd find it hard coping on her own, but she's capable and strong. I admire her."

"She's done better since that arsehole died," John says bitterly, gesturing down. "I hope that bastard's burning right now."

Surprised at his vehemence, I can't stop my eyebrows rising. "You didn't like Lee?"

"He was a cocky son of a bitch who always thought he was too good for her, which is ridiculous, because she was worth a hundred of him." He looks at me then and claps me on the shoulder. "Look after her. She's very precious to us."

"I will." I watch her bend down from behind Finn's chair to slide her arms around his neck and hug him, and he laughs.

John gives me an appraising look, then smiles. "You're fond of the boy." It's a statement, not a question.

"I am. He's determined and resilient, and he's made excellent progress."

"Mainly because of you, from what I hear."

"It's all his own doing. He's worked very hard."

John nods. "You're a good lad. I'm glad Missie's found you."

Amused to be called a lad, but touched by his words, I put Zelda's crate near the back door, then go inside with Pippa as she gestures for me to follow her. "Come on," she says, "I'll show you around."

The house is large and sprawling, on two levels and mostly open plan. It's been modernized, but I can see its nineteenth-century heritage in its traditional sash and leadlight windows, the wraparound balconies, and the log fires. The kitchen is huge but looks well-loved, and the dining area has an indoor-outdoor flow to the paved area. The living room is big but comfortable—numerous throws and cushions bring color to the suite, there are dog beds and toys everywhere, and on the walls, interesting works of art mingle with grandchildren's paintings.

There are six bedrooms and three bathrooms. Finn's room—obvious from the LEGO and books they keep for him there—is on the ground floor. I think it was probably a study that they've converted for him so he doesn't have to use the stairs. They're clearly well off, which surprises me, as Missie and Sandra's home is small and nowhere near as luxurious as this. I guess John was the one with the money. I'd be surprised if they haven't offered to help Missie out with Finn's care, but I'm pretty sure that money is tight for her, even with the insurance money, as I doubt she's spent much of it on herself. I know people who don't have money are often too proud to accept it when it's offered. I'll have to work on that with her.

In the upper bedroom, Pippa and I stand by the window looking over the glorious view across the vineyards, the cellar, and winery.

"Nice place," I say.

She nods. Then she turns to me. "I wanted to say thank you. For everything you've done for Missie and Finn."

"It's my pleasure. He's worked hard."

"Mm." She slides her hands into the pockets of her trousers and studies her feet for a moment. She's very like Sandra, a few years older, with gray hair gathered in a loose bun at the nape of her neck, and blue eyes a shade lighter than Missie's stormy ones. "I know it's not my place," she says, "but I love my niece and Finn a lot. And I need to make sure you're aware of just how vulnerable they both are."

So that's why she brought me up here. "I understand."

"You obviously care for them both, and John and I, and Sandra, are so grateful for everything you've done. But..." She hesitates, then speaks quickly, as if she's worried she won't be able to get the words out. "They both like you. I mean, *really* like you. And I just want to say, I know it's early days, and the last thing a guy wants is a conversation about Where This Is Going, but if you're not planning to hang around for long, it might be better for you to make the break earlier rather than later. Because I think they could both fall heavily for you, in their own ways."

I meet her eyes. She flushes a little, but holds my gaze, lifting her chin. She's really concerned about them, and I think it's taken a lot of courage for her to speak up. I wonder whether she's voicing Sandra's fears for her? The two of them seem close, and I have a feeling Sandra wouldn't want to say that to me directly.

"I know what you're saying," I tell her. "And you don't have to worry. I'm not going anywhere."

She frowns. "It's just that they've been through so much, and you seem very nice, but a successful guy like you must have a busy lifestyle, and perhaps in the future you'll—"

"Pippa, I'm going to marry the girl. I'd have proposed already, but we've only been on one date, kinda, so I figured she'd probably say no. But it's on the cards, just so you know."

She stares at me. "Propose? Are you serious?"

"Yeah. I know it's only been one date, but I've been in love with her for a year, so…"

"I thought you only met at the end of March."

"I was rounding up."

A smile slowly spreads across her face. "You really like her that much?"

"I'm crazy about her."

Her smile turns mischievous, making her look not unlike her niece. "She's a lucky girl."

"I'm the lucky one. She even comes with a ready-made family. How cool is that?"

Her eyes glisten then. "You've been so good to Finn."

"Well, we're not there yet. But I hope that next year he'll be getting out of my helicopter and walking unaided over to your house. That's my goal."

"You're very driven, aren't you?"

"I know what I want, and I do my best to get it, if that's what you mean."

She chuckles. "I can see why she likes you. I'm half in love with you myself."

I give a short laugh. "Don't say anything to her about all this, okay? All in good time."

"Sure. Come on. I'm sure you want to get on your way to Wellington. You're the best man at the wedding, right?"

"Yeah. I've got a couple of events planned." I tell her about them as we walk back downstairs to join the others, and she laughs out loud, prompting everyone to look over as we approach.

"What's so funny?" Missie asks curiously.

"It's a secret," she teases. "Let's just say I think you're in for a show over the next few days."

I sit beside Missie and accept the glass of lemonade she hands to me. "I'm in charge of entertainment," I explain.

"Oh God," she says. "I'm guessing it's all highly organized. He has OCD," she tells the others.

"I have *mild* OCD. I like things to be orderly."

She winks at them. "OCD," she mouths.

I meet her eyes and raise an eyebrow, and she gives an impish giggle.

"I think she's still on your naughty list," Finn says, and everyone laughs.

We finish our drinks while we talk, and then eventually Missie says we should get going. She gives everyone a kiss goodbye, and I hug Finn and shake hands with the others.

"Thank you so much for looking after Zelda," I say. The puppy is currently flaked out on the flagstones, knackered from running like a maniac around the house with the other dogs. "I hope she behaves."

"She's beautiful," Pippa says, "I think we'll have a lot of fun together."

John brings us a whole crate of wine for us to take to the wedding, which I'm very touched about. We wave goodbye, and then I take the crate, and Missie and I walk across the lawn and through the gate to the paddock where the helicopter is waiting.

It's a gorgeous day, not a cloud in the sky, which is a brilliant blue. It's *hot as*, and apparently the weather is going to stick around for the next few days, which is terrific news for Damon's wedding.

I secure the crate in the back, and we get in the helicopter, Missie in the front seat this time, and don our headphones. I do all the safety checks, and then eventually I lift the machine into the air, and we head northeast across the Cook Strait to Wellington.

"How are you doing?" I ask Missie.

She's been looking at the view of the coastline and the meeting of the Tasman Sea and the Pacific Ocean, but now she looks across at me. She's wearing sunglasses so I can't see her eyes.

"I'm good," she says. "Thank you for whatever you said to Pippa."

"What do you mean?"

"She thinks the sun shines out of your backside."

"There's a joke there about Uranus…"

"I mean it," she protests. "You've completely won her over. Of course. You're so charming."

I wonder briefly whether she's comparing me to her late husband. She told me that Lee charmed her and talked her into bed. "I hope you don't think I was being insincere."

"Aw, Alex. Of course not. There's just something about you that makes women go gooey."

"Are you including yourself?"

"Definitely. I turn to melted caramel whenever you're around."

"That's a nice thing to say."

"I used to think you were so serious and stern, but you're not. You have an exoskeleton yourself, don't you? A protective shell. But inside you're a real softie."

"If you say so."

"I do." She surveys me for a moment, while I check the instruments and start the descent into Wellington. "You told me that you've got more cynical as life has thrown things at you. Are you ready to tell me what yet?"

I head the helicopter across the hills of Wellington toward the suburb of Brooklyn. "Maybe later. When we're on our own."

"Okay." She looks down. "Where are we going?"

"To Damon's parents' place. I have to warn you—it's palatial. He and Belle are getting married in church, but everything else is being held at Brooklyn Heights."

"We're staying there?"

"Yeah. He, Saxon, and Kip all had separate apartments while they were in their late teens. We're staying in Kip's."

"Where's he staying?"

"Oh, he and Saxon don't live far away so they'll just Uber home at the end of the day. They're good guys, you'll like them. You'll get to meet everyone over the next few days—practically everyone I know. Lots of people flying in from all over the country. Damon's cousin, Titus, works in Auckland with a group of guys we both know well, and they're coming down too."

"I'm looking forward to meeting everyone."

"Missie, something I should have warned you about is that I want Damon and Belle's big day to go as smoothly as possible, so all joking aside, my organizational skills have gone into overdrive."

She smiles. "That's okay, I guessed you'd be pretty busy. I'm happy to stay in the apartment, or I can help you if you like."

"Oh." I didn't expect that. "Yeah, that would be cool. I do have one thing I'd like to ask."

"Fire away."

"I know you haven't met her yet, and she has her bridesmaids and friends looking after her. But keep an eye on Belle for me, would you? And let me know if you think there's anything I should know or that I can do for her."

"Of course." She waits as I clear my descent with Wellington Tower and head the helicopter to the landing spot at the top of the steep hill on which Brooklyn Heights is built. Then she says, "Did it bother you when you found out that your best mate was seeing your sister?"

"When she was younger, I always told my mates—including Damon—that she was off limits. But actually I was relieved when I found out they were dating. I didn't like her ex, and she needs someone... understanding. I knew Damon would always treat her right."

I don't elaborate, and Missie doesn't push it. Instead, she watches as I lower the helicopter onto the H-pad and turn off the engine.

Chapter Twenty

Missie

Oh my God. He said it was palatial, but I just thought he meant a bigger version of Aunt Pippa's place.

The mansion—because that's the only word for it—looks as if it's on at least three stories and possibly more. I can see the main house with a terrace at the top, another huge terrace above an enormous pool beneath it, and further down what I think must be the separate apartments Alex mentioned. The whole place is surrounded by a botanical garden with native plants and waterfalls, and a cable car that links all the terraces and decks.

The heli-pad is right at the top of the hill, and as we get out, we have a spectacular view of the whole property, the city, and across Lyall Bay to what I think is Petone on the other side.

"Holy shit." I stand there, stunned, mouth agape.

Alex chuckles as he goes around to collect our bags. "Pretty impressive, eh?"

"I didn't realize we had a royal family in New Zealand."

"It's one of the biggest properties in the city. If not the whole of the country."

"Damon's parents must be really well off!"

"His dad invented a computer graphics card that was better than anything else around at the time. It made him an absolute fortune."

I knew that Alex was wealthy, mainly through his actor mother, as well as through the patents for the medical equipment he's invented. And I knew Damon and his brothers were rich. But it's only now that I realize just what people I'm mixing with.

"Does everyone you know have money?" I ask, taking my case from him.

"Mostly."

"Oh God, I'm so nervous."

"Aw. Don't be. You'll know some of the people there, anyway. James, Henry, Gaby, Tyson, Aroha, and Juliette, probably…"

"Probably?"

He hesitates. "I don't think things are good between Juliette and Cam."

"What happened with her and Henry on the twenty-first?"

"I don't know. Neither of them will talk about it." He shoulders his bag and slings his suit carrier over the same shoulder. Then he takes my hand with his spare.

"What about the guys from Auckland?" I ask as we walk down the path. "What do they do?"

"Mack invented a supercomputer. He's like Einstein but with better hair. Huxley owns a business club—he's a financial whizz. Titus—Damon's cousin—is into Artificial Intelligence, and he's made major breakthroughs in IVF with it."

"Jesus."

"Missie, don't worry, all their partners are really nice. You're going to fit in great. Come on. Let's go and meet everyone."

We start walking down the steps toward the house. My mouth has gone dry. "I should have worn something smarter. I thought I was going to be able to change first."

"Look at me," he says, "I'm hardly wearing a suit."

But his chinos and shirt look expensive, he's styled his hair this morning, and he practically oozes wealth and sophistication. I'm a primary-school teacher with cut-down jeans that still bear the glitter from making Christmas decorations with the kids on the last day of term. He's told me that a couple of the wives here have babies—I have an eleven-year-old son. Even though I'm only twenty-eight, I'm sure I must be ten years older than what I'm convinced most of these girls are going to be. I can't believe that all of these rich men are like Alex, who for some crazy reason is interested in me—surely most of them will have married young models? What on earth will we have in common?

He leads me down a neat pathway to a driveway and a car park—Jesus, this house has its own car park. It's full of cars. Half a dozen young men and women dressed in white shirts, black trousers, and silver waistcoats are either parking the cars or carrying luggage down to the house.

"Are they staff?" I ask.

"Yeah. They hired a wedding company, and there'll be a lot of staff around for the next few days, waiting and whatnot."

One of them, a pretty young woman with shiny blonde hair in a ponytail, approaches with a smile and says, "Morning, sir, ma'am. Are you here for the wedding?"

"Yes," Alex says, "Alex Winters and Missie Macbeth. I'm the best man, and we're staying in Kip's apartment."

"Oh, of course, nice to meet you both. Would you like to go straight to the apartment? Or shall we take your bags down so you can join the others on the terrace?"

"That would be great," he says, making my heart skip a beat. She beckons one of the guys over, and the two of them take our bags.

"Thank you," I say, and they both smile before heading off to the cable car.

"Don't panic," Alex tells me as we head along the path toward the house. "You look amazing."

"I'm so nervous. I hope I don't say something stupid. Do I look okay?"

He stops walking. I look at him in surprise, my eyes widening as he pulls me toward him. Other guests are pulling up in cars, and staff wandering around, including two gardeners brushing the paths and tidying the hedges, but Alex ignores them. He lifts my sunglasses onto the top of my head, takes my face in his hands, and lowers his lips to mine.

My face flushes, but I don't fight him, because he's a hell of a kisser, and I know he's trying to reassure me. I close my eyes against the bright sunshine and concentrate on the feel of his lips on mine, the warmth of his hands on my skin. He kisses me gently, taking his time, and I sigh, my panic dying down a little.

He lifts his head, and his eyes hold a sultry heat. "Stop. Worrying," he instructs.

"Yes, Dad."

His expression turns wry as he takes my hand, and we start walking again. "And don't call me that or I'll be dragging you down to the apartment and we'll never get to meet anyone."

My eyebrows rise. "You like being called Daddy?"

"No…"

"Alex…"

"Stop it," he scolds, and nods at one of the guys in silver waistcoats who directs us around the house toward the terrace below it.

There's no more time to tease him, because the scene opens out before me. The top terrace is a wide, open space with a neat lawn. It's dotted with attractive mosaic floors with ocean-inspired patterns that are topped with round tables and elegant white chairs. A canopy of white fairy lights covers the whole terrace, and there's a huge Christmas tree near the house that's also covered with outdoor solar lights.

The place is full of people—old and young, sipping drinks, eating from the trays of canapes the waiters are taking around, and talking and laughing. There are kids and babies and dogs, and it's a beautiful, chaotic scene that immediately makes me feel better, because although I know I'm going to have to talk to people, it's not the same having half a dozen people staring at you across a dinner table, asking questions.

"Alex!" Damon spots him immediately and crosses the lawn to come and greet him. Like Alex, he's dressed casually but also manages to look wealthy and sophisticated in a light-pink shirt and smart stone-colored chinos. "I saw the helicopter come in and thought it must be you. Good to see you." The two of them exchange a bearhug.

He turns to me then and smiles. "And you came! I'm so glad." He gives me a kiss on the cheek. "Where's Belle—she's been so looking forward to meeting you. Belle!" He calls to a pretty young woman with brown hair who's wearing white jeans and a blue top, and beckons as she looks over. Oh, so this is Alex's youngest sister? She's not unlike Gaby, a little shorter, a tad younger and prettier. She spots us, and her face lights up.

"Alex!" She runs across and throws her arms around him, then moves back and beams a big smile at me. "You must be Missie! I've heard so much about you, and I've been dying to meet you."

"Oh dear." I smile back as we shake hands. "All good things, I hope."

"Oh God, yes, Alex doesn't stop talking about you. It's all 'Missie this' and 'Missie that.'"

"Belle," he says, exasperated.

"Well, you do! It's great to meet you at last."

"This is such a beautiful place to have a wedding," I tell them.

"Oh, it's like a fairytale palace," she says. "I was totally intimidated when I came here. Still am, really. But Mae and Neal have organized

everything. They're Damon's parents. Come on, let me introduce you."
She slides her arm through mine. "We're going to be best friends," she
states.

"She doesn't normally talk quite this much," Alex tells me. "You
need to cut back on the coffee, Belle."

She pokes her tongue out at him and leads me away, over to an
older couple who are standing talking to some of the staff. "Mae,
Neal," she says, "I want you to meet Missie. She's Alex's girlfriend."

I glance at him as he follows us, wondering if he minds me having
that label when we've only had one date, but he just shakes hands with
Neal while Mae kisses my cheek.

"So pleased to meet you," Mae says. She's in her fifties, but looks
younger, with blonde, slightly wavy hair, and blue eyes several shades
lighter and more dazzling than mine.

"And Alex, I'm so glad you're here. He's been invaluable," she says
to me, "helping to get everything organized. I don't know what I
would've done without him." She gives him a hug and teases, "Who'd
have thought that shy twelve-year-old nerd would have grown up into
such a gorgeous man?"

"Still a nerd, though," Damon says.

"Damn straight," Alex says. "Forever and always."

She grins. "How's your mum?"

He slides his hands into his pockets. "All right."

"And your dad, and Sherry?"

"They're good, thanks."

"I'm glad. Neal, get them a drink, would you?"

Damon's dad flags down a passing waiter, takes two glasses of
champagne from him, and passes them to us.

"Thank you," I say. "You have a beautiful home."

"It's very useful on days like this," Mae says. "When my baby boy
is getting married."

Damon rolls his eyes, and Belle and I chuckle. "Come on," Damon
says. "Lots of people to introduce you to."

Leaving them behind, he leads us through the guests to a table
looking out over the view of the city. It's full of people, some sitting
down, others standing and talking. Most of them look to be around
our age. I'm relieved to recognize some of the faces, and spend a
moment saying hello to Juliette, Henry, James, Gaby, Tyson, and
Aroha, who I remember from the quiz night.

"Let me introduce you to everyone else," Damon says. "Everyone, this is Alex's girlfriend, Missie. Missie, these guys are all down from Auckland, you've probably heard Alex talk about them all—that's Mack, and his wife Sidnie, my cousin Titus and his wife Heidi, Victoria and her wife Evie, and that's Huxley and Elizabeth with little Teddy boy." I say hello to them as they all wave. "And these are my brothers," he says. "Kip and his wife, Alice, and Saxon and his wife, Catie. And their boys are Liam and Aidan."

Alex mentioned that Damon's brothers were identical twins, but I'm still oddly surprised at how alike they are. They're not unlike their younger brother—Damon's a couple of inches taller and a few pounds heavier.

"Sorry, which is which?" I ask as they come to shake hands with me.

"Kip wears glasses," Damon states.

"Until they decide to play a trick on you and swap," Alice says, and Catie nods as if to say That happened to me, too!

I chuckle and shake Kip's hand, say, "Pleased to meet you," then turn to Saxon and do the same.

"Hey, Missie," Saxon says. He's standing, bouncing one of his boys, who has bright red hair, the same as Catie's. He glances at Alex, then gives me an appraising look. "You seem like a nice girl. So why are you with this miserable old fart, then?"

"Saxon," Catie scolds as everyone laughs.

"He's got a point," Alex says, giving me a rueful look.

Wanting to defend Alex, because he's not really grumpy deep down, I say mischievously, "Because he's really, really good in the sack."

There's a moment of stunned silence, during which Alex stares at me, his eyebrows slowly rising. Then everyone bursts out laughing, and his lips slowly curve up.

"That's the first time I think I've ever seen you speechless," Saxon tells him. "I like her already."

"Thank you for that," Alex says to me, amused.

"See, why can't you say nice things like that about me?" Huxley says to his wife.

"I would, if you didn't fall asleep during sex," Elizabeth retorts, and everyone laughs and goes ooooh!

"I only did that once," he points out sarcastically.

"Twice," she says. He thinks about it, obviously realizes she's right, and pulls an 'eek' face at everyone.

"Huxley! You did *not* fall asleep while making love with your wife," Sidnie scolds.

"In my defense," he states, "Elizabeth was due to get up at five a.m. for a Zoom call with Titus, so—"

"Wait," Titus says, "how did it end up being my fault? I wasn't even in the country!"

Huxley gives a short laugh and continues, "So I took the night shift, and Teddy decided at two a.m. that there were far more amusing things to do than go to sleep, so I was awake for four hours. And then Elizabeth came back to bed just as I was dozing off at six and decided I deserved a prize for my parenting skills, and it was so pleasant and relaxing that I just kind of dozed off..."

"Nice to know my technique is so great that it sends you to sleep," Elizabeth says tartly.

He pulls her onto his lap and whispers something in her ear, and she pushes him, then giggles and says, "Naughty boy."

"You're lucky," Aroha says out of the blue. "Not everyone has an excuse as good as that."

Everyone looks at her, puzzled for a moment. Then Juliette's eyes widen, and she stares at James, who's wincing with embarrassment. "James!" she declares. "Please tell me she's not talking about you."

Henry and Alex laugh, and Tyson says, "Jesus, bro. Seriously?"

James gives Aroha a wry look. "Thank you," he says, half-amused, half-sarcastic.

"What's this?" Elizabeth asks. "When did this happen?" And the others sit up at the news that something's going on between James and Aroha.

James looks at Aroha and says, "Go on then. Clearly the world needs to know what an idiot I am." His eyes challenge her to confess it all.

She sees he's annoyed, though, and drops her gaze, maybe regretting her outburst.

James studies her for a moment. He's obviously embarrassed that she's told everyone, but I know he likes her, and I'm sure he regrets what happened. His lips curve up.

"I'd had a lot to drink," he says, "and it was very late. I took her home, promised her the best sex of her life, then fell asleep before I could get her knickers off. It wasn't my greatest moment."

Everyone laughs, pleased he decided to make fun of himself rather than be offended.

"So what's the plan this afternoon?" I ask, smiling at Titus as he gets up and gestures for me to take his seat. Old fashioned, but very sweet.

"Paintball for the guys this afternoon," Alex says.

"Ooh. Who's likely to win?"

"Mack, probably," Huxley says. "He's a sprinter. Broke all sorts of records before he got old and past it."

"That's true, unfortunately." Mack pats his stomach. "I'm getting a paunch."

"No, you're not," Sidnie scoffs. "But you do groan when you get up out of a chair now."

"I do that, too," Huxley says, and a couple of the others nod.

"You realize none of us is going to be able to walk after the game," Titus points out.

"Jesus," Damon says, "you bunch of old farts."

"You're only twenty-seven," Saxon states. "Some of us are heading toward thirty at a rate of knots."

"For God's sake, just bring him back in one piece," Belle says.

"Especially his family jewels," Elizabeth states. "You don't want to spend your wedding night icing his nuts."

"Some people are into that," Huxley tells her as everyone laughs.

"Don't worry, I'll keep an eye on him," Alex promises his sister.

She blows a raspberry. "That's what you said when you were both eighteen, remember?"

"Ah, jeez," Alex says.

I grin. "What happened?"

"It was after they graduated from high school," Belle explains. "A group of them decided it would be a good idea to go camping in one of those Department of Conservation lodges, even though they were both supposed to be going on vacation the next day with Damon's family. They all got drunk, Alex passed out in a bush behind the lodge and nobody knew where he was for twelve hours, and Damon fell in the river and got swept over the waterfall."

"Don't exaggerate," Alex says as everyone chuckles, "it was only four hours."

"And the 'waterfall' was six feet high, and I was perfectly fine," Damon adds.

"You caught a chill and had to stay in bed for three days," Saxon reminds him.

"That was just Mum being over-zealous," Damon says. He grabs Belle's hand. "Come on. We need to mingle." He leads her away, taking the opportunity to kiss her.

"They seem very happy," I comment with a smile.

"I never thought he'd be the sort to enjoy all the pomp and ceremony," Kip says, "but he's having the time of his life."

"Talking of which," Mack says, "what's this I hear about you getting married? That was sneaky."

"We didn't want a big do," Kip states, putting his arm around Alice. "So we eloped."

"It was lovely," Alice states, sliding her arms around his waist. "We went up to Lake Tekapo. It was the middle of winter, and at night we could see the southern lights. So romantic."

"We did the same," Heidi admits. "I didn't want a big white wedding, so Titus and I went up on Dartmoor and tied the knot, just us and a couple of friends as witnesses."

"So what's the plan for the next couple of days?" Sidnie asks.

"Stag night and hen party today," Alex says.

"Lots of fun things planned," Alice says to me with a smile. "But nothing too alarming, no strippers or anything. Both of them just wanted to be with their friends and family."

"Are you sure Belle would want me to come?" I ask, surprised.

"Of course!" all the girls say. "You're her sister-in-law," Alice points out.

I give Alex an embarrassed look, but he's talking to Henry and James and doesn't appear to have heard her.

"We've only had one date," I say to the others, not wanting anyone to think I'm overstepping the mark. "And now I realize I've already told you he's great in bed, which means I put out on the first date. How embarrassing."

"Took me about twenty-four hours," Sidnie says cheerfully, and Mack grins and nods his agreement. "And anyway," she adds, "Alex looks at you as if you're prime steak, so I'm not surprised."

"Three hours after meeting Kip on Tinder," Alice says. "And I second Sidnie's comment—he obviously sees you as juicy medium-rare."

"One hour after meeting Saxon," Catie says. "He knocked me up on our one-night stand. I third the comment, with blue-cheese sauce."

"And truffle fries," Elizabeth finishes. "He's crazy about you, girl. Go on. Say you'll come. We all want to get to know you better."

"Okay," I say, touched that they seem to want me there, and flustered that they all think Alex is into me.

"What was that about steak?" Alex asks, leaning on my chair behind me.

"Nothing," Sidnie says, fluttering her eyelashes at him, and the rest of us giggle.

"This is the kind of thing we've got to get used to over the next few days," Mack says. "They're totally going to gang up on us."

"I'll cope." Alex plants a kiss on the point where my neck meets my shoulder, and I shiver.

Elizabeth chuckles and changes the subject, but Alex kisses up to my ear and murmurs, "I haven't forgotten about that compliment you gave me."

I turn my head to look up at him. "Surely I don't deserve punishment for that?"

"No, it was the nicest thing anyone's ever said about me. It definitely deserves a reward."

"What kind? Dinner? A bottle of champagne?"

He waits for a moment, his breath warming my ear. "How about I go down on you and take as long as I can to make you come real slow," he whispers.

I blink. "I feel a bit dizzy. I think it's the sun."

He chuckles and gives me a quick kiss on the lips. "Soon as we get to the apartment. Just so you know."

Ooh.

He straightens, and the conversation moves on, but I'm filled with a glow now that's not going away anytime soon. This guy only has to say half a dozen words and I turn to mush.

Now that's a serious superpower. All he needs is a cape and tights, and he'd be more than a match for Superman.

Chapter Twenty-One

Alex

More guests arrive throughout the morning, and we spend a pleasant hour or so wandering around, talking to Damon's friends and family, many of whom I remember from childhood. At twelve-thirty Mae announces lunch is ready, and we take a plate and help ourselves to the amazing spread laid out on tables in front of the house.

"You know so many people," Missie comments as we pause to get a cup of coffee from the barista working in the kitchen.

"I spent a lot of time here," I tell her. "Damon and I went to the same school, and the atmosphere wasn't always great at home, so I often stayed over. When I was eighteen, my folks divorced. Kait moved to LA, and my dad went back to Christchurch, where he was from. I'd applied and got in at Vic uni, though, so Damon suggested I stay here with him. We shared his apartment for a couple of years."

"Oh, I didn't realize that." She accepts her coffee, and we walk over to an empty table to eat our lunch. It's slightly tucked away, at the edge of the garden, in the shade of a large palm tree.

The food is magnificent—a dozen different salads, homemade breads, meat and vegetarian dishes, lots of fish and seafood. We tuck in, talking about all sorts of things, and we've nearly finished eating when she says, "So why didn't you stay here when you graduated? Why return to Christchurch?"

I poke at some of the potato salad on my plate with a fork, my appetite disappearing.

"You don't have to tell me," she says. "I'm sorry, I didn't mean to pry."

"It's okay. I was going to tell you at some point. It might as well be now."

She puts her hand on mine. "Are you sure? I don't want to make you sad on such a beautiful day."

I look across the terrace. Neal is a big muso and loves all types of music. It was always playing whenever I was here. Today, he's chosen a playlist of love songs. At the moment, Dinah Washington is singing *What a Difference a Day Makes*. In the center of the terrace, everyone has moved back to leave a space, and in the middle of it Belle is dancing with Damon, her arms around his neck. They're moving slowly, talking and laughing, but they both look so happy that my throat tightens.

Missie's right—it's a beautiful day, and nobody should be sad at weddings. And yet, for some reason, I know it's the right time to tell her.

"It happened when I was eighteen," I begin. "Gaby was fifteen, and Belle was twelve. Kait and Dad hadn't been getting on for a while. Kait was never an easy person to live with. She suffered from depression, she was moody, and a drama queen. I don't mean to sound mean, but I guess it was because she was an actor, and there was always some kind of drama going on, when she wasn't away filming."

Missie's hand tightens on mine, giving me the confidence to go on.

"They argued a lot," I continue. "Blazing rows. If we were there, Gaby and I would take Belle out for an ice cream or something, just to get her out of the house. I was in the last year of secondary school. I hated the atmosphere, and although I felt bad leaving the girls, I slept over here as often as I could. One of those times, I woke the next morning to a text from Gaby to say that Kait had walked out."

"That must have been a shock," Missie says.

"It was a shock, but not a surprise, if that makes sense? We knew things were bad. It was only this year though that I found out Dad had been having an affair for six months with Sherry before Kait moved out."

"That's your stepmother?"

"Yeah. I didn't know—Kait told Belle at Gaby's wedding earlier this year. A guy called Tom had been working on one of Kait's movie sets here in New Zealand, and he'd apparently made a pass at her a few months before, but she'd turned him down. When she found out about Sherry, though, she went straight to him and moved in with him."

"On the rebound?"

"Yeah, I'm sure it was to punish Dad, although I think he was just relieved to see the back of her." I sigh. "I'm being harsh. She had genuine feelings for Tom, I know that. She loved him, which just makes the whole thing so much worse."

Missie frowns. "I'm guessing that's not the end of the story."

"Not by a long shot, no. Dad moved back to Christchurch to be with Sherry. Gaby and Belle went with him. But they used to fly up and stay with Kait and Tom most weekends. Mae and Neal suggested I stay with Damon so I had some consistency. I was more than happy to do that. I was about to take my Level Three exams, and we were both working hard. So I stayed here. I didn't see much of Gaby and Belle for the rest of that year. I was angry with Kait, but I hoped she might settle down a bit now she had Tom. She used to walk all over Dad, but Tom stood up to her more, and I thought that would be good for her."

Missie's blue eyes study mine. "What happened?" she asks softly.

"Just under a year after Kait and Dad broke up, I'd finished my exams, and I was on a rare visit down to Christchurch, staying with Dad and Sherry for a few days over Christmas. It was Boxing Day, and the girls were up with Kait and Tom. We were halfway through a movie—it was *Mission Impossible*. I'll never forget it. An Uber pulled up outside the house, and Sherry went to the window and said it was Kait with the girls. They came in. Kait was white as a sheet and both the girls were crying."

I run a hand over my face, still torn up over the memory. "Kait didn't say hello or even take off her coat. She just blurted out that Tom had been sexually abusing Belle."

Missie covers her mouth. "Oh, no…"

"Apparently it had been going on all year, from when Belle and Gaby started staying with them. To her credit, when Belle finally told her, Kait walked out with the girls, went to the airport, and got on the first plane to Christchurch—she didn't stop to talk to Tom. She brought them straight to Dad."

"What did he say?"

"He just started shaking. He was so angry that he was upset, you know? Belle saw it and started crying and said, 'I'm sorry, Daddy,' and he broke down in tears. It was the only time I've ever seen him cry."

We sit in silence for a minute or so while I fight with the familiar hollowness inside me that I always get when I think about that day. Gradually, the sunshine, the music, the conversation and laughter, and the way Missie is stroking my palm with her thumb banishes the shadows, and my heartbeat returns to normal.

"What happened then?" she asks eventually.

I clear my throat. "Dad rang the police, and they came around and took statements. Tom was arrested. They found out that he'd also abused girls at the local sports center, where he worked part-time. He went to prison for ten years. He was released this year on parole."

"Oh, shit. Does Belle know?"

"No. Damon does. He didn't know what had happened at the time, but when they started dating and I realized she hadn't told him, I did. She wasn't very happy with me about that, but I didn't care. I thought he deserved to know. I wanted him to be able to protect her if he needed to."

"Do you know where Tom is now?"

"I know where he is every minute of every day. Damon and I hired a security firm to make sure someone is always following him."

Her eyebrows rise. "Seriously? Is that legal?"

I purse my lips. "Maybe I shouldn't have told you that."

We study each other for a moment. Then her lips curve up.

"He won't do it again," I say vehemently. "I'll make sure of that. And I'll know if he comes within a mile of Belle."

"Good," she says. "I'm glad."

I blow out a breath and run my hand through my hair. "Both Damon and I have a problem with guilt. Damon was involved in an accident in a sea cave when he was young—one of his cousins died, and his other cousin, Kennedy, lost her arm. He has survivor's guilt and PTSD and fuck knows what else. Now he's president of the Women's Refuge here in Wellington."

"Oh wow, I didn't know that."

"But he still feels guilty. And I..." I hesitate. "It's why I eventually moved back to Christchurch when I graduated, to spend more time with Belle. Which was dumb really, because when she was eighteen she decided to go to university here in Wellington. Did you know she's a qualified lawyer?"

"No!"

"I don't think she's going to practice, although she is going to help the women at the Refuge with legal advice. Anyway, I was able to spend a few years with her, but it never got rid of the guilt. If I'd been around more, maybe I would have seen what was happening, or even been able to stop it before it began. But I was selfish, and only concerned with my own happiness. And I'll never forgive myself for that."

"Oh, Alex. You were eighteen. You were practically still a child yourself."

"I could legally drink, get married, vote, and fight in battle. I wasn't a child."

She cups my face. "It wasn't your fault. Or your mum's, or your dad's, and certainly not Belle's. It was Tom's fault, and he's the only one who needs to bear any responsibility."

I turn my head and kiss her palm. I don't agree, but I'm not going to argue with her.

"Poor Belle," she says, lowering her hand. "Do you think she's been able to put it behind her?"

"Yes, I do, and Damon has helped a lot with that. She's never talked a lot about it, but I think she's had trouble… you know… with men, a bit. Maybe that's why she didn't tell him initially, and perhaps that helped, because he didn't have to take it into account when they were together. I know she idolizes him, and he worships her, which is sweet."

She wrinkles her nose at me. "Alex Winters, saying something is sweet. I didn't think I'd ever see the day."

I lean forward. I love that she listened to my story with patience and kindness. "Maybe it's time we retired to the apartment for a bit," I murmur. "You know, to have a rest before the game."

"Is that in air quotes? 'Rest'?"

"Maybe."

Her eyes glow. "Come on, then."

We rise from the table, and our plates are immediately whisked away by one of the waiters. We thread through the guests and spot Damon standing talking to a couple of his older relatives, over by the cable car. We wait until he spots us, and he excuses himself with a smile and comes over.

"We're just going to the apartment for a rest before the game," I say.

"Sure," he replies. "See you at three."

"Are you having a nice time?" Missie asks him.

"I'm having a fabulous time, and so's my fiancée. She really is the Belle of the ball." We both chuckle, and he grins. "She's looking forward to her hen night," he adds. "She's so glad you're going, Missie. She said she's looking forward to telling you all Alex's dark secrets."

"I have so many," I say.

"She did mention that she's found photos of when we were all in the band," Damon states.

Missie's eyebrows shoot up. "You were in a band?"

"Yeah, with Saxon and Kip. They were fifteen, we were thirteen."

"Jeez," I say. "I thought I'd burned all the photos."

"We wanted to be the Arctic Monkeys," Damon says.

"What was your band called?"

Damon and I both say at the same time, "The Antarctic Coyotes."

"That's a great name," she declares, laughing. "Why aren't you famous?"

"Because we were terrible," Damon replies. "You were pretty good on the drums."

"I was awful, it's okay to say it. You could sing, and Kip's always been a guitarist. Saxon was a terrible bass player, though. It was one of those phases you go through when you're kids. It didn't last long."

"Jesus," Damon says, "I've just remembered, that was when we both had our hair bleached."

"We didn't get out much so we were as pale as vampires," I tell Missie. "We both looked like Spike from Buffy the Vampire Slayer."

She giggles. "Oh I've totally got to see those photos now."

"Over my dead body."

"I'm sure that can be arranged."

I take her hand as Damon laughs. "Come on. See you later."

He waves goodbye. We walk down the path that runs beside the terrace, then cut through the garden to where the cable car sits waiting by the platform. Missie climbs in and I sit opposite her, we press descend, and it slowly lowers down.

"Look at that," she says, peering through the palms at the pool. "It's huge!"

"That's where the guys are hanging out tonight." I gesture to a group of guys who are erecting a large screen by the poolside. "They're showing *Extraction 2*."

"We're going to watch *Mamma Mia*."

"Oh, your favorite! Talk about stereotypical."

"Yeah, it should be fun. And apparently there'll be some entertainment afterward. God knows what that will be."

"Male strippers?" I suggest.

"Ah, I hope not. I can't imagine Belle wanting that. Or Mae organizing a show in her garden. But I guess it's a possibility. I might sneak off if it is. It's not my thing."

"You don't like to see men taking off their clothes?"

"I'd watch you," she says. She leans back in her seat, and her eyelids drop to half-mast.

"Girl, I'm so hot for you that it'd be a very short show. I'm betting it'll be six seconds tops before I'm naked."

She laughs, her eyes lighting up. "Promises, promises."

We smile at each other from across the car. She's been delightful today, especially once she relaxed, saying hello to everyone I've introduced her to, chatting to all the old aunts and uncles, playing with the kids and dogs, holding babies and charming everyone with her bright smile and pleasant nature.

"I adore you," I tell her.

She wrinkles her nose at me. "That's a nice thing to say."

"I'm going to show you how much when we get into the apartment."

Her lips curve up.

I check my watch. "We've got about ninety minutes. Should be enough."

"Won't it sap your strength? Maybe we should wait until afterward."

"Nothing saps my strength when you're around, Mistletoe Macbeth." I grab her hand and pull her up and onto my lap. She squeals, then puts her arms around my neck, and she crushes her lips to mine.

I feel surprisingly content after sharing my story with her, as if she's cleansed me of all the darkness and shadows that have been hiding in my soul since that day ten years ago. Despite the terrible things that have happened to her, she's like the ray of sunshine pouring in through the glass, and the smell of the roses outside the car. She's summer to my winter, the best thing that's ever happened to me, and I want to show her how I feel about her, because actions speak louder than words.

The car comes to a stop with a slight bump, and she stands up, giggling as she sees a gardener clipping the hedge a little further down who obviously spotted us kissing, judging by his smile. "I feel like a naughty teenager," she admits, opening the door and stepping onto the platform.

"I know what you mean." I take her hand and nod to the gardener as if he hasn't just caught us snogging like a couple of fourteen-year-olds.

Laughing, we head across the terrace past the first apartment to the one in the middle. "This is Kip's," I explain, producing a key from my pocket. I slide it into the lock, open the door, and step back for her to precede me.

She goes inside, and I follow, locking the door behind me, and leaving my shoes there. This place is as familiar to me as my home in Christchurch. These are one-bedroom apartments, although they all have a study, and Mae and Neal turned Damon's into another bedroom for me when I moved in. Today, though, I take Missie's hand and lead her through to the main bedroom. It's large and sun-filled, the walls pale cream, the bedding brilliant white. A couple of Kip's beloved science fiction movie posters hang on the side wall. It feels like a happy room, but then maybe that's just because Missie's in it.

The sliding doors facing onto a small private patio with pots containing bird-of-paradise plants that glow in the sunshine with their unusual orange and blue flowers that resemble the birds that gave them their nickname. I open the doors a little to let in the smell of summer.

Our bags are already here, waiting for us. There are mints on the pillows, and I know the kitchen will be stocked with food and champagne and the best whisky. Mae and Neal know how to make their guests feel welcome.

Missie glances around, looking at the furnishings, but eventually her gaze comes back to me, her eyes lighting up as I close the distance between us.

"I've thought about nothing else except this since we parted," I murmur, putting my hands on her hips and backing her up to the wall. She meets it with a bump, and looks up at me with big eyes as I move close to her.

I cup her face and study her mouth. "You're trembling," I observe. "Are you cold?" I'd be surprised—the air con is on and it's a pleasant temperature in the room.

She shakes her head.

"Frightened?"

She shakes again.

"Nervous?"

Another shake.

I frown.

"I'm excited, Alex," she whispers. "I want you so badly. I've watched you all morning, with my family, with Damon's, with your friends, and everyone thinks you're grumpy, but you're not. You're so warm and friendly with everyone, and you're gentle and kind, but you're so fucking sexy you make me ache…"

I lower my head until my lips are just brushing hers. "I haven't forgotten that nice thing you said in front of my friends. I know it was a joke, but—"

"It wasn't a joke. You are really, really good in the sack, and I'll tell everyone who cares to listen."

I touch my tongue to her bottom lip, and her lips part with a sigh. I stifle a groan. I'm already hard as a rock, and I could easily toss her on the bed and thrust us both to a climax in minutes. But she deserves more than that. She deserves as much pleasure as a woman can stand. And I'm determined to spend a lifetime showing her what she means to me.

Chapter Twenty-Two

Missie

Is this man for real? He holds my face and kisses me with agonizing slowness, tenderly and yet with passion, as if I'm the most precious thing he's ever seen, and he's worshiping me with his mouth.

I meant what I said to him—I've been watching him all morning, and I just love the way he is with people. He's the perfect best man—he's been introducing himself to everyone, telling them to come and see him if they need anything, getting old aunties cushions and drinks and the kids treats, and always keeping the conversation flowing, so nobody feels uncomfortable. We work quite well together in that way, as that's what I'm like, too. Lee hated social gatherings like this and would hang around out on the outskirts being sulky and monosyllabic until he was able to join his friends, and it's been nice to have someone by my side who's so similar.

Oh my God, I'm more than half in love with him, and falling more and more with each minute we spend together. I wanted to play this cool, to take my time, but it's impossible with the way he treats me.

Like right now—he could have torn off my clothes, tossed me on the bed, and screwed me all the way to heaven in minutes, and I wouldn't have complained. But he doesn't. Instead, his tongue teases mine, giving slow, sensual thrusts, while he sinks his hands into my hair, stroking with his thumbs and sending shivers all the way through me. He presses up against me, using his height and weight to pin me to the wall, and leaving me in no doubt that he's turned on. He's showing me that he wants me, but that he's not going to give into his desires, not yet anyway.

Still kissing me, he begins unbuttoning his shirt. "I want to feel you," he murmurs. "Your skin against mine."

"Okay." I know better than to complain that it's broad daylight. I'm going to have to get over my nerves about being naked with this guy. My stretch marks don't seem to affect how much he wants me at all.

I take off my top while he removes his shirt, and then, still kissing, we unbutton our trousers and remove them, too. He takes a moment to admire me in my lacy cream bra and knickers, and then he unclips my bra and slides the straps down my arms. He hooks his fingers in the elastic of my knickers and draws them down my legs until I step out of them. Finally, he removes his boxers, and now we're both naked, and I sigh at the sight of all that taut, tanned skin. He's young, fit, and healthy, muscular, and toned, like an underwear model. I'm still shy of my body—I don't exercise as much as I should, plus I've always had big boobs, and after having a child, nothing's as tight and high as it used to be.

But he cups my breasts with a sigh, and strokes me as if I'm a perfect Aphrodite, worshiping me with his hands. I love the way he touches me, skimming his fingers over my ribs and back, and I can feel my body reacting to him, goose bumps popping out on my skin, my nipples tightening, and down below I'm swelling and growing moist, ready for when he slides inside me.

He's still kissing me, but as I tremble again, his lips curve up against mine, and he gives a short laugh. "Come here," he scolds, taking my hand and leading me over to the bed. "It's like trying to make love to a girl in the Arctic." He draws back the thick duvet in its brilliant-white cover, and we both climb on the mattress. He falls back, bringing me with him so I tumble on top of him, then draws the duvet over us, and we snuggle down beneath it.

"There," he says, tucking the duvet around me. "Better?"

"I wasn't cold." I'm still trembling. "It's you, Alex. It's all you. Just looking at you turns me to caramel." I wish I could explain how I feel about him. How seeing him makes me catch my breath. How I can't think about anything else when we're not together.

We look into each other's eyes for a moment, and the affection I see in his makes me catch my breath. I think he feels the same way about me.

Something shifts between us, an understanding, maybe, a realization. It's as if we've reached a checkpoint in our relationship, a moment when both of us can feel this turning into something deeper. Officially it's only our second date, but of course it's been going on much longer than that. He's been seducing me since day one, when he took me for a walk in Hagley Park. I'm sure he doesn't take all his clients out for a romantic walk through the park. Now I know him better, it wouldn't surprise me if he'd planned it. But we'd never met— I'd literally just walked into his office—so he couldn't have had any idea that we'd be attracted to one another. He must have just found me attractive right away, even though I was a mess, my brain scrambled with thoughts of Finn's treatment.

He looks to the side, and I follow his gaze to the colorful bird-of-paradise plants in their pots on the patio. It's a beautiful day, the sunshine pouring through the sliding doors, bringing with it the smell of the mown grass and flowers in the gardens, and in the distance the faint sound of music and laughter from the terrace way above us.

Alex tucks a strand of my hair behind my ear, and I look back at him to see him watching me. Softly, he starts singing *You Are My Sunshine*, and he smiles as he tells me that I make him happy. Then he slides his hand to the back of my head and brings it down so he can kiss me.

His lips move across mine slowly, and I open my mouth so our tongues can play together, and sigh as he brushes his hands down my back. He keeps his touch light, skimming his fingers across my skin, from my shoulders, down either side of my spine, to my hips, across my bum, then back up the sides of my ribs before he finally cups my breasts. I feel him sigh as he lets them rest in his palms, and he rubs his thumbs across my nipples.

"So soft," he murmurs, taking the tips between his thumbs and forefingers and teasing them. I mumble something unintelligible as I feel them harden, and groan when he flicks them, making his lips curve up.

Without warning, he puts his arm around me and lifts up, turning me over, so in seconds I'm on my back and he's on top. "I want to taste you, Mistletoe Macbeth," he states, kissing around to my ear to nip the lobe. He touches his tongue to the inside and blows on it, and I shudder. "I bet you taste amazing," he states, his voice little more than a growl.

"Ah, maybe I should just pop in the shower…"

"Not a chance." He begins to kiss down my neck, big wet kisses, using his tongue, tasting me as he goes, and occasionally sucking, which makes me shudder.

"Oh God, don't give me hickies," I beg. "I don't want to have to go to the wedding in a burka."

"I'll only do it in places it won't be seen." He kisses to the top of my breast and sucks.

I squeal. "Alex!"

He laughs—it wasn't hard enough to leave a mark. Pushing up my breast, he fastens his mouth over my nipple and sucks again, and I moan and writhe beneath him.

"Stop wriggling."

"You're making me ache."

"I haven't even started yet, baby girl." He swaps to the other nipple and does the same there, teasing it with his tongue and teeth, sucking and licking, until I'm sure I could come just by him doing that.

At that point, he leaves them and kisses down my belly, shifting beneath the duvet, and moves between my legs. Pushing up my knees, he lowers down, and I sigh and stretch my arms over my head as I close my eyes.

This is heaven—the sunshine and the huge white duvet and Alex's tongue sliding down into my folds. Oh man... he's so good at this. He goes all the way down and slips his tongue right inside me, then licks slowly all the way up. Ahhh fuck... With just the tip, he circles my clit, and then he does it all over again.

"You taste fucking amazing," he says, his voice muffled beneath the duvet.

I cover my face with my hands. "Oh God..."

"Mmm..." He slides two fingers gently inside me, and I feel him press up as he strokes them in and out.

Gradually, I have an out of body experience, my spirit ascending out into the sunshine and up to the fluffy white clouds of heaven as he arouses me. It doesn't take long before I feel all the tiny muscles inside me begin to tighten, but he obviously feels it too, because he withdraws his fingers and kisses my thighs, waiting for the waves to die down before he starts again.

Oh shit, he's going to edge me until I beg him to let me come, just as he promised he would.

I groan, arching my back, and he strokes the outside of my thigh as he licks me again, teasing my clit with short flicks of the tip of his tongue. He does it for ages, drawing me right up to the point of coming, then stopping, and either blowing lightly on my swollen skin, or kissing my thighs, my belly, anywhere except the place I want to be kissed.

"Ah, Alex…" I beg, "please…"

"All in good time, baby girl." He eases his fingers inside me again. "Jesus, you're so wet."

"Oh my God. I wonder why?"

"That's such a fucking turn on. I'm so hard for you right now."

"You know I'm going to pay you back for this, right?"

"I don't care. I'm having the time of my life down here." He returns to sliding his tongue through my folds, and I bite my bottom lip as every muscle tenses in response, lifting up onto my elbows.

"Relax," he scolds, stopping and kissing my thigh.

"I can't…" I'm almost panting.

"I'm not starting again until you lie down."

I flop back, cursing him, and pull a pillow over my head.

"Good idea," he says. "You can muffle your screams."

"I've never screamed during sex, and I don't intend to start now."

"We'll see." He licks me from the bottom all the way to the top.

I crush the pillow to my face to hide my loud moan, and I feel him laugh as he strokes inside me.

"It's going to feel so good when you come," he says with annoying confidence.

"I might have a coronary first."

"Ah, Missie. I'm never going to wash again."

I can't reply. I'm going to come whether he wants me to or not.

But my orgasm remains tantalizingly out of reach, and I realize I'm totally under his control, and he's only going to let me climax when he's good and ready. I lose all sense of self, all hope of dignity. I beg him to have pity on me, but he makes me wait, and wait… I'm almost crying with it, close to calling out our safe word, shit, what was it? Some tropical fruit… mango? No, pineapple. The word hovers on my lips… I can't take much more…

But then he murmurs, "All right, sweetheart. Hold on tight."

He curves his fingers up and presses, and at the same moment he covers my clit with his mouth and sucks hard. Oh fuck. He's waited so long that I expect it to hit like a train, but it doesn't. It creeps over me, agonizingly slow, a contraction of every single muscle inside me, oh holy fuck, it's almost unbearable, squeezing, tightening… And then the pulses slam into me as if I'm being hit with a tennis racket. It's going on forever… I cry out into the pillow at the blissful beauty of it… my body jerks, eight, nine, ten times as he continues to suck… and then all of a sudden it's too much and I squeal and say, "Oh my God, stop! Stop!"

He rears up and throws off the duvet, moves up my body, and in two seconds he's inside me. We both give a loud groan. I force my eyes open and look up at him, and he bends and kisses me as he starts to move. Oh jeez, he's all wet…

"Please don't say that was all from me…" I plead.

"We might need to change the bed," he says with a wicked laugh. Lifting up onto his hands, he starts to thrust hard. His eyes are so hot I'm sure they could set me alight. He's moving fast, driving down into me, and even though I've just come, the orgasm seems to be hovering around, intent on making a reappearance.

To my surprise, he pauses then, though, and withdraws. Aw. But I should know better—he's not stopping. Instead he moves next to me and kind of under me, lifts my leg across his hips, and enters me from behind, and I'm lying there spreadeagled and completely uncaring as he arouses me again with his fingers and tugs my nipple with his other hand, and oh holy Jesus this guy is going to be the death of me…

He fucks me hard, and it's only minutes before I feel my muscles start to tighten again. Luckily this time he doesn't stop, he just demands, "Come for me, Missie," and I say, "okay," and he says, "good girl," and we come together, him thrusting us all the way to the finish line, then holding me tightly as our bodies lock together as if we're one statue carved from the same piece of marble.

And then we flop back with a groan, turning into limp noodles in the space of seconds.

"Holy shit," he says, still inside me.

"You can't keep doing that," I complain. "I'll be a shadow of my former self. Not every orgasm has to be an eleven out of ten."

"Are you seriously complaining?"

"A little bit."

"That's it. We're going again."

I groan. "I couldn't, not in a million years."

"I only need a second."

"Alex! I need a snooze, a cup of coffee, and a steak sandwich before I can even think about coming again."

That makes him laugh, which starts me giggling. He says, "Ow," and withdraws, then pulls me into his arms, and I snuggle up to him. He pulls the duvet back over us, taps his watch to set a forty-five-minute alarm, then holds me tightly.

"You're some girl," he says.

"Is that a polite way of saying I'm a right tart?"

"Po-tay-to, po-tah-to." We both laugh.

He kisses my ear. "I'm serious. You're a special girl."

"Nah. I'm just me." I kiss his neck. "Thank you, though, for making me feel like me again."

"What do you mean?"

"I've been in mum mode for so long, especially this year. I've put Finn first for a long time, and I've kinda lost touch with me, you know? I haven't painted much, or gone out, and I certainly haven't had sex… I've felt old before my time. There are other women my age out there who are partying and clubbing and meeting guys on Tinder and having the time of their lives, and I'm responsible and dependable and reliable and other words ending in 'ible'. Or 'able'. But right now I feel young and sexy." I yawn.

"You are young and sexy."

"Yeah, but I feel it now. And that's all down to you."

He kisses my nose. "All I've done is hold up a mirror and show you who you still are inside. Now, go to sleep."

"I'm not tired."

"You'll be asleep in less than a minute."

"No, I won't."

That's the last thing I remember saying before I doze off.

Chapter Twenty-Three

Missie

Later, Alex heads off to the minivan to join the guys heading out for the paintball game, and I take the cable car up to the house. On arriving, I discover that Mae has turned the top terrace into a beauty salon, with lots of beds set up under a shade sail, and a whole team of beauticians brought in to provide massages, facials, manicures, pedicures, waxing, and every other treatment you can think of as part of Belle's hen party.

Most of the women who have already arrived are taking advantage of it, and I spend some time to talking to them all as we move between the treatment areas. Everyone's so friendly, and it's not long before I feel as if I've known them all forever.

I can't remember the last time I went to a beauty spa, so this is a real luxury for me. I indulge in a hot stone massage and a pedicure, and then I find myself sitting next to Belle as I have my fingernails painted. We can order coffees from the barista in the kitchen, and Mae's also set up a cocktail bar, which is how I end up with a pina colada in one hand while the beautician does the nails of the other, while Belle sips her mojito and lies back with her eyes closed and gives a long sigh.

I glance at her and smile. She seems so happy. But it's impossible not to think about what Alex told me about what happened to her when she was young. I can't imagine how awful that must have been. I'd never mention it, of course, but it explains a lot about how protective he is of her, and Damon too, I guess.

"Are you excited about your big day?" I ask her.

She opens her eyes and smiles back. "I am, although this whole week has been fun. It's been so cool to spend time with Damon's family."

The two beauticians move away to paint someone else's nails while our coats dry, leaving us alone. Belle glances around, making sure nobody can overhear us, then says, "Do you find it all a bit intimidating? I have to admit I do sometimes."

"I know what you mean," I admit. "The house is huge! Although I thought you and Alex were used to this kind of lifestyle?"

"God, no. I mean, Mum's super rich, but she lives in LA. My dad and Sherry are just ordinary people. They have to save up for vacations like everyone else. Their house is in the suburbs, just a normal three-bedroom place. Alex has done well at Kia Kaha, and he's good with money, mainly because James has a financial head on his shoulders, and he's shown them all how to invest what they've earned. I've got money in the bank from Mum, but I live quite normally. So I'm not used to all this." She waves a hand around at the sumptuous property.

"I feel like royalty," I admit.

She grins. "They're the nicest people, though, maybe because they weren't born into money. The boys were, of course, but Neal and Mae were in their twenties when they became rich. They're both so lovely and supportive, and they've been great to Catie and Alice too. Has Alex told you much about them?"

I shake my head.

"Saxon had a one-night stand with Catie in Auckland, and she left in the middle of the night, so he didn't know where she went. She turned up at his office in Wellington for a temp job four months pregnant."

"Oh wow."

"Yeah. She'd had a tough life, and was practically penniless, and refused Saxon's help, but of course he won her over eventually. He absolutely adores her."

"Their babies are gorgeous. They must have been a surprise!"

"Yeah, he didn't expect twins, I'm sure."

"Alice said she met Kip on Tinder?"

"Yeah. Her mum—not sure if you've met Penny?"

"She's the one in the wheelchair, right?"

"Yes. She has Multiple Sclerosis. Alice looks after her twenty-four-seven and has done since she was about fifteen, I think, so she'd never been on a date with anyone. They lived in Gisborne. One day she went on a rare trip to Wellington and signed up on Tinder. She ended up meeting Kip! Talk about lucky. But it was so brave of her. I don't think I could've done that."

"God, me neither."

"They had a one-night stand, but he fell for her and chased her down. Such a romantic story."

"True, but then so is yours," I say, and smile.

She looks at her toenails and wiggles her toes. "That's true, more than you could know. Although I suspect Alex has probably told you some, if not all of it." She gives me an appraising look.

"A little," I say softly.

"He must like you. He doesn't talk about it, not even to Damon until earlier this year. What happened… it hit him very hard and turned him quite cynical and broody. He didn't used to be like he is now. He's so wary of people. Till you get a couple of drinks in him, and he loosens up."

"Yeah, Juliette told me that. I like him a lot. I'm very lucky to have met him. I can't quite believe he's interested in me."

"Aw, Missie. I've never seen him like this with a girl. He's head over heels for you."

I blush. "That's a nice thing to say."

"I know my brother better than almost anyone, and I'm telling you, he's crazy about you. So don't be put off if he plays it cool."

The beauticians come back to check our nails, and Belle and I talk for a while about other things, but inside I feel this warm glow at the fact that his sister thinks he's head over heels for me.

"So what else do you have planned for the rest of the day?" I ask Belle when our nails are done.

"Gaby's organized it all," she says, "with the help of the bridesmaids." Her sister is her Matron of Honor, and Catie, Alice, Kennedy, and her friend Jo are the other bridesmaids. "After this, we're going to watch Mamma Mia!"

"I love that movie!"

"Yeah, me too. Mae and Neal have a cinema in the house, so—"

"A cinema!"

"Well, a small one, but yeah. There'll be a buffet and more cocktails or champagne while we watch it. Then later they've organized something else. I don't know what."

"Strippers?" I tease.

She pulls an 'eek' face. "I hope not. I'd be so embarrassed."

"I'm sure they wouldn't want to embarrass you."

"No, I did ask them not to do anything like that. Alice promised I'd enjoy it, so I'll just have to wait and see." She grins. "Are you ready?"

I wiggle my fingers. "Yep, all done."

"Come on, then."

With everyone beautified and relaxed, we make our way inside. The cinema room has a large screen that takes up almost all the front wall with a projector, and two rows of comfortable seats, with lots of beanbags for those who prefer to lounge on the floor. A long table to one side groans with food, and we spend a while helping ourselves to pizza, southern-fried chicken, a variety of salads, kebabs of roasted vegetables, and loads of other dishes. Most of us opt for another cocktail, and we take our food and drink to a seat and put our feet up to watch the movie.

Most of us have seen it multiple times, and we sing to all the songs and say all the lines, laughing and joking while we eat and drink.

When it finally comes to an end, Gaby tells us we have half an hour or so before the next entertainment starts. She shepherds us all outside and announces we're going to watch the sun go down while we drink champagne, so we follow her out, collect a glass of champagne, and sit together on the blankets spread out on the lawn to the side of the house, facing west. Someone brings a couple of boxes of chocolate truffles, and we start work on those as we sip the champagne.

The sun is heading toward the horizon, and the sky has turned orange, purple, and dark blue. Venus is already out, and as the sun sets, more stars begin to appear on the velvet background. Ooh, the world is starting to get hazy. I should make sure I intersperse the alcohol with water. I'm having such fun, though. I'm so glad I came.

The staff have surrounded us with citronella candles to keep us free from any nighttime insects, and although it's not too cold, there are a couple of deck heaters to take any chill off the evening air. Mae and the other older women are up on the terrace sitting in the chairs, chatting, so it's just us younger girls on the blankets, talking and laughing. There are fourteen of us: Me, Gaby, Belle, her friend Jo, Sidnie, Elizabeth, Victoria, Evie, Heidi, Catie, Alice, Kennedy, Aroha, and Juliette.

Elizabeth and Catie have put their babies to bed, and they're being watched by a nanny. We're all able to relax without responsibilities and just be ourselves, and we're all determined to enjoy it.

"I'm so tipsy," Belle admits, blowing out a long breath. "I've lost count of the glasses of champagne I've had."

"It would be a pretty poor hen party if you didn't get wasted," Gaby tells her.

"Good point." Belle looks around her friends with a fond smile that gradually turns mischievous. "Okay, I've got an idea."

"Uh-oh," Jo says.

"No, it's a great idea," Belle protests. "I've got an admission to make. You lot already know." She points at Gaby, Aroha, and Juliette. "I've only got the courage to tell the rest of you now I'm drunk, so here goes… I'd never had an orgasm until I met Damon."

We all stare at her, our laughter dying away.

"Seriously?" Jo asks. "What, not even on your own?"

Belle shakes her head. "For various reasons, I'd just never had one. And I told him the night he drove me home for Gaby's wedding." Her eyes gleam. "He pulled over in the car and told me he'd give me an orgasm right there if I wanted one."

Heidi's jaw drops. "In the car?"

"Yep. So I said yes."

"And did he?" I ask.

"He did. It was fucking amazing." We all squeal, and she laughs. "The rest is history. But anyway, the point of me telling you was that I have a lot of ground to make up. So I want all of you to tell me something amazing about your sex lives. Come on! I need you to teach me!"

"Oh God," Gaby says, "you are so drunk."

"Oh, and you're completely sober? Come on Gabs. You can start. You can't pull the whole 'oh but Tyson's in a wheelchair' thing now he's walking. I know the two of you are at it like rabbits."

"We are," she admits, giving us all a sheepish look. "He told me he wants to make up for lost time. And we're trying for a baby, so…" She stops as everyone cheers, and laughs. "The doctors said the accident might have affected his fertility, so I'm quite relaxed about it, I'm just happy to wait and see what happens, you know? But he's determined to put a baby in me. It's turned into quite a thing." She rolls her eyes.

"Oh God," Catie says, "Saxon's the same! He totally has a… what do they call it? Impregnation fetish." It takes her three goes to get the word out.

Alice grins. "He found you really sexy when you were pregnant the first time, didn't he?"

"Yeah. It made him so horny. Especially when he discovered I was producing milk."

"Oh, I'm so glad I'm not the only one," Kennedy admits. "Someone told Jackson when I was breastfeeding that orgasms made the milk spurt out, and he made it his life's work to get me to hit the wall or the ceiling." We all giggle again.

"What about Titus?" Belle asks Heidi. "Has he turned all English, like Mark D'Arcy? Does he ask before he comes?"

"He does seem very polite," I say.

She grins. "Not in bed. No... recently we've... ahh... discovered anal sex." She chuckles as we all squeal.

"Do you like it?" Belle asks curiously.

"Yeah, as long as there's lots of lube and he takes his time. It's pretty hot."

"Anyone else?" Belle asks.

Sidnie pops a chocolate truffle in her mouth. "Yeah, Mack likes glazing my donut."

That makes us all burst out laughing, and it's a good few minutes before we get our giggles under control.

"I want to ask you something," Heidi says to Elizabeth, who lifts her eyebrows. "Last time we were home, I called in on Saturday morning to pick up the cake you ordered for Mum's birthday. It was, like, ten a.m., and Hux came to the door. He said you were still in bed and winked at me. He was wearing a gray T-shirt, and he looked like someone had sprayed him with a water pistol. I said, 'You're all wet,' and he laughed and said, 'It's Elizabeth's fault,' but he wouldn't elaborate."

"Oh my God."

Sidnie pokes Elizabeth with her toe. "Come on, spill the beans."

She laughs. "I can't."

"Elizabeth!" Belle protests. "You have to! It's the rules!"

"Jesus," Evie says, "don't tell me. I bet he made you squirt."

Elizabeth covers her face. "Oh God, don't." She lowers her hands, and her face is scarlet. "It just happened one day, and he's such a kinky bastard, he got all smug and proud of himself, and now he thinks it's great fun to make it happen."

"How do you do it?" Belle asks, fascinated.

"You have to massage the G-spot," Sidnie says. "It helps if you have a full bladder."

"Don't tell me, Mack…"

She snorts. "He's a sexpert in every department."

"I get so embarrassed," Elizabeth says.

Sidnie nods, "Yeah, me too. Doesn't make any difference."

"These men."

"I know."

"Alice?" Belle asks. "Come on, confess. I just know Kip's got to have a few aces up his sleeve."

"The second time we had sex," she says, "he inserted a piece of ice where the sun doesn't shine." We all whoop, and she laughs. "I was so innocent," she admits. "I had no idea men did things like that."

"I know what you mean," Belle says. "Damon's thing is toys. Have any of you got a rose?" Evie and Victoria giggle, and Belle grins. "Looks as if you two have."

"Magic toy," Evie says.

"What does it do?" Juliette wants to know.

"It sucks," Belle says. "I mean, all orgasms are amazing, but the rose…" She rolls her eyes.

"I'm totally getting one of those," Sidnie says, and everyone else agrees.

"We'll do a bulk order," Elizabeth says, and chuckles.

The waiter comes around with a bottle of champagne to refill our glasses, so we fall silent, trying not to laugh as he makes his way around. He's in his thirties, and quite good looking, and he gives us an amused look as he fills the last glass, then walks away, and we all giggle like fourteen-year-olds.

"I don't know if I dare ask Jo for tips," Belle says. "She's polyamorous and she has a Dom."

All our eyes widen as she pushes Belle bashfully. "Tell everyone all my secrets," she scolds.

"Do you call him Daddy?" Catie asks. She reaches for a chocolate. "Saxon likes that."

"I do," Jo admits as we all chuckle. "A lot of guys seem to like it. It makes them feel in control and powerful."

"Do you call Hux Daddy?" Sidnie asks Elizabeth.

"Only when he's been a good boy," she says, and winks.

Aroha sighs. "I don't have any stories to share, sorry."

"Not even with James?" Juliette teases.

Aroha sighs again, but doesn't answer.

"Aw," Belle says, "you never know, maybe he'll come to his senses over the next few days. What about you?" She asks Juliette. "Where is Cam, anyway?"

"At home. He didn't want to come." She studies her fingernails. "Things aren't great at the moment."

Belle glances at me, then at Gaby. "Is there someone else in the picture?"

"No." Juliette takes a truffle. "Maybe."

"Henry's a big guy," Sidnie says. "I like big men."

"I wonder if he's big all over," Belle says.

"He is," Juliette says, then laughs as Gaby pokes her. "I thought you meant his feet!"

"Juliette! You have to tell us the deets."

But she shakes her head and looks at me for deflection. "Come on Missie, what about Alex? Tell us something interesting about him."

I have a mouthful of champagne, trying not to sneeze as the bubbles go up my nose. "Actually I do have something interesting."

"Ooh," they all go.

"He has no refractory period at all."

Their eyebrows all rise. "You mean..." Elizabeth asks.

I nod. "It just doesn't go down. He's ready to go again straight away."

"That happens to Mack," Sidnie says. "Not every time, but sometimes."

"How are you still walking?" Belle asks.

I giggle. "With difficulty."

"Don't know what all the fuss is about," Victoria says. "Our vibrators are permanently hard."

We all laugh. I know Victoria and Evie are a couple, and also that Victoria is a transgender woman. She's absolutely gorgeous, tall and beautiful, and I know she married the striking police officer Evie not long ago.

Gaby glances across the lawn at someone, then says, "Oh, okay, looks like it's time! Come on everyone. We're going down to the bottom terrace."

Somewhat unsteadily, we all make our way down the steps to the terrace on top of the pool. I know the guys came here after their paintball session. They had a swim and watched a movie while they had dinner brought down to them, and we could hear their laughter occasionally. Now it's relatively quiet down there, so I don't know what's going on.

On the terrace, several rows of seats face a square tiled area. Behind it, a makeshift stage has been erected in the middle of which stands a single microphone on a stand with a table to its right. To the far side a DJ is setting up in front of a turntable, and speakers have been placed around the terrace. There are also lights set up all the way around, one of which is shining on the microphone like a spotlight.

Puzzled and curious, we all take a seat. More champagne is brought around while everyone sits. Behind the girls, the older women join us, laughing and joking. I have no idea what's going to happen. Belle looks nervous, and I don't blame her.

The sun has set now, and the sky has darkened, with just a mild blush to the west, the rest of it turning a beautiful midnight blue. There are more deck heaters down here, though, so even though I'm only wearing a sundress, it's not cold.

Someone cheers and a couple of others whistle.

"Oh my God," Elizabeth says, "it's Alex."

Surprised, I follow her gaze to the right of the stage. She's right— he's climbing the couple of steps onto the stage. He's wearing a black suit, extremely well fitting, as all his suits are. This one's a three piece, as I can see a waistcoat beneath his jacket. He's wearing a white shirt and a dark tie. I'd say he looks sophisticated, but his hair is flopping over his forehead, and he looks a bit… disheveled, which detracts a little from the refined appearance he's probably trying to project.

He's holding a whisky glass in his right hand which is half-filled, and he places it on the table next to the microphone. He beckons to one of the staff, and when the guy walks up to him, asks for something, and the guy nods and goes off. Alex then straightens and approaches the microphone.

"Evening ladies," he says as he adjusts the mic, lifting it a few inches and tightening the screw on the side. Everyone cheers and claps. He looks at me then and winks before smiling at the rest of the women in the crowd. Flicking back the sides of his jacket, he slides his hands into his pockets. "I've been asked to provide some entertainment while you wait for the guys to come," he says.

There's a big cheer, and he obviously realizes what he's said and gives us all a wry look.

"While you wait for the guys to *arrive*," he corrects. "Jeez. I can see what kind of mood you're all in tonight." Everyone whoops again. "Actually," he says, "a friend of mine, Amanda, is a comedian, she was supposed to be doing an innuendo routine tonight, but she can't be here, so I've got to fill her slot."

I burst out laughing, and he looks across and chuckles. "Thanks, love. It helps to have your girlfriend in the crowd." While we all laugh, he accepts a bottle of water from the guy who hands it to him, unscrews the top, then drinks half of it. "Ahhh…" he says, putting the lid back on. "That's better. I've got to water down all the alcohol." He puts the bottle on the table, then points at Elizabeth. "That's your husband's fault. I was trying not to drink too much, but every time I looked away, he filled my glass up."

No wonder he looks disheveled—he's three sheets to the wind. Ohhh… I like sexy, intoxicated Alex. He's enchanting every girl in this audience, but I'm the only one who gets to take him home. I remember then that Juliette told me he used to do stand-up comedy when he was at uni. This is going to be one helluva experience.

"Right," he says. "Where was I? Oh yeah. Innuendo. Well, there's much more where that came from."

Chapter Twenty-Four

Alex

"A woman walks into a bar and asks the bartender for a double entendre," I say. "So he gives her one."

Half the girls laugh, and the other half try not to, and fail. I chuckle and have a mouthful of Scotch. Part of the reason for drinking is Dutch courage. I've been the keynote speaker at international conferences and given a presentation to the prime minister and her cabinet, but it's much harder getting up in front of a crowd of young women. I know most of these girls well, and they're all gorgeous and kind-hearted, but I have no doubt they'd eat me alive if they sensed an ounce of weakness.

"A naked man broke into a church," I say. "The police chased him around and finally caught him by the organ."

That causes more than a few giggles, and my lips curve up. "Oh, you like that one? Okay. Here's another knob joke. My penis…" I stop as they all cheer and laugh. "Hold on," I protest, "let me tell the joke. My penis was in the Guinness Book of World Records…" I stop once more as they all cheer again. "Girls! For God's sake. This is going to take all night."

"We don't mind that," Sidnie calls.

I grin and try again. "My penis was in the Guinness Book of World Records." I wait a few seconds, and say, "but then the librarian told me to take it out."

They all burst out laughing. Then someone yells, "Get your kit off!"

I raise my eyebrows. "Seriously? Here I am, delivering quality comedy, and you just want to see my boxers?"

"Whooooo!" They all cheer, and I laugh and have another swig of whisky. I go to say something, but they just cheer again, and I have to wait until they finally let me speak.

"I'm sure the last thing Belle wants is to see her brother take his clothes off," I say wryly.

"I don't mind seeing you be humiliated," she calls.

"Fair enough." Ah, fuck it. It's Belle's hen party. Don't they deserve a bit of fun? Plus, I want to show off for Missie.

Still holding the glass, I point it at them and say, "Okay, here's what I'm going to do. I'm going to tell each of you a joke, and if I can't make you laugh, I'll remove a piece of clothing, okay?"

I glance at Missie. Her eyebrows have risen almost to her hairline. "I am so going to regret this in the morning," I tell her. "I apologize in advance. I'm a little tipsy."

"More than a little by the look of it," Gaby calls.

"Maybe. So be kind to me."

"Not a chance," she says.

I give her a sarcastic look, then run my gaze along the front row until it falls on a young blonde woman with a mischievous smile. Titus's girl is also Huxley's baby sis. I've met her many times, and she's really sweet, so hopefully she'll be good to me.

"Heidi! Okay, you're first."

"Oh God."

"Don't worry, I'm always gentle the first time. Ask Missie."

Missie rocks her hand from side to side, debating the issue, and they all laugh.

I grin at Heidi. "Okay, I'll even tailor the jokes to you. You're a primary-school teacher, right? Why did the student do multiplication problems on the floor?"

"I don't know."

"Because his teacher told him not to use tables."

She meets my gaze, but manages to keep a straight face. Then she shakes her head, lifts her hand, and beckons to me to remove a piece of clothing.

"Really?" I feel an impending sense of doom. "The very first joke?"

"Get 'em off, Winters."

They all laugh and whoop.

Ah shit. I didn't think this through. I thought they'd play along. That was a stupid mistake. They're really going to make me strip.

Mumbling to myself, I toe off one shoe and push it away.

"Give me another joke," Heidi yells.

"It's my game," I tell them, "I make the rules," but someone yells, "Chicken!" so I blow out a breath and stick with Heidi. "Okay. Why do seagulls fly over the sea? Because if they flew over the bay, they'd be bagels."

Against her will, she gives a short laugh, then says, "Dammit."

I smirk and have a mouthful of whisky.

"That's not a teacher joke," she complains.

"Hey, I've got the whole audience to get through, and I'm not wearing that many clothes. I'm going to use every trick at my disposal." I walk along the stage a little and gesture at Catie. Saxon's girl is quiet and shy, but she's a terrific computer programmer, and we've talked a lot about coding.

"Catie," I say. "Here we go. An SQL query goes into a bar, walks up to two tables, and asks, 'Can I join you?'"

She gives a peal of laughter, and the others all say, "Aw, Catie!"

"It was funny!" she protests, still laughing, and gives me a clap. "Nice one."

I grin and move on to the next girl. "Alice in Wonderland."

She folds her arms and raises an eyebrow. Kip's girl does podcasts where she interviews science fiction and fantasy authors. I listen to her every week, and we've often talked about books we're reading.

"How many ears does Captain Picard have?" I ask. "Three. A left ear, a right ear, and a final front ear."

She bites her bottom lip, shakes her head, and flicks her fingers at me.

"Ah, damn." I toe off my other shoe as they all cheer. "All right," I say, moving my shoes aside. "Round two. How did Darth Vader know what Luke was getting for Christmas? He felt Luke's presents."

That makes her laugh, and she curses herself, but gives me a clap.

With a grin, I move on. "Sidnie. Hmm." I remember her maiden name and give her a mischievous look. "A clean beaver always gets more wood."

She laughs immediately, then yells, "Aw, that was below the belt, literally!"

"Hey, whatever works." I move to the left and point at Juliette. "Your turn."

She gives me a challenging gaze. "Do your best."

"Okay. Physio jokes. Hmm. I had a patient come in complaining about lower leg pain. I told them it's going tibia okay."

"Not even close," she says, and beckons at me.

I huff a sigh, look down, then take off a sock, almost falling over in the process. "Goddammit."

"Come on Alex, you can do better than that."

"I'm impaired."

"It's your own fault."

"It's Huxley's fault. All right. What kind of Physical Therapy exercise do lazy people do? Diddly squats."

She laughs, then screws up her face and says, "Oh fuck."

I chuckle and move on. "Victoria!"

"Yeah, go on," she says. "You know you want to."

I press a finger between my eyebrows. "Lesbian joke overload." She's the first person to make jokes about her sexuality and she's a good sport, so I have no problem with teasing her about it.

"Give it your best shot," she calls.

"What's a lesbian dinosaur called? A lickalotopus."

"You're kidding me," she says. "That's seriously the best you can come up with?"

Mumbling, I take off my second sock and toss it on top of my shoes. This one'll get her. "What's the difference between a chickpea and a lentil?" She shakes her head. "I bet you've never had a lentil on your face."

It takes her a second, but then her lips curve up and she gives a short laugh, while the rest of them burst into giggles. "Yeah, all right," she says, "that was pretty good."

"I can't believe you're sinking to this level in front of the groom's mother," Gaby calls out.

I glance over at Mae, who's laughing as much as the rest of them. "What do you mean?" I reply. "She's the one who taught me most of these."

"I did not!" Mae protests, still laughing.

"You told me the Barbie one," I remind her, giving her a reproachful look.

She glances around and admits, "I did do that."

"What's the Barbie one?" Gaby asks.

"Why isn't there a pregnant Barbie doll?" I say. "Because Ken came in another box."

Gaby laughs, and I say, "Success!" and move on.

"No!" she complains, "that's not fair."

"I told you, I make the rules. Aroha! *E mutunga kore ana taku aroha ki a koe.*" It means 'My love for you is endless.' She pokes her tongue out at me, and I smirk. "Beautician jokes. Hmm. Okay. Fifty dollars in hair extensions were stolen from a hair salon in Riccarton. Police are combing the area for clues."

She laughs without meaning to. "That was terrible," she says.

"I know." I grin and move on. "Elizabeth."

She folds her arms. I know she's going to do her best to make this difficult for me.

"Chemistry jokes," I say. "Right. What do you do with a sick chemist? If you can't helium, and you can't curium, then you might as well barium."

The others all whoop, but she shakes her head and flicks her fingers at me.

I remove a cufflink, show it to her, and put it on the table. "Okay. What happened to the man who was stopped for having sodium chloride and a nine-volt in his car? He was booked for a salt and battery."

She shakes her head, flicks her fingers.

I glare at her, then, grumbling, remove my second cufflink, and put it on the table. I study her for a moment as I sift through some jokes in my head. She lifts her eyebrows.

"Two chemists go into a bar," I say. "The first one says, 'I think I'll have an H_2O.' The second one says, 'I think I'll have an H_2O too.' And then he died."

She snorts a laugh, then yells, "Dammit!"

"H_2O_2 is hydrogen peroxide," I explain to the rest of the crowd, and they all chuckle as I have another mouthful of whisky.

"Okay," I say, putting my glass down, "Belle. What's the difference between a lawyer and a gigolo? A gigolo only screws one person at a time."

"A lawyer joke?" she complains. "Alex, seriously?"

I blow out a breath and look down at myself. I slide off my tiepin and put it on the table. Belle has recently qualified as a lawyer, but her first love is magic, and she's very good at it.

"Right. 'What's your father's occupation?' the schoolteacher asked. 'He's a magician,' Jack said. 'How interesting. What's his favorite trick?' the teacher asked. 'He saws people in half,' Jack answered. 'Wow! That must be amazing to watch,' the teacher said. 'Do you have any siblings?' And Jack said, 'One half brother and two half sisters.'"

Belle laughs. "Yeah, okay," she says. "That was pretty funny."

I chuckle and turn to the young woman next to her. She's watching me, a small smile on her face. "Ah, Missie." I say. "Oh light of my life. My beautiful baby girl."

Everyone whistles, and she blows me a kiss. Man, she's so fucking gorgeous. She'll be good to me, right?

"Missie's an artist. Sweetheart, if you're ever sad, I'll let you draw things on my body. I'll give you a shoulder to crayon."

To my surprise, she doesn't laugh. Like Elizabeth did, she folds her arms, shakes her head, then beckons at me, and it's only then that it dawns on me.

"Ah, no. You're going to make me strip naked, aren't you?"

She nods, and everyone cheers and whistles.

"Ah, shit." I take out my pocket square and toss it on the table. I'm running out of non-clothing things to take off.

"Tell her some rude jokes!" one of the girls yells.

"Rude jokes?" My lips curve up. "How rude?"

"The rudest ones you know!" Sidnie calls.

I scratch my head. "Rude but respectful," I mumble, giving them a wry look as they all giggle. This is a totally different audience from a group of guys. There's no way I can reveal half of my repertoire.

I'm conscious of the crowd growing as the guys who aren't taking part in the next entertainment and some of the staff join at the back. Great. Everyone's going to be here to watch my humiliation. Oh well. Serves me right for thinking I was good at this.

"Okay." I have a swig of whisky. "What does a guy call receiving oral while eating a steak?"

She shakes her head.

"Fellatio Mignon."

The others laugh, but she shakes her head and flicks her fingers.

Mumbling, I slide the end of my tie out of the knot, then remove it and drop it onto the rapidly growing pile of clothes.

I study her for a moment, wincing as I undo the tight top button of my shirt. She winks at me.

"I saw a dildo the other day described as 'nine inches long and realistic.' I thought, well, which is it?"

Catie gives a peal of laughter and the others all join in, but Missie shakes her head and flicks her fingers.

Keeping my gaze on hers, I undo the buttons of my jacket, then let it slide off my shoulders. Everyone cheers as I toss it to one side.

This is turning into a battle of wills. Still holding her gaze, I say, "What's the difference between hungry and horny? Where you stick the cucumber."

A shake and a beckon, and a whoop from the crowd.

"Dammit." I huff, unbutton my waistcoat, and that joins the jacket.

Now I just have my shirt, trousers, and underwear. Holy shit. This is getting serious.

I blow out a breath. "The nurse at the sperm bank asked me if I'd like to masturbate in the cup. I said, 'Well, I'm pretty good, but I don't think I'm ready to compete just yet.'" I chuckle as the girls dissolve into giggles. "I made myself laugh then."

But Missie shakes her head, straight-faced. Jesus, she's really going for it.

Glaring at her, I unbutton my shirt and slide it off. They all cheer. I toss it aside.

Right, this calls for extra effort. I remove the mic from the stand, then jump down from the stage and walk forward to stand a few feet from her. The girls all whoop and clap. Missie lifts her chin and gives me a challenging look, determined not to be intimidated.

"What's the difference between a G-spot and a golf ball? A guy will actually search for a golf ball." I point at her. "Now, you know that's not true."

Everyone cheers. But Missie shakes her head and gestures at my trousers.

Fuck me. With one hand, I undo my belt buckle, then slide it out through the loops. I hold it in my hand for a moment, tapping it against my leg, letting my lips curve up. "You realize I'm going to make you pay for this later," I tell her, amused.

The girls all go, "Ooooh," and she blushes and presses her hands to her cheeks. I laugh and toss the belt onto the stage.

I hold her gaze. "Why can't Miss Piggy count to seventy?"

"Don't know."

"Because every time she gets to sixty-nine she gets a frog stuck in her throat."

The girls all burst out laughing. But Missie holds my gaze, keeps a straight face, and shakes her head.

"Missie!" I beg, "Come on! Don't make me do it!"

But she just beckons at me.

"Ah, man." I give her the mic to hold, then, keeping my gaze on hers, I undo my trousers and slide down the zipper. Shit, am I really going to do this? I can't back out, though. I'd never live it down.

Slowly, I push my trousers over my hips and let them fall. Luckily I'm wearing a new pair of black boxer-briefs. I pick up the trousers, toss them onto the stage, and take the mic back from her. There's no point in acting coy—I'm standing in front of a group of gorgeous twenty-something girls in just my underpants—so I put my hands on my hips and let them ogle. They all laugh and cheer.

My Missie's eyes are hot, though, and full of desire. She lifts her chin. "One more piece of clothing, Alex, unless I'm very much mistaken."

"You're really going to make me do this?"

She flares her eyes.

I have no idea what's going to happen if I can't make her laugh.

"Right." Standing in front of her, I keep my eyes locked on hers. We survey each other with amusement for a moment. I think about different jokes, discarding them, looking for one I know will take her down.

Eventually, I say, "What's the difference between anal and oral sex?"

She gives a small shrug.

"Oral sex makes your day. Anal makes your hole weak."

Despite her best efforts, she gives a short laugh, then covers her face and groans with feeling, "No….!"

"Missie!" they all yell. "Aw, no!"

Relieved, I bend and kiss the top of her head, then turn back to the stage and mount the steps. Thankfully, I can see the guys waiting behind the partition at the end of the stage, so I refix the mic to the stand and say, "Luckily, it's time for the real entertainment. Thank you, ladies, you've been a terrific audience."

Chapter Twenty-Five

Missie

My heart is still hammering as Alex retrieves his clothing. Wow, that was close. I have no idea what he'd have done if I hadn't laughed. Would he have stripped? Aw, dammit. But his naughty joke, and the mischievous look in his eyes, had been my undoing.

I'm totally bowled over by his performance and the way he controlled the crowd. I'm pretty certain his suggestion of stripping as he told his jokes was planned, but it was a brilliant idea, and the girls reacted so well to it, playing along.

We all whistle and boo as he picks up his trousers and puts them back on. Then Damon appears, and our boos turn to cheers. He looks at Alex and says into the mic, "Dude, what the fuck? You were only supposed to tell jokes."

"They made me do it," Alex mumbles, buttoning up his trousers. He pulls on his shirt, although he leaves it undone, then quickly adds the waistcoat and jacket before sitting on the edge of the stage to pull on his socks and shoes. "It's a feral crowd, I'm telling you."

Damon laughs and turns to face the audience. "How are you doing, girls?"

"We love you!" someone shouts.

He grins and blows a kiss to his fiancée. "You all right, sweetheart?"

She nods, looking up at him with complete adoration. He smiles. "Are you ready to be entertained?"

We all yell, "Yes!" and it turns into a loud chorus of whoops as the rest of the guys come out. They're all wearing the same black suits, and it's clear from their boisterous manner that they're 'a little tipsy', in Alex's words. They're all there: Damon, Saxon, Kip, Mack, Huxley, Titus, Alex, James, Henry, Jackson, even Tyson, moving exceptionally well and with no walking stick in sight.

They form a line on the stage, with Damon at the mic. He winks at Belle and says, "We've got something a little special for you now."

Alex nods to someone at the back, and the white lights around the terrace dim, leaving the spotlight on Damon, and another on the DJ to the side. A bass beat starts playing—a pounding, heavy heartbeat, and at the same time, colored lasers jump into life and flash around the stage.

As the music starts, my eyes widen, and I glance along the lines of girls, seeing the same realization reflected in their faces. We all recognize the song—it's *I Scream* by the Kiwi band Paua of One, and oh my God, the lyrics are absolutely *filthy*. It earned an Explicit tag and was banned on all the radio stations, but it still managed to become famous across the country, and any time it comes on in a nightclub, it immediately has everyone up dancing.

And now the guys start moving to the beat, in the semi-darkness, with the stars behind them and the laser lights flashing across the terrace. They've obviously been practicing this, because all these gorgeous, sexy men are moving together, and oh wow, if that isn't the hottest thing I've ever seen.

Damon moves closer to the mic and adopts the same breathy tone as the band's singer as he murmurs, "Let me hear you scream…"

We all scream in response, and he smirks as he begins to sing. He directs the lyrics to his fiancée, but it's impossible not to feel as if he's singing to all of us.

"It's summer, baby, and it's hot tonight,
I'll hold your ice cream, baby, gonna take a bite,
Hey it's melting, baby, and it's time to strip,
Let me lick it, baby, suck up every drip…"

As he says the word 'strip', the guys all start unbuttoning their jackets, and we all scream as if they're The Beatles. Wow, Damon delivers the lines so sexily, leaving no doubt as to exactly what he's thinking about licking up, and Belle covers her mouth with a hand, probably blushing, although it's too dark to see.

"Lie down, baby, now I'm melting too,
Gonna melt my ice cream over you…
Lie down baby, and open wide,

Want you to take my ice cream all inside…"

Oh, holy shit. I don't think I'm going to make it through this song in one piece. I hear Belle say, "I think I'm going to faint," just along from me, and I know what she means.

The guys are all singing together now.

"Take it, take it, take it inside,
Gonna take what I give you, gonna open wide,
Gonna melt on my tongue, gonna taste so sweet,
Girl I'm coming for you, are you coming for me?"

As one, they all let their jackets drop and toss them into the audience. The girls scream, and the guys laugh as they break into the chorus together.

"Ice cream, you scream, scream for me,
Love every flavor in your recipe,
I wanna lick your chocolate and strawberry,
Ice cream, you scream, scream for me!"

Every time they say the word scream, we all do as we're told.

As the song progresses, the guys strip off their waistcoats, then finally their shirts. It doesn't look as if they're going to go as far as Alex had to, which is a shame, but once they're naked from the waist up, they all jump down from the stage as the guitarist goes into a wild break, and they come right up to the girls and dance in front of us.

Alex pulls me to my feet, and the others do the same to their girls. Out of the corner of my eye I see James go to Aroha and Henry approach Juliette, and both girls let the guys pull them up and start dancing.

Alex slides his arms around me, and I turn so my back is to him and wind my hips to the music, so my butt is nestled against him. He moves with me, and we dance together, the heavy beat vibrating right up through me, so I can feel it in every bone in my body.

Damn, that's sexy. The guy can move, and even though he's only resting his hands lightly on my hips, I feel his touch like a laser burning through me.

When the guitar break comes to an end, he turns me and plants a swift kiss on my lips, then he and the others return to the stage for the final part of the song. The lights flash across them, and then the music ends, and we all cheer and clap as they come forward and take a bow together.

The DJ immediately switches to Nine Inch Nails' *Closer*—another filthy song—and the guys grab their shirts and jump back down from the stage to come over to us. Saxon spins Catie into his arms and the two of them start dancing, and that's enough to get the rest of us up. As the singer tells us exactly what he wants to do to us *like an animal*, we all cheer and laugh.

We dance for ages, the DJ playing non-stop dance songs, old and new—Post Malone and ABBA, Doja Cat and Disco Inferno, Taylor Swift and Michael Jackson, all mixed up together.

After a while Alex instructs everyone to change partners, and we continue to do this for ages, until I've danced with most of the guys at the party. I dance with Huxley, who makes me laugh the entire time, and Saxon, who I struggle to keep up with because he's so good on his feet, and Henry, who's surprisingly agile for a big guy, and Jackson, who's not a great dancer, but who seems to be enjoying himself anyway.

I've just danced with James when a slow song comes on—John Mayer's *Slow Dancing in a Burning Room*.

"Ooh, up close and personal," James says, pulling me close, but Alex comes over and says, "Don't even think about it," and James chuckles and goes off to find someone else.

"Don't tell me you're jealous," I scold Alex as he pulls me into his arms.

"He's far too good looking," he says. "Disco is one thing, but I don't want any other guy having a slow dance with you."

I'm wearing high-heeled sandals, so he's only got a few inches on me, and I lift my arms around his neck and press up against him as we move to the music. He kisses me, and we indulge in a long smooch that soon has me tingling all over.

We dance for ages, talking and looking into each other's eyes, while around us our friends do the same. It's warm and sultry, and he's gorgeous, and I'm having the time of my life. I feel fifteen again, without a care in the world, and I wish it could go on forever.

But of course all good things come to an end, and eventually, around two a.m., people start drifting off. Some go to the house if they're staying there, others like Kip and Saxon and their girls get an Uber home, and a few go to nearby hotels in the city.

Alex waits until Damon and Belle have gone down to their apartment, and he's about to start helping clear up when Mae takes him by the shoulders and gently steers him toward me. "Take him home," she tells me. "The staff will clear up."

I slide my hand into his, and together we walk over to the cable car. We get inside and close the door, and Alex presses the button to descend to the bottom level.

He sits opposite me, arms stretched out along the back of the seat. He never did his shirt back up all the way, and although he's now wearing his waistcoat and jacket, he looks disheveled and sexy.

We meet each other's eyes, and smile.

"I can't believe I got down to my underwear in front of all those women," he says. "I'm never going to live that down."

"Aw, you're kidding me? They were all half in love with you by the end of your routine. Including me."

"Only half?"

"Maybe a little more than half."

We both smile again. Damn, but the man is sexy. He's looking at me with half-lidded eyes, and if I didn't know better, I'd be convinced he was thinking about me naked. A ripple of desire runs through me.

"Damon said he's had a fantastic day," I tell him. "He said everything you organized went smoothly."

"Yeah, it was good fun."

"Did you plan the comedy strip or was that improvised?"

"Improvised. I realized it was a mistake as soon as Heidi refused to laugh." But he chuckles, showing he's not upset about it.

"Would you really have gone all the way?" I ask curiously.

"I guess we'll never know. Incidentally, did you laugh at that last question on purpose, or were you really trying to get me to strip naked?"

"I was really trying to get you to strip naked." I give him a mischievous smile. "You promised you'd make me pay for it later."

He doesn't reply immediately. He observes me for a moment, just a small smile on his lips, before saying, "You had me at lunchtime."

I roll my eyes. "That was hours ago."

"I'm sure you're very tired. I'll still be there in the morning."

The car descends, the only noise the light clack of the wheels on the track. Outside, solar lights illuminate patches of the garden, but in here it's dark and quiet. Alex's eyes glitter.

I know we're both inebriated and tired, but my instincts tell me he's not being truthful with me. He said *I'm sure you're very tired*, not *I'm very tired*. He's saying what he thinks I want to hear, no doubt wary after being criticized for wanting sex too much in previous relationships.

I know nothing about his exes and I don't particularly want to know, but I do feel a surprising twinge of jealousy at the thought of him being with other women. I don't want him to think about them, and I don't want to be judged by his previous experiences.

"I thought you wanted to make me scream," I say.

His eyes take on a dangerous glint. "Missie…"

Leaning back, I slowly hitch up my skirt. When it's above my knees, I part them. Ever the gentleman, he refuses to look for a moment. I hold his gaze and lift my eyebrows. He sighs, gives in, and glances down. His eyes widen, and then he gives a short laugh before he tips his head back and closes his eyes. "Jesus Christ," he says.

"What?" I ask innocently.

He drops his head and gives me an amused glare. "Have you been going commando all day?"

"Only the last few hours."

His knee is bouncing now, his motor well and truly running. "Naughty girl," he says.

"Oh, I am." I place my hands on my knees and slowly draw my fingers up my inner thighs. He watches me, looking sulkily aroused.

My hands reached the top of my thighs. Feeling reckless, I slide a finger down into my already moist folds and swirl it over my clit.

Then I bring it up to my mouth and suck it.

"Jesus." He laughs and looks away.

"Mmm," I murmur, making a show of sucking my finger, even though he's trying not to look. "So wet already. That's from watching you, Alex. You looked so hot up on the stage. I've been thinking about you all evening. Kissing me. Touching me. Sliding inside me."

The car shudders to a halt by our stop. He looks back at me, and I lick my lips. "Don't you want to be inside me? Don't you want to fuck me like an animal?"

He throws open the door, then grabs my hand and pulls me out of the car. "Are you trying to make me embarrass myself?" he says roughly, closing the door and then dragging me along the pathway toward the apartments.

Ooh, I've riled him up. Heart racing, I run after him as fast as my high heels will let me, hoping I don't fall over.

We get to the apartment, and he fumbles with the key, manages to get it in the lock, and opens the door. We fall in together, laughing, and close the door behind us.

Immediately, our mouths meet, and I throw my arms around his neck and slide my hands into his hair, while he turns me so my back is to the wall. He pushes up against me, his young, strong body hard against my soft one, from the broad chest to his muscular arms to the very obviously interested part of him that's pressing against my belly.

I tug at the back of his jacket, and he lowers his arms so I can yank it off his shoulders, and he lets it drop to the floor. He begins to move me back toward the bedroom, still kissing me, as the waistcoat follows the jacket, and the shirt follows the waistcoat. Next he gathers my dress in his hands and lifts it up over my head, and my bra follows seconds later, so now all I'm wearing are my high heels.

I undo his belt, and he toes off his shoes, pulls off his socks, and then his trousers join the rapidly growing pile of clothes on the floor.

Now we're both naked, and as we reach the bedroom, I remove my sandals, not wanting anything to get in the way. Ooh, now he's a lot taller than me. I find that such a turn on.

I pull back the duvet, then climb on the mattress and pull him on top of me. We bounce and laugh, and then he crushes his lips to mine, delving his tongue into my mouth. Man, this dude can kiss. I sink my fingers into his hair and scrape my nails lightly over his scalp, and he groans and tears his lips away from mine so he can kiss down my neck.

Seconds later, he closes his mouth over my nipple, and I arch my back as he sucks.

"Harder," I whisper. He does as I ask him, and I moan, bite my lip, then finally squeal as he increases the pressure. He laughs and rolls over so I'm on top of him. "Be careful what you wish for," he says, and brings my head down to kiss me.

Mmm… I like inebriated, fired-up Alex. He was good before, but now he's abandoning his good-boy behavior and turning into the animal I knew he was deep down.

I know he's thinking we need foreplay for a while to get me ready, but I've been watching this guy for hours, and I'm so hot for him, I'm melting, just like in the song.

I move astride him, and before he can stop me, I wiggle my hips until I feel the tip of his erection parting my folds, and then I push down, impaling myself on him.

"Jesus," he says, his fingers digging into my hips. He groans and closes his eyes. "You need to warn me when you're going to do that."

I bend, kiss up to his ear, and nip it with my teeth.

"Ow," he says, but he swells inside me, and strokes his hands up to my breasts.

"Boy I'm coming for you, are you coming for me?" I whisper.

"Ice cream, you scream, scream for me," we both sing, and laugh.

I push up and start moving properly, driving him in and out of me. The moonlight slants in through the open curtains, falling across the bed in a sheet of silver, like a black and white photo of the sunshine-filled scene earlier in the day.

Alex looks like a Greek statue, his muscular arms like marble, his strong features like something Michelangelo might have carved. He's so fucking handsome. I can't believe I've been lucky enough to have a man like this in my bed.

I lean over him, still moving, and kiss him hard, and he cups my breasts and tugs my nipples with gentle fingers.

"Come on Alex," I tease, taking bites out of his jaw and his ear. "Is that all you've got?"

"Jesus. I don't want to hurt you…"

"I'm not made of china." I kiss down his neck, then fasten my mouth at the place where it meets his shoulder and suck hard.

"Missie… ouch, you're going to leave a—ow! Fuck!" He rears up, twisting and tossing me onto my back.

I give a triumphant laugh as he starts moving inside me. "Oh yeah, now you're talking. Give me all you've got."

"Just how drunk are you?" he says, amused, lifting my legs higher, around his waist, as he thrusts hard.

"Not so drunk that I can't tell how turned on you are." I slide my hands around his back, dig my nails into his skin, and draw them down.

"Ahhh… fuck." He shudders and grabs my hands, his eyes flaring.

"Yeah, about time." I meet each thrust of his hips with one of my own. "Come on, Alex. Fuck me hard. You know you want to."

"I told you, be careful what you wish for."

"Ooh." My heart racing, I taunt him, wondering how far I can push him. "Promises, promises. You're such a good boy. Far too good to let the naughty side free."

He stops moving and his eyes narrow. Uh-oh.

Moving back, he withdraws, then flips me over onto my stomach in one easy move before positioning himself between my legs. In seconds, he's pushed up my knee, pressed the tip of his erection down through my folds, and then without any warning, he thrusts forward, hard.

I groan and bury my face in the pillow.

"What?" he asks, kissing the back of my neck. "You give it, but you can't take it?"

"Holy shit."

"Lie down baby, and open wide," he sings in a low voice in my ear, "Want you to take my ice cream all inside…"

"Ah, fuck."

He sets up a fast rhythm, thrusting hard. I try to lift up onto my elbows to give myself some purchase, but he places a hand in the middle of my back, pushing me down again, then wraps my hair around his hand and yanks my head back.

"This what you want, baby girl?" he murmurs. He crushes his lips to mine, plunging his tongue into my mouth, and I moan and open my legs wider to give him better access. He takes advantage of the position and rides me hard, filling the air with the smack of his hips against my butt, the sensual sounds of sex, and our deep groans, as he fucks me right through to the weekend.

"Ah, ohhh…" I can feel my orgasm building, and for a moment I wonder whether he's going to stop and edge me again, but then I realize he's close to coming himself. Instead, he drives harder, thrusting me all the way over the cliff, and as my body clenches around him, he shudders and stills, spilling inside me.

We stay like that for ages, gasping for breath as our bodies take over, and then they finally release us, and we both collapse forward onto the pillows.

Ah jeez, he's heavy on top of me. Our skin is sticking together, and his breath is hot on my ear. He grunts and withdraws, but doesn't move off me.

"Fuck," he says.

"Yeah," I reply, with feeling.

Lit by the moonlight, we fall asleep, not even bothering to draw the duvet up.

Chapter Twenty-Six

Alex

I come to my senses gradually, as if I'm swimming from the dark depths of a pool toward the sunlight at the surface.

I open one eye. I'm lying sprawled on my front, arms tucked under a pillow. The space next to me is empty. I extract my hand and squint at my watch. It says 08:09. Wow. I haven't slept past seven a.m. for years.

With some effort, I push up onto my elbows and look around. The curtains are open, fluttering in the breeze from the gap in the sliding doors. Jeez, that sunlight is bright. I can't see Missie, but I can hear her in the kitchen. It sounds as if she's making coffee. So she hasn't done a runner, then.

I run my tongue over my teeth. My mouth tastes like someone's boiled socks in it. Luckily I wasn't sick last night, not that I remember, anyway, despite having drunk enough whisky to fill a swimming pool. I crashed out, and I didn't even rouse to visit the bathroom.

Talking of which—my bladder is about to burst. I stumble out of bed, visit the bathroom, wash my hands, splash my face with water, glare at my reflection, then go back into the bedroom. I open my case, find some clean boxers and a pair of track pants and put them on, then wander out.

Sure enough, she's in the kitchen. She glances at me as I come out, does a double take, looks at my hair, then laughs. "Wow."

Wincing against the harsh sunlight, I run a hand through my hair, then scratch the stubble on my chin. "Morning."

"It's the Walking Dead," she says. "You look like you need a cup of coffee."

"More than I need air to breathe." I go around the breakfast bar into the kitchen and take the cup she pushes over to me. I have a big mouthful and sigh as I swallow. Ahhh… that's heavenly. "Thank you."

She sips her own drink, watching me over the rim with much amusement. Although she clearly hasn't been up long—she's wearing my shirt and her hair is also unruly—she looks amazing, whereas I look like a werewolf.

"Don't mock me," I mumble, leaning a hip against the worktop. "I've got one hell of a hangover."

She laughs. "I'm not surprised." She extracts a bottle of water from the fridge and fishes a couple of Panadol out of her bag. "Take these," she instructs.

I swallow the paracetamol with a glug of water. "I feel as if I've been run over. It's Huxley's fault. I was doing all right until he started topping up my glass."

She giggles. "You were pretty wasted."

"Did I really strip in front of all those women?"

"Yes. And you did a mighty fine job of it, I have to say."

I brush a hand over my face. "I can't believe I did that."

"You were amazing, Alex. Such a good sport. And so funny." She moves closer and runs a finger down my chest. "I got you right down to your boxers."

"I haven't forgotten."

"You made me pay for it, though." She gives me a mischievous smile.

I think about how, when we got back, I held her down and thrust us both to a climax in minutes. Jesus. What a Neanderthal.

"Aw," she teases, "Mr. Bashful. You're almost blushing."

"I'm so sorry."

"Oh my God, don't apologize. Best thing that's happened to me all week."

"You're a naughty girl."

"I'm going to make it my life's work to lead you astray."

I chuckle. She slides her arm around me, then lifts up and presses her lips to mine. I accept the kiss, then move back and pull a face. "Don't. I smell awful."

She nuzzles my neck. "You smell heavenly."

"I can smell myself, Missie, and it's not heavenly."

"It's manly. You smell all warm and sexy and pheromone-y. You drive me crazy, Alex. Have I told you that?" She kisses the hollow at the base of my throat.

I sigh, put down my coffee, and wrap my arms around her. "I'm crazy about you, too."

She hugs me, then moves back a little so she can look up at me. "I've got a bone to pick with you, though."

"Oh dear."

"From now on, we need to be honest with each other where sex is concerned. You put words in my mouth last night, and that's not fair. If I'm too tired, or not in the mood, I'll say so, okay?"

"Okay."

"And you do the same. Don't have sex with me just because I want it."

"Sure."

She narrows her eyes. "You don't mean that, do you?"

"If you think I'm ever going to turn down sex with you, you're seriously misguided. I'd summon up the energy even if I'd just run a marathon."

"But there are going to be times when you don't feel like it."

"I never not feel like it when you're around."

She purses her lips at me. "Did it occur to you that I might feel the same way?"

My eyebrows lift. I think about it for a moment. "No. But even so, I'll never assume."

"Why?"

"Because I'm a gentleman."

"You're also old-fashioned. Some girls like sex as much as guys."

"Hmm."

"You don't believe me?"

I frown.

"Alex," she says patiently, "I bet I can out-sex you."

"I sincerely doubt it."

"I've changed my mind. I'm going to make it my life's work to wear you out."

"You're welcome to try," I say, amused.

"Challenge accepted." Her eyes hold sultry desire.

We study each other, and my skin prickles at the thought that this gorgeous young woman wants me. "Even though I look like this?" I gesture at my head.

"Your hair is pretty wild. What have you done to it?"

"I don't know. Must be the way I slept. Nothing to do with someone running their fingers through it last night."

She giggles.

I look at my reflection in the window and pat it. "This bit won't stay down. And I need a shave. I look like a yeti."

"An adorable one." She kisses me. "Let's sit outside for a minute," she says softly. "It's a gorgeous morning."

We take our coffees out onto the patio. I put up the umbrella, and we sit in the shade, stretching out our legs.

"What time does the rehearsal start?" she asks.

"Three p.m. at the church."

"So what's happening this morning?"

"My parents are arriving. Dad and Sherry's flight lands at twelve. Kait's been in Auckland for a few days but hers will arrive around the same time. They'll both be here for lunch."

"Oh." She widens her eyes. "Are you sure you want me to meet your parents?"

"Why wouldn't I?"

"It's a bit... serious."

"That's true. I forgot you were a one-night stand."

"Alex! You know what I mean."

"They're important to me. I want them to meet you, because you're important to me."

"I am?" She pokes me with her toe.

I just roll my eyes and drink my coffee.

"I'm a bit nervous," she says. "Do you think they'll mind that I have a son?"

"Why would they?"

"Wouldn't they prefer it if you had met someone who was... you know..."

"An eighteen-year-old virgin? We've been through this already. I'm not the heir to the throne. I'm sure all they want is for me to be happy. Besides, you're only twenty-eight. You're hardly drawing your pension."

She smiles. "Thank you."

"For what?"

"For making me feel young again."

"Aw. You're welcome. Can't say the same though. I feel about a hundred this morning. I'm sure I creaked when I got out of bed."

"That's what you get for screwing me senseless. It's called karma."

I give a short laugh and finish my coffee. "Okay. I need a shave and a shower."

She finishes the last mouthful of her coffee. "Can I join you?"

I sigh at the thought of having her naked and slippery in the shower. "Sure."

We go into the bathroom, and I run the sink full of hot water, then retrieve my shaving gel and razor from my wash bag.

She perches on the edge of the bath. "Do you mind if I watch?"

"No. You can shave me if you like."

Her eyes light up. "Really?"

"Yeah." I hand her the gel.

"You'll have to show me what to do," she says.

"You never did it for Lee?"

"No." She doesn't elaborate.

I lean over the sink and splash hot water on my face, then we swap places, and I perch on the edge of the bath. She squirts some gel into her palm and rubs her hands together until it turns to foam. Then she cups my face and spreads the foam across it. I close my eyes for a moment, enjoying the movement of her fingers across my skin.

"Have all your girls done this?" she asks.

I open my eyes. "All the hundreds of girls I've been with?"

She smooths the foam across my chin. "I just wondered."

"No, Missie. You're the first I've trusted with a razor."

She draws a line of foam above my top lip. "I don't understand why you're single."

"I'm not."

She blinks as if I'm admitting to being secretly married, then realizes I'm referring to being with her, and her lips curve up. "You're smart. Rich. Handsome. Why aren't you married with six kids?"

"I guess I was waiting for the right girl."

Oh, she likes that answer.

"Like this," I tell her, showing her how to draw the razor up my neck and across my cheeks. She begins to shave me, frowning as she concentrates.

"I want to make something clear," she says, the tip of her tongue sticking out of the corner of her mouth as she draws the blade up my neck.

"I'm at your mercy," I point out. "You've got a razor to my throat. You can tell me whatever you like."

"I just want to say that I know you're wealthy, but that's not why I'm dating you."

"I know that," I say, amused.

"I don't earn a bad wage," she continues as if I haven't spoken. "That pays the bills and gives me a little spare, and Finn and I don't need much."

"What about the insurance money? I'm sure Lee took out the life policy so you'd be provided for if something happened to him."

She turns and washes the blade in the sink. "I'm glad he had the policy, because it has enabled me to take care of Finn, and for that I'm thankful to him. It was the one redeemable thing he ever did for me. But I know it was for Finn. It certainly wasn't anything to do with me."

She comes back and continues shaving me.

I watch her, sensing her hurt, and puzzled by the fact that anyone who was with this beautiful girl wouldn't want to take care of her and treat her like the most precious thing in the world.

Glancing up, she meets my eyes. "It's beyond your realm of understanding, isn't it?"

"Yeah."

She bends and kisses me, then moves back with a blob of foam on her nose. I chuckle and wipe it off.

She scrapes the razor up my cheek and washes it in the sink. "It's funny to think of you with other women. Jealousy is a new sensation for me."

"You needn't be jealous. I didn't feel the same way about any of them that I feel about you."

She stops and stares at me. "We've only been dating a few days."

I shrug.

She studies me, then continues shaving me. "I've never felt it before, even when I thought Lee was cheating on me."

"Well, that's one thing you'll never have to worry about with me. I would never cheat."

"I know." She shaves my cheek. "I trust you."

"I trust you too. Hence the razor in your hand."

She draws it up my cheek. "Did you love any of the girls you were with?"

"I was fond of them, of course. But dating is about trying each other on to see if you fit, right? And they didn't quite fit."

Her gaze meets mine for a moment. Then she continues shaving me. "What were they like?"

I lift a hand to the back of her neck and pull her head down for a kiss. She laughs as I smear shaving foam all over her nose and cheeks.

"I'm guessing you won't tell me." She wipes her face.

"I don't think you really want to know about my ex-girlfriends. I think you want to know whether *we're* going to fit."

"Maybe. I suppose only time will tell."

"Hmm."

Her lips curve up. "What?"

"Nothing."

"Alex! People always think they're going to fit at the beginning, right? And it's only as time goes by that you realize it's not going to work?"

"I imagine it happens that way for most people."

She looks into my eyes. "I might drive you crazy after a few weeks or months."

"That's true."

"You might think, jeez, that woman is annoyingly cheerful, or wow, she really gets on my nerves."

"I think it's more likely you'll wonder what you're doing with this grumpy old fart, as Saxon called me."

She scrapes the razor carefully beneath my nose. I press my lips together to give her better access, watching her.

When she's finished, she rinses the razor. Then she puts her arms around my neck. "That's never going to happen," she says, her voice husky, and kisses me.

I bear it for as long as I can, then get to my feet and cup her face in my hands. "I want to taste you," I murmur.

"Not until I've had a wash."

"Fine." I turn on the tap in the shower. "I'll wash you first. Then I'll taste you."

"Oh," she says helplessly.

I take her into the shower cubicle, pour shower gel onto the puff, and wash her top half, taking time on her breasts. Then I cover her bottom half in foam, turn her so she's leaning on the glass, and wash between her legs, my fingers slipping through her folds, until her breath is coming in ragged gasps. Only then do I turn her back to face me, drop to my knees on the shower floor, and slide my tongue inside her, licking and sucking as the shower cubicle gradually fills with clouds of steam.

*

Much later, we go up to the house for lunch, and join Mae, Neal, Dad, Sherry, Kait, Gaby, Tyson, Damon, and Belle, picking at platters full of sliced meats and cheeses, various breads, and olives and chutneys. Well, all of us except Kait. I don't think I've ever seen her eat in public.

"So," Sherry says, "what have you all been up to today?"

For a moment, I can only think about Missie's slippery body in the shower, and I say, "Uh…"

Next to me, Missie hides a smile, Gaby smirks, and Belle giggles.

"I forgot you were all young things with loads of energy," Sherry says as everyone laughs.

"Actually we went for a walk through the gardens," I reply.

"You have an amazing array of plants here," Missie says to Mae.

"Oh are you a gardener?" Kait asks.

I glance at her. I know her well enough to hear the bite behind her words.

Missie just laughs, presumably missing the sarcasm. "God, no. I know next to nothing about plants. But I can appreciate a beautiful display."

Kait puts down her serviette. "May I borrow your bathroom?" she asks. She directs the question to Neal.

"First down the corridor on your right," he says, gesturing at the nearest door.

She rises and walks toward the house.

"Do I need to say it?" Dad asks once she's out of hearing.

"Mason," Sherry warns.

"She's drunk," he says bitterly.

"She's had two glasses of champagne," Gaby replies sharply.

"She smelled of alcohol before she started on the champagne," Dad states.

I glance at Damon, who's looking at his fiancée. Belle's eyes are downcast—this is the last thing she wants at her wedding.

"She's been snotty since she got here," Dad says, "and she was rude to Missie."

Missie glances at me, unsurprised by the comment, so she obviously did pick up on Kait's sarcasm. "I don't think it was directed at me," she says. "No offense taken."

"If she keeps on like this," Dad says, "I'll—"

"Dad," I say mildly. He glances at Belle and has the grace to look ashamed.

I get to my feet. "I'll talk to her." I bend and kiss Missie on the top of her head. Then I walk across the terrace toward the house.

Inside, I can hear staff in the kitchen, and the vacuum cleaner on deeper in the house, but here it's cool and quiet. I stand by the window, looking out at the view, and wait for Kait to exit the bathroom.

When she eventually comes out, she sees me and rolls her eyes.

"He's sent you to have a word with me," she states sarcastically.

Hands in my pockets, I don't reply, I just hold her gaze, and eventually the tension leaves her shoulders.

"Come and sit down for a minute," I say gently, gesturing with my head toward the room along the corridor. It's a quiet reading room overlooking part of the garden, with a small library of books and a coffee machine, the sofa and chairs decorated with colorful throws and bright cushions.

Kait lowers herself onto the sofa, and I sit in the chair opposite her. She sits stiffly, looking uncomfortable and miserable as she glances around.

"What's up?" I ask.

My feelings toward my mother are complicated. She's a very difficult woman, what some men would call high maintenance, and certainly not easy to live with.

From the age of eighteen, I blamed her for the breakup of her marriage. I know Dad tried hard to make it work, and I also know how difficult she can be.

But Belle's revelation that Dad's affair with Sherry began before Kait left shocked me deeply. Nobody knows what goes on inside a marriage. Dad can be stubborn and unsympathetic, and I'm not sure how understanding he was of Kait's struggle with depression. The fact that he cheated on her upset me a lot, especially as he's always acted like the hurt party because of what happened with Tom.

And deep down, I know I've blamed her for what happened to Belle. *She* walked out, she chose Tom, and she didn't notice what was happening to Belle for a whole year.

But I've spent a lot of time thinking about it this year. Putting myself in her shoes. She's an actor who lives in the spotlight. Every word she says, every pimple she has, every time she has a bad hair day, it's splashed across the media. She doesn't eat because she knows if she puts on a pound, someone will notice, and she probably won't get that role she's been hoping for. Her life is about control. And she loves her career. I get my drive from her, not my father, and she's always been supportive of me. She's harsh on Gaby and Belle, but ultimately I think it's out of love—she wants her girls to be resilient, and to be able to cope in this harsh world.

"Is it about Ryan?" I ask. She broke up with the actor earlier in the year.

But she shakes her head. "That's done."

"Are you seeing anyone else?"

"No."

"Why not?" She's beautiful, accomplished, and rich. There must be hundreds of guys who would be thrilled to have her on their arm.

But she just shrugs and looks away.

I frown, frustrated. "You don't have to talk to me, but you're on the verge of alienating everyone else here this weekend. And speaking of which, I don't appreciate you being snarky with Missie. She hasn't got a spiteful bone in her body."

Her gaze comes back to me then. I wait for a spiteful comment, but to my surprise she says, "She's lovely, Alex. You seem very taken with her."

"I am."

"How long have you been dating?"

"Not long, but she's been coming to Kia Kaha since March."

"Is it serious?" I just lift an eyebrow, and her lips quirk up. "She's a lucky girl."

I shrug. "Gaby wouldn't say so."

"Gaby adores you, and you know it. I wish I could have met Missie's son."

"He's a good kid."

"He'll be very lucky to have you as a stepfather."

My eyebrows rise. It's the first time I've thought of it like that.

"You've been lucky," she says softly, "to have Sherry, and Mae and Neal."

"I didn't think you liked any of them," I say wryly.

"I'm jealous of them, Alex. They got to be with you, watch you grow into a man. I know it was all my fault. And I love my job. But that doesn't mean I'm not sad at what I did, and what I missed out on. Everyone has someone. Except me." Her eyes fill with tears.

"Hey." I get up, go over and sit beside her, and put my arm around her. She stiffens for a moment, then curls up on the seat and leans against me.

"It wasn't all your fault," I tell her. "We are who we are. I know what your job means to you, and I understand it better now I have my own business. It's hard to fight ambition and drive. You've had a successful career, and you still managed to bring up three kids."

"He hurt her, Alex." Her voice is little more than a whisper. "He hurt my little girl, and it's my fault."

"No, it's not. I talked to Missie about it, and she said it wasn't your fault, or mine, or Belle's or Dad's—the only person who was at fault is Tom, and I think she's right. You were a victim too. You mustn't forget that."

She starts to cry. I dig out the serviette I'd stuffed in my pocket and hand it to her. "Come on," I scold gently, "the mother of the bride is only allowed to cry for happy reasons."

"Sherry is the real mother of the bride." Normally that would be a spiteful comment. She's always been jealous of Sherry, and the two have got by with an uneasy alliance because of us kids. I like Sherry because she makes Dad happy, and she's been good to the two girls, but privately I'm much fonder of the relaxed and open-hearted Mae, who took pity on the lad who was so mixed up and angry, and gave me both the support and freedom I needed as I entered adulthood. My feelings toward Sherry have also cooled somewhat since I found out she had an affair with Dad behind Kait's back, although I've made sure not to let it show.

"No, she's not," I tell Kait now. "That role is yours and yours alone. Belle doesn't blame you for what happened, Mum. It's been ten years, and Damon's helping her to move on."

She looks up at me then with watery eyes. "That's the first time you've called me Mum for years."

"Well, maybe we're all making steps forward."

She rests her head on my shoulder. "Thank you."

I kiss the top of her head. "You're the famous Kaitlyn Cross. Don't let anyone tell you otherwise. And hey, you never know, there might be some eligible young bachelor here you can snap up. Just please don't let it be one of my mates."

Chapter Twenty-Seven

Missie

After Alex follows Kait, there's an awkward silence at the table. I take out my phone and send a chatty text to Finn, wondering whether I should excuse myself, as the others clearly want to talk about what just happened, but don't want to do it in front of me.

Then Mae says, "Would you like me to give you a tour of the gardens?"

"That would be lovely," I reply. I wasn't joking when I said I know nothing about plants, but I'm guessing she wants to get me away from here.

We rise, and I follow her to the end of the terrace, where we begin walking slowly down the path through the beautiful gardens.

It's been eye-opening watching Alex interacting with the three mother-figures in his life. With his birth mother, Kait, he's cautious and a little wary, more reserved than he is with the others, but equally he's defended her a couple of times when his father has been openly hostile. With Sherry, his stepmother, he's friendly and polite. But it's clear to me that his favorite out of the three of them is Mae. With her he's physically affectionate, giving her hugs and kisses on the cheek, and he laughs more when she's around.

I understand why. Damon's mother obviously adores him, and in their relationship I can see reflections of the past—the boy who came looking for an escape from the turbulent atmosphere at home; the young man who was traumatized by what happened to his sister and who she took under her wing; and the grown man who has been so supportive of her son. By letting him live with them for a while, Mae provided some stability in his life, and Alex, being Alex, is devoted to her because of that.

"I love the hostas," Mae says, gesturing at the light-blue flowers, "they're my pride and joy."

"They're beautiful." I stop to admire them. "You know I was serious when I said I know nothing about flowers, right?"

She laughs. "Yeah, I know. I thought you needed an escape."

"I appreciate that. I had the feeling they didn't want to talk with me there."

"It's nothing to do with you." She links arms with me as we continue to walk. "They don't like talking about it in front of me, either. It's an old family problem."

"Alex has told me some of it."

She gives me an appraising look. "He doesn't normally talk about it, but I'm not surprised he told you." She smiles. "He obviously likes you a lot."

"I hope so," I say, blushing. "And he's very fond of you."

"Ah, well, all boys want to do is play music and game. They want as little drama as possible, and he found that at our house. But they still need guidance, of course. You know all about this, though, having one yourself. It's a shame you didn't bring him. I'd like to have met Finn. Maybe next time?"

I nod, pleased that she thinks I'll be coming back. "He's a good boy," I say as we descend the steps through the ferns that tower over our heads. "He's had a very tough year."

"Of course, losing his father and all."

"Yes, and with all the physical troubles. He was never that much into sports—like you said about Alex, all he wants is his LEGO and his computer—but suddenly not being able to go outside and play when he felt like it was a real shock. Having to be a part of the Learning Enrichment Department at school, being classed as disabled, needing a wheelchair, not having control of his bodily functions—it left him feeling very angry and resentful."

"Toward the world?"

"Mostly toward his father, unfortunately."

"That must be very hard for you."

I'm beginning to see why Alex likes her so much. "It has been difficult. Has… Alex said much to you about what happened with Finn's dad?"

"He did tell me a little. I hope that was okay."

"Of course." So Mae is the one he confides in. I find that strangely touching. "Finn's had to carry the burden of knowing about his father's affair for a long time, so it's good in one way now that it's all out in the open."

"And it's also good that the first anniversary is out of the way. I know it doesn't erase all the difficulties, but it does help a little, I've found."

"Oh, definitely, if only because I've finally been able to date Alex. It didn't feel right before that. Of course after finding out about Lee's affair, I was angry that I'd waited, but deep down I know it was the right thing to do. I'm just glad Alex didn't meet anyone else this year!"

"He's been very patient," she says. "It says something about his feelings for you."

I frown at her. "Oh, I'm not the reason he hasn't dated in a while. We've only been involved for a few weeks."

She gives me an amused look. "Missie, you are absolutely one hundred percent the reason that Alex hasn't dated this year. He told me that Finn said you thought it would be wrong to date anyone else until a year had passed. So he waited."

I stare at her. "What?"

"He rang me the day he met you and told me he'd seen the girl he was going to marry." She gives me a mischievous smile. "If he was prepared to wait a year, it says a lot about his feelings for you."

"You mean nine months," I correct faintly. "We met at the end of March."

"Of course," she says. "I was rounding up." She looks at me curiously. "You really didn't know?"

I think about his words that puzzled me on the way home from the trivia night: *I've waited this long—I'm not going to rush things now. I want to take my time to get to know you.* And then I think about how he took me and Finn on at Kia Kaha. How he's been so kind to Finn, even getting a puppy so Finn can play with it. How he brought THOR to his school and helped Finn look so cool to all his friends. How he came to my classroom afterward. How he sat in a fur suit in the baking heat for four hours to help me out.

How he helped my boy to walk again.

Oh God. I've been so blind.

"He loves Finn," she says. "He's impressed with his resilience and determination. And he thinks you're amazing for how you've supported your son and worked so hard. He's crazy about you, Missie. Never, ever think otherwise. He might be reserved, but he'll be loyal and devoted to you. I love all my boys—they're all kind, generous sweethearts, and they all adore their girls. But Alex is the most serious of them all, and the deepest thinker. If he's decided you're the one for him, there's not much you're going to be able to do about it."

Tears prick my eyes, and I press my fingers to my lips.

"Aw," she says, and immediately puts her arms around me and gives me a hug. "I'm sorry if it's a bit overwhelming, but it had to be said. These guys worry about looking weak or being vulnerable, and they don't realize sometimes it's best if they lay all their cards on the table."

I clear my throat, trying to stop my head from spinning. He told her that first time we met in his office, when we went for a walk through the park, that he was going to marry me? I can't believe it. We haven't even said we love each other yet.

But of course I do love him, with all my heart. We might only have been having sex for a week, but we've been getting to know one another for a year. Rounding up, as Mae said. Funny how she used the same wording as him.

"It's difficult for him having Kait here," she says, interrupting my thoughts, and we start walking down again. "Especially with Sherry and me. His loyalties are split, and that makes him uncomfortable."

"I can see that. He obviously has a difficult relationship with his mother."

"Oh yes. I've always tried to defend her. In many ways I admire her a lot. Do you know much about her?"

"Not really, only what you see in the papers."

"She became famous a little later than most actors—she'd already had Alex and Gaby when she landed the role in *Station Zero*, and her career took off. Mason pressed her to stay in New Zealand rather than move to Hollywood, but of course she had to go there for filming, so she was absent a lot, and the care of their family fell to him. She loved him, I think, but her job put a strain on their relationship, and eventually it broke them. There was all the traveling, and of course he was jealous of her co-stars, understandably so. I don't think she ever had a relationship with any of them, but it must have been hard for him to see her at all the parties with other men."

"And he started seeing Sherry?"

"Yes, before he broke up with Kait, which hit Alex very hard. He's always blamed Kait for the breakup of their marriage, and he feels very guilty about that. He's quite angry toward his father right now, although he'd never show it."

"Has he spoken to Mason about it?"

"Not to my knowledge. Kait told Belle at Gaby's wedding, and then Belle confronted her father. He admitted it, at least. And then she went and told Alex. He was very upset about it. It's one reason he feels for Finn. Boys are so protective of their mothers."

"Alex is very fond of you," I say, smiling.

She gives a bashful smile back. "I do think of him as a son. I've known him since he was twelve."

"What was he like?" I ask, admiring the rose bushes. On our left, the water in the pool sparkles in the bright sunshine.

"Shy. Quiet. Handsome." She smiles. "He's always had that strange lock of hair that refuses to lie flat."

"I know the bit."

"He and Damon used to follow the twins around. Saxon and Kip were always very good with them, although they used to get them into a lot of mischief."

I chuckle at the thought of the four boys getting into trouble.

"Of course they spent a lot of time with Neal," she says. "He was happy to talk about computers for as long as they were willing to listen, which was pretty much all day, every day."

"Oh, I didn't realize that's where Alex's love of computers came from."

"Yes, that's all they talked about. Well, computers, gaming, the All Blacks, food, and occasionally girls." She winks at me.

"Did you meet any of Alex's exes?" I ask curiously. "He doesn't like to talk about them."

"Yes. He's only had three girlfriends that I know of."

"What were they like?"

She smiles. "Do you really want to know?"

I wrinkle my nose. "Maybe not. He's just so private, such a closed book. I wonder why he broke up with them? Or did they break up with him?"

"Honestly, I think all of them were mutual separations. Alex's relationships have always been carefully thought out. They were nice, quiet, pleasant girls who, if I'm perfectly honest, seemed to have had little to make them stand out from the crowd. I think he wanted to date girls who were uncomplicated and low maintenance, because his life was so turbulent."

I frown, puzzled as to why he finds me attractive, when I have all these issues with Lee and the accident to overcome.

But Mae says, "That's why you're so special. You have heaps of personality, and he's so different with you."

"Really?"

"Oh God, yes. He lights up like a Christmas tree when you're around. You might not notice it, but we all do. He can't take his eyes off you. He's very different with you."

We've reached the bottom of the path, on the level of the apartments. "I might stay here," I say to her, "and get ready for this afternoon."

"Of course. I'll catch the cable car back."

"It's been lovely talking to you," I tell her. "Thank you so much."

"You're very welcome here, Missie, and I'm always happy to chat about Alex and the others. Neal's smart—a lot smarter than me—and the boys are the same. I'm not saying I'm dumb by any means, but these guys are gifted, and sometimes it's difficult being on the outside of that. Us girls have to stick together, you know?" She smiles and comes forward to kiss my cheek. "I'll see you later."

"Yes, see you." I wave, and she walks away, back to the cable car.

I let myself into the apartment, which is cool and quiet. I consider making myself a coffee, but I think Alex might be back soon, so I decide to wait until then. Instead, I go out onto the patio and stretch out on one of the cushioned deckchairs beneath the shade of the umbrella. I can smell the roses and the faint scent of chlorine from the pool further up the hill. It's not an unpleasant aroma.

I send Finn a Snapchat, telling him how I'm doing, and just a minute later get a photo back of Zelda tearing around the garden with the other dogs, and a brief message saying how much he's enjoying himself.

Putting down my phone, I lie back, thinking about what Mae said.

Alex waited for me. He didn't pressure me, or rush me to get over Lee. He just calmly supported us both while he helped Finn walk again, until the time was right.

I'm so touched that my throat tightens, and I have to fight against the prick of tears again. What have I done to deserve this guy? This whole family, in fact? I know that if Alex and I stay together, I'll be seeing a lot more of Mae, Damon, and all the others, because they're clearly all very important to him.

I've done nothing at all to deserve it. I'm so lucky.

Swallowing hard, I close my eyes, letting the warm sunshine soothe me, and trying to believe I'm worth all the trouble.

*

A shadow falls across me, and then I feel the press of lips against my own. I open my eyes to see Alex looking at me upside down, leaning over the deckchair.

"Hey you," I say, smiling up at him.

"Hey." He comes around and sits on the chair next to me, then reaches out to take my hand. "You okay?"

I nod. "How long have I been asleep?"

"Not long. I came straight down after I found out you'd left."

"I went for a walk with Mae."

"Oh?"

"She's so lovely, Alex. I can see why you love her so much."

He narrows his eyes. "Has she been telling you all my secrets?"

"A few." I smile. "How's your mum?"

He sighs. "She's okay. Vulnerable. Lonely."

"Oh of course, she broke up with Ryan Webster didn't she?"

"Yeah, some time ago. I thought I might ask Henry or James if they'd mind looking after her over the next couple of days. Do you think that'd be a huge mistake?"

"Are you asking me if one of them might make a move on her?"

"Kinda."

"Then ask Henry, not James."

He laughs. "Yeah, all right. Neal told me one of his friends has a crush on her."

"Oh really?"

"Yeah. His name's Simon and he's a lawyer. Apparently he's seen all her movies multiple times and he's dying to meet her. He's coming to the wedding tomorrow. He might not be her type, of course."

"Maybe not, but it's always nice to know when someone's interested in you, isn't it?"

"Yeah." He leans forward on the deckchair, so his lips aren't far from mine. "You might be surprised to know there's someone not so far away who's very interested in you."

I look up at the terrace. "Are you referring to the gardener who was working on the hostas?"

He chuckles and touches his nose to mine. "Actually someone a lot closer than that."

I look up into his warm brown eyes. I knew he liked me. That he desired me. But Mae's revelation about how he's waited for me has completely spun me off my axis. I'd taken his calm, reserved manner as a lack of emotion, but now I know how wrong I was. She said, *These guys worry about looking weak or being vulnerable*, and I realize he was probably concerned about revealing how he feels about me because he didn't want to come on too strong, and he wasn't sure how I feel about him. We haven't been dating long, after all.

But I think about the past nine months, how many times he's been there on Finn's treatment days, and how he's hung around to see me to talk, so we can get to know each other, even though we weren't officially dating.

We've been falling for each other since the moment we first met, and I just didn't realize it.

"I love you," I say.

His eyebrows lift, and he stares at me in surprise. "Oh," he says.

My lips curve up. "I'm just saying. I don't expect you to say it back. But I wanted you to know."

His eyes are filled with affection and delight. Softly, he says, "I love you too."

And he bends his head and kisses me, while the afternoon sunshine warms us through.

Chapter Twenty-Eight

Alex

I'm a tad nervous about the wedding rehearsal—not because of my part in it or because I'm worried that it won't be well-organized, but because I'm conscious that my family might play up.

Following Missie's advice, I have a chat with Henry and ask him if he'd do me a favor and look after Kait for me. "Unless you've got yourself another date," I say.

"Nope," is his reply, so I guess he and Juliette haven't yet worked out their differences. Anyway, he's happy to oblige, and when he sees Kait approach the luxury coaches that are taking us all to the church, he immediately strikes up a conversation, then asks her to sit next to him, and all the attention stops her from casting daggers at my father, who's always ready for an excuse to get annoyed at her.

Our destination is a beautiful church called Old St. Paul's. It's wooden, constructed from New Zealand native timbers painted white, built in a Gothic revival style. Its exterior is modest, but it's stunning on the inside, with large, colorful stained-glass windows, native timber columns, and embroidered furnishings. I like it because although it's consecrated, it's non-denominational, and any type of wedding can be held here, whether it's religious, civil, or LGBTQIA+.

Damon and Belle are having an Anglican ceremony, which surprised me initially as Damon didn't go to church when he was younger, but I knew that was to do with him losing his cousin when he was ten, and Belle has told me he's rediscovered his faith since they got together.

My family isn't religious, and we've never been to church other than to attend other people's weddings and christenings, but Belle has embraced Damon's faith, and the two of them have been attending church, and undertook a course in marriage preparation. This amused me when he first told me, and I teased him about it, but since then I've been thinking a lot about marriage, and I've come to admire them both for their dedication and commitment.

About fifty people are attending the rehearsal and the dinner tonight, but there'll be around a hundred for the service and reception tomorrow—friends, family, and work colleagues arriving from all across New Zealand and Australia—and another hundred or so coming for the evening do. It's a huge event, and privately not something I'd be interested in, but Damon and Belle seem to be loving all the funfair.

Damon and I are wearing matching medium-gray suits, not quite as smart as the dark-gray morning suits we've got for tomorrow, but still British-cut—formal and elegant. Missie's wearing a beautiful pale-yellow dress that's perfect for a summer wedding, and the sexiest pair of high-heeled sandals I've ever seen.

Mik, the wedding coordinator, and his team show everyone where they're going to sit, and then he runs through the ceremony. He's warm and funny, and I can see everyone gradually relaxing as he makes it clear that everything is going to go smoothly, and they'll easily deal with any hiccups that happen on the day.

My stomach still flutters though. Why am I so anxious? It's not like me. I look at Belle and Damon then, though, holding hands in front of the altar, and I realize why I'm feeling like this. Both of them have had huge obstacles to overcome in order to be here today. Damon's loss in his youth caused him all sorts of problems, and what happened to Belle had a severe impact on her, and, I'm sure, continues to do so.

My baby sister has been through the ringer, and I wasn't there for her. I don't think that guilt will ever completely go away, no matter what I do for her from now on. I wish I had a magic wand and could wave it and make everyone's pain disappear, but I can't. We're all stuck with it, and the only thing we can do is work through it as best we can, and move on.

"If we could have the rings now," Mik says to me.

I stare at him. "Sorry?"

"The rings please, Alex?"

My mouth opens, but no words come out.

"Bro," Damon says with much amusement, "that was your one job." A ripple of laughter passes through the crowd.

"I didn't realize I needed to bring them for the rehearsal," I say, embarrassed. "I'm so sorry. I was worried about losing them. They're in the safe in the apartment."

"It doesn't matter at all," Mik says, sliding a hand into his trouser pocket. "I happen to have a couple of spares so we can practice the exchange." He brings out a small case and hands it to me and carries on.

I look at Belle and mouth, "Sorry!" She laughs and gives a small shake of her head, and her eyes sparkle. I glance at the crowd, not surprised to see most of my friends looking a combination of sorry for me and amused. Lastly, I look at Missie. She winks at me and blows a kiss, which makes me feel a bit better, but I still curse myself under my breath.

After he finishes going through the ceremony, Mik talks about signing the register, then moves everyone outside and explains where the photographs will take place. I'm standing at the edge of the crowd, and Missie threads her way through to stand beside me.

"You okay?" she murmurs, slipping her hand into mine.

I look at where Belle and Damon are standing, also holding hands, and my heart twists. "I'm such an idiot."

"Alex."

"The one job I have, and I blew it."

"Alex."

I blink and look at Missie.

"It doesn't matter," she says. "It's just a rehearsal. You'll bring them tomorrow, and that's the important thing."

I inhale, then blow it out slowly, but I don't say anything.

"They know you're there for them," she says. "What's done is done. Leave the past where it is and think about the future." And she lifts up onto her tiptoes and kisses me.

I sigh, shocked and yet somehow not surprised that she's able to read me. When she moves back, I look down into her eyes, my heart swelling. Earlier today, she told me she loved me—something I did not expect to hear. I knew she liked me, that she found me desirable. But we've not been dating long, and I wasn't sure she'd be open to declarations of love so soon. I wish I'd broached the topic, but I didn't want to send her running for the hills.

It doesn't matter who said it first, though. The important thing is that we both know we're serious about the other, and that's opened me up to a world full of sunlight.

"By the way," she says, her voice teasing, "what's your middle name? And don't tell me it's 'diplomatic'. I mean your real one."

My eyes widen. "What?"

"At the trivia evening, Tyson said Gaby runs Hepburn Education, and he also called her 'Gabrielle Audrey Winters-Palmer.' I assume your mum was the fan of Audrey Hepburn? Then, when they ran through the vows, Mik called Belle 'Michelle Marilyn Winters—after Marilyn Monroe, I'm guessing?"

Damn, she's astute. I nod slowly. "Mum loved the old movie stars."

"So what's yours?"

"I'm not telling you."

She laughs. "It can't be that bad."

"It is. Now shush, Mik's talking."

We listen to him as he rounds up, and Missie doesn't push me. But the bright hope I was feeling in my heart has dimmed a little.

I guess I'll have to tell her my middle name one day. In itself it's not the end of the world, not unless she makes the connection. Hopefully she won't. I don't plan on telling her my secret, even though there have been times I've been desperate to blurt out the truth.

But there's no time to dwell on it, because we all head for the coaches to go back to the house, and everyone's talking at once, and as soon as we get back, I have things to do. More people are arriving, and I want to make sure everything goes smoothly, so that Damon and Belle have nothing to worry about.

Mik and his team are well in control of the organization, though, and although I have a few odd jobs to do—sorting out a couple of rooms in nearby hotels for last-minute guests who decided to come, thanking guests for presents and taking them inside, running a few errands for Mae—everyone seems happy and positive, and gradually I begin to relax.

First, cocktails are served on the lower terrace, and then we move to the upper terrace for dinner. Tomorrow it will be a sit-down do, but today it's a buffet, where guests help themselves before finding a seat at one of the round tables. Several large food stations line the back wall with an amazing array of options, including a charcuterie station with meats, cheeses, and fruits, an oyster bar and a seafood spread, a taco station, a colorful vegetable assortment with various dips, and several sweet options, including a fantastic cupcake table. Waiters move between the tables serving champagne and wine, including the wine from Missie's uncle, which turns out to be fantastic, or taking drinks orders for the bar that's been set up to one side.

Eventually, when most people have chosen their food and are seated, Mae pushes a plate in my hand and tells me to help myself before I pass out from hunger. I do as she bids and take it over to the seat beside Missie, who says, "I got you a glass of champagne."

"I was only going to drink water today," I reply, having a big bite of a taco filled with shredded chicken, black beans, lettuce, and salsa, topped with grated cheese. "Oh God, that's good."

She chuckles. "Hair of the dog. Do you know why it's called that?"

"No."

"Because the cure for rabies is supposed to be the hair of the dog that bit you."

"Seriously?"

"Yeah. Go on, just one, then we'll just have soft drinks tonight, okay?"

I nod, pleased she understands.

Gradually, I start to relax, as my stomach fills, and the champagne threads through me. I'm surrounded by my family and friends, and it's wonderful to have Missie by my side. She's friendly and funny, she joins in the conversation, and I can see that everyone likes her.

I'm glad Mae took her for a walk earlier. The two of them seem to have hit it off, which is important to me, probably more so than whether Kait likes her or not, although I'd never admit that to my mother. Henry's doing a fine job entertaining her today, and she's currently sitting between him and James, so she's having a great time.

A waiter comes up and asks if anybody would like a drink from the bar. "I'll have a gin and tonic, please," Huxley says.

"Do you want a squirt of lemon in that?" Sidnie asks him.

Elizabeth coughs into her champagne. Huxley glances around the table, his lips gradually curving up as the girls all giggle.

I look at Missie, who's trying not to laugh. "Private joke," she says. Elizabeth has turned scarlet, though, so I can guess what the joke was about.

Amused, Huxley puts down his serviette and says, "I'm going to get a bit more food. Do you want to come with me, sweetheart?"

"Thank you," Elizabeth with relief, and she gets up and follows him over to the food stations. She buries her face in his shoulder, and he laughs and hugs her as he murmurs in her ear.

"That was wicked," Heidi scolds Sidnie.

She giggles. "I couldn't resist."

"We might have overshared last night," Missie reveals.

"Oh God," Mack replies.

"Yep," Sidnie states, "they know all your dirty secrets now."

"Dirty being the operative word," Alice adds. "I'll never look at a glazed doughnut the same way again."

Sidnie bursts out laughing, and Mack looks at her and raises an eyebrow, which just makes her laugh more.

"Talking of which," Victoria says to Saxon, "have you knocked your wife up again yet?"

"I'm working on it," he says.

"Incessantly, from what we hear," Victoria says.

He gives Catie an amused look, and she also turns the color of a tomato.

Kip grins and reaches for his glass of water, and Belle says, "Do you want some ice in that?"

Now it's Alice's turn to go scarlet, and the rest of us laugh as his eyebrows rise.

"Can't a guy have any secrets?" Kip complains.

"Oh, we had great fun last night," Belle says.

"Yeah, we're putting in a bulk order of roses after Belle's revelation," Sidnie states.

Damon laughs and kisses his fiancée's temple. "I see."

"Roses?" I ask.

"It's a suction vibrator," Sidnie says helpfully.

"Ah."

Sidnie winks at me. "They're useful if the guy wants a break, although I understand you don't tend to need one…"

"Jesus," I say, and the girls all giggle.

"Sorry." Missie looks embarrassed.

"Hey, I'd much rather you share that than you all be laughing because it's so small."

"Definitely no problems there," she says, and everyone else chuckles.

"Anyway," Damon says, "moving on… speeches time, Alex?"

I glance around. Most people are coming to the end of their dinner, and the waiters are refilling glasses. It's nearly seven p.m. now, and although it'll be light for another couple of hours, the sun is low on the horizon, and the sky is a deep blue above us and a warm orange-gold over the hills to the west.

I put down my serviette, stand, and catch Mae's eye. She nods, so I pick up a glass, and tap it with a spoon. It takes a while, but gradually everyone falls quiet.

As we're in the open air, Mae has arranged for a lapel mike for the speeches, so I clip it to my shirt collar and then address the guests.

"Good evening, everyone," I say. "I think I've met most of you by now, but just in case you slipped through the net, I'm Alex Winters, Damon's best man and Belle's brother. I'll be giving my proper best man's speech tomorrow, but I wanted to say a few words today, as it's a special occasion, with the bride and groom's closest family and friends here. I didn't really know where to start so I thought I'd trawl the internet. After a couple of hours I'd found some really, really good stuff. But then I remembered that I was supposed to be writing a speech, so…"

Belle bursts out laughing, which makes Damon laugh, and that sets everyone else off. "Thanks, sis," I say to her, and she blows me a kiss. "All right, so I'll keep this short and sweet," I continue. "I thought I'd tell you a story about me, Damon, Saxon, and Kip."

"Oh jeez," they all say.

"When Saxon and Kip were fifteen, and we were thirteen, we decided it would be a great idea to form a band," I say. "And thus the Antarctic Coyotes were born." Everyone laughs, and I hold up a hand. "Damon told me that Belle had found some photos of us. Well, I happened to mention it to Mae, and she let it slip that she had some old video footage…" I nod at Neal, who's linked his laptop to a projector that's directed at a white screen they've erected for this purpose. He presses play, and the four of us appear on the screen, performing in our band.

We all look so young! Kip and Saxon haven't changed that much, although their faces are baby smooth rather than bearded as they are now, but Damon and I have the most vivid bleached hair. Everyone whistles and cheers, and the four of us start laughing.

"I'm so sorry," I say to Damon. "I didn't realize it was that bad." We listen for a minute. We're not great. Damon can sing, and Kip's guitar playing is terrific. I'm absolutely terrible on the drums, though, and Saxon's bass is clearly out.

"Anyway…" I make a gesture across my throat, and Neal laughs and cuts the video, making everyone boo. "Ah, but I have a story to tell about that day," I continue.

"Ah no." Damon puts his hands over his face.

I try not to laugh. "Believing that we were going to be the next big thing, we decided we'd hold a concert, and we invited a group of friends over to watch us, including, I have to say, several rather pretty young women." Everyone whistles, and I grin. "We played a few songs, which were, as I'm sure you can guess, terrible. Then we decided we'd all go for a swim. Except we'd forgotten we'd bleached our hair. So this happened."

Neal puts up a photo on the screen of Damon and I taken up close after our swim, with our bleached hair that's turned a beautiful shade of lime green. Our hair is awful, but it's a great photo of the two of us, so young at thirteen, forgetting our worries for a while and laughing at Neal, who's taking the photo.

"Surprisingly," I continue, "the two girls we had our eye on were not interested in becoming groupies for the Antarctic Coyotes."

I glance down at Missie, who's chuckling away. Then I look at Damon, who's smiling at me. "Damon's been my best mate since the age of twelve," I say. "He's helped me through some tough times, and he's still the guy I turn to whenever I need someone I can rely on. He's smart, resourceful, and he's incredibly good-looking, which is really annoying." Everyone laughs, and I smile back at him. "He's an amazing best friend, and even though I once told him I'd kill him if he touched my sister, Damon, I'm thrilled you're going to be my brother-in-law."

He laughs and gets up, and the two of us exchange a bearhug.

"Thanks, man," he says in my ear, holding me there. "I'm so glad you're here."

"Always," I tell him. "I'm glad she's got you."

He tightens his arms, then releases me, and I give him the mic and sit down.

I reach out to hold Missie's hand, pleased when her fingers close around mine.

"Like Alex said," Damon begins, "we'll keep the main speeches for tomorrow. But I have a few things to say today. I want to thank my parents for all their support over the years. How the two of you have put up not just with the twins but with me and Alex as well, I'll never know, but I'm so glad you were there for us, and I know I'm speaking for all of us when I say how much we appreciate you and what you've done for us."

I get to my feet, and so do Kip and Saxon, and the four of us clap Neal and Mae. Neal puts his arm around his wife, and Mae presses her fingers to her lips, clearly touched.

"Next I want to thank Kip and Saxon," Damon says. "You guys have always been great brothers. I know everyone says twins have a special connection, but I can honestly say you've never made me feel awkward or on the outside because of that. We're guys, so we don't get to say it often enough, but I love you both."

They get up and exchange bearhugs, while everyone else goes *Awwww!*

"Alex," Damon says once the twins have sat. He looks down at me and smiles. "We met on the first day of high school, when we were placed in the same form class. We all had to stand up and tell the rest of the class something about ourselves that we were proud of. And Alex stood up and said he had a level eighty paladin on World of Warcraft, and I thought, 'I want to be friends with that guy.'" He grins as everyone cheers, and I chuckle.

"I know you said your sister was off limits," Damon continues. "I'm sorry about that, bro." He gives an embarrassed grin as everyone laughs. "We did fight our affection, for several years, but I think it was always going to end this way. And I'm glad, because it means I get to have you not just as a best mate, but as a brother-in-law. You're a fantastic guy, and I couldn't ask for anyone better for that role."

We have another hug as everyone cheers. Wow, this is turning into a soppy evening, but I guess if you can't say these things at a wedding, when can you say them?

"Lastly," Damon says as I sit, "I want to thank my beautiful bride-to-be. She was only six when I first called her Belle, and the word is as apt now as it was back then. Sweetheart, I'm crazy about you, and although I think you're more than aware of that, I'm hoping this'll convince you even more." He nods to his father, who starts up some music. I laugh. It's the Beatles' *Michelle*, and as McCartney's voice rings out across the terrace, Damon joins in and sings the words to her.

I watch her blush and laugh, then stand and dance with him as he sings, while everyone around us claps and fights against shedding tears. Then I look at Missie, not surprised to see her also trying not to cry.

Chapter Twenty-Nine

Missie

After the food, there's music and dancing, although it's all a little more sedate than it was last night. Both Alex and I have only had the one glass of champagne, and I know he wants to have his wits about him for Damon's sake.

I watch him doing his best man duties—making sure Damon and Belle have whatever they want, keeping an eye on our friends so they're never without a drink, getting wraps for the girls when it gets cold, handing out cushions for the old aunts, welcoming and entertaining all the time, bewitching everyone with his gentle wit and his warm smile.

If I wasn't in love with him before this, I'd have fallen for him tonight. I thought he was sexy last night, dancing with the other guys and doing his comedy routine, but there's something about a man who's a good host, who's genial and capable, and who genuinely cares about the people around him. He's smiled more tonight than in all the time I've known him. Am I anything to do with that? I hope so.

In between his errands, he's always at my side, and he often takes my hand and brings me with him to introduce me to someone he's known a long time—often, I have to say, Damon's relatives rather than his own. It's clear that he's very fond of the Chevalier family, and from the way the favorite uncles and second cousins react to him, I can see they think of him more as Damon's brother than his friend, and certainly someone they're very fond of.

There is someone that I haven't had a chance to talk to yet. The sun has now set, and the terrace has been lit by fairy lights that sparkle against the darkening sky. When Alex is off helping Mae organize something, I spot Kaitlyn Cross on her own, sipping a glass of water and studying her phone. Henry's been looking after her for most of the day, but he's currently talking to Mack and Saxon by the bar, so I go over to her.

She looks up in surprise, as if she's unused to people approaching her, although surely it must happen all the time. She's very beautiful, far too thin, but her makeup is immaculate, and her clothes are obviously expensive.

"Hello," I say. "We haven't really had a chance to talk yet. Do you mind if I sit with you for a bit?"

"No, of course."

"Tell me if you'd rather be alone," I say, "but I was hoping to wheedle some secrets about Alex from you."

She scans my face as if suspicious that I'm mocking her. "I think you should talk to Sherry or Mae if you're looking for information about Alex."

"Aw," I say, "they're both lovely, but it's not the same as talking to his mum."

Her lips curve up at that. "He did live with me until he was seventeen," she says.

"Of course, all the formative years. He talks about you all the time." It's a white lie—as a mother, I know it's what she would want to hear.

She's not fooled, but her smile broadens anyway. "I can see why he likes you," she says.

"He thinks I'm a pain in the butt because I'm so upbeat," I tell her. "Was he always this grumpy?" Too late I realize the event that might have changed him, and bite my lip.

But she just chuckles. "I've always thought of him as serious rather than grumpy. I think it stems from being puzzled by people—he's taught himself not to react. Nowadays, I would have him tested to see if he has ADHD or something, but it wasn't something so widely talked about when he was young."

"I hadn't considered that his seriousness might be due to him being on the spectrum," I say, surprised. I deal with children who have it all the time, but I hadn't made the connection with Alex. "He was terrific last night when he did his comedy routine. Wouldn't that rule it out?"

"No, not at all. I used to think ADHD was another name for naughtiness, for kids who couldn't sit still, or who misbehaved and didn't do as they were told. I've talked to several parents whose children have it though, and it covers a lot of different symptoms. He has the hyper-fixation, the intensity that people with ADHD have. If he's playing a computer game, for example, he has to stay there until he finishes the level or beats the bad guy. It drove me mad when he was young because I thought he was just being naughty, but it almost physically hurts him to walk away from something that's incomplete."

"I never thought of it like that," I say softly.

"He likes to be organized and have everything in its place because his mind is always elsewhere, and he forgets where he's put things. He sets five alarms for everything because he's terrified that he'll become involved in a task and forget appointments. He has trouble calming his mind, which is why he's often up late. All the signs are there, but I didn't see them when he was young."

It makes me look at him in a different light. The way I've teased him for being OCD, for being so grumpy, for all his alarms.

"No wonder he was so upset when he forgot the rings," I say.

"Oh, I really felt for him. He prides himself on doing his research and knowing all the rules and regulations. He'll still be kicking himself for not having gotten that right."

"He must have been very good at school."

"Yes, he's always been bright. By the time he started school, he was reading and writing, and he knew all his colors and shapes and could tell stories. Did you know that he wrote poetry?"

I smile. "Yes, he did tell me."

"He's always done that, right from a kid. He used to write them for me." Her expression turns wistful.

"Did you used to read to him?" I ask, hoping the memory will comfort her.

"Oh yes. We read all the Narnia books together and Harry Potter. I miss the kids being that age. They were all very sweet."

"Maybe you'll have grandchildren soon?" I suggest. "Gaby and Tyson are trying for a baby, aren't they?"

She nods. "He's not sure about his fertility after the accident, but hopefully it'll happen for them."

"And of course Damon and Belle will probably want children."

"I'm sure."

"They'll be so excited to have such a famous Nanna. A movie star! How wonderful."

She smiles. Then she gives me a mischievous look. "I think maybe my first grandchild might be a step-grandchild?"

Oh, she means Finn! I give an embarrassed laugh. "Oh, Alex and I have only been dating a week or so."

"Yes, but he told me ages ago that there was this woman whose son was having treatment at Kia Kaha, and she'd been through a tough time, so he was having to wait a while before he asked her out. But he said she was the most beautiful girl he'd ever met, and he was crazy about her."

Heat floods my face. "Oh. Goodness."

She reaches out and touches my arm. "I'm sorry I was rude to you yesterday."

"Were you? I don't remember."

"You're being very nice about it, but yes, I was, and I am sorry. It wasn't you—being with Sherry and Mae makes me realize how much I've missed out on with my children, and it brings me down." She hesitates. "Alex said he'd told you about what happened."

I wasn't going to bring it up, but the fact that she has suggests she wants to talk about it. "Yes, he told me yesterday." I look across at where Alex is standing talking to Damon, and feel a swell of relief that he's such a kind, loving man. "My own experience is very different, but my late husband was violent at times. Not with Finn, with me, but I used to worry that he would hit Finn." I look back at Kait. "I walked out once, but I went back because I thought it would be better for Finn. I regret that a lot. I was frightened about being alone. It's not the same as what you went through, of course, but I just wanted to say from one mother to another that I can't imagine how horrific it was for you, and I admire you so much for the way you walked out that day."

She looks stunned. "Thank you." Her eyes shine. "It was a very difficult time."

"Of course. I think it says a lot about the way you brought up your kids that they've all turned out to be so great. Belle and Gaby are lovely young women, and Alex is just… he's a fine man. Honorable, loyal, and strong, and a lot of that has to be down to you."

Her bottom lip trembles, and a tear tips over the edge of her lashes. "That's a lovely thing to say."

"Aw." I put my arms around her automatically when I see her emotion. For a second she stiffens, but then she relaxes, and we exchange a long hug.

Over her shoulder, I see Alex and Damon looking over. Damon says something, and Alex nods. Then he smiles, and I smile back.

"Sorry," I say as I release Kait. "I forget not everyone's a hugger."

"Don't be sorry," she whispers, dabbing a tissue to her lashes. "I appreciate it. It's been a while since I've had a sincere hug like that."

"Are you making my mother cry?" Alex appears in front of us and raises an eyebrow at me.

"Yeah, I was telling her how you got right down to your boxers in front of a crowd of women last night," I tease as she composes herself.

"Close but no cigar," he says, and Kait laughs.

"He was very good," I tell her. "Has he always told jokes?"

"Oh yes. Completely deadpan, which I always found hilarious. What was your favorite when you were a kid?"

"What does a cloud wear under his raincoat?" he says. When I shake my head, he answers, "Thunderwear."

I giggle, and he smirks. "I've still got it."

The music has changed to a slow Ed Sheeran song, and Alex holds out his hand to his mother. "You don't mind?" he says to me.

I smile. "Of course not."

"You don't want to dance with me," Kait scolds.

He flicks his fingers at her. "Stop arguing and come with me before the music changes."

"I didn't think you liked Ed Sheeran," she says, taking his hand and letting him lead her away.

"I love Ed Sheeran. You know I have a thing about ginger hair." He takes her to the dance floor, and I see her laugh as he turns her into his arms, and they begin to dance.

Someone appears in front of me, and I look up to see James holding out his hand. "Finally got a chance to dance with the most beautiful girl at the party," he says.

"Aw, you're such a smoothie." I take his hand though and let him lead me to the space in front of the DJ near to where Alex and Kait are dancing. James pulls me toward him and slides his other hand around my back, resting just above my butt. Alex reaches out and moves it up a few inches, and Kait and I laugh.

We turn slowly to the music, lit by the twinkling fairy lights. "Are you having a good time?" James asks.

"I am, thank you. It's funny being without Finn. I've been a mum for so long I'd forgotten I was still me."

He smiles. "I can see how that might happen."

"What about you? Are you enjoying yourself?"

"Yeah, free food and drink and good company, what's not to like?"

"No Cassie though?" I say.

He sighs. "No, that's over."

"I'm sorry."

"Eh, I think we both knew it wasn't a long-term thing. I drove her nuts."

"I can't believe that."

"I'm a pain in the arse," he says. "Vain and shallow." He smiles.

He's an exceptionally good-looking guy, tall and muscular, with dark hair and attractive blue eyes. He smells great, too. He's obviously aware of how gorgeous he is. He's a lot cockier than Alex, and very self-assured, although he still seems nice with it.

"But... no Aroha either?" I tease.

He meets my eyes and gives me a wry look. "I snatched defeat from the jaws of victory there."

"Aw. She obviously likes you. Aren't you going to try again?"

"Eh, I blew it. She's not going to touch me with someone else's bargepole."

"You might be surprised. Maybe if you romanced her a bit. Turned on the charm, you know? You were very self-deprecating when you admitted falling asleep, and I could see she liked that."

His eyebrows rise. "Really?"

"Yeah."

He thinks about it. "I don't know. I think she was pretty upset by what happened."

"What did you say when you woke up?"

"Uh... I didn't say anything. I was embarrassed. I wrote a note saying I hope she slept well and left."

I gape. "You didn't stay and talk to her?"

"Um, no."

I sigh. "Oh, James."

"I didn't think she'd be interested."

"No wonder she's upset. You should at least have apologized in person."

He looks suitably ashamed. "Yeah, probably."

"Maybe take her to one side and say sorry. It is a magic word and nearly always makes things better."

"All right," he says. "Maybe I will." The song ends, and he says, "Thanks for the dance."

"Thank you for asking me, and good luck."

He gives a mischievous smile, then turns to Kait and holds out his hand as another slow song comes on. "Would you do me the honor?"

"I wouldn't," Alex says, "he'll take a selfie and it'll be up on Instagram before the song's over."

Kait laughs and accepts James's hand. "I'll survive." The two of them start dancing.

Alex pulls me toward him and slides a hand around to the base of my spine.

"You were very territorial when James did that," I comment as we begin to move to the music.

"Only I get to touch your bum," he says.

"Oh, that's the rule, is it?"

"I'm having it typed up and laminated as we speak."

I chuckle and run a finger along his jaw. "I need to return the favor you granted me earlier."

His eyebrows rise. I run my tongue briefly over my top lip, and his lips curve up.

"Maybe we should go now," he says, "I think the party's wrapping up."

"Alex! No, we can't sneak off. You'll have to wait."

He sighs. "You're such a temptress."

I lift up and kiss him, and he chuckles.

"Thank you," he says. "For talking to Kait."

"Oh, it was nice, I've been wanting to talk to her since she came here. She told me all your secrets."

"Really?"

I give him a curious look. "Hmm, and now I'm wondering what you're worried I'm going to discover. It can't be worse than the bleached hair, surely?"

"God, no," he says. "That was a great photo of me and Damon, though. I'm going to have a copy printed and framed for both of us."

"I'm sure he'll be delighted to be reminded of his worst hair day."

He chuckles and spins me around, and I laugh, happy to be in the arms of the man I love.

*

It's several hours later before we finally leave the party, as Alex wanted to wait until the end, to make sure everyone knew where they were staying, and that nobody needed any help.

We left Belle up at the house where she's staying tonight, and traveled down in the cable car with Damon, who's just made his way over to his own apartment alone. Alex is going over there tomorrow, and he'll be spending the morning with him before the two of them make their way over to the church at three p.m.

"Belle said you're welcome to join her in the morning," Alex says as we let ourselves into Kip's apartment. "She'd love to have you there while she gets ready."

I sit on one of the dining chairs to take off my sandals. "That's very sweet, but she's got her bridesmaids, and Kait and Mae and Sherry, and probably half a dozen other people, too. No, I'll be fine here. I might go up and have a swim, then I can take my time getting ready."

"Okay. You don't mind me leaving you?"

I smile, walk over to him, and begin to walk him backward. "Of course not. You're the best man."

"I hope you realize that's an honorary title."

I shake my head, guiding him back to the sofa, then push him so he falls backward onto his butt. "I'm convinced I got the best deal out of all the girls at the wedding."

His brow furrows. "I'm not so sure about that."

I toss a cushion onto the floor, then lower down between his legs onto my knees. "Why don't we take a look?"

He gives a short laugh, then sighs as I undo his belt and slide down his zipper. "Um… it's late, and I'm sure you're tired. You don't have to—" He stops as I look up at him.

"Alex," I say patiently. "You're gorgeous, I'm crazy about you, and I've been thinking about this all evening. You're going to have to get used to the fact that I'm going to be a very demanding girlfriend."

"Oh," he says faintly.

I release his erection from his boxers, meet his eyes while I moisten my lips, then lower my head and take him in my mouth.

He exhales in a rush, the tension leaving his body, and slides a hand into my hair as I proceed to tease him with my hands, lips, and tongue.

"Mmm…" I murmur, casting coquettish glances up at him as I lick him.

He scoops my hair over my shoulder so he can see my face, his eyes darkening as he grows more aroused. "You're so fucking beautiful," he whispers.

Ooh, he's swearing, that shows how turned on he is. Excited, I make sure he's well lubricated and stroke him firmly while I lick and suck, and it's not long before his breathing deepens and his hips begin to move, thrusting him deeper into my mouth. I slide my lips down his length, doing my best to take him all the way, and he groans and slides his hand to the back of my head, holding me there for a few seconds before letting me continue. Fuck, that's hot, and I can feel myself getting turned on, too.

"That feels so good," he says, "Jesus, Missie, you're so good at this…"

"You taste amazing," I tell him, continuing to stroke with my hand. "Are you going to be a good boy and come for me?"

He gives a short laugh and studies me through half-lidded eyes.

"I want to taste you," I tell him, running my tongue up from root to tip. "I want to swallow down everything you've got."

He groans and tips his head back on the sofa. Ohhh… he's close. While I give firm strokes, I tease him with my tongue, then close my mouth over him and suck as hard as I dare.

Yep, that does it—he clenches his hand in my hair and then gasps as his climax hits, filling my mouth with several long jets. I swallow it all, and when he's done, he flops back with a long groan before opening his eyes and giving me a helpless look.

Interested, I close my hand around him and stroke him slowly.

"Ah," he says, twitching as it's obviously sensitive. I slow my hand. He's still erect, and only a shade less hard than he was. He sighs, eyes half-lidded, watching me as I avoid the head and just concentrate on the shaft. Only fifteen seconds pass before he's fully hard again, and letting me stroke all the way up.

"You're a marvel," I say, getting to my feet and shimmying out of my knickers.

"Bed?" he asks.

I shake my head and climb astride him. "Here." I move down his thighs until our bodies are flush. He's still in his suit, and I'm still wearing my dress, and somehow that's even hotter than if we were doing this naked.

He moves a hand beneath my dress, slips it down my front to my mound, then slides his fingers into me. He groans. "You're wet."

"Of course I'm wet." I kiss him. "Going down on you turns me on."

With a thumb resting on my clit, he slides two fingers inside me, and I moan and drop my head back, moving my hips to encourage him to stroke me.

"We should go to bed," he whispers, cupping my breast with his other hand and teasing the nipple with his thumb.

But I shake my head, lift up and wait for him to remove his hand, then position myself so the tip of his erection is parting my folds. "No time for that." I lower down, and we both sigh as he slowly fills me up.

"Ah, Missie." He holds my butt with both hands, pulling me toward him so he can slide further inside me. "That feels so good."

"This is going to be quick," I tell him. "Get ready."

He groans as I start to rock my hips. He's buried right inside me, and I don't need to move much, because my clit is pressing against him, and just these small movements are enough to make pleasure ripple through me.

I hang on, though, wanting him to come again, but it's not easy. "Tell me when you're ready," I say through deep gasps, trying not to grind on him.

"Ah, I'm so close," he says, his fingers digging into my hips.

Suddenly I'm wearing too many clothes, and I rip my dress over my head and toss it away, then tear off my bra, and the breath hisses through his teeth as he cups both my breasts and covers one nipple with his mouth.

Oh yeah, that works, and I know it's turning him on, too, as I continue to move on top of him, driving us both to the edge. He teases both of my nipples with his teeth and tongue, then tips his head back, his eyes gleaming in the moonlight as he looks up at me.

I hold his face and kiss him, and he grips my hips and gives several hard thrusts, making me gasp. I can't hold on any longer, but luckily he whispers, "I'm gonna come," and so I give in and let my orgasm sweep over me.

Ahhh… the beauty of coming together… clamping around him with such strong pulses… feeling his cock twitch inside me… knowing he's also experiencing that exquisite tension deep inside… feeling so blissfully happy because I've given him pleasure…

Ooh, sex is soooo good when it's done right. I'm never ever going to get tired of doing this with him.

Chapter Thirty

Alex

The next morning, at around eight-thirty I stroll across from Kip's apartment to Damon's and knock on the door. I've had a shower, but that's all. He answers it, yawning, in a pair of track pants and with his hair all over the place.

"Did I wake you up?" I ask with a grin.

"Nah. I was just getting up." He goes in, leaving me to shut the door. "I've spoken to the kitchen and they're bringing breakfast down."

"Cool."

"Patio?"

"Sure. Looks like it's going to be a nice day."

He leads the way. "Forecasters said it could rain in the evening."

"Nah. I've booked good weather all day, she'll be right."

He chuckles, and we sit at the table.

"Dude," I say, "you're getting married."

"I know! How weird is that?"

"It's a bit… you know… adult."

"Yeah. I'd rather be playing Call of Duty and eating a family-size pack of Doritos."

We both chuckle, because that pretty much summarizes our childhood.

"Have you heard from Belle?" I ask.

Damon smiles. "Yeah, we spoke on the phone for an hour last night."

"Isn't that illegal in the Law of Weddings?"

"Nah, apparently it's the visual thing that matters. She's happy. She's had a great few days."

"Ah, that's good. I'm glad."

The front door opens, and we wait as a couple of the staff come into the house with two large boxes.

"Jesus," I say, amused, "how much food did you order?"

He grins. "We're out here!" He waves to the two guys.

They bring the boxes through, and we stand and help them unpack. Oh wow. There are two cooked English breakfasts consisting of two fried eggs each, bacon, tomatoes, mushrooms, two sausages, a separate pot of baked beans, a rack of toast, and a pot of spicy chili chutney. There's also a plate of warmed croissants, a jar of strawberry jam and a jar of marmalade, a pack of softened butter, two small bottles of cold orange juice, and two large piping hot lattes in cardboard takeaway cups.

"Fantastic," Damon says, "thanks, guys."

They leave us to it, and Damon and I sit, look at each other and laugh, then tuck in.

After we've eaten, he has a shower, and then at ten the barber turns up, and we both get a proper shave, so close that my skin feels as if I'll never grow a beard again. One of the beauticians gives us a manicure, and the barber styles our hair, leaving us all ready for the day, apart from our clothes.

Saxon and Kip turn up, and the four of us play a game on the PlayStation together, laughing like kids as we race around a track, crashing into obstacles and blowing each other up.

When we've had enough, we sit and chat for a while, and then Henry, James, and Tyson arrive. James has brought a bottle of twenty-one-year-old Glenfiddich Gran Reserva that he admits cost him nearly fifty grand, and after lunch is delivered, we open the whisky with reverence and argue about the tasting notes while we eat the pulled-pork rolls, loaded ranch potato skins, and jalapeno poppers.

At one-thirty, Dad and Neal turn up, already dressed, and so does Mik's friend Tama, who's in charge of the men's wardrobe. Much hilarity ensues as the rest of us start getting ready. The guys, who are doubling as groomsmen and ushers, are all wearing black morning coats over dark-gray trousers and waistcoats. Damon and I have silver embroidered waistcoats and white cravats. Tama ensures that our cravats are tied properly and are neatly pinned, that we all have a pocket square and a boutonniere—a single white rosebud tucked into our buttonhole.

By 2:15 p.m. we're all suited and booted. Even Saxon is wearing shoes rather than his usual Converses today, and I have to say all the guys look superb all dressed the same.

"Ready?" I say to Damon as I hear cars pull up outside.

He has a last look in the mirror, then blows out a breath. "No."

I grin at him. "You know you're going to make her cry."

"Is that a good thing?"

I pull him toward me for a bearhug. "Good luck, bro."

We hug for a moment, and I feel the weight of our friendship wrapping around us like a blanket—fifteen years of gaming, laughing, working, talking, and supporting each other. We've hardly ever argued, and he's always been there if I needed him.

And now he's marrying my sister. I know I'm not Belle's father, but I feel a strange sense of passing on the responsibility of looking after her. I don't have to worry about her anymore. Damon is more than capable of fighting off both physical and emotional demons, and I know he'll always be by her side.

He lets me go, and I can see he's feeling emotional as well. "I'm going to blub today, I can feel it," he says.

"I bawled my eyes out at the altar," Kip says. "Alice thought I'd stubbed my toe."

Damon laughs. "Come on. Let's go."

We make our way to the cars, and soon we're heading for the church. We arrive in plenty of time, and the guys give Damon bearhugs and get ready to shepherd everyone to the right place, while the two of us head inside and make our way up the central aisle to the altar.

It's quiet at the moment, with only a scattering of early guests. A couple of Mik's crew are putting finishing touches to the flowers, and the priest is talking softly to the choir who will be singing during the service.

Hands in his pockets, Damon studies the altar, lost in thought, and I wonder whether he's thinking about God and the vows he's about to take. Or maybe he's thinking about Christian, the cousin he lost as a boy. Leaving him to his thoughts for a moment, I look around the church. The afternoon sunlight is streaming through the tall stained-glass windows, casting colored jewels onto the deep-red carpet, and turning the beautiful rimu and kauri wood a deep orange-brown.

I look back at Damon to find him watching me. He smiles. "Would you get married here? You don't have to be religious."

"It's a beautiful setting."

"Maybe we should have had a double wedding."

I snort.

"Don't tell me you haven't thought about it," he says.

I don't reply, looking up at the beams in the high ceiling. "Did you know it's called a nave after the Latin, *navis*, which means ship, because it looks like an upside-down hull of a boat?"

"I didn't," he says in surprise.

We look up at it for a moment.

"Are you thinking about Christian?" I ask.

"Yeah."

"Thought so."

"I was wondering if he'll be here to watch the wedding."

"I'm sure that if it's possible, he will be." I give him a wry look. "I bet he wouldn't forget the rings."

Damon laughs. Then he checks his watch and blows out a breath. "I'm starting to get nervous."

"I would imagine every groom does at this point."

"She'll definitely turn up, won't she?"

"Belle?" I give him an amused look. "She's had a crush on you since she was six. Someone would have to lock her up to stop her coming here today."

He breathes in, then out slowly, giving me a look that says, *Jesus, I hope so.*

"How did you know?" I ask, curious. "That she's the one, I mean?"

His lips curve up. "Because I couldn't stop thinking about her. When we weren't together, I found it hard to concentrate on anything else. I wanted to be with her all the time. She's my soulmate." He gives me a wry look. "Now you can mock me. I know you don't believe in all that shit."

"I didn't," I say.

He lifts an eyebrow. "But now you do? Oh dude, you've got it bad."

"Tell me something I don't know." I sigh. "I should have brought our Nintendo Switches. We could have had a game of Mario Kart while we were waiting." We both laugh.

People are starting to filter into the church, and Saxon, Kip, and the others hand out orders of service and direct the guests to the pews. James brings in Alice's mum in her wheelchair, and it makes me think of Finn. He's Snapchatted me a few times since we've been here, sending me photos of Zelda with the other dogs, and telling me what he's been up to. I asked him whether he's doing his exercises, and he sent me a selfie of him crossing his eyes and sticking out his tongue, which made me laugh.

It reminds me that tomorrow we're heading back to pick him up, and I give a little sigh. It would have been nice to have some more time with Missie, just the two of us. But it's been good staying at the apartment, and I have to be thankful for the time we've had.

Gradually, the church fills. To my surprise, I realize I'm nervous too, mainly for Damon, but also because I'm going to see Missie. Weird. I only left her this morning. But when I glance down the aisle and suddenly see her walking with Kait, my stomach does a strange somersault, and I inhale, my heart lifting.

She's wearing a champagne-colored dress in a kind of nineteen-twenties style, the underskirt falling to mid-thigh, and the whole dress overlain with layers of fringe in the same color that swish as she moves, the bottom layer reaching down to her calves. She has a matching clutch, and the sexiest high-heeled strappy sandals. Her hair is pinned up in an elegant twist, with one long curl by her cheek. She looks a million dollars, and so gorgeous I have to hold back from dashing down the aisle and sweeping her up in my arms for a kiss.

She sees me and gives a little wave, and I wink at her before smiling at Kait, who, I have to admit, also looks stunning today in a dark-blue jumpsuit. The two of them slip into a pew together. As mother of the bride, Kait's supposed to sit at the front, but she obviously feels more comfortable sitting with Missie, and that warms me all the way through.

Everyone's here now. As I scan the pews, I can see all our friends and family, and as my watch buzzes on my wrist, letting me know it's 2:55 p.m., I see movement by the church door. James is there, watching the scene, and he looks down at us at the altar and gives us a thumbs up with a smile, telling us that Belle and the bridesmaids have arrived.

"She's here, bro," I tell Damon, and he inhales deeply, then blows out a relieved breath. I laugh and clap him on the back. "Come on, let's get you married."

A few minutes later, Belle appears with Mason. She waits for the bridesmaids to finish tweaking her dress, and then the music starts, and they begin walking down the aisle.

I glance at Damon, who only has eyes for his bride, then look back at my sister. It's the first time I've seen her gown. She's gone for a dress with a gazillion layers of tulle, and she looks like a fairytale princess, with a glittering tiara, a big veil, and thousands of twinkling stones sewn into the tulle that sparkle in the sunlight. She looks so happy, it makes my throat tighten with emotion. She's made it through the tough times, and now she's marrying the man of her dreams.

Beside me, Damon swallows hard.

"She looks all right," I say.

He gives a short laugh and rubs his nose. "Yeah."

She approaches the altar, and Mason brings her forward, then steps back, his job done. Behind her, Gaby, Catie, Alice, Kennedy, and Jo are dressed in long light-green gowns embroidered with colorful flowers that are perfect for a summer wedding.

The music slowly dies away, and the priest smiles at the congregation and begins his service.

It's been years since I've been in a church, and, like most of the guests I would think, I don't know many hymns. In New Zealand we have separation of church and state, so we don't have any religious teaching at our schools unless they're faith-based, and therefore kids don't learn hymns unless their own family is religious. But Damon and Belle have opted for Christmas carols as it's that time of year, which most of us know, so we sing to *O Come All Ye Faithful*, *Oh, Little Town of Bethlehem*, and *Silent Night*, which gives a great festive flavor to the wedding.

It's a pleasant, touching service, carried out in the summer sunshine, with the smell of roses drifting in from outside to mingle with the scent of the polished pews. Halfway through, one of Saxon's twins, who's being looked after by a nanny, begins crying, and Saxon takes his boy and walks around the church with him, showing him the brightly colored tapestries while the priest carries on, unbothered, adding to the feel of this being a place for families to celebrate together.

A ripple of light laughter passes around the church when it's time for me to produce the wedding rings, and Damon gives me an amused look, but I extract them from my jacket with a flourish, and he and Belle chuckle as I wink at them both and hand them over.

I stand to the side as they say their vows, and my stomach flips as Damon slides Belle's ring onto her finger. In the past, I've thought rings possessive and old-fashioned—you don't own your wife, and it feels as if you're saying you don't trust her, that if she doesn't have a ring, there's nothing to stop her pretending to be single.

But watching him slide it onto her finger, and seeing him give her a smug smile, suddenly I understand. They're committing to each other, promising to love no other for the rest of their lives. The ring is a token of their vows. But it's also a way for him to show other men that she belongs to him, and nobody else can touch her. Hmm. I kinda like that.

Wow, I thought I was a twenty-first century guy, but I've practically turned into a caveman. Am I going to drag Missie off by her hair and chain her to the kitchen sink, too?

I glance at her and find her watching me, looking amused, as if she can read my thoughts. She pokes her tongue out at me, just a tiny bit, but it's enough to make my lips curve up.

They finish saying their vows, and then Damon kisses Belle as the choir starts singing. She's his now, and I feel a sudden and surprising surge of emotion, the voices rising through me, lifting me up to the rafters with their beautiful song.

We make our way outside for the photographs, and Missie comes up to me and slides her arm around my waist.

"Look at you," she says, "Mr. Beautiful."

"I think you mean Mr. Ruggedly Handsome."

"Beautiful and handsome." Her eyes twinkle. "You look amazing in that morning coat. You make my mouth water."

I chuckle and put my arms around her. "And you look stunning in that dress."

"Thank you."

"I want to take it off."

"Now? I think the priest might complain."

I nuzzle her elegant neck and the soft spot behind her ear, revealed where she's pinned up her hair. "I've thought about you naked for the entire service."

"I thought I saw a stroke of lightning come through the window and hit you on the forehead."

I chuckle and kiss up her jaw to her mouth.

"Don't smudge my lipstick," she complains. Pouting, I touch my lips to hers lightly, and she sighs. "You drive me crazy," she grumbles.

I kiss her nose. "Until later, sweetheart."

We have hundreds of photos taken in the church grounds on the lawn amongst the trees, and then eventually it's time to go back to the house. There, Belle and Damon welcome their guests on the bottom terrace, where we have cocktails and canapes beneath the shade of the marquee, and then eventually we make our way up to the top terrace. Here, round tables have once again been laid with white cloths, but this time it's a proper sit-down do, and Missie sits next to me at the top table while we eat the magnificent meal.

We're served caprese skewers, crab cakes, lobster rolls, and vegetarian spring rolls to start, followed by grilled chicken, seabass, or roasted red pepper tartlets with summer vegetables for the main, and peach and blueberry cobbler, strawberry shortcake, and ice cream for dessert. All the bread has been made here, and although champagne and other wines flow, the bar is kept busy serving a range of cocktails.

After the meal, it's time for speeches, and this time mine is a little longer, filled with stories of when Damon, Belle, and I were young. I get a huge round of applause afterward, so I guess I did okay, and Missie's eyes glow as she whispers, "You were amazing."

The speeches done, we move back down to the lower terrace, which has been set up for dancing, with a live band and a DJ. The evening guests begin arriving, and I'm kept busy with making sure everyone's happy and comfortable, as well as dancing with Missie as much as I'm able.

At one point, when we're dancing to a slow song, she says, "Oh Alex, look," and I glance over to see a tall, gray-haired, good-looking guy approaching Kait with Neal. "That must be Simon," Missie says.

We watch as Neal introduces them, and they shake hands. Simon keeps hold of hers and obviously asks her to dance. She looks doubtful, but he says something that makes her laugh, and then she nods and lets him lead her onto the dance floor.

"Nicely done," Missie says with admiration.

"I don't know whether to congratulate him or console him," I reply.

Missie smacks my arm. "Don't be mean. Kait's lovely."

I chuckle. "She looks good today, I have to admit."

"She looks amazing. I hope they hit it off."

They obviously do, because after their dance, he gets her a drink, and then I see the two of them walking through the gardens, talking. I'm pleased for her, especially today, when it feels as if everybody's with someone. She's been to hell and back, and she deserves some happiness.

It seems to be catching, because later I see Juliette and Henry talking, which pleases me. Missie has told me she spoke to James last night, and I had a dance and a chat with Aroha, too, and did my best to convince her that he's a good guy. Now, I see the two of them dancing together, so I guess we've mended a few bridges.

Later, I'm up on the top terrace, running an errand for Mae, when my phone rings in my inside pocket. I take it out, surprised to see Finn's name. I answer it, heading into the house and going through to the library, where it's nice and quiet. "Hello?"

"Alex?"

"Yes, hey Finn. Everything all right?"

"Yeah, it's all cool here. Is it okay that I rang you? Are you busy?"

"No, I'm good to talk. What's up?"

"Um... I wanted to ask you something. My best friend called me—"

"Robbie?"

"Yeah," he says, sounding pleased that I remembered. "His parents are taking him and his brothers to their bach on the coast tomorrow, and he asked me whether I'd like to go with him."

"Oh, okay. That sounds fun."

"Yeah, and they said I could bring Zelda. I know she's your dog, but I thought... um... you and Mum could have some more time together on your own."

Smiling, I sit on the sofa and stretch out my legs. I miss the puppy, but I know she'd love a trip to the sea, and it would make Finn the happiest boy alive. "Nothing to do with you wanting Zelda for a few more nights?"

"Busted," he says with a laugh. "But I really did think it would be nice for you and Mum. Grandma said she might go over to Mike's place, and I didn't want Mum to be on her own. Last New Year's Eve was horrible. And..." He hesitates.

"Go on," I say.

"It's just... I don't want to... you know... get in the way..."

I frown. Getting to my feet, I wander over to the window and look out at the fantails hopping from branch to branch in the trees. "Finn, you're not and will never be in the way of me and your mum. You're very important to both of us, and you'll always be number one in her eyes."

"Yeah, I know, but… I want her to have someone. She deserves it. And I know I can be a pain, and I don't want to put you off."

"You're not a pain. If anything you're a bonus. She comes with a ready-made family. How cool is that?"

He's quiet for a moment. I'm not quite sure what's bothering him. Is he jealous of my relationship with Missie? Or worried that I'm expecting to walk in and want to boss him around like a father?

"Look," I add, "I want you to know that I'm not expecting to replace your dad. That will never happen."

"What if I want you to?" he says.

My eyebrows rise. "Oh."

"I just mean that if you and mum, you know, get married and stuff, I'd like that. I wouldn't call you Dad if you didn't want me to, but if you did, you know, I wouldn't mind…"

Emotion tightens my throat, and for a moment I can't speak.

"I'm sorry," Finn says, "I shouldn't have said all that."

"It's okay."

"I just meant—"

"Finn, it's all right. I'm very touched. This is new for both of us, and it's good that we can talk about it. I like your mum a lot, and I have done for a long time. But we've only been dating a week."

"Yeah, of course. You need time to make sure you want to stay with her."

"Well, no, I know I want to marry her."

"Oh!"

"But she's had a tough time, and I want her to be sure. If it does happen, though, it'll be good for both of us, won't it? Me and you? We'll be great friends, and we can support your mum and look after her together."

"Yeah," he says. He sounds thrilled, bless him. "I'd like that."

"All right. But I don't want you worrying that you're in the way. You're one of the main reasons I like being with your mum. You're a good kid, and I'd be honored to be a part of your family. Okay?"

"Okay."

"All right. Look, I've got an idea about the next few days. Leave it with me. I'll get back to you shortly, okay?"

"Yeah, thanks Alex."

"No worries. Speak to you soon."

I end the call and think for a moment.

I'm incredibly touched by his words. I feel as if he's given me his blessing to take the next step with his mum, and that means a lot.

I bring up my contacts and dial the number of a friend of mine. We chat for a while, and then, filled with hope, I finish the call and head back down to the bottom terrace.

Chapter Thirty-One

Missie

I'm sitting on the lower terrace, chatting to Kennedy and having a cuddle with her little boy, Eddie, before she puts him down for the night. He's about eighteen months old, and he's plump and beautiful, quite happy playing with a plush toy dog and sucking on its hard paws that are obviously designed for teething. We've been talking babies because Kennedy is around seven months pregnant with her second.

"I'd love a water birth," Kennedy says.

"Would Jackson be there for it?" I ask.

"God, yeah. He'd be in the pool with armbands and a snorkel."

That makes me laugh. "Aw, how sweet. Lee didn't come to Finn's birth. He went out with his mates, wetting the baby's head before it had even arrived."

"Oh no." Her brows draw together. "How awful for you."

"He wasn't interested in the pregnancy at all. He found it all quite distasteful."

"I know some men can be like that, and I kinda get it, you know? It's all a bit alien-like and weird, and I think sometimes they get frightened about the birth. I'm glad Jackson's not like that, though. It was such a relief to have him there." She picks up Eddie's dog as it falls to the floor and passes it back to him, then gives me a mischievous look. "So... you and Alex... I'm going to be really nosy now. How serious is it?"

I give a shy laugh. "I don't know. I like him a lot. We've only been dating a week. But..." I bite my bottom lip. "Mae told me that on the day he met me, back in March, he rang her and said he'd found the girl he was going to marry."

Her face lights up. "Oh, wow. How romantic! Did you have any idea?"

"Not at all! I thought he found me annoying. You know what he's like, so serious and hard to read."

"Yeah, he's always been like that."

"How long have you known him?"

"Since he first came to the house. Me, him, and Damon were all twelve. The two of them have always been good to me. They've never been the sort of boys who pulled your braids, you know? They were always protective of me. Still are. He's a lovely guy, Missie. You've fallen on your feet there." She glances across the terrace and smiles. "Here he is, on the hunt for you, I think."

I look up to see Alex walking toward us. Most of the men have taken off their jackets during the evening as it's so warm, but Alex is still wearing his. He looks suave and sophisticated today, with his hair tamed into a neat swept-back style, and his neatly shaven jaw. God, he's gorgeous.

"Hey you two," he says, smiling at us. "Sorry to interrupt, but can I have a word, Missie?"

"Of course." Surprised, I hand Eddie back to Kennedy, then rise and let Alex take my hand and lead me to a quieter spot in the gardens. "What's going on?" I ask when he stops and turns to face me.

"I had a call from Finn," he says. My eyes widen, and he says, "Don't worry, he's fine, no problems at all." He explains that Robbie has asked Finn to go with him and his family to the coast with Zelda, and that Mum is talking about spending New Year's with Mike.

"Oh," I say softly, sad and pleased for her at the same time.

"Are you okay with that?" He cups my face, stroking my cheek with his thumb.

I nod. "Of course. She deserves to be happy, just like Kait."

He clears his throat. "Look, it's entirely up to you—I'd understand if you'd prefer to spend New Year's with Finn. But I made a quick call to a friend of mine who owns a luxury villa out at Akaroa. It's a beautiful place—I went there for a party one year. And he said it's free until the second, because he's away in the Northland till then. So… I wondered if you'd like to go with me?"

My heart lifts. I wasn't sure what was going to happen when we got back to Christchurch. "You wouldn't rather spend New Year's Eve here?" I know Damon and Belle aren't leaving for their honeymoon until the end of the first week of January, and the family is seeing the New Year in together.

But he says, "I'd rather spend it alone with you. We'd have some quiet time to talk."

My gaze drops to his mouth. "Just to talk?"

"Well, you know… It has a huge bed that looks out over the sea. It's pretty impressive."

"And we would just talk in this bed?"

There's a lamppost behind me with a Narnia-style lamp that comes on at dusk. Alex moves me up against it and lowers his head. "We needn't get up for two whole days," he murmurs.

"Oh… I like the sound of that."

He touches his lips to mine. "Uninterrupted orgasms. As many as you can handle."

I sigh. "You've talked me into it."

He chuckles and kisses me properly, then moves back. "Okay, I'll call back and book the villa. Do you want to ring Finn?"

"Yes, will do."

"I hope you don't mind that he called me. We… had quite a chat." He smiles.

I don't know what that means, but I'm encouraged by his smile. "You don't mind that he called you?"

"Of course not. I was quite touched." He kisses me. "Tell your mum that I'll pick them both up in the helicopter and take them back to Christchurch tomorrow. We'll wait for Robbie's parents to pick Finn up, then we can head off to Akaroa."

"Sounds like a plan. Do you need to set five alarms now?"

He gives me a wry look. "Every time you mock me, I'm making a note."

"Ooh."

"I've still got the spatula. That's all I'm saying." He lifts an eyebrow, then walks off, taking out his phone to make the call.

Chuckling, I take my phone out of my purse. I've got another few days alone with him! I don't know what a luxury villa is, but I'm very interested to find out.

I call Finn and let him know that he can go to the beach with Robbie, and have a chat with Mum and explain what's happening. Then I return to the party, filled with excitement at the thought of the next few days.

*

It's a great party, and I spend several hours drinking champagne, dancing with Alex, with some of the other guys, and with the girls on our own. I also talk to as many of his friends and family as I can. I chat to Gaby and Tyson for a while, and then Mason asks me to dance. I haven't had much of a chance to talk to him yet, so I accept, and we move slowly around the dance floor.

He makes me a little nervous, I don't know why. He's a secondary-school teacher, and it shows—he's obviously used to keeping groups of teenagers in order, and he's quite no-nonsense.

But he says, "I'm so glad Alex brought you to the wedding. He's been talking about you for a while, and it's great to finally meet you."

"Likewise," I say. "It's been amazing to meet all his friends and family."

"So you're a primary-school teacher?" he asks.

"Yes, and you're at Maldon High School?"

"That's right. We've just had an ERO inspection."

"Oh, you poor thing!" It's easy to commiserate over our shared dislike of government inspections, and we spend the rest of our dance together talking about how teaching has changed over the last five years, and what we think of the curriculum.

When the music finishes, Mason's smile holds genuine warmth, and he says, "Thank you for the dance, Missie. It's lovely to meet Alex's girl. I think you're going to be very good for him," which is a nice compliment, and it's a relief that both Alex's parents seem to like me.

Midnight comes and goes, then one a.m., and I finally start to flag. People are still dancing, talking, and laughing, but my feet are aching, and I'm really tired.

I can't find Alex—I think he's up at the house helping Mae with something—so I track down Damon and Belle instead. I give them both a hug, and ask them to tell Alex I've gone back to the apartment and not to rush, because I know he'll want to stay until the end.

I walk slowly down the steps to the bottom level and let myself into the quiet apartment. I can hear the music playing, but it's in the distance, and I'm too tired for it to disturb me.

Going into the bathroom, I take off the beautiful dress I bought for this occasion, remove my makeup, then slide beneath the cool covers and curl up, hugging the pillow. I've had a wonderful day, and I appreciate how Alex has made me feel like a member of his family, introducing me to all the people who are special to him. I have a small family who I love very much, but it's great to think that all these people are going to be a part of my life going forward, providing that Alex and I stay together, and at this moment, there are no signs of that changing.

I think about what he said when he asked me if I'd like to go to Akaroa with him: We'd have some quiet time to talk. What does he want to talk about? The future?

The only thing I'm really worried about is how Finn and I would fit into his life. I don't have any concerns about him and Finn, as they obviously get on really well. It's more that I know I need to think about Alex's career. I know he's a workaholic, that he's spoken in front of the Prime Minister, and that he travels regularly to Australia and elsewhere for business. His company is doing really well, and he's told me they might expand to Australia and possibly even the UK and the States. Is it possible that he might want to move to another country? Or at least travel frequently?

I believe that stability is so important for children, and especially for Finn, after what he's been through. Plus of course I have a job too.

I don't want to come down all heavy when we've only been dating a week, but equally I think we need to talk about where we're going, because I've already fallen for him heavily, and if our long-term goals are very different, it would be better to end things now.

Hugging the pillow, I inhale the smell of the roses through the open window. I don't want to think about that. It's going so well, and I'm a big believer in positive thinking. One way or another, hopefully we'll be able to work things out.

I close my eyes, and within seconds, I'm asleep.

*

I rouse when the bed dips behind me, and then I feel Alex's arm slide around my waist.

"Hey," I murmur. "What time is it?"

"Nearly three a.m."

"Wow."

"I know." He yawns and moves up close to me, nestling into the pillows.

"You didn't mind me coming back without you?"

"Of course not. I wanted to wait until the end in case Damon or Mae needed anything."

"I knew you would." I turn over to face him, and we snuggle up together. "I missed you," I whisper. He's naked except for his boxers, and his skin is warm. He smells amazing.

"Mmm." His breathing is already deep and regular. I think he's nearly asleep.

Smiling, I tuck my head beneath his chin, and I feel him kiss my hair.

I close my eyes, and go back to sleep.

*

The next morning, despite Alex only having had four and a bit hours' sleep, we're up, packed, and back at the house by nine, where we join all those who stayed over for breakfast on the terrace. We spend a couple of hours eating, talking, and laughing, but eventually it's time to say our goodbyes. I go around hugging and kissing all my new friends before Alex and I head up to his helicopter.

It's a bright and breezy day, promising a touch of rain later on, but we don't mind now the wedding is over.

"Do you think Damon and Belle were pleased with how it went?" I ask into the mic as Alex flies southwest over the Cook Strait, heading for Blenheim.

"They had a great time," he says, his voice coming through my headphones. "Mae was thrilled with how it went."

"And was Kait okay?" I saw him talking to his mum at the end.

"Yeah, she got on really well with Simon, and they've made arrangements to see each other again."

"Oh, I'm so pleased!"

He sends me a smile. "I've never known anyone who finds such pleasure in other people's happiness the way you do."

I shrug. "Doesn't everyone feel like that?"

"Most people are only concerned with themselves."

"I guess. It's alien to me. I'd much rather give than receive presents, for example. I know I'm a people pleaser. That's why it's been so nice having some time just the two of us. I feel like I've rediscovered myself all over again." I blush. "That sounds a bit pretentious, but..."

"No, I know what you mean. I would think that's quite common for mums, especially after what you've been through."

I think about that as he heads down the coast, and I look out of the window, thrilled to see the fluke of an orca rising out of the sea. "It's true that this year, especially, I've devoted myself to Finn's recovery, and what with that and teaching, there's not been a lot of time to concentrate on myself. I don't regret it, because Finn is and will always be my baby boy, and he means the world to me. But it is nice to think about what I want for a change."

"So what do you want?"

I glance across at him, and my lips curve up.

He chuckles. "Well, we've got two whole days for that, so I hope you're ready because I intend to wear you out."

"I can't wait." I'm so excited, I'm almost jumping around like a toddler. Alex looks gorgeous today—he's wearing dark jeans and an All Blacks rugby top, his hair is ruffled, and he hasn't bothered to shave this morning. He looks gorgeous and sexy, and I can't wait to get him into bed.

First, though, we have to pick up Finn and Mum, and Alex sets the helicopter down at Pippa's place. We walk over to the house and say hello to everyone, and it's midday now, so we agree to stop for a light lunch, eventually returning to the helicopter around one-thirty. Alex puts Zelda in her crate, then helps Finn into the front seat, and we all buckle ourselves in. We wave goodbye as the helicopter lifts into the air, and Alex flies us back to Christchurch.

Finn is full of it—he's had a fantastic time, he's flying in a helicopter, and now he's going away with his best friend for a few nights. Mum's also bright and perky, obviously excited at the thought of spending some time with Mike alone.

So none of us is disappointed to be returning. When Alex lands at the airport, Mum, Finn, and I Uber back to the house so we can all repack for the next few days, while Alex returns to his house with Zelda, takes her for a long walk, and makes sure she has enough food and all her bedding before returning in his Audi to my house.

Mum's already left to be with Mike, and Robbie's folks turn up just half an hour later. I introduce them to Alex, and he makes sure they're happy to take Zelda before transferring her in her crate to the back of their car. The boys pile into the back, and then we wave goodbye as they drive away.

Alex turns to me then. "So it's just the two of us."

I lift my arms around his neck. "How lovely."

He wraps his arms around me and kisses me. "Shall we get going?"

"Are we driving?"

"Only to the airport. We'll go by helicopter." He speaks so casually, and I wonder whether I'll ever get used to flying around the countryside like that.

He flies us southwest from Christchurch to the Banks Peninsula. I know he mentioned the town of Akaroa, so I'm expecting the villa to be near there, but to my surprise he continues to the north coast, over the amazing landscape of forests and rolling hills, until he eventually sets the helicopter down in a field near a clifftop path. Smiling at me, he takes our bags and leads the way along the path and over the crest of the hill, revealing the sparkling waters of the Pacific laid out before us.

"Jesus, Alex."

"Not a bad view," he says.

"Understatement of the year."

He chuckles, heading down to the property. "This is Seaview."

I'd expected a luxurious house, but I couldn't even conceive of a place like this. I hope there's no chance of a tsunami, because the long, narrow, stone-built house sits at the end of the track, right on the edge of the beach, feet from the currently calm waters of the Pacific. It spans most of the tiny bay, surrounded by tussock grass, with high hills on either side, and not another property in sight.

A Range Rover is parked in front of the house. Alex walks past it, opens the front door, and calls out, "Carl?"

A man who looks to be in his fifties with gray hair appears, and the two of them shake hands. "Missie, this is Carl Collins," Alex says. "Carl, this is Missie."

"Pleased to meet you," Carl says, offering his hand. "I'm the property manager. Please, come in."

The place needs a property manager? Alex gives me a mischievous smile and gestures for me to precede him.

I walk in with an open mouth. The whole front of the house is glass and faces the sea. All the windows have shutters, but they're currently all open, and the place is filled with light.

While Alex chats with Carl, I walk through the property, discovering all the rooms. I've never seen anything like it. The front of the living room has no wall! It's literally open to the elements, which I find puzzling until I realize it has automatic shutters that can roll down at night. But at the moment they're open, revealing an unimpeded view of the bay, as well as of a huge hot tub *and* a pool. It feels as if the house is floating on the open sea.

There's a spotless kitchen, a bathroom with a shower and a large bath that has sliding doors with views over the bay, and two bedrooms. Both of them also have sliding doors leading to the deck. Clearly, the place wasn't built that long ago, and all the furnishings look pristine.

I come back into the living room to hear Carl telling Alex that there's champagne in the fridge, a selection of wine in the rack, and spirits in the liquor cabinet. He opens the fridge and shows us several plates stacked neatly with covers. "As you ordered," Carl says to Alex, "just put it in the oven for thirty to forty minutes."

"Thanks, Carl."

"You're welcome. Have a lovely stay. And Happy New Year!"

"Happy New Year to you, too!" I'd forgotten it was New Year's Eve.

He waves and goes out, and soon we hear the Range Rover heading up the hill. In a few minutes, the sound of the engine vanishes, and all I can hear is the sound of the waves and the cry of seagulls.

"What's on the plates in the fridge?" I ask.

"I hope you don't mind—I took the liberty of ordering dinner for tonight. They specialize in degustation."

"What's that?"

"A tasting menu, basically, concentrating on appreciating food." He looks at a piece of paper that Carl had left on the counter. "There are Sweetbread Crisps, Te Matuku Oysters, Trevally Celeriac, and Salted Venison to start, Ruakākā Kingfish and Caviar, Scampi, Roast Duck with Wasabi, and 55-Day Aged Beef for mains, and Quince and Caramel Doughnut, Coconut, Blueberry, and Sorrel, and Petit Fours to finish. Sounds good."

"My God, Alex, you are such the King of Understatement. It sounds amazing."

He grins and opens the fridge. "Want a glass of champagne?"

"Oh Jesus, yes. I could get used to this lifestyle."

"It doesn't suck," he says, opening the bottle. I find two glasses in the cupboard, and he pours a generous amount in each.

"What do you want to drink to?" he asks.

"To us." I touch my glass to his.

"To us."

We both have a mouthful of champagne. The bubbles go up my nose, and I laugh, spinning away from him and going over to the view. I stop then, eyes wide. "Oh! I just saw a dolphin!"

"Yeah, and we'll probably see seals too." He comes up behind me and slips an arm around my waist. "Do you like it?"

I turn in his arms. "It's amazing. It must cost a fortune to stay here."

"Five thousand a night, I believe."

My jaw drops. "Five thousand?"

He laughs. "Luckily I know the owner."

And it sounds silly, but even after my visit to Brooklyn Heights, and everything else I've experienced with him, this is the first time it's really sunk in just how rich he is.

"What are you doing with me?" I ask softly. "I'm a nobody. I'm just a primary school teacher with a penchant for Jaffa Cakes. I'm not rich, or famous, or particularly clever."

He tips his head to the side, studying me. "You are smart."

"Not like you."

"There are different kinds of smart. I know nothing about art. I want you to teach me. I want to find out all about your passions." He kisses me, quick and fierce. "You fascinate me, Missie. You have a heart as big as the ocean. You care about so many things and so many people. You're incredibly unselfish. It's as if you're made of sunshine and diamonds, you just shine so brightly. You dazzle me, and I'm completely crazy about you."

I blink, taken aback by so many compliments crammed into one sentence. "Thank you," I whisper.

He cups my face. "I still don't think you believe me. Maybe actions can prove what words can't." And then he lowers his lips to mine.

Chapter Thirty-Two

Alex

Although I don't normally throw my money around, I'm glad I chose this place, because Missie is clearly wowed by the villa, and I'm human enough to want to impress her.

Today she's wearing incredibly short denim shorts and a lemon-colored tee that clings to her breasts, and she looks even more appetizing than the food I know is going to be spectacular. She's like my very own tasting menu, and half of me is starving and wants to eat her in one bite, while the other half wants to take my time and savor her, from the roots of her hair to the tips of her toes.

I should let her settle in… maybe have a dip in the spa or go for a swim… or even have a nap for a while as I only had four hours' sleep… but I'm too keyed up, buzzing with energy, thrilled to have her all to myself for two days. Anyway, she said I should be honest with her about sex, didn't she? And the truth is that I want her, right now.

I settle for kissing her slowly, keeping her up against me with a hand pressed to the base of her spine, while she threads her fingers through my hair and murmurs her approval as my mouth slants across hers. Ahhh… she tastes sweet, of champagne and strawberries, the taste of summer. In fact, that's what she's like—a snippet of a New Zealand December, with the hot, sultry weather, the excitement of Christmas, and the hope that the new year brings, all wrapped up in a beautiful package.

"Mmm," she murmurs, moving her hips and obviously feeling my erection. "Already?"

"I'm like a kid at the beach. I can't be bothered to put on sun lotion and a hat. I want to jump right into the water."

She chuckles, her tongue darting out to meet mine. "Don't you think we should wait until it gets dark? Hey, if we wait until nearly midnight, we could have sex that lasts a whole year."

"That sounds like a great idea. We'll definitely do that." I slide my hand down to the bottom of her shorts and run my fingers along the top of her thigh.

"Alex, you must be tired, honey, don't you want a rest? I'll still be here in a few hours."

I groan, brushing my lips up her jaw to her ear. "Don't make me wait. You're so soft, and you smell so good..."

"But—"

"Sex now, and then sex again later. I promise."

"Oh! In that case, go ahead."

I laugh, take her glass from her hand, and put it with mine on the counter. Then I pick her up, wrap her legs around me, and carry her through to the bedroom.

The sliding doors here are wide open, filling the room with the sound of the waves and the smell of the ocean. It's about four p.m. now, and the sun is a long way from setting, but it's starting to head toward the hills, and the waves are topped with gold.

I lower Missie onto her back on the bed, then stretch out on top of her. I kiss her for a long, long time, enjoying the taste of her, and the feel of her soft mouth against mine. Her sighs make me thrust against her slowly, arousing us both.

"Alex..." she murmurs, "you're driving me crazy..."

"That's the idea." I move back and pull her up so I can take off her T-shirt. Next I unbutton her shorts and remove those, leaving her phone on the bedside table, and then finally her bra and knickers join the growing pile on the floor.

"Now I know how turned on you are," she teases, "not bothering to fold up the clothes."

"That's the last thing on my mind." I watch her lie back, and I tug my top off and let that drop, then take off my jeans, placing my phone beside hers.

"This feels very decadent." She stretches as she looks out at the ocean. The sunshine pouring through the windows has painted her skin a buttery yellow.

"The best sex always is." Starting at her neck, I begin to kiss down her body.

"It's probably the word I'd use to describe making love with you," she says.

"Decadent?"

"Mmm. You make me feel wicked."

I kiss over her collarbone and down to her breast. "You are wicked, Missie. *Wicked as*. Even in church, you made my thoughts turn to sinful things."

She buries her fingers in my hair and sighs. "I've always been such a good girl."

"Not deep down. Beneath the surface, I think you were born naughty." I close my mouth over her nipple and suck hard, and she squeals.

"Alex!"

I chuckle. "Scream if you want. I don't care."

"What's got into you?"

"You." I swap to her other breast and tease the nipple to a peak with my tongue. "You're all I think about. You're all I've thought about for a whole year."

"Nine months. Yeah, I know, you're rounding up."

I tug the tip of her nipple, and she moans. "Serves you right for being cheeky," I say.

"Alex…" She groans as I kiss down over her tummy. "Don't kiss my stretch marks."

I ignore her and kiss them anyway, then carry on down over her mound. "So soft," I murmur, parting her legs. I settle down between them and peruse her for a moment.

"Jesus." She covers her face. "Don't stare."

"Why? You're beautiful. Look at you, just begging to be tasted." I run a finger down through her folds, smiling as I find her already swollen and moist, then press either side of her clit. "Look at that. It's asking me to tease it."

"Oh God."

"Such a tiny thing. But it gives such pleasure." I kiss it, and she shudders. I blow gently on the sensitive skin. She moans, so I do it again.

"For fuck's sake," she says. "I swear you could make me come in seconds if you wanted."

Smirking, I lick the little button, then tease it with the tip of my tongue.

"Ahhh... Alex..."

I continue to arouse her, as slowly as either of us can bear it, with my lips, my tongue, and even my teeth, grazing them gently on her tender skin. At the same time, I brush my fingers through her folds, then turn my hand palm up and slide two fingers inside her, massaging firmly on the swelling I find a few inches in. Her hands clutch at my hair, the bedcovers, the pillows, and she writhes beneath me, tilting up her hips as she tries to get me to work faster.

I want to draw it out for hours, to make her beg, but I'm too turned on, and in the end, as her breaths become ragged and her chest starts to heave, I cover her clit with my mouth and suck. She cries out and tightens her fingers in my hair, so I suck harder, and harder still...

She comes with a squeal, pulsing around my fingers, then pushes me away with a loud, "Ohhhh!"

I laugh, lift up, rid myself of my boxers, then move over her. Her cheeks are flushed a sexy pink, strands of her hair are stuck to her cheek, and she looks all flustered.

I pull a pillow down to the side of her hips, then with one hand I roll her onto her front, on top of the pillow, so her hips are slightly propped up. I move between her legs, pushing up one of her knees, then stroke the tip of my erection down through her moist folds until it presses against her entrance.

Leaning over her, I push my hips forward and, very slowly, bury myself inside her until I'm fully sheathed in her velvet warmth.

She groans. "Are you trying to spear me to the bed?"

I ease back. "Sorry baby. Too deep?"

"Just... aaahhh... give me a minute to adjust. You're not a small man."

"You say such nice things." For a while I give short thrusts, letting her grow used to the position while I kiss her back and neck.

"I'm so hot," she complains. "Why do you never let me turn on the aircon?"

"I like you sticky and slippery."

"Jesus. You're disgusting."

"You're only just figuring that out?" I lower down on top of her, sliding my arms beneath her shoulders, and kiss her as she turns her face to look at me.

Lifting a hand, she sinks her fingers into my hair, curls them into a fist, and tugs.

"Ow." I wince.

"Serves you right," she says, not letting go.

I sigh and continue to thrust, despite not being able to move my head. "It's not going to stop me."

"Aren't you going to berate me?"

"No. You can do whatever you want to me." I kiss her ear and tug the lobe with my teeth, liking her possessive touch.

She groans as I push a little deeper. "Famous last words. You don't know what I want to do to you."

"Just name it."

"Give you a love bite somewhere visible."

I kiss down her neck and touch my tongue to the skin there. "I'll wear it with pride."

She sighs. "I want to tie you to the bed and do wicked things to you."

"Whatever you like, baby girl."

"Seriously?"

"Whatever lights your candle."

"I might want to insert things in naughty places."

"As I recall, you've already done that, and I survived."

"You'd be at my mercy."

"That sounds like heaven."

She looks over her shoulder at me, releasing my hair. "You'd really let me?"

"I'm yours, Missie. One hundred percent. As long as you know it goes both ways." I thrust hard, without warning, and she clutches hold of the pillow.

"What do you want to do to me?" she whispers, gasping with each thrust.

"Unmentionable things."

"Fuck me like an animal?"

"Definitely fuck you like an animal." I lift up and show her, thrusting hard.

She groans as I plunge into her. "I love that you're such a nice guy normally. Such a gentleman. I don't know why it makes me so hot when you're so filthy."

I laugh, give a couple more thrusts, then pull out of her, and she flops onto the pillow.

"Turn over," I say, a bit more gently, and she shifts onto her back. I slide into her again, and this time I lower down and kiss her mouth.

"I could say I want to fuck you all the time," I murmur against her lips, and she shivers. Then I add, "But it wouldn't be true."

She looks up into my eyes. "It wouldn't?"

"No. Because fucking with feeling is called making love. I want to make love to you, Missie. Again and again, the last thing before we go to bed, in the middle of the night, first thing in the morning, and in broad daylight. I want to make love to you hard and fast, and slow and gentle, and everything in between. I never want to stop making love with you."

She sighs. "I love you."

"I love you too." I move up an inch, making sure I'm grinding against her clit, and she moans, her eyelids fluttering closed.

"Open," I instruct, and she does as she's told, looking up at me with hazy eyes.

I thrust inside her while we watch each other, kissing occasionally, and there's something magical about gazing into her deep-blue eyes as we tease our bodies slowly to the edge. After a while I lift up onto my hands, increasing the pace of my hips, and she matches each thrust with one of her own, so we're moving together like the waves in the ocean.

"Alex," she says, teeth clamping down on her bottom lip, "I'm going to come…"

Now I know she's close, I give in to the urge I've been fighting hard for so long, and I slam into her, riding her all the way through her climax, as she cries out and digs her nails into my back. I don't stop there, though, but continue on, feeling the heat building, the heavenly tightening inside me, and then I still and shudder as I come, pouring my heart and soul into her, a feeling that's so overwhelming, it's like a tsunami of emotion and sensation, and all I can do is wait for it to pass.

*

A while later, I fetch us both a glass of cold water to quench our thirst, and we lie looking out at the ocean, with Missie facing away from me. We're a few inches apart, because it's so warm, and I've finally relented and turned on the aircon. As the cool air washes over us, along with the sea breeze from outside, I brush my fingers over her damp skin, wanting to touch her.

I lift her long dark hair off her neck and onto the pillow, then stroke down from her jaw to her throat, over her shoulder, along her ribs, into the dip of her waist, and over the swell of her hips. Then I return up the small of her back, following her spine. I write my name on her skin with light strokes, and she shivers.

"Cold?" I ask.

She shakes her head. "It feels as if you're branding me."

"Maybe I am." I write again, Alex, Alex, Alex, over and over. She won't be able to see it, but it'll always be there, beneath the surface.

We lie there quietly for a while, listening to the gentle brush of the waves raking their fingers through the pebbles, and the cry of the seagulls as they dip and soar in the air currents.

I'm convinced she's dozed off, but then, out of the blue, she says, "It's funny. You know when you say you've known me for a year?"

My hand stops. "Yeah."

"And then you say you're rounding up? Mae used that exact wording."

I study her back. She has a mole on her shoulder blade. I draw a circle around it. "That's weird," I say.

"Mmm."

I lean forward and kiss the mole. "Need to pee. I'll be back in a minute."

"Okay." She sighs, making herself comfortable on her tummy.

I get up and pull on my boxers, then walk to the door and turn to look back at her. The duvet is draped over her hips, but her back is bare. The sun has moved a little, but the bed is still bathed in orange-gold light, and it's as if she's caught in amber. She'll stay preserved in my memory like this forever. No matter what happens.

Frowning, I turn away and leave the room.

Chapter Thirty-Three

Missie

I think I doze for a minute or two, but I'm roused by my phone vibrating on the bedside table. Without moving the rest of me, I reach out a hand and pick it up. It's a text from Belle. Smiling, I bring it up.

Belle: *How do you like Seaview?* <smiley face>

Me: *OMG. It's amazing! Have you been here?*

Belle: *Yeah, Damon took me there a few months ago. Have you seen any dolphins yet?*

Me: *Yes! Alex said we might see some seals, too.*

Belle: *I'm so glad you like it.*

Me: *What are you up to? Having another party?*

Belle: *Yeah, everyone's here. We missed you two! But I hope you have a lovely time.*

Me: *Not long till your honeymoon!*

Belle: *No, I'm super-excited. It's going to be a good year. Traveling across Europe, and then when we get back, did I tell you that I'm starting my own company doing parties for kids?*

Me: *No, you didn't! Oh that's fantastic!*

Belle: *Yeah, I was going to call it Winters' Wonderland, but of course I'm a Chevalier now. I'm trying to think of names. I thought maybe The Magnificent Monroe, LOL.*

Me: *Oh, after your middle name!*

Belle: *Yeah, I thought it was funny!*

Me: *Oh, talking of which, Alex won't tell me his!*

Belle: *Haha I'm not surprised. It's Clint.*

That makes me laugh out loud.

Me: *It's not too bad. I don't know why he wouldn't tell me.*

Belle: *You know what he's like. Mr. Eastwood doesn't exactly wear his heart on his sleeve. Anyway gotta go. Happy New Year!*

Me: *Yeah, Happy New Year xxxx*

I put down the phone. Shifting onto my side, I pull the duvet up and look out at the view.

Something's bothering me. I've heard the name Eastwood before.

Alex comes back into the room, and I look over my shoulder to discover he's carrying our glasses, topped up with champagne, and a box of something under his arm.

He climbs on the bed, and I sit up, propping myself up against the pillows, and take my glass from him.

"Found some chocolates," he says, putting the box between us. He opens it, revealing an array of gorgeous truffles.

"Mmm." I choose one and bite it in half, sighing as it melts on my tongue. Then I have a sip of champagne, enjoying the blend of flavors.

I look out at the view again. The sea is the color of saffron in the late afternoon sun. The sky is a glorious blue, although there are clouds on the horizon, promising rain later.

I have the other half of the truffle and look at the two circles of melted chocolate on my thumb and forefinger.

Then it pops into my head. Where I've heard the name Eastwood before.

Alex is lost in thought, staring out at the view, but he smiles as I turn to look at him. When I don't look away, he says, "What?"

I don't say anything for a moment, thinking hard. I must be wrong. It doesn't make sense.

"What?" he says again, amused.

"I had a text from Belle," I say softly.

"Oh? How's she doing?"

"Good. She told me that when she gets back from her honeymoon, she's setting up a company doing parties for kids."

"Yeah, she's pretty good at it."

I watch him carefully. "She said she was thinking of calling herself The Magnificent Monroe. Because her middle name's Marilyn."

He goes still, studying me, the shutters coming down behind his eyes. Jesus, I was right.

"And Gaby told me she runs Hepburn Education," I continue. "Because her middle name's Audrey."

He still doesn't say anything.

"Belle told me your middle name's Clint."

He puts his glass on the bedside table, then turns back to me slowly.

SERENITY WOODS

"So," I say, "I'm thinking that maybe you use the name Eastwood sometimes. Like, for example, an insurance company?"

We study each other for a long time. I wait for him to explain, but eventually I realize he's not going to say anything.

Eventually, I say, "I don't understand. You own the insurance company that Lee's policy was from?"

He runs his tongue over his top teeth. "Not quite."

"What do you mean?"

He breathes in, then lets it out slowly. "It's not a real insurance company."

I blink. "What?"

"I made it up as a way to give you the money."

My eyes widen, and my jaw drops. I go to say something, but the words refuse to come as questions fly around in my head. "That doesn't make sense. The policy paid out in January. That's before I met you."

"But not before I met you."

I frown. "You're not making any sense."

He moves the box of chocolates off the bed, then sits back against the pillows. "Last December, I went to the hospital for a regular meeting I have every week to discuss which patients will benefit from therapy with MAX. The doctor took me on a walk through the ward, and that's when I saw her."

"Who?"

"She was sitting by the bedside of a young lad, her elbows on the rail that stopped him falling out, watching him sleep. She looked tired and tearful, she wasn't wearing any makeup, and her hair was up in a scruffy bun. Her clothes looked wrinkled, as if she'd slept in them. But she was the most beautiful girl I'd ever seen."

His brown eyes study me. Holy fuck. He's talking about me.

"I asked the doctor who she was," he continues. "He told me her name was Mistletoe Macbeth, that she'd just lost her husband in a car accident, and she was there with her son, who'd suffered a spinal column injury. 'It's bad,' he said. 'The kid won't walk again. No point in wasting your time on him.'"

"Oh God. Dr. Michaels."

He nods. "I decided right then and there that I was going to get Finn walking again, no matter what."

I remember talking to him about Dr. Michaels on the first day I met him in the park, and the quiet anger I felt radiating from him.

"I watched you for a long time," he says. "You didn't see me—you were lost in thought. But I was absolutely captivated. You'd just lost your husband, though, and your son was badly injured. I couldn't even bring myself to talk to you, because you were obviously grieving. At one point you even started crying. I watched you, and I wanted to walk in and take you in my arms and hug you, but I couldn't. So instead I went back to Kia Kaha, and I told the guys we were going to start work on an exoskeleton for kids. I began drawing plans for THOR that evening."

My jaw is still sagging. "You built THOR for Finn?"

He nods. "That poem I read to you? I wrote it that night." He gives a mischievous smile.

We study each other for a moment. My head is spinning.

"And the money?" I ask eventually.

"I knew you'd need things for Finn, and I wanted you to be able to get them. So I invented an insurance company and transferred the money to you."

I'm absolutely blown away. "Who knows all this?"

"Hardly anyone. I only told Damon a few days ago."

"And Mae?"

He nods. Of course, that's how she knew he'd met me a year ago.

"So when I came to Kia Kaha the first time, when I met the guys, they didn't know?"

He shakes his head.

"You took me to the park," I say faintly. "You were so kind."

His lips curve up a little. "I'd waited a long time to talk to you. I wanted to get you to myself."

No wonder he'd been so unreadable. He must have been watching himself closely to make sure he didn't let it slip that he'd seen me before. And now I know him a little better, I think maybe he was nervous, too. He created THOR for Finn, for me. I know that some of the other guys weren't sure about taking on a single mother, and he must have had to restrain himself from making it obvious that he wanted me there. He waited three whole months to talk to me. And he waited a whole year to date me.

"Why didn't you tell me?" I whisper.

He looks embarrassed. "I thought you might think I was stalking you. Not every girl likes secrets, even if it's all done with the best intentions." His expression softens. "Plus, you thought Lee had taken out the policy for you. I didn't know anything about your relationship at the time, but later you said it was the only redeemable thing he'd done, and I couldn't take that away from you."

I look away, out at the sea. Lee didn't take out the policy. He didn't do it for me, and he didn't do it for his son.

Did he love me? I'm not sure. Certainly not at the end. I presume he loved Finn, although I don't think he ever told him. He was a selfish, vain man who needed to be admired in order to love back, and once I lost the stars he put in my eyes as a girl, it was never going to work between us.

Just like how I convinced myself he wasn't having an affair all year, I've clung to the idea that at least he wanted to provide for Finn, clutching hold of it like a life raft to convince myself that I didn't make an immense mistake by getting pregnant and marrying him. But the truth is that the guy was an arsehole, and now I'm free.

There, at last, I've finally brought my deepest, darkest feelings into being. I've done it time and again this year, taking my guilt, my resentment, my anger, my pain, and making them real like a golem.

I talked about golems in my class once. One of the students had been playing a computer game where he had to fight one, and he asked me what it was. I told him that a golem is a creature from Jewish folklore formed from a lifeless substance that has been brought to life. It has Hebrew letters on its head that read 'emét,' which means 'truth.' To destroy it, you remove the first letter, making the word 'mét,' which means 'dead.'

I created the misery I've felt this year myself, taking something that didn't exist and breathing life into it. My eyes sting, and for a moment I can't catch my breath.

"Don't cry," Alex says. "I'm sorry. This is why I didn't want to tell you."

He thinks I'm crying because I'm devastated that Lee didn't create the policy for me. I face him, wiping away my tears.

"I'm not crying because I'm disappointed, Alex, I'm crying because I'm relieved. I'm glad Lee didn't take out the policy. All this year, I've been crushed by guilt, and it's all been so pointless. He was having an affair. He didn't take out the policy. He didn't care for me or Finn. And I'm fucking glad he's dead."

Then I burst into tears, because of course I don't mean that, and I cover my face with my hands and sob. Alex puts his arms around me and says, "Ah baby," and when I lean against him, he holds me tightly, kissing my hair and stroking my back while the tears stream down my face.

He holds me for ages, maybe ten or fifteen minutes, while I cry until there are no tears left. At one point he grabs a handful of tissues from the box on the bedside table, and then he holds me again, until my sobs die down, and all that's left is raw, clean grief, like a stone that's been turned over and over again by the sea until all the edges are worn away, and it's smooth and shiny.

"Jesus," I say, pushing myself upright. I'm all stuffed up, and I know I must look a sight. I blow my nose several times, wipe under my eyes, and get rid of all the tissues.

Then I curl up beside Alex, leaning on the pillows, facing him.

"Better?" he says.

I nod.

His brows draw together. "Do you hate me?"

I blink a few times. "Hate you?" I study his now-familiar face—the stubble on his jaw, his beautiful brown eyes. "Which bit should I hate you for? Giving three hundred thousand dollars to a girl you hadn't even spoken to? Building a piece of expensive, technical equipment to help my son walk again? Being kind and patient to him? Finding a way to give him a puppy without giving him a puppy? Making him feel special with all his friends at school?"

He purses his lips.

"For taking me with you to your sister's wedding," I continue, "and introducing me to all your friends and family, and making me feel like a valued part of your life?"

I move a little closer to him. "For waiting a whole year—twelve whole months, and that's not rounding up—for me to get my act together, without dating anyone else, even though you're a sex maniac?"

His lips curve up. My gaze drops to them as I imagine kissing him again.

"For making love to me?" I whisper. "Making me feel a million dollars, over and over again?"

"Well, if you put it like that…" He gives a rueful smile. "I am sorry I lied to you, though."

"You never lied, because I never asked. The worst you did was the whole rounding up comment." I frown then. "So does that mean that when Mae said you called her the day you met me, that was back in December?"

He nods. "The evening of the twenty-first, when I got home from the hospital."

I look at him in wonder. "She said that you told her you'd met the girl you were going to marry."

His lips twist. "I might have said that."

"I don't understand. You hadn't even spoken to me! I might have been a horrible person. Or have hated sex! How could you say something like that?"

He takes my hand in his and interlinks our fingers. "In the church, I asked Damon how he could be sure that Belle was the one, and he said, 'Because we're soulmates.' I've always scoffed at that kind of thing, but I realized then, that's how I knew. It was as if I recognized you in that hospital room, even though we'd never met before. I think you're my soulmate."

My eyes water again. "Will you stop? I'm going to bawl all night."

"I don't care." He lifts my hand and kisses my fingers. "When I said that to Mae, I meant it, and I still mean it. I want to marry you. I'll ask you properly, on one knee, with a ring, when I have one, but you should know right now that it's coming. I don't care that we've only been dating a week. I fell in love with you the moment I looked into that hospital room, and what I felt only grew as the months went by, and I got to know you and your son. Finn's a great kid." He hesitates.

"What?" I say, amused.

"He told me he'd like it if we got married. And that he wouldn't mind if I asked him to call me Dad."

My jaw drops again. Finn!

"Obviously, that would be up to you," Alex says quickly, "and I told him I wouldn't want to replace his father. Whatever Lee was like, he was Finn's dad, and he always will be. I don't care if he calls me Alex—hell, I call my mother Kait. But I want you to know that I want Finn to be a part of my life. I'd like to adopt him in time, if you're amenable to it."

Despite my emotion, it makes me laugh. "That's so you."

"What do you mean?"

I mirror his voice. "'If you're amenable to it.'"

His lips curve up. "Are you mocking me?"

"A little bit."

"Come here." He pulls me on top of him, then rolls so I'm pinned beneath him. I let him, because it's what I want anyway, and I just sigh as he kisses me until I'm seeing stars.

"You're really not mad at me?" he says eventually, brushing my hair away from my face.

"Of course not. I'm so touched by everything you've done that it makes me want to cry all over again. I'm madly, crazily in love with you, Alex. How could I be anything else?"

He looks relieved—the daft guy actually thought I was going to be angry with him.

"Kiss me," I tell him. "Kiss me again. Don't ever stop kissing me."

So he does, while the waves stroke the pebbles, and the sun sinks slowly toward the dark-blue sea.

*

Later, we eat dinner together out on the deck, talking as the sun goes down, and watching the sky and the sea turn from gold to red to purple to black. The stars come out, and a silvery path on the water leads all the way to the moon that hangs in the sky like a Christmas bauble.

We talk about the past—about Belle and that difficult time, about his friendship with Damon, about Lee and all the problems we've had. We talk about the present—the wedding, our families, what Finn and Zelda are getting up to.

And we talk about the future. I tell him that I know his work is important to him, and I want to support his career, but that I also want stability for Finn. He says he understands, and that he has no intention of moving either abroad or in New Zealand. He loves Christchurch and Kia Kaha, and he has lots of plans for things he wants to do there.

"Besides," he says, "your job is here. Why would you want to move?"

I just smile.

He says that he wants me and Finn to move in with him. I have no hesitation in saying yes. My current house belongs to my mother, which she bought after my father died, so it doesn't hold many memories for me. Besides, it wouldn't surprise me if she moves in with Mike soon.

"One thing about moving in with you," I say, "is that Finn's going to be there."

"Ah. I was hoping he might stay with your mother."

I push him, because I know he's joking. "What I mean is, we'd have to… you know… keep the noise down a bit. And it rules out having sex anywhere but the bedroom."

"Not during the day." He smirks.

"What do you mean?"

"I'll pick you up in your lunch break and take you home, then we can shag ourselves senseless on the kitchen table, or anywhere else you fancy."

I giggle. "Yeah, all right."

"Do you think Finn will mind moving?" he asks.

"Will he mind being around Zelda all the time, having a pool, a PlayStation, and someone to play games with? Hmm, let me think." I pretend to ponder.

He pokes my chair with a toe. "You love to mock me."

"I really do." I put my feet in his lap, and he begins to massage them. I watch him, feeling love bloom inside me like a rose.

"I know we touched on it before, but do you want children?" I ask after a while.

He thinks about it while he strokes the sole of my foot with his thumb. "You want an honest answer?"

"Always."

"I honestly don't mind. You've been through childbirth, and you've got an eleven-year-old son, so if you say you don't want to go through it all again, I'd understand. I love Finn, and I'd be happy to call him my son." He lifts my foot and kisses my toes. "But if you said you wanted a baby? I wouldn't be devastated." He smiles.

"Are we really going to do this?" I murmur.

He lowers my foot. "Do what?"

"Be together. Be a couple. Get married."

"Looks like it."

I glance at my watch. "It's 11:38."

"Oh, wow. We'd better get started then." He leaps to his feet. "Only you take so long to get going."

I snort as he leads me through to the bedroom. "Yeah, right. Don't be too quick or it'll all be over by midnight."

He laughs, pulls me into his arms, and presses me up against the wall. "Oh, I have no intention of rushing. I want to make the most of finally having you in my arms." He kisses me, delving his tongue into my mouth. "I love you, Mistletoe Macbeth."

"And I love you, Alex Winters. Happy New Year."

"It will be," he says, "with you by my side." And then he lifts me and carries me to the bed, so that we can make love for a whole year, just as he promised.

Epilogue

Six weeks later

Alex

"Stop it," I say to Finn. "She's already suspicious."

He giggles, but bites his top lip as his mother approaches, carrying three ice creams.

She hands them out, giving us a suspicious look. "What's going on?"

"Nothing." Finn offers his ice cream to Zelda, who eats some, and then he has a bite himself.

"You shouldn't do that," Missie scolds. "She might catch something from you."

Finn snorts and continues eating, and I grin.

"It's a beautiful day," I say. It rained quite a lot in January, but February has been warm and humid, even in Queenstown, which is normally one of the drier cities in New Zealand. The three of us are on vacation, enjoying the beautiful town on the shore of Lake Wakatipu. It's known for its outdoor activities like skiing and bungee jumping, neither of which Finn is up for yet, but it's also holding this year's New Zealand Science Fiction and Fantasy Convention, which all three of us were eager to visit.

We've had a great couple of days being nerds together, and we're going back home tomorrow. Finn's already started at his new high school, and so far things seem to be going well, helped in no small part by the fact that he's worked extra hard on his physio in the New Year, and he's made significant progress.

Now, as he finishes his ice cream, he gets to his feet, walks over to the rubbish bin, and deposits the wrapper. Missie watches him, then looks at me, her lips curving up. He's not exactly running yet, but his movement improves every day, and she's thrilled.

I finish my own ice cream and say, "Shall we walk down to the lake?"

"Sure," she says. Together, with Finn holding Zelda's leash while he talks to her non-stop, we walk down Queenstown Bay Beach to the edge of the lake.

Finn looks up at me, eyes dancing, and I nod. He stands back, holding Zelda, barely able to contain his excitement.

Missie's looking out at the view across the lake and hasn't noticed our exchange, and therefore she stares at me, startled, when I suddenly drop to one knee and take her hand.

"Don't look surprised," I say. "You knew this was coming."

Her eyes widen and her jaw drops. "Oh my God."

I nod at Finn, who produces the box from his pocket and opens it. The solitaire diamond glitters in the sunlight. It was a huge risk letting him carry it, but I wanted to show him that I trust him, and, bless him, he's hardly taken his hand out of his pocket, making sure it's there every five seconds.

"Mistletoe," I say, "will you marry me, and make me and Finn the happiest guys in the world?"

Her eyes fill with tears, and she presses her fingers to her lips. I knew it would get to her if Finn was present when I proposed. He's almost as much a part of this as she is, and I want her to see that he approves.

"Mum!" He glares at her.

"Yes," she squeaks.

I laugh and get to my feet. "You had me going there."

She throws her arms around my neck. "Yes, yes, yes!"

"Aw." I hug her, then give her a long kiss.

"Don't look, Zelda," Finn says. "Mum, put the ring on!"

She laughs and moves back, and Finn takes it out of the box and hands it to her. She slides it onto her finger, then moves it around to watch it catch the light.

"Is it real?" she asks, breathless.

Finn rolls his eyes. "No, Mum," he says sarcastically, "he got it out of a cracker."

"Don't be cheeky to your mother." I put my arm around his neck, and we wrestle for a moment.

"Will you two stop?" she complains. "This is supposed to be a romantic moment." She sits on a nearby bench and gives Zelda a kiss as she goes up to Missie. "There, you understand, don't you girl? These men never grow up."

Finn and I sit on either side of her, and she looks at us both before returning her gaze to the ring. "Thank you," she whispers.

"You're welcome," Finn says, and I chuckle.

She looks up at me. "Mistletoe Winters," she says. "I kinda like that."

"Can I be Finn Winters?" he asks.

Neither of us had considered that, and we both look at each other. Missie lifts her eyebrows, looking a little embarrassed. She doesn't want to assume.

I look at Finn, whose face is filled with hope.

"I'd love you to take my name," I say huskily. "And to call me Dad, if you want to. But it's up to your mum."

"I'd like that," she squeaks.

"Yes," Finn says, pumping his arm. "Cool."

She puts her arms around me and buries her face in my neck. "Don't worry," I tell him. "They're happy tears."

"Yeah, I know," he says. "When are you going to get married?"

"I thought maybe next spring. September? October?"

"Can I be the ring bearer?"

"You're far too old for that. I'd like you to be the chief groomsman."

His face lights up. "Really?"

"It comes with quite a lot of responsibility—organizing guests, helping Damon—the best man—if he needs anything."

"Cool. Wait till I tell Robbie. Hey, I meant to tell you, we can't beat that last boss in Robot Wars. Do you know how to do it?"

I explain how to turn off the power grid with the giant wrench, drawing patterns on Missie's back, while she sighs against my neck, and Zelda barks at the waves.

Newsletter

If you'd like to be informed when my next book is available,
you can sign up for my mailing list on my website,
http://www.serenitywoodsromance.com

About the Author

USA Today bestselling author Serenity Woods writes sexy contemporary romances, most of which are set in the sub-tropical Northland of New Zealand, where she lives with her wonderful husband.

Website: http://www.serenitywoodsromance.com
Facebook: http://www.facebook.com/serenitywoodsromance

Made in United States
Orlando, FL
29 December 2023

41856159R00185